FINDING LORD LANDRY

LUCY LENNOX

Cover Art: Natasha Snow Designs
Cover Image: Michelle Lancaster
Editing: One Love Editing
Proofreading: Jodi Duggan

FINDING LORD LANDRY

When a secret enemies-with-benefits situation turns into the world's most public fake marriage…

The world knows me as Landry Davis, supermodel. A beautiful face and killer abs that have spawned a hundred fantasies.

To my friends, I'm simply Landry, the snarkiest (read: most fun) member of our billionaire brotherhood.

But to Kenji Toma, the gorgeous and oh-so-capable personal assistant I've been in love with for years, I'm "effing Landry," the charming slacker who disappears for weeks only to resurface in trouble. His favorite enemy-with benefits. A man he refuses to fall in love with (though I've tried) and also can't resist managing (a fact I'm not too proud to take advantage of).

What none of them know is that I have another title—in fact, a whole other life. One I was born into. One that comes with sprawling estates, a coronet, and a metric ton of familial and political expectations. A life I've kept secret for way too long... and hope to keep secret for just a little while longer.

At least until I learn Kenji is in danger.

When all my money and fame can't save the man I love, I don't hesitate to use long-hidden political power to whisk him to safety, even though it means outing myself as Viscount Hawling, the elusive heir to the Davencourt earldom...

And pretending the man who loves to hate me is actually my doting husband.

ONE

KENJI

"Do you have any soup?" Landry demanded. "I'm starving, but I shouldn't have solids until after tomorrow's shoot."

"No. But there's a ramen place on the corner. You should go there," I said, emphasizing the word *go* so there was no confusion.

Landry ignored me, stretching his long, lean body on my bed. "What about lemon? Why don't you ever have fresh lemons when you know I need lemon in my water to chug down as much as I have to drink."

I tried my hardest not to look at the miles of bare skin on offer. He was preening. The man didn't know how to be any other way than arrogant about his body, but then again, if I'd had a body like that—one people paid millions to display their clothing on—I might preen, too. Unfortunately, on Landry, the preening was not only insufferable but also irresistible.

Not that I'd ever admit that out loud. To anyone. Even on pain of death.

"I'm not your valet..." My words trailed off because while I wasn't his valet, technically, I was his executive assistant. And an argument could be made—for other people, not Landry—that an executive assistant should, in fact, consider supplying the things a man needed for his job.

He turned onto his side and propped his head on his hand. His long, blond hair was enticingly tangled, as if the man had just had the hungry fingers of a lover in it.

I cleared my throat. "You need to leave."

He kicked off the sheet and ran his fingers down his thigh and back up the *inside* of his thigh while giving me a familiar look.

I pressed the button on my mindfulness app and asked, "What does Chaska Inira say about staying calm when provoked?"

"When emotions rise like stormy seas, seek the still waters beneath. A provocation is but a test—a mirror reflecting the mastery of your own peace. Do not wrestle with the storm; instead, anchor yourself in understanding and let the tempest pass."

Chaska's melodious voice soothed me as I finished folding my pajama pants and placed them into the suitcase. Even though I'd had the Louis Vuitton bag for over two years now, I still treated it like a spoiled princess. Who paid this much for a Rollaboard? No one rational, that was who. People with more money than sense.

"Told you you'd like it," Landry said knowingly, nodding toward the suitcase.

"And I told you I didn't want Louis Vuitton. I wanted a Samsonite just like the one you ruined," I muttered. I wasn't lying, per se. It was true that I had wanted a simple replacement for my old, trusty carry-on. But when he'd given me this one anyway... well, I hadn't cried about it.

Landry sat up and peered into the suitcase. "Did you iron those? Who the fuck irons pajama pants? Wait. Is that a cummerbund? And what kind of retreat is this? I thought you were staying in a yurt with yaks and ringing metal bowls or something."

I ignored Landry's voice and tried to focus on the one in my head that was actively counseling me against murder.

I was still waters, and Landry was the damned tempest.

"I don't see why you have to go halfway around the world to listen to more of that 'live, laugh, love' nonsense. You should stay here," Landry continued. He reached into the suitcase for my bow tie, but I slapped his hand before flicking it away.

"Sex is over. Our time together has come to a not-regrettable end," I informed him.

He settled back onto the pillows and put his hands behind his head. This had the—probably intended—effect of popping out his defined biceps. I bit back a sigh. While I didn't necessarily like the man himself most days, Landry was fucking incredible in bed. His body was a very fine specimen, and he was particularly talented with his tongue.

I'd also discovered a few years ago, when we'd made the unfortunate decision to hook up "just this once," that Landry Davis happened to be the world's most generous lover.

I wasn't sure what Chaska would say about fate taking a glorious talent like Landry's and wrapping it in an immature, self-absorbed package, but I doubted the answer would help me find lasting peace. Dwelling on Landry never did.

As if he could hear my thoughts, the man in question ran his hand down his chest to his cock, which was still flaccid against his thigh after he'd orgasmed while balls-deep inside of me.

I cleared my throat. "I'm flying to San Cordova in six hours. I will be gone for four weeks. And to answer your question, it's a mindfulness retreat at a luxury island resort... as I've already told you."

Not that he'd listened. Not that he'd actually heard me or cared.

His face widened into a knowing grin. "Ha! You can't give up your Apple Watch and charging station. Or your daily lattes. Admit it. You had to pick a retreat with amenities."

I shot him a look while pressing the button on my app again. "What does Chaska say about self-care?"

"To nurture yourself is not selfish; it is sacred. Your body, mind, and spirit are vessels for your journey, and they must be tended with care. Just as the sun does not apologize for shining or the river for flowing, you must not hesitate to honor your needs. Rest when you are weary, nourish yourself with kindness, and seek joy without guilt. Only when your own cup is full can you truly pour into the lives of others."

"See? I'm going to fill my cup, asshole," I said before closing my suitcase and yanking the zipper.

Landry sat up again. "Take me with you. I'm good at filling cups. Pretty sure I filled your cup a few minutes ago, and I don't recall any complaints."

To my extreme horror, I felt my face heat.

This was unacceptable. He needed to go.

"Absolutely not. The retreat's been sold out for weeks, and San Cordova is a small place where you'd be bored to tears anyway. Not a single dance club on the whole island," I told him solemnly. "Nothing but the resort, a British historical something-or-other, a copper mine, and a very large number of coffee plants."

"What if... what if *you're* my scene?"

It took me a moment to comprehend what he was saying. I blinked up from my carry-on bag. "Me? How do you mean? Surely you can find someone else to wet your dick." The idea of him having sex with someone else made my stomach revolt the same way eating brussels sprouts did. Or the idea of beans on toast.

"Not for that. I mean..." He stopped and flared his nostrils. "Never mind. Wait. What happened to our monogamy rule?"

I glared at him. "Don't use that word."

"Which word? Monogamy?" He flicked his hair back. "It wasn't my idea, if you recall. When we first got together—"

"No, *rule*. Calling it a rule implies that this is... that we are..." I pressed my lips together. "There are no expectations here, Landry. You can fuck anyone you want, whenever you want." I clutched the packing cube in my hands tighter than absolutely necessary. "We're not together."

He'd suggested it before, most recently at Christmas, but I'd made it very clear I was not interested. It was purely physical or nothing at all.

Landry's gaze, when it met mine, was unexpectedly heated. "When we first *fucked*, you said there wouldn't be a repeat. Then, when there was a repeat, you said it was only because I hadn't slept with anyone else in between and you needed to ensure I wasn't carrying... what was the exact phrase you used? Ah, yes, '*Manky ho germs.*' You said if I ever wanted to touch you again, I needed to keep my dick to myself."

"That... doesn't sound like a phrase I would use," I lied, packing the few remaining items that needed to go in my carry-on.

In truth, I remembered the whole exchange—my flash flood of jealousy at the idea of Landry putting his hands and mouth on anyone else and the equally violent flare of relief when he'd shrugged and agreed—but a man couldn't be held responsible for what he'd said or thought before he became enlightened.

"Anyway, it doesn't matter anymore," I continued. "I'm leaving. You'll have to find someone else to... meet your needs."

I almost added the words "while I'm gone," but that would have been self-defeating. One of the biggest draws of spending four weeks in mindful meditation with very limited outside contact was the promise that it would help me realign my priorities and re-center my goals and dreams.

In other words, it would help me focus on the things I actually wanted out of life... and stop being distracted by the man I couldn't seem to stop wanting in my bed.

He stood up and stretched, making an entire meal out of the thing. Acres of golden skin took up too much space in my small bedroom, and I nearly groaned.

I focused instead on the painting of Three Daughters I'd

splurged on during my first trip to Majestic, Wyoming, and let out a slow breath. The mountain range wasn't as breathtaking as Landry's body, but it was a close second. The artist had captured the mountains in the golden hour just as the sun dipped below the horizon, casting warm, amber light over its jagged peaks and the peaceful river in the foreground.

I'd spent a lot of time in Majestic over the last few years as most of the men I worked for—Landry's best friends—had found a home there, but I'd never found the particular spot depicted in the painting. Someday, though, I liked to imagine building myself a fortress of solitude there—

"Is that what you really want, Kenji?"

The sound of my name in Landry's voice made something inside me whimper.

Something *dreadful* inside me.

Something unnecessary and unwanted.

And stupid.

It took me several long seconds to remember we'd been talking about Landry getting his *needs* met, and when I did, my voice came out snippier than usual. "Yes. Why wouldn't I?"

He threw up his long arms. "Oh, I don't know... maybe because we've been together for three fucking years?"

"We're not together!" I cried. "How many times do I have to tell you that?"

"Have you been with anyone else since that first time?" he demanded, though he knew the answer.

I jabbed the button on my app. "What would Chaska say about getting rid of unwanted pests?" I gritted out.

"Every creature has its purpose, but not every purpose belongs in your space. Approach with respect, for even the smallest intruder has its role in the great web of life. Seek balance first: understand what draws them, and gently remove what invades. If they persist, guide them away with firmness but without cruelty. Harmony is not

in the destruction of others, but in creating boundaries that protect your peace."

I snapped my fingers and pointed at him. "Boundaries."

Landry pulled his jogging tights off the floor and began tugging them on. He'd been in the middle of a run last night when I'd texted him to ask how he wanted to RSVP for the Baxter-Hicks gala. Instead of responding with the answer, he'd asked if he could stop in to take a leak and get a drink of water.

I should have known it would end up with the two of us naked and spent. It always did.

"It's only four weeks. I can self-service for that long. Unless..." Landry gave me a piercing look. "Are you planning on sleeping with other people on your retreat? Is that it?"

My heart gave an annoyingly wonky *thump.* "That... is none of your business."

"Chaska Inira," he said in that stupid, singsong way he always said the man's name. "I'll bet you want to get into his ceremonial robes, don't you? Who wouldn't? I've seen pictures, you know. He's an attractive man."

"He's married to his purpose," I said loftily.

"So are you," Landry pointed out. "Doesn't keep you from getting some on the side."

I took in a deep breath. "I do not have plans to sleep with my guiding light, no. And looking after the five of you could hardly be considered 'purpose.' More like 'circus.'"

When I'd accepted the role of executive assistant to five billionaires who called themselves "brothers," I'd assumed they'd settle down with age. That my job might even—*gasp*—become boring. Now, between babies, horses, business and recording contracts, and watching each of those idiots fall in love, my days were busier than ever.

Landry reached for his shirt. I took one last appreciative look at his chest, shoulders, and abs before the fabric separated me from them.

"Why can't you give me a straight answer?" Landry's voice was tight with frustration. "You're so fucking cagey."

"I'm going to San Cordova to focus, Landry. To anchor myself for the year ahead. To learn new techniques in mindfulness and meditation. No, I do not plan on asking the faith healer—or anyone else for that matter—to put his dick in my person while I'm trying to focus on myself."

Landry made a little growling noise in his throat. If my dick hadn't been spent already, it might have perked up at the sound.

I walked around the bed and poked the center of his chest with my finger. "But I'm also not making any promises to you about who I am or am not sleeping with. That wasn't the deal."

"It was literally the deal."

"No. I said I wouldn't sleep with you again if you *had* slept with other people. I didn't ask for promises, and I didn't give any."

I started to pull my hand away, but Landry grabbed my wrist and held on. The warm strength of his grip made my stomach tighten. "Don't go," he said softly. "Please don't go."

Oxygen suddenly became scarce in the room while red alert beacons flashed in my hindbrain. *Do not let a man keep you from following your dreams,* I reminded myself. *What do you want?*

Him, my stupid fucking heart cried.

Peace, my hindbrain insisted. *Focus. Success. Growth. Mindfulness.*

Dick, my still-sore ass added helpfully.

Our eyes met and held. Landry leaned in.

For a split second, I thought about it. Thought about giving in, agreeing to stay with him, and trying to turn this enemies-with-benefits thing into something real and good.

But then I remembered why that would be the worst idea ever:

I knew Landry Davis. Knew everything there was to know about him.

He was a professional supermodel and *un*professional playboy. He was charming and intelligent. He loved his friends.

But he was also allergic to taking things seriously, being responsible, or following through on anything, as evidenced by the number of times he'd begged me to rebook his missed flights, post his bail, or fly across the world to solve whatever international incident he'd stumbled into that week. "I was bored," he'd say with a shrug, back when I bothered asking why.

He also happened to be competitive as fuck... which was why I couldn't trust his sad eyes or any of the stuff he'd said to me at Christmas about wanting a relationship.

Landry wanted to win. And there was no way on earth he was going to win me. Once he did, he'd just get bored of me, too.

"I'm going," I said, trying to soften my response to a less antagonized, more neutral tone. "This is important to me."

He let go of my wrist and moved his hand up to cup the side of my face. "I know it is. I'm sorry."

I blinked at him in surprise. Landry Davis didn't do sorries. Or serious. "O-okay then."

"Can I at least kiss you goodbye?"

Again with the not-enough-oxygen thing. Maybe while I was gone, I could put in a maintenance request.

"We don't do kissing," I said, turning around and looking for my shoes.

I found them on my feet.

"Just this once?" The teasing tone was back in his voice, putting us back on much firmer footing.

I rolled my eyes at him. "Do you ever stop provoking people?"

"Not if they're this fun to provoke, no."

"Put on your shoes and grab your things. My Uber is going to be here in three minutes."

He pulled on his running shoes and grabbed his keys and phone off the nightstand, shoving them in the pocket of his high-tech running jacket. "You're going to be at the airport five hours before your flight?"

I shouldered my carry-on and extended the handle of my rolling suitcase. "Lounge access for the win. I have a lot of work to do before I land in San Cordova and put my electronics away."

He reached for my suitcase and wheeled it out of the bedroom and to the apartment door, giving me a chance to double-check the thermostat and lights before locking up.

We made our way to the half staircase and up to the street. The Uber was already waiting in the gray shadows of late afternoon.

"This is me," I said, reaching for the suitcase handle. Instead of handing it over, Landry moved to the trunk of the vehicle and loaded it up. I swung my carry-on into the back seat of the car and turned to say goodbye.

Before I knew what was happening, Landry had pulled me into his arms and kissed me. One of his hands was on my face, fingertips tangled in my hair. His other arm was banded around my back possessively as if I were the only thing standing between him and salvation.

And his lips...

My head swam from the unfamiliar taste of his mouth. The sheer strength of his kiss. The nearness of his face. The way he moved my face and my body exactly where he wanted it while he completely devoured my mouth.

I whimpered and clung onto him, seeking more—much, much more—until some vague memory suggested this was against the rules and I should stop.

I wanted to laugh. Stop? Stop this? Who in their right mind would stop this? This was a world-ending kiss. The kind of kiss that sent soldiers off to war and welcomed them home again. The kind of kiss that sunk ships and invaded cities.

The kind of kiss that changed absolutely everything and crumbled walls that had been built meticulously, brick by brick, over three years.

The kind of kiss that drew a deep line in the sand between the Before time and the After.

The kind of kiss that couldn't in its right mind be possible between enemies with benefits.

I whimpered again. Landry's hold on me tightened.

And then it was gone. I reached out and slammed a hand on the car to keep from falling over.

"Safe travels," Landry said in a strangely gruff voice before turning around and walking away.

I stared after him in shock.

There was a reason I'd never allowed myself to kiss Landry on the mouth. And now, after three years and countless hookups, I finally felt pretty damned clear about what that reason was.

Because kissing him even just once would have devastating consequences.

TWO

LANDRY

I raced down the street with my heart already pounding and my head spinning and ran for two solid hours until my legs shook and my stomach cramped. By the time I reached my building, the taste of Kenji's kiss was already stronger in my memory than on my tongue.

Damn him. Damn him to fucking hell for not giving me a chance.

Our argument at Christmas played through my head for the millionth time. I'd tried to make my case—to convince Kenji to take a chance at turning our physical relationship into something more, something with actual, confessed feelings—but he'd soundly rejected me.

"You're incapable of a serious relationship, Landry," he'd said. *"And you don't know who you are or what you want. Why would I want to be with someone like that?"*

It had cut deep, mostly because he was right in some ways... just not for the reasons he thought.

Exhausted and heartsore, annoyed at both Kenji and myself, I took the elevator up to the penthouse, trying to think up a way to keep myself distracted for the next four weeks so I didn't accidentally find myself jogging in the neighborhood of San Cordova, pretending to need a bathroom just so Kenji might invite me in.

When the elevator door opened and I noticed a suitcase in my entry hall, I realized my distraction had arrived, but it was *not* the pleasant sort I'd been hoping for.

Fucking fuck. I leaned forward and braced my hands on my knees, concentrating on taking a deep breath and letting it out. *Jesus Christ. Just what I do not need right now.*

"I can hear you out there cursing silently, Everett," Nan's voice called from the kitchen. "Might as well face the music."

Nancy Bayliss was my father's majordomo. The woman who'd been half housekeeper, half auntie to me growing up and the person most likely to call me on my bullshit.

Second only to Kenji, of course.

"How did you get in here?" I asked, coming around the corner and seeing her making herself at home with my kettle and the tea things. "And you know I prefer *Landry*."

Nan's hair was pulled back in its usual twist, but a few silver-brown strands were loose around her face. Her clothes were a bit wrinkled, which wasn't usual for her—it was clear she'd just flown in—and her smile looked tired.

"What makes you think I don't have a key? I manage all of the family properties for you and your father."

I moved over to the cabinet to get a glass and fill it with cold water from the fridge. "This isn't a Davencourt property. It's my personal one, and we both know it."

She rolled her eyes. "Fine, then. I sweet-talked your doorman. It turns out he has a beloved Cornish Rex. I grew up with Cornish Rexes. That was all it took. Oh, *and* I gave him a tin of Walker's Shortbread from the airport Duty Free."

I snorted. Bruce was a sucker for shortbread, so I'd asked Nan to send me some homemade shortbread from the cook at the family's Scotland estate to go along with Bruce's holiday bonus last year. Nan never forgot a detail, nor did she refrain from using one to her advantage when needed.

"This isn't a good time, Nan."

She picked up two full mugs and tilted her head toward the sofas in the living area. "Have a cuppa with me. We need to talk."

I was filthy. Covered in sweat and probably still reeking of sex. But something in her tone alerted me to the fact this was serious. I followed her to the sofa and sat down.

Nan took a careful sip of her tea before glancing at me. "Your father's health is deteriorating."

"His health or his memory?" I asked. "Because you have a hard time saying the words. Dementia. Alzheimer's." The words weren't hard for me to say. Accepting what they meant for him and for me, however...

Her lips firmed. "He's no longer able to do his job, Landry. I've been trying to tell you for a while now, but you've continued to ask for more time. Well, I'm afraid that's no longer an option. If you leave it much longer, your father might reveal your identity by accident. We need to get him out of the public eye and into a quiet retirement on the estate. And you need to take your place as the future Earl of Davencourt."

Nan's words were a calm statement of fact, yet they made my heart ricochet around my chest.

"Dad can simply take leave." I felt like I was reciting lines from a script, replaying a conversation we'd had several times. "Our publicists can tell everyone he's dealing with health issues. Cora's already handling the family charitable foundation, and I'm managing the estates remotely. The only part of it I'm not doing is the glad-handing bullshit—"

She lifted a sculpted eyebrow. "And a little thing known as the House of Lords."

I made a sound of disgust. Inheriting the earldom after my

father passed was one thing; serving in Parliament was another. Besides, things were different now. A seat in the Lords wasn't passed down from father to son anymore. A replacement was carefully selected from a list of hereditary peers in a by-election. And as I had no interest in politics, I would be a terrible choice.

However, fifteen generations of Davencourts before me had been willing to take their place in the House of Lords, and I couldn't—wouldn't—be the first to throw off legacy. It was unthinkable. Instead, I would put myself forward when the time came and expect a polite, but quick, rejection.

Nan seemed to think otherwise. "You are a hereditary peer. The Right Honorable Everett Landry Davencourt, Viscount Hawling," she said, as if I'd ever been able to forget. "Your father has served in the Lords for forty years. He's spoken to Teddy about you taking his place, and the prime minister would like to meet with you to discuss it." She tilted her head and studied me. "There's only so long a young peer can be off 'finding himself.' Your gap year has become a gap decade, I'm afraid. You're needed back in England."

The press of lifelong family expectations was a familiar weight on my shoulders. "This is why he let me hide," I reminded her a bit desperately. "He didn't want me to feel this pressure."

Even if I wasn't selected for Parliament, I would be expected to re-enter high society, be the face of the Davencourt earldom, which involved rubbing elbows with other peers, influencing politics to benefit the family's holdings and purpose, marrying within my station, and playing pretty peer at charity events. It all seemed so staid and boring. The opposite of who I was and the life I wanted.

Nan nodded. "Who do you think arranged everything? Your father. And I'm happy it worked. Considering you chose the most high-profile career possible, it's frankly a miracle you've managed to keep your title under wraps this long."

Nan was right, but then again, I hadn't exactly planned on becoming a fashion model. And I sure as hell hadn't planned on becoming a world-famous one.

Fortunately, the long-haired blond with perfect skin and chiseled abs on the cover of fashion spreads was unrecognizable from the scrawny teen with military-short mousy-brown hair, spots, and a belly a bit rounded from pints at the pub with his mates. I'd left school before going into sixth form and had spent two years studying for my A-levels with private tutors while watching my mother's final struggles with lung disease. I'd been the late-in-life miracle child, which meant I'd had to watch my parents suffer from age complaints and illnesses way too soon. My father had witnessed the toll my mother's decline and death had taken on me, which was why he'd agreed to my desire to run away from my life and start over somewhere new—somewhere people didn't know I was the long-awaited "Davencourt heir," potentially on the cusp of becoming one of the largest landholders in the United Kingdom outside of the royal family.

I'd meant to sneak away just long enough to have a normal college experience in America. My father had insisted on an Ivy League education, but otherwise, he'd gone along with my request for a temporary name change, a glow-up, and a fresh start.

But the expectation had always been there, a giant noble anvil hanging over my head, stamped with the family crest and crusted with hundreds of years of expectations.

"I'm not ready," I whispered to Nan now. Even I could hear the emotion in my voice. I cleared my throat. "Not yet. I need more time."

"That's what you said last time we discussed this." Nan set her tea down and scooted closer before squeezing my arm. "Is this about a man?"

I clenched my back teeth together. "That makes me sound pathetic and childish."

She laughed. "It's not pathetic and childish to want to find love, darling. It's very normal."

I huffed. "Nothing normal about this situation, I promise you. I'm not sure love is in the cards with this one. At least... at least not on his side."

I, of course, already loved Kenji more than was healthy. My side wasn't the problem. But Kenji had already decided I wasn't a good bet for a relationship... and that was *before* he learned that I'd been hiding the truth about my name and title, the work I spent half my time doing, and my family responsibilities.

Nan reached for her tea again and sat back, kicking off her shoes and tucking one leg underneath the other. Despite being in her mid-fifties, Nan remained trim and fit. Managing the upkeep of the Davencourt estate was no small position, and Nancy Bayliss had held the job for decades.

She studied me as she sipped her tea, and I tried not to squirm. She'd known me since I was nothing but skinned-kneed and gap-toothed. If there was a secret to be had, Nan would suss it out.

"Unrequited love? How very Shakespearean."

I sighed.

She gave me an empathetic smile. "So tell me about him, this man of yours. Is this simply a crush, or are you two actually seeing each other?"

I stalled for time with another sip of tea. Now that I was cooling off from the run, my sweat-damp clothes were turning cold and unpleasant. The gray January day outside the wall of windows in my apartment didn't do much to warm me. "Neither, really. I mean... both?"

Nan let out a soft laugh. "Well, that's clear as mud."

I took another sip and glanced at her out of the corner of my eye. "It's Kenji."

She opened her mouth, then closed it again. "Kenji, as in... your executive assistant?"

"You make it sound inappropriate," I snapped.

Nan lifted that damned eyebrow of hers but didn't say anything.

I gritted my teeth. "It wasn't like we planned it." My heart thumped a little faster as I remembered that night. "He was angry. I was... also angry. Anyway, it just happened."

"You mean sex," she said. "You slept with him."

My face heated. Nan matter-of-factly discussing my sex life was somehow worse than if it had been my own mother. I nodded.

"Recently?"

Very recently. As in, just a few hours ago. I coughed and took another sip of tea. "Three years ago, the first time," I mumbled. "It's been off and on since."

She nodded slowly. "And you have feelings for him, but you say he doesn't necessarily return those feelings."

I inhaled sharply through my nose. "He acts like he doesn't," I admitted. "Hell, he acts like he hates me. But then sometimes..."

I thought back to the nights Kenji had allowed himself to fall asleep with me—the times he'd curled against me, searched for my hand, and tucked his face into my shoulder, trusting me implicitly when he was too exhausted to remember all the reasons he didn't want to trust me.

I let out a breath. "I just want him to give us a chance. Give *me* a chance. Let me prove to him that I..."

Nan patted my arm. "Have real feelings for him?"

"He doesn't know. About my family." I darted a glance at her. The look of empathy on her face bordered a little too close to pity. "And I can't tell him. Not now. Not after all this time. He'll think I'm even less responsible than I am."

Her smile dropped. "You're the most responsible man I know, Landry. You have two full-time jobs and manage to live a double life without anyone outside the family being any the wiser."

"Yes, well. Lying but doing it well probably isn't a point in my favor." I winked.

Trying to lighten the mood was pretty much my default setting, but it was harder than usual in that moment. I needed to leave off this unpleasant topic so I could search for my equilibrium. Kenji's departure was still too raw, and I was nearly shivering from cold in my running kit.

I stood. "I need to shower and change before I run us both out of here with my stench. Give me a few?"

I didn't wait for her response, simply disappeared down the hallway to my bedroom. The firm press of her stare followed me all the way.

As I made my way into the bathroom and turned on the water jets, I wondered at her making such a long trip. Things must be serious with my father, even though he'd seemed okay in December when I'd visited last. I'd stopped in London on my way back from a job in Paris and spent a week listening to my father tell me stories from his travels to Africa in the 1980s to visit his late brother, stories I'd heard a thousand times before and could recite word for word. When he wasn't regaling me with the same old shit, he became sentimental about how he'd met my mother or about Davencourt Park, the country estate where our ancestors had lived for hundreds of years, though *he* hadn't lived there full-time in ages.

I hated those visits. Every time I walked into Hawling House in London, I felt invisible chains tightening around my chest. Grief at the slow loss of my father was one part of it. The clock ticking on my freedom was another. And though I'd always known there was an expiry date on my life as Landry Davis, I wasn't ready to give it—*me*—up.

I stood under the pounding hot water and let it wash away the dirt and morose feelings. I had no business feeling sorry for myself because one of my many sources of untold wealth was demanding my attention.

What right did I have to throw a pity party? None whatsoever.

I replayed moments from my night with Kenji. The clench of his stomach muscles as I ran my tongue around his nipple. The sound of his breath catching when I murmured the word *beautiful* into his skin. The scent of his shampoo as I wound a long strand of his hair around my finger and tugged.

I groaned into steamy air. The man was sex on two legs. He was putty in my hands when we were naked together, but he was so fucking stubborn outside of the bedroom.

He was regimented and strict. Exacting and professional. Scarily—*sexily*—competent. The only time Kenji seemed to allow himself any pleasure was during sex or his damned meditation sessions. And knowing I was the man who got to glimpse the softness behind that hard shell, who got to light the fuse that made his tightly leashed control explode in a white-hot shimmer, felt like a privilege far more precious than anything else Everett Davencourt *or* Landry Davis could possess.

All these thoughts of Kenji made my dick hard as usual. I stroked myself off to memories of being inside the hot clench of his body. By the time I dried off and pulled on clean clothes, I was shaking from hunger and exhaustion.

When I returned to the living area, I saw takeout bags from Katz's deli. My mouth watered immediately. "I can't eat that. I have a shoot in the morning." It came out whinier than I'd intended, but my disappointment was real. Katz's pastrami was world-famous. Nan couldn't help but order it as soon as she landed every time she came to New York.

"I wasn't sure, so I also ordered you an avocado quinoa salad with hard-boiled eggs." She gestured to the dining table by the window. "Have a seat, and I'll get you a... well, I guess you don't want too much water, do you?"

I let out a breath. "No. They want abs."

We sat down and started eating. After a few minutes, she couldn't hold back her strong opinion. "When are you going to stop torturing yourself with this ridiculous diet?"

There was no point in arguing with her because she was right. For the past year, I'd begun hating my modeling career. I'd taken fewer and fewer jobs, only keeping enough of them to be able to still call myself a professional model without feeling like a fraud. I didn't need the money. Not only had I been born into obscene wealth, but I'd tripped into a second fortune when a group of university friends and I had invented a software program that had sold for billions. And then there'd been my modeling career.

I had more money than sense.

But I also had more money than purpose. If I didn't want to be the earl yet, and I didn't want to be a supermodel, and I didn't want to help run the tech incubator company my friends and I owned, then what was I? *Who* was I?

"...you don't know who you are or what you want. Why would I want to be with someone like that?"

Kenji was right.

"I don't know how to stop," I admitted before filling my mouth with enough salad to keep from saying more.

"You tell them you're done. Hell, you tell them you have to go home and take over the family business. They'll understand, especially when they learn who you really are."

"You make it sound so easy."

"Not easy, maybe, but simple. Your father needs you, Landry. And it wasn't like you were going to hide from your responsibilities forever."

"I have a couple of weeks free after tomorrow's shoot," I offered. "I was going to use that time to deal with estate business remotely, but I can do it in London and check on Dad."

She studied me. "And while you're there, we can make a plan

for you to meet with the prime minister to talk about serving in the Lords."

"Not yet." I held up a hand. "Please, Nan. This is not my agreement to make anything official. It's my agreement to come check on Dad and help out, okay?"

I expected her to argue further or at least call me out for being in denial, so her sigh of relief surprised me. "I'm just happy you can come. I'm sure once you see the state of things, you'll feel ready to finally take your place where you belong. Back home with us."

I tucked into my salad despite the nerves churning up my stomach.

Maybe Nan was right. I wanted to retire from modeling anyway, things with Kenji seemed to be in a perpetual stalemate, and managing the estate already took a lot of my time and attention. Would it really be so bad to claim the role of heir publicly?

It didn't take long for me to learn that the answer to that question was an unequivocal *yes*.

THREE

KENJI

I stepped off the plane into a tropical paradise. Despite the first-class seat and the large amount of work I'd been able to finish overnight, eleven hours of flying had left me feeling stiff and restless. The warm air sliding under my hair and across my skin was a much-needed improvement over the cold, dark city I'd left behind.

The island nation of San Cordova was sunny and breezy. Rolling hills in the near distance were striped with regimented rows of coffee plants, and the mountains beyond were covered in the deep green of tropical trees. Seabirds swooped lazily over the water on the other side of us, and the sun's reflection danced on the waves.

There was a sense of peace here, completely the opposite of the bustle of the city. As I moved with the other passengers through customs and into the luggage hall of the tiny, open airport, I forced myself to drop my shoulders and leave the stress of New York behind.

I was here to relax. To focus on myself. To be mindful and meditative. To anchor myself for the coming year and reflect on the previous one.

To take stock of where I was in my life, what I wanted, and what changes I needed to make.

I stood up straighter and brushed the wrinkles out of my trousers just as my phone buzzed with a message from one of my bosses in the Brotherhood.

BASH

> I know you're on vacation, but do you know who we use for liability insurance? I can't find it anywhere.

My blood pressure inched up.

> Why? What's going on?

BASH

> Don't worry about it. Was his name Jim Something? Jed?

I took a deep breath and pulled up the contact for Jessica Covey before sharing it with Bash.

BASH

> I was close. Thanks!

I slid the phone back into my pocket and stepped forward to grab my suitcase when the luggage attendant flung it off his metal cart and into the collection area. Several other tourists were doing the same, and I wondered which ones were there for the retreat.

Near the exit doors, an attractive young man in a clean white tank and tan linen pants with leather sandals held up an iPad with the name of the retreat on it.

"Hi, I'm Kenji Toma," I said, nodding toward his tablet. "I'm one of your arrivals."

A grin split his warm brown skin as he reached for the handle of my rolling suitcase and handed it off to a man standing slightly behind him who was wearing a uniform branded with the name of the hotel. "Excellent. We're just waiting for two more, and then we'll head to the resort. How was your flight?"

We made the necessary small talk as a younger woman and an older man approached to claim the other spots in the transport van. They all continued their friendly chatter as the van bumped along the local streets, passing open-air markets and run-down storefronts interspersed with flashier souvenir shops. It reminded me of a trip to an island in Belize I'd made with the Brotherhood several years ago. They'd spent the week scuba diving and lounging in the sun while I'd taken the opportunity of having them all together to get critical papers signed and nail down business decisions and planning details.

Now, finally, I was set to have a relaxing island vacation of my own.

The warm air floated in the open windows of the van. Once we'd left the small city center, the air carried a slight floral scent mixed with the salty tang of the ocean. Soft steel-drum music playing from the van's speakers sent a clear message to my body that it was relaxation time.

Unfortunately, I didn't speak that language. I hadn't in the years I'd worked for the Brotherhood and, if I was honest, not before that, either. How did you relax when your idea of a good time was achieving goals? I wasn't sure, but I was here to learn.

My body remained tense for the remainder of the drive along the coast. I gazed out of the window toward the ocean and wondered if Landry had made it back to his place without incident. It had only been six months since he'd been clipped by a car crossing a street on one of his runs, and I worried about him.

Not because I cared about him more than I cared about any of the other members of the Brotherhood I worked for, of course. Because I didn't. But because I would have a mountain of hospital bills and scheduling changes to manage if...

I closed my eyes and took a deep, cleansing breath, remembering what Chaska said about stress.

"To avoid stress, begin by anchoring yourself in the present moment. Breathe deeply, for every breath is a reminder that you are alive, and life is resilient."

I inhaled for four long seconds, held it for a beat, and then exhaled slowly before opening my eyes. The waves continued to tumble rhythmically in the distance, a reminder that this world was way bigger than anything I could ever have to be concerned about.

My phone buzzed again. I knew I needed to turn it off, but old habits were hard to break. I'd turn it off when I reached the hotel.

LANDRY

Did you make it okay?

My heart did a little pirouette. Before I could stop myself, I typed a response.

Aren't you supposed to be at your shoot?

LANDRY

Finished already. Slayed, obvi. How's the weather? According to my app, it's sunny and warm there.

I took a photo of the sea with the afternoon sun glinting off it and hit Send.

LANDRY

Well, fuck me.

No thanks.

A photo of Landry's devastatingly beautiful face popped up in the window. He was wearing a teasing, knowing grin that completely called bullshit on my response.

And he was right. If there was one thing about Landry I couldn't deny liking, it was his talent in bed. I'd let him fuck me pretty much whenever and wherever he wanted. And I *had*. Frequently, despite my better judgment.

I stared at the photo and drew my finger over a flyaway wisp of blond hair caught by the wind.

"That your man?" the lively woman next to me asked, startling me into nearly dropping my phone.

I quickly clicked my screen off and cleared my throat. "Oh, er. No? No. I work for him. At work."

She looked at me knowingly. "If I worked with someone that good-looking, I'd never get anything done. He looks like a famous actor or something."

I didn't explain that she probably subconsciously recognized him from something. Landry got that a lot, people knowing they knew him "from somewhere" but not being able to put their finger on it.

"He's actually a cocky asshole," I muttered. "Sometimes the most annoying things come in lovely packaging."

Her smile faded until her eyes lit up. "Oh my gosh. You're so right. I once got a wall mirror from a home decor store, and it came with this super-sick custom box with a magnetic flap closure. Inside was just the fastener to hang the mirror on the wall. Here I thought there'd been a gift with purchase."

"No," I said, hiding a smile. "Just a basic screw with a beautiful presentation."

She tried to think of other examples, mentioning the collectible glass jar she'd bought Nutella in at Christmas and the pink tissue paper and satin ribbon that her everyday sports bra had been wrapped in at the shops.

"But back to this guy in your phone. What do you do for him?"

I clicked my screen on and glanced down at the photo. Just seeing Landry's face, the pert nose and piercing eyes, did something to me. *Orgasm, mostly*, I thought.

I bit my lip and tried to stay focused. "I'm an executive assistant. He's one of my bosses."

The woman, who'd introduced herself as Lindsey, bounced her eyebrows. "Are the others that pretty?"

I sighed. "I mean, kind of."

"So, like, you make them coffee and do their... accounting and stuff?"

"I do whatever needs to be done," I said. "Scheduling, negotiations, project management, communications and correspondence, crisis management, you name it, I'm probably in charge of it."

She turned in her seat to face me as if settling in for a salacious story. "Oooh. What kind of crisis management? Anything good?"

I thought of some of the doozies. Handling a man who'd fraudulently claimed to be the owner of Bash's company. Untangling Silas from an accidental Vegas marriage to a stranger. Navigating Dev's sudden fatherhood to a baby he didn't know he had. And finally, dealing with multiple threats against Zane's life while he was on a world tour.

"No," I said, hearing my voice squeak a little. "Mostly regular stuff. Now that you mention it, I do grab a lot of coffee."

She gave a dreamy sigh. "I wouldn't mind fetching coffee for that one."

"What do you do?" I asked out of politeness.

"I'm a lifestyle influencer."

There were many, many ways of responding to this, but in the end, I said, "How interesting. Do you enjoy it?"

By the time we'd pulled into the resort's porte cochere, I regretted asking. Lindsey seemed interested in creating social media content while she was at the retreat, which was an interesting choice for a follower of Chaska Inira.

One of my favorite Chaska quotes, which I kept in a widget on my tablet as a helpful reminder, read: *True presence is found in the quiet between thoughts. In the spaces where we are not distracted by the pull of distant voices, we learn to enjoy the simple act of being, without the urge to seek what's elsewhere.*

Seemed Lindsey hadn't gotten to that module of Chaska's mindfulness course yet.

I glanced down at my phone. Landry's bright eyes and pouty lips stared back at me mockingly, and my stomach twisted with want.

I turned the phone off with a sigh. It was possible I could use a refresher on that "seeking what's elsewhere" business myself.

But that was one of the reasons I was here at the retreat. Obviously, I was eager to study mindfulness with a master, but I was also eager to get a little distance from Landry. Remaining in an enemies-with-benefits situation with him wasn't going to get me to my goals.

I was here to focus on my goals.

As we entered the large, open-air lobby with views of the ocean out the opposite side, I spotted tasteful signage for the retreat. One of the signs read: *"Step Away to Step Within: To fully embrace the peace of this retreat, we invite you to turn off your devices and tune in to the rhythm of the present moment. Let the world outside rest while you journey inward. Your mind, heart, and spirit deserve this time of undivided attention."*

Right. It was time. I was well aware of my phone addiction, and I'd gone to great lengths to prepare for my monthlong absence from my job and my commitments by training an assistant and preparing my army of support staff. It would be fine. The world—and the Brotherhood—could survive without me.

I couldn't imagine someone like Lindsey would respect the strong suggestion to pack away all electronic devices, but I reminded myself that was none of my business.

When I pulled out my phone to power it down, the image of Landry's face flirted back up at me from the screen.

I didn't want my last message to be such a rude dismissal, even though I'd been joking.

> I'm turning off my phone. Please take care of yourself. And... don't do anything stupid.

I took one last look at the photo before turning the device off and storing it in the pocket of my suitcase so I wouldn't keep reaching for it out of habit.

Then, I stepped up to the reception desk to begin my "journey inward." The sign was right. My mind, heart, and spirit deserved this time of undivided attention.

———

Fuck undivided attention. I'd only made it two weeks before I was going out of my mind from all of this undivided attention and fucking meditation.

I'd tried my hardest to let go, to teach myself that my own mind-body connection was what mattered and that the connection to others was secondary. But I craved connection to my life, to my family, to the Brotherhood, to... well, to anything that wasn't cold-pressed juice "rich with antioxidants," mindful reflection, and picture-perfect serenity.

"Kenji! I thought you were at a monastery in Borneo," my grandmother said with a laugh when she picked up the phone.

I smiled. "Wrong continent, Baa Baa. You're probably thinking of Mom and Dad. Aren't they cruising around Southeast Asia until April?"

"So *they're* the ones in Borneo?" Another peal of laughter was followed by a *tsk*ing sigh. "Who can keep up? For two people who never took a vacation their whole lives, they sure get around. And so do you, come to think of it."

She wasn't wrong. After decades of frugality and scrimping to make ends meet, my parents had finally retired five years ago, and my father had been determined to enjoy every single day of his retirement. They'd been cruising nearly continuously since then and loved every minute of it.

I couldn't talk, since I traveled constantly while working for the Brotherhood.

"I'm at a retreat off the coast of Ecuador," I reminded her. "In a tiny island country called San Cordova. And it's a luxury resort for Westerners, complete with Wi-Fi and coffee pods in the room—"

"Oh, that's right! You were supposed to be silent for a month."

I let out a breath. "Not *silent*, but..."

"Not working on your computer?" she teased. I could hear the smile in her voice.

"No."

"And so."

It was so like her, that expression. I grinned. "And so. I realized I missed my Baa Baa. How are things in Boca?"

Instead of interrogating me, she went on to give me all the hot goss from her retirement community. It reminded me of the way she used to catch me up on her soap operas when I had to go back to school in the fall after watching them with her all summer long. And the stories were just as outlandish.

I leaned back in the hammock on my terrace and let the familiar cadence of her voice wash over me. When her update finally wound down, there was comfortable silence for a beat.

"You know," she began gently. "I've been reading that book you gave me at Christmas. I read a very interesting part the other day. Let me find it... ah, here it is. *Mindfulness is a powerful tool, but it is not the only tool. Sometimes, the heart calls for connection.*"

"You made that up," I said with a surprised laugh. While it was true I'd included a book of Chaska's wisdom in her holiday gift package, I knew without a shadow of a doubt she wouldn't have cracked it open and actually read it.

"It sounds like him, though, doesn't it?" she snickered. "And maybe it's something he'd say. He's there with you. You could ask him."

I let out a breath and lowered my voice in case anyone's terrace was too close to mine. "He's here, but he's not..." I tried to think of a respectful way of saying it. "He's a bit impressed with himself."

The man was as magnetic in person as I'd envisioned, but he was also, surprisingly, a conspicuous consumer. "He wears a Prada cross-body bag," I admitted in a whisper.

The sound of her tittering laughter made me laugh, too.

"Oh, honeybunch," she said affectionately. "Not all life lessons are easy ones."

"What lesson am I supposed to learn from this? Because the only one that keeps coming to mind is that I'm an unrepentant workaholic. I tried repenting, but it didn't take. I didn't think that was possible."

"Did it ever occur to you that Chaska himself might be enjoying life in moderation rather than attempting extremes? No vow of silence. No vow of poverty. Simply... taking time out to reflect and be intentional. Perhaps you can take a lesson from him and check your email periodically. In moderation."

The idea of checking my email gave my heart a little jolt of excitement. "You think?"

"We all have our security blankets," she teased. "Maybe for you, it's not a Prada bag but your spreadsheets."

After ending the call with Baa Baa, I moved back into the room and allowed myself to start up my laptop and check my email. Unfortunately, a type A workaholic had put someone else in charge of the damned thing for the month, and everything seemed to be in order. There were absolutely no fires to put out.

The idea that someone else had been able to take over for me without turning everything into a chaotic nightmare was... depressing as fuck.

I clicked through the tidy folders until I froze on the one named Landry. Inside were several emails from Lamar Duane, Landry's agent. On most of them, I was only copied on the email. Landry had insisted his agent keep me in the loop since I maintained a master calendar for him and managed his travel arrangements.

But one of the emails had been sent directly to me and didn't even copy Landry.

Why is he doing this, Kenji? Did something happen? I thought I'd have at least a few more years with him before he decided to pursue a different career.

I read the email two more times and then went back to read the others in the Landry folder. They were emails about his retirement from modeling. About decisions not to renew various contracts, to pull out of whatever projects he could pull out of, and to determine whether or not to announce his retirement or simply fade away.

I scrambled for my phone and powered it on to send him a text.

> What the fuck? You're retiring?

It was late, but New York was only an hour later than San Cordova. I waited for a response.

> LANDRY
>
> It's four in the morning. And why do you have your phone on?

Four? It was only 11:00 p.m. in New York.

Answer my question.

My phone rang, the shrill blare of "I Don't Need a Man" by Pussycat Dolls in the quiet room scaring the hell out of me.

I quickly pressed the button to answer it. "Tell me you're not quitting as some kind of... grand gesture," I began.

When his familiar voice came over the line, my eyes began to sting. Maybe I was allergic to long-distance phone calls all of a sudden. "Not everything is about you, Kenji."

Great. Now, my pride was stinging, too. "No, I know. That's not what I meant. I just... what's going on? Where are you?" I asked, scrambling for his calendar to see if I'd overlooked a European job that would have put him in a different time zone.

"England. My father isn't doing well."

His voice was rough from sleep, but I could also hear the strain in it. Since I'd rarely heard of him visiting his father, I realized something must be very wrong for him to be there.

"Are you needed at home? To take care of him?"

The subject of Landry's family was a touchy one, and he rarely talked about them to me or even anyone in the Brotherhood. We knew he had dual citizenship, due to having an American mother, and that she'd died after a serious illness while he'd been in high school. We also knew he was an only child.

But that was *all* we knew.

The Brotherhood seemed to think Landry's reluctance to discuss his early life was because he'd grown up poor—maybe even as poor as Zane had—but privately, I wasn't so sure. There was a quiet but arrogant confidence about Landry that reminded me of people with old money—*big* money, the kind that came with power—which made me wonder whether there had been some kind of drama he didn't want to share. Had his parents been into something shady? Had one of them done time for something he didn't want us to find out about?

Possibly, I'd watched too many of Baa Baa's soap operas.

In any case, it was clear I'd never know the truth. Anytime I asked in even the most casual way, Landry would shut me down with a firm "Let's not talk about that, hmm?" or distract me with his talented lips and tongue until I couldn't remember my own past, let alone his. All of which just went to prove that Landry might trust me to manage his billion-dollar investments and legal matters, as I did for the rest of the Brotherhood, and to keep a handle on his modeling career... but when it came to his family matters, I didn't have the right security clearance to know a damn thing.

Which was one of many reasons Landry Davis annoyed the fuck out of me. He claimed to want a serious relationship with me, yet *he* was the one putting up giant barbed-wire roadblocks to keep me at arm's length.

No one owed anyone else all the gory details of their past. I believed that. But at a certain point, his omissions had started to feel like a lie. And if Landry couldn't be honest with me, any hope of a serious relationship was dead in the water.

"No, my father..." Landry began, stopping himself before continuing. "He'll be alright."

I held back a sigh. "Is he sick? Is it temporary? Maybe you could hire him some help and make sure he's getting medical care—"

"No. He has help and doctors and everything. It's just... I feel pressure to be here."

There was a thread of stress in his voice that made me wonder if this issue with his father had led to his sudden retirement from modeling.

"Are you... are you planning on moving back to England? Helping him more permanently?"

"No, god no. *No.* I'm just here for another few days, then I'm headed to Majestic for Lellie's birthday."

"You're avoiding my original question," I pointed out. "What brought up the idea of retirement?"

I heard the rustle of bedsheets and imagined bare-chested, messy-haired Landry in bed. "You're alone, right?" I blurted before he could say anything.

There was silence on the other end. "Not exactly..."

I sucked in a breath. "Oh." My stomach soured, and my heart contracted. I swallowed. *Oh.*

"As for retirement, I just decided I'm done starving and dehydrating myself for money. I don't need the money, and I'm past the point of feeling like the ego stroke makes up for it. Besides, it's time. I don't want to start getting polite rejections as the industry begins to prefer the younger guys."

I bit back a scoff at the idea he was anything other than in the highest demand. Landry Davis was considered one of the most beautiful men in the world, and that wasn't about to change when he got a few more years under his belt.

"I can't say I'm disappointed to hear it," I admitted. "The schedule was killing you. Not to mention the physical demand it's been taking on your body."

He let out a sleepy laugh. "There are physical demands on my body I'm more interested in these days than the ones from modeling."

His innuendo reminded me he wasn't alone. "Right. Well... I should let you get back to... whoever."

"Are you jealous?" he asked incredulously. "*You?* The man who all but begged me to go fuck someone else when he left?"

"I did not," I snapped. "I only wanted to make it clear that you didn't have to do without simply because I—"

The rhythmic buzz of a cat's purr came over the line. I waited a beat to make sure I was hearing what I thought I was hearing.

"Is that... is that a cat?"

"Kenji Toma, may I introduce you to the ever-faithful yet ever-finicky Lady Bayliss of Kent. Otherwise known as Turkey."

I was stunned speechless. "A cat? You have a cat?"

"My father has a cat. Well, more accurately, his... helper, Nan, has a cat. But she tends to defect to my room whenever I'm visiting. What can I say? I'm a joy to sleep with. At least someone thinks so."

He made it sound like he visited fairly regularly, which made me wonder if he'd managed to stop in on his way to and from European jobs and I just hadn't known. I wanted to ask him about it, but I was more interested in determining if the cat was the only thing keeping him warm at night.

"So... when you said you weren't there alone..."

"I'm snuggled up with Turkey."

The swell of relief I felt was borderline disgusting and humiliating. I swallowed. "Right. Well, I should let you go regardless. Why did my text wake you up? Don't you mute your phone at night?"

Landry hesitated. "Certain contacts are allowed to break through."

I was secretly touched by this. Until the asshole opened his mouth again. "You know, in case I'm arrested and need someone to bail me out."

It wasn't funny because it had actually happened. More than once.

"Maybe if you made an effort not to get arrested, you wouldn't need to receive my calls in the middle of the night."

"True. I wouldn't *need* to. But Kenji?"

"What?"

"I'd still *want* to. Good night."

I stared at the phone as he ended the call. Within moments, a photo flashed up in our text window.

A sleepy Landry was full-spooning a beautiful gray-and-white cat. The man had a shit-eating grin on his face, but all I could focus on were his hands, casually stroking the cat.

His fingers were long and strong, familiar. Those hands had touched me absolutely everywhere. Had spent hours as devoted servants to my pleasure. Had teased and tormented me until I broke, crying out for release.

Those long fingers had been inside of me, probing, pressing, stretching. They'd tangled in my hair and teased my skin with the barest of caresses.

I stared at them, remembering.

Landry Davis was an incredible lover. In bed, he was kind and generous, attentive and aware. He was hyperfocused and dedicated. He was loving and committed.

But the second we got dressed and back to our real lives, he shifted seamlessly into the flippant, unserious playboy narcissist who treated his past like a state secret.

Which was the real Landry?

Even after all these years, I didn't know.

At Christmas in Majestic, he'd seemed crushed after he'd made the play for something more than enemies with benefits and I'd politely declined. I'd assumed, for good reason, that his disappointment came from childish annoyance that I'd said no to him. That he hadn't *won*.

Now, I wondered whether I'd read the situation wrong. Whether there had been actual feelings involved—

But it didn't matter. At least, it shouldn't. Until Landry Davis figured out who he was and began trusting me with the truth of his past, any chance at a deeper connection was never going to happen.

I shut down my laptop and turned off my phone again.

Which was how I missed the first news alerts.

FOUR

LANDRY

"Dear god. It's only nine o'clock. Aren't you supposed to be on American time?"

I glanced up from my laptop screen to see my cousin shuffle into the large kitchen of our family home in Regent's Park. She gave me an affectionate peck on the cheek before helping herself to the kettle.

"Good morning to you, too." I sat back and stretched, grinning. "How's my favorite equestrian prodigy? Planning to reach new heights in the jumps this morning?"

"Not today. I canceled my ride in favor of a lie-in for once." Her long curls bounced around her shoulders as she reached up to find the tea she wanted in a cabinet before placing the bag in her mug. "Too cold and wet, even for me."

"No riding?" I asked in mock surprise. "However will a gently bred girl like yourself pass the time, dahling?"

She managed to glare at me and fill her mug at the same time. "I changed my mind. Piss off, Landry. You sound like my mother."

I laughed out loud.

Though Cora was only a few years older than I was—and had

been living here with her mother since I was ten—we hadn't been particularly close as kids. At first, she was grieving the loss of her father, but then we'd been off at different schools. During all that time, Aunt Lydia had never ceased attempting to micromanage Cora's education, hobbies, wardrobe, and boyfriends.

Unfortunately for Aunt Lydia, Cora was more resistant to being managed than I was.

Now that we were adults, Cora and I weren't just friends but allies. Two of the few people on Earth who knew the truth of my father's condition, not to mention the truth of my identity. And since Cora ran the Davencourt family foundation and I managed the Davencourt holdings, we worked together often on family business, even though most of it was done long-distance.

Cora brought her tea to the old wooden table, scarred and faded from a century of use, and slumped into the chair opposite me with a yawn. "Where is everyone?"

"My father had a doctor's appointment. Just an eye exam," I assured her when she looked at me sharply. "He and Nan should be back shortly. Before Reg left for the market, he mentioned your mother was at the salon, preparing for her trip to the Maldives. And I assume everyone else is occupied." I waved a hand vaguely toward the rest of the house and the office wing beyond, where the small hive of very discreet staff kept the house clean and maintained, the clothing laundered, the accounts tidy, and the schedules under control.

She gave a tiny grunt of acknowledgment before taking a sip of her tea and relaxing in relief. "God, that first sip is so good."

I studied her for a moment. Faint dark circles were just visible beneath her eyes, if you knew how to look beneath the concealer. "You look done-in. Rough night as a socialite on the mean streets of Mayfair?"

My teasing was a cover for genuine concern, and her amused eye roll said she knew it.

"You mean Belgravia," Cora corrected, tugging the sleeves of her wool jumper down to cover her hands. "Art auction at the Gagosian Gallery. A lovely evening... for the most part." She shrugged. "I'd planned to chat with Colin Garner from the *Times* about getting us some good coverage for the Hearts of Hawling Dinner, but he was called away early for a breaking story. Civil unrest somewhere in Ecuador, I heard."

My ears perked up. Thankfully, Kenji wasn't in Ecuador but several hundred miles off the coast. Still, I couldn't help asking faux-casually, "Ecuador? Really? I haven't seen anything about that online."

She shrugged again. "Something about a risk of toxic gasses at a copper mine? I didn't get the whole story because Mother pulled me away so she could 'introduce' me to Rupert Mehra, a man I've known since sixth form." This time, her eye roll was less amused. "Then, when Rupert asked how preparations for the charity dinner were coming—his sister Amelia is a co-chair of the Montrose Initiative, so he knows the last few weeks can be intense —Mother changed the subject." She shook her head. "The woman acts like the past two hundred years were all a fever dream and potential suitors might be scared off if they discover I have goals and a purpose to my life."

I pretended to think about it. "Goals and purpose *are* fairly terrifying. Have you tried being a dilettante like the Davencourt heir?" I batted my lashes at her.

Cora snorted. "Mmhmm, that's you, alright. Sowing your wild oats all day. Not a single thought in that pretty head." She cast a glance at my laptop. "By the by, I saw your memo this morning about the strategic allocation of funds to the Davencourt Foundation's upcoming initiatives in arts and education. Just a little something you threw together between your mani and pedi, I presume?"

I smiled. "You know I hate to be bored."

"Of course. It has nothing to do with you being a fucking *genius*." She sipped her tea for a moment, then set the mug down. "Mother did mention last night that you were planning to step away from your modeling career." It came out like a question.

"Did she?" My smile evaporated. Though I felt secure in my decision, I hadn't announced it to the family yet since I knew they'd start making assumptions about *why* I'd made it. "How... resourceful of her. I only told my agent a couple of days ago."

"You know my mother could teach MI6 how to ferret out information. I was just thinking..." Cora drew a sharp breath, then sat forward and exhaled it in a rush, bringing a torrent of words with it. "I'm not sure if you're aware, but Sir Jonathan Porter has been talking quite a lot about a proposed heritage tax *and* a bypass through Davencourt Park. If you could just meet—"

"Cora," I warned, knowing she was right. While I wanted to pawn her off on my dad for issues like that, we could no longer trust him to carry on a meeting without getting confused or repeating his stories.

Cora bit her lip. "Landry." She managed to imbue those two syllables with a wealth of sympathy and frustration.

"I'm not staying," I told her. "I fly out in a few days."

Her face dropped. "But... Ed really needs you here. *We* need you here. It's not just that people are starting to ask questions about you and that it's getting impossible to keep putting them off with tales of far-off adventures. There are *real* issues for the estate —for the family—that need to be handled delicately. We need someone who can be in Surrey, meeting with people at the Park. We need someone in the House of Lords who—"

"I know." I cut her off to keep from rehashing everything Nan had already told me. "But Cora, I also have a *real* life in the States. A career. Friends. I... I can see Dad's Alzheimer's is progressing, but the solution is for him to retire from office and get a care plan in place. Just because I'm not modeling anymore, that doesn't mean I'm prepared to take over my dad's political career right away. Besides, I would make a terrible MP. I wouldn't even get selected, so it's a nonstarter."

She pressed her lips together in thought before shaking her head. "I think you're wrong. This country—and the Lords—need fresh young energy. I think you should give it serious thought."

I braced my hands on the table and shoved up from my chair to make a fresh coffee. "I've done little *but* think about it since I've been here. Look, the Palace and the prime minister know where I am, and *they* haven't asked me to take my father's place—"

"Not yet," Cora said flatly, which was more than a little chilling. She took another sip of tea and studied me. "Nan says this is about a boy."

"Jesus." I let out a weary laugh and did what I'd been trying *not* to do practically every moment since I'd crawled out of bed this morning: I thought of Kenji.

Kenji, who of course—of fucking *course*—hadn't been able to make it more than two weeks into his monthlong electronics sabbatical without checking his phone because the man thrived on challenge and lived to be needed.

Kenji, who'd called me the moment he'd heard about my modeling retirement, clear concern for me in every word he'd spoken, though he'd tried to hide it.

Kenji, who'd been jealous—there was no other explanation for it, despite all his talk about "no promises" and "no expectations"— when he'd thought I was curled up with another man, and who'd sounded incredibly relieved when he'd learned my bedmate was just a very large cat.

Kenji, whose voice had been a lifeline of sanity when I'd felt like my life was spinning inexorably out of my control.

"He's not a *boy*," I said belatedly. "And Nan needs to keep her thoughts to herself."

"Tell me," Cora commanded.

I sat back down with my coffee, gripping the warm mug with both hands. "Not much to tell. I'm in love with a man who calls me his 'enemy with benefits.' He's the most beautiful, sexy, intelligent, capable person on the planet. He's prickly as a hedgehog and has a heart like a marshmallow. And he thinks I'm an incompetent twat because at one point, I had the brilliant idea that if I kept messing up my life, he'd have to keep fixing it, and any attention was better than none." I summoned a self-deprecating smile. "Still think I'm a fucking genius?"

Cora's blue eyes widened. "Oh, Landry. Nan said it was a tricky situation, but..."

"Nan is a master of understatement." I blew out a breath.

"Does Kenji know about, uh..." She waved her hand around the historic kitchen with antique copper pots hanging from hooks and the old brass servant bells still hanging on a board by the door to the butler's pantry. "You being the earl?"

Of course she'd figured out right away who I'd meant. It wasn't like I'd never spoken about him to her.

"Viscount," I said instinctively. "I am still Viscount Hawling. I won't be earl for many years, hopefully. And no, I haven't told him about my fucking *hereditary peerage*, Cora. God." I laughed shortly. "I wanted the guy to like me. Kenji believes in working hard and achieving your due through diligence and dedication—"

"You work hard!"

"I work hard managing land and investments that were handed to me at the entrance of my mother's cervix. That's a bit like saying I work hard carrying all of my heavy piles of cash around."

"Don't be crass. You can't help being born into wealth. It's what you do with it that counts. And you do amazing things. This morning memo alone was a testament to your talent in structuring budgets, optimizing disbursement timing,—"

"You know how your mother believes anyone born above

Hampstead Heath is a fundamentally good person? Imagine the inverse of that," I instructed. "Kenji is a... a reverse snob. He thinks a person's worth is directly related to how hard he works. You should hear the way he talks about our friend Zane's sacrifices for his fans, or Dev staying up all night helping his mare deliver a foal, or Bash for winning a cutthroat negotiation, or... or... Silas for landing another new consulting gig. When I landed the Armani contract, he said, 'I'm surprised they went for a blond when brunets are more classic.'" I ran a hand through my carefully high-lighted locks and shot her an aggrieved look.

Cora bit her lip, fighting a grin. "I *have* often said I liked your hair better when it was—"

"Zzzzzt." I made a cutting motion through the air. "I'll have you know, this color takes an astronomical amount of commitment to achieve. No one outside the family would guess it's not natural unless they've seen up close and personal that my carpet doesn't match my curtains."

Cora's smile slowly faded. "Landry, have you considered that Kenji *can't* truly love you when you haven't let him truly know you? The real you, I mean. You *are* a hard worker."

I rubbed a hand over my stomach, where hot coffee churned. "That's just it. He *has* known the real me. He knows Landry Davis. And Landry Davis has made some questionable decisions."

Kenji knew things about me that no one else did. He knew about my obscene wealth—by which I meant my *second* round of wealth, which had come when the Brotherhood and I had sold our software program, and the *third* round, which had come thanks to my modeling career—and how I liked to manage and donate it.

He knew I considered the Brotherhood my chosen family and that I sometimes cried listening to Zane's songs—especially the happy ones he'd been writing recently—because, of all the broth-ers, Zane was the one I felt most protective of.

He knew about my love for cheese curls—the American snack

food that might or might not contain actual cheese—a love that I would not divulge to my personal trainer or modeling agent under any circumstances.

He knew I liked classical music but hated opera, that I couldn't sit through a movie in the theater or at home without licorice whips, and that I thought lobsters were strange and terrifying.

In other words, he knew everything about me that was important to know.

At least everything *I* thought was important to know.

I was aware *he* wouldn't see it that way once he learned about my family.

"This—" I waved my hand around the ancient kitchen a bit desperately. "—this isn't me, Cora. This is Everett Davencourt, Viscount Hawling. Someone I never wanted to be."

Cora's face softened with sympathy. As the person next in line to inherit my father's estate if I died without a child, she knew better than anyone the responsibilities that came with this privilege. While she'd no doubt manage everything better than I would, she'd never once implied she had any desire for it to come to her instead of me.

"It *is* a part of you, though," she said quietly. "You might not want the position, but being a Davencourt is as much a part of you as... as being a Yale graduate. As being a model."

I said nothing. I wanted to argue that being a peer was *over there*, something that wasn't relevant to my current life and therefore didn't count, but we both knew it was more like an alarm clock I'd hit Snooze on one too many times.

"You could always walk away," she ventured. "Go back to the States and forget all about this. I selfishly want you to serve in Parliament because it would be good for England. But I love you, and I want you to be happy."

"Why?" I gave her a sidelong look. "Eager to take on the House of Lords yourself, cousin?"

She let out a loud bark of laughter that set her brown curls bouncing again. "Not for love or money. And think of my poor mother, Landry. How would she introduce me at parties? 'This is Cora. She loves riding, children, the color pink... and delivering blistering speeches about tax reform to the Economic Affairs Committee'? Forget matchmaking for me—she might never get *herself* another date." Cora laughed again, and this time, I joined in.

"No," I finally said once our amusement died out. "Without even pretending to consider your mother's romantic prospects, I wouldn't walk away permanently. I'm a Davencourt, as you said."

I loved my family. I was proud of my ancestry. I cared about doing my duty and upholding the legacy I'd been born to.

Just... not *yet*.

"I'm going to tell Dad and Nan tonight that I'm happy to continue doing what I'm doing, and I'm even happy to plan more time here in London working behind the scenes, but I won't be ready to go public as Everett Davencourt and put myself in the running for Parliament for a few years. Maybe after my face is no longer plastered on bus stops all over London and I'm not quite such a person of interest. If I came forward now, can't you just see the headlines? 'Viscount Armani' and 'The Long-Lost Lord of the Runway.' It would be unbearable."

Cora inhaled and let it out. "I hate to admit it, but that's a fair point." She reached across the table and laid her hand on mine. "Nan and Uncle Ed might not be happy, but they'll understand, just like I do."

"Will they?" I smiled wanly. "Dad might say he does, but I'll probably have to keep explaining it to him over and over again every time I come back."

Cora winced. "God, you're right. You will do, won't you? Have to keep explaining it."

I nodded once. "Sometimes he's so *there,* and then all of a sudden, he's—"

The familiar creak of the swinging door leading into the kitchen alerted us that we weren't alone.

"—in Ecuador, you said? Your friend from the *Times?*" I finished, jumping back to the only other thing I could think of.

Nan and my father came in through the door, pulling off their coats and hats.

"Er, not Ecuador, exactly? It's a little island nation off the coast." Flustered, Cora stood up to help my father remove his coat.

Meanwhile, my stomach dropped. "Island nation? What island nation?" I asked.

Nan smiled at Cora. "Hello, love. How was the auction last night?"

"Great—" Cora began.

"What nation?" I repeated.

My dad took the seat next to me with a huff. "Can't see a damned thing."

Nan patted his shoulder as she passed. "It's the drops. You had your eyes dilated. Let me fix you some tea."

"Cora," I said, louder now. "Which island off Ecuador? Was it San Cordova?"

She spread her hands. "I honestly don't remember."

"Everett." Dad turned toward me with a big smile, reaching out to squeeze my arm. "I didn't know you were popping round. How are things in New York?"

There was a familiar beat of silence while everyone in the room changed gears and silently acknowledged he was having a moment.

"They're good. I thought I'd come check in and see how you're doing," I said. There was no point in reminding him I'd already been here a week and had spent most of that time in his study with him.

He brightened at this unexpected pleasure. "Can't complain. My memory's not what it was, but Nan says it's stress. I've taken a little break from work, but I'll be right as rain in a bit."

I pressed my lips together and nodded. He'd been lucid enough when he'd gotten his original diagnosis, but as the disease had progressed, it had become impossible and unfeeling to break the Alzheimer's news to him at every turn. It was much easier to brush it off as stress and change the subject.

He thanked Nan for the cup of tea once it was in front of him. "Oh, Everett, Henry Goodwin was asking after you the other day. Wanted to know if you might like to try on the suit of armor he found in an old trunk." He let out a laugh that brought a smile to my face, even though Henry Goodwin had been dead for at least five years and the suit of armor joke was twenty years old.

"You tell him I'm too pretty to be encased in rusty old armor, Dad."

"Too right," he barked before his face softened. "You have your mother's looks, thank god."

Nan took the seat next to Cora and glanced between us. "What's happening in San Cordova? Isn't that where your friend is?"

I nodded absently while I searched for news on my phone.

San Cordovan Government Betrays Miners

Copper Toxins Threaten Island Nation

Citizens of San Cordova Protest Government Corruption

I scanned the articles and murmured a few of the details as I came across them. "Looks like there was a breakdown of the filtration system that limits exposure of toxic particles and gasses. I guess this would usually trigger a shutdown of mining activity until they can get it up and running again, but the government granted the mining company an exception and extended the allowable exposure time..." I continued reading. "There are allegations of government corruption and bribes. It mentions a history of similar broken promises. The people are protesting."

Nan frowned. "Do you think your friend is safe?"

"I talked to him last night," I said, trying to reassure both of us. "He sounded fine. So far, it seems fairly benign. No violence has been reported."

"Good."

I tried calling Kenji, but it went directly to voicemail. I shot him a text.

> Are you reading the news? What are they saying about the protests there?

I sent him links to the news articles but quickly realized I was being overly dramatic. Angry copper miners didn't have a beef with the tourists, and from what the articles said, the environmental toxins were dangerous to people working in the mine, not necessarily tourists several miles away.

Still. I worried. There was only one airstrip on the island. It was conceivable protests could impact Kenji's ability to get out of there safely if things escalated.

I forced myself to get a grip and calm down. Kenji was smart and travel savvy. He was also fairly risk-averse. He could handle himself. Thankfully, he was staying in the kind of high-end resort that would keep its customers apprised of the situation in town.

Still, I groaned in relief when my phone rang many hours later.

"Sorry it's so late," Kenji said as soon as I answered. "Were you asleep?"

"No. I was too worried," I admitted.

I'd managed to keep my cool for the rest of the day and through an interminable dinner with the family. If Davencourts weren't too civilized to yell, people across the park would have heard how displeased the family was by my proposed two-year delay in stepping forward as the heir. As night came without a phone call from Kenji, though, my anxiety had ramped up.

In desperation, I'd even tried to lose myself in Netflix since their algorithm had my personality on lock somehow and they always suggested the best shows, but that hadn't worked, either. There was nothing new since the last time I'd logged in a couple of weeks before.

"Yeah, well..." He let out a breath. "I had my phone off until I overheard some of the guests talking about the situation in town."

"What are they saying?"

"Resort management is acting like it's no big deal, as if the locals protest over every little thing. But several of the guests are concerned enough to leave early."

I hesitated, worried my asking him to leave would have the opposite effect. "Kenji... I think you should consider—"

He cut me off. "I called to get a flight just in case, but they're all full."

I let out a breath of relief. "I'll send the plane."

"There's no point. They're not approving any new aircraft into the island's airspace. Apparently, the media attention has made it a zoo at the airport, and they could barely handle their air traffic on a good day."

I was surprised to hear a hint of nerves in his voice. Kenji was never nervous. He always had his shit together with several different backup plans, all with their own shit together, too. He was the most quietly confident person I knew, and nothing ruffled him.

"What are you going to do?" I asked. "Is there anything I can do to help?"

"The managers of the resort are assuring us we're safe where we are. That they have plenty of supplies even in a worst-case scenario, and they have armed guards at the resort gates. Obviously, Chaska himself is encouraging everyone to remain calm and stick around."

I could only imagine. "Let me guess. He said something to the effect of... *'Whatever storm rages around us, remember—it will pass, as all storms do. Together, we will weather this moment. Peace begins here, with you.'* Or some bullshit like that."

The warm rumble of his laugh made me grin like a fool. "You're learning. A few more of those and you'll be well on your way to being a die-hard apostle. I should bring you back a meditation robe and incense-burning kit."

"Are you worried?" I asked softly. "You must be if you're trying to get out of there."

He cleared his throat. I knew that trick. It was his way of shoring up and getting on with it. Here in England, it was famously known as the stiff upper lip. "No. I'm just ready to get home. It turns out I'm not particularly good at relaxation."

"You don't say?" I teased. "I figured you'd go through iPad withdrawal at first, but you'd rally and embrace the sunshine and fruity cocktails eventually. I half worried you'd decide to chuck it all and become an islander."

"Not all of us have a billion dollars, Landry," he reminded me. Thankfully, there was no bite in his voice. The Brotherhood paid him very, very well, and part of his compensation over the years had included stock options in our various lucrative endeavors. Kenji Toma was doing just fine, financially speaking.

I leaned back in my bed and stretched out, throwing one arm behind my head. "What would you do with a billion dollars if you had it?"

I half expected him to scoff and make a short remark before chivvying me off the call. So I was surprised when he actually humored me.

"Well, for one, I'd splurge on something ridiculous like the Pearl Royale chess set by Colin Burns. But then I'd have to have a room fitted out with custom lighting to do it justice. Which means I'd need to buy a place."

Kenji currently lived in a small apartment between the park and Lenox Hill, which was very convenient to work, but it was also half-underground and didn't have its own laundry machines. My fingers itched to buy him a nicer place and give it to him anonymously. But since he was neck-deep in all of my financial business—at least the non-Davencourt side of things—it would have been nearly impossible to pull it off, even if he'd been willing to accept an anonymous gift. Which... considering the Brotherhood's history of trying to give him perks, would have been a disaster.

Not that I hadn't decided to do something very stupid anyway. Something I'd probably never tell him about or show him. Still, it was nice to spoil him, even if I couldn't tell him about it.

"You should buy a place anyway," I suggested. *Or move into mine.*

"I'd send my grandmother a Birkin bag so she could show it off to all her friends."

"No you would not," I said with a bark of laughter. "You would never spend that much on a bag you know she'd never use."

I could hear the smile in his voice. "No. You're right. But maybe I'd send her a good knockoff so she could still brag about her rich grandson."

"She already brags about you," I said without thinking. As soon as the words were out of my mouth, I winced and prayed he wouldn't read into it.

"And how would you know that?"

Fuck.

"I've met her, remember?"

"Landry, you met her for five minutes when I brought her by the office once to show her where I work."

"I, ah... I..." The truth was I'd flown down to Florida on my way to London. At Christmastime in Majestic, Kenji had said he was ready to let his grandmother set him up with a nice man, and I'd be damned if I'd let her choose anyone other than me. I'd made a beeline for the Vista Bonita Active Seniors Community in Boca Raton, Florida, to plead my case. It had been a good visit—Kenji's grandmother was nearly as quick-witted and sharp-tongued as her grandson, and spending a few hours with her had temporarily dulled the worst of my craving for the man—but the results of my efforts remained unclear.

"Don't all grandmothers brag about their successful, handsome grandsons?" I said vaguely.

"Did yours ever brag about you?"

I thought back to my memories of my paternal grandmother. My mom's mother had passed on when I was too young to remember her. But my grandmother on the Davencourt side had been a warm, loving type, even if she'd been a bit formal in public. "Yes, actually," I said. "She once told the..." I stopped myself from saying *Queen*. "Lady in charge of our community that I had perfected the art of folding a napkin into a blooming lotus. The woman was very impressed. I, on the other hand, wanted to die of embarrassment."

Hearing his chuckle released some of the tension in my shoulders. "I can just picture you now, all skinny and knock-kneed, folding napkins for your grandmother like a good lad."

"I wasn't always skinny," I corrected. "And in that story, I was fifteen," I joked.

The rich, dark sound of his laughter floated down the line. His voice still sounded warm when he asked, "How's your dad? And don't pretend everything's fine. You wouldn't be there comfort-snuggling the cat if it was."

I grimaced at this reminder of how much I'd kept from him—not just my title but my father's health, too. It had been easier to pretend I was off on an unidentified jaunt somewhere for fun than to explain I was visiting home because it meant fewer questions about my family, about where I was from. In reality, I visited my father quite a bit. I just... didn't exactly tell Kenji and the rest of the Brotherhood about it.

Cora's words from earlier hit me in the solar plexus. *Kenji can't truly love you when you haven't let him truly know you.*

I glanced across my bedroom to the intricately carved wardrobe, mentally traveling along every familiar divot and swirl in the design. It was an exercise I'd done a million times before, sometimes out of boredom and sometimes just to distract my mind from other things.

"He, ah..." I sucked in a breath. "He has Alzheimer's, Kenji."

The silence lasted several beats. "I'm so sorry. Is it a recent diagnosis?"

I clenched my jaw. "No."

The single-word answer was like the blade of a guillotine, cutting off any intimacy we'd created. I knew it was hypocritical to expect him to give me a chance at a real relationship when there was so much I was hiding from him.

"Oh."

"I'm sorry I didn't tell you."

"Not necessary. You're entitled to keep your private life to yourself."

I could hear the stiff formality in his voice, the tone that he took when he wasn't sure of his role among the Brotherhood. When he returned to the comfort of his distant role where emotions played no part in his relationships.

"I don't want to keep my..." I stopped when I realized that was exactly what I was doing, what I'd always done. "I don't keep my private life to myself because I don't trust you, Kenji. I hope you know that."

"I don't know that. What other reason would there be?"

Because I don't want you to look at me differently.

Because I'd rather have the scraps of a relationship than lose you entirely.

Because I've kept this secret for so long, I worry you'll hate me when I tell you the truth.

I closed my eyes and tried to decide how much to tell him. It wasn't exactly a conversation I wanted to have when we were literally on opposite sides of the world from each other. "It's complicated," I finally admitted.

Kenji hesitated. "Well, that explains it."

I let out a breath. "Kenj—"

"Are we having phone sex or what?" he asked, dropping the personal subject matter like a hot potato.

My jaw ached with the realization I'd fed right into his usual preference.

To keep things physical and shallow. To avoid emotions at all costs.

To never get past enemies with benefits.

But as always, I'd take whatever pieces of Kenji Toma I could get.

"That depends," I said, hearing the false casual tone in my voice. "What are you wearing?"

FIVE

KENJI

A vulnerable Landry was my Kryptonite.

It didn't matter that he'd lured me into talking about my dreams, then admitted he'd been withholding the truth about his father's illness. It didn't even matter that he'd literally *it's-compli-cated* me when I'd admitted it felt like he didn't trust me.

Hearing the sadness in his voice as he talked about his dad was enough to make me want to fix it.

I was good at fixing things. I made a living fixing things. But I couldn't fix this.

I could, however, distract him from it temporarily.

As expected, Landry ended the call immediately and dialed me back using FaceTime. Ever since the one time he couldn't turn an existing call into a video call, he gave up trying. Now, he insisted on ending the call and starting a new one. It was ridiculous... but endearing.

Seeing his face made my chest constrict. "Hi," I said stupidly. For some reason, all the saliva on Earth pooled in my mouth at once.

"Hey, gorgeous."

Landry's eyes were warm, and the edges crinkled with affection. People paid lots of money to look into those eyes, and here I was, getting the laser focus for free.

"Hi," I said again.

"Get naked," he replied with a grin.

"You've forgotten who the boss is in our getting-naked relationship." My hands betrayed me, propping my phone on the nightstand before reaching for the buttons on my shirt.

"I haven't forgotten." He yanked a cable-knit sweater over his head, leaving his long hair messy. "Naked. *Now.*"

I'd swear he added an extra-growly vibration to his voice when he commanded me in bed—something too low for the human ear to hear but that my dick responded to like a dog whistle.

"Hey. I could give or take this little session," I said, making my greatest attempt at a bold-faced lie to date. "Consider it a pity fuck." My shirt slid off my shoulders and onto the tile floor of my room, and then I reached for the waistband of my shorts and shucked them down.

Landry's eyes popped out of his head. "Is that a *Speedo*, Kenji Toma?"

Heat rushed to my face. "It's a beach resort. I was on the beach."

"In *that?* Straighten up. Give daddy a little show." The edges of his mouth quirked up, and his eyes brightened. I couldn't help but devour his sculpted chest and shoulders, even though he still had a T-shirt on.

I rolled my eyes but stood a little straighter and turned so he could see my ass. I hadn't spent half my life doing squats at the gym to miss an opportunity to see this man's expression get even hungrier.

He let out a low wolf whistle. "Pan up and down. Step a little away and let me see your legs. Fuck, Kenj."

I lifted one of my legs in an exaggerated froggy cowboy maneuver and made a stupid face. "I'm not a cam boy. You get what you pay for on this channel."

He laughed while yanking off his shirt. "Okay, okay. But don't take them off yet." He unbuttoned his jeans and shimmied out of them, leaving a tight-fitting pair of black-patterned boxer briefs I recognized from an ad campaign he did once.

Landry's blue-green eyes came closer to the camera. "Okay, *now*. But tease me a little while you do it."

My cock was already getting hard, jutting out the front of the suit and pulling the waistband away from my lower belly. I ran my fingers down my chest and snuck them into the opening. Landry made a low groan.

I secretly loved turning Landry on. He was so easy, so expressive. But the commanding edge to him during sex made me want to roll over and show him my fucking belly.

Preening in front of him, watching him react, was one of the ways I retained a little control over the situation. Otherwise, I'd most likely collapse into a puddle of submissiveness... which would be absolutely unacceptable.

If Landry knew exactly how much I craved him, I'd never hear the end of it. And if he ever learned how much his slightly cocky, teasing way turned me on, he'd be insufferable.

I closed my eyes and leaned my head back, feeling the soft brush of my hair slide down my bare back. I stroked my cock inside the suit and let out a sigh of appreciation and relief.

"That's it," Landry murmured. "Cup your balls. Let me see the tip. Are you leaking?"

His voice washed over me, making my skin prickle and my nipples tighten. I used one hand to push down the front of the suit while I stroked up with the other and revealed my cock head, sticky with precum. I smoothed my thumb over it and brought it to my mouth, making a show of tasting it and sucking it.

"Oh fuck," he breathed.

I opened my eyes and met his before pulling the suit completely off and using both hands to stroke and cup and tug myself.

"Kenji, fuck," he said, over and over again. He yanked off his own underwear and lay on the bed, stretching out until his cock stood up from his neatly trimmed pubes.

I'd made fun of him once, early in our time together, for being excessively manscaped. He'd explained it was a professional requirement. That was the first time I'd stopped to think about how many people had seen Landry naked. About how many people got to have a say about how he maintained his body.

And it had made me white-hot with anger and jealousy.

I sat back on the bed and pulled my feet up so he could see my hole. The noise he made ramped up my heart rate. I ran a finger lightly over the crinkled skin and imagined it was Landry's teasing touch.

"That's it," he said. "Push it inside for me. Finger yourself."

I curled my toes but refused to do as he'd said. It felt too good keeping us both on the knife's edge.

"Kenji," he growled. "Where's your lube?"

I swiped a finger over my slit and moved the sticky precum down to rub over my hole. He sucked in a breath and growled my name again.

The lube was under my pillow. I reached for it and poured some into my hand before moving it back down to stroke my cock. "You're so impatient," I warned.

"Turn around on all fours. Face down. Ass up. Give it to me."

My cock jerked in my hand. I wanted to do what he said, and if he'd been there with me in person, I would have obeyed him right away. But for some reason, this... this distance... doing it over a screen... made me less compliant. Part of me felt like if I gave him everything he wanted, he wouldn't come back for more. And I didn't want to delve too deeply into *that* fucked up line of thought.

Instead, I pressed my finger inside, just the tiniest amount.

He groaned and closed his eyes, jacking his own cock faster for a few strokes. It was shiny already. He must have lubed it up when I wasn't looking.

His voice held a growl. "Do what I say, Kenji."

"Make me."

He opened his eyes and met mine through the camera. "You know if I was there, you would move where I put you and do what I ask, right?"

My breath came in shallow gasps as the tantalizing sensation of my orgasm began. "That right?"

"You like to be good for me. You like it when I tell you what to do."

"Never," I said on a gasp. My release was *right there*.

"Put another finger in. Do it now."

The second finger caused a delicious stretch. A slick sucking sound broke the silence as I moved them in and out.

"Another," he commanded.

As soon as I felt the resistance of a third finger, my orgasm slammed into me, causing me to cry out. The sound of Landry's broken curses added to the mix. Hot spunk landed on my stomach and fist and filled the air with the scent of sex. I opened my eyes in time to catch Landry with his head thrown back, tendons in stark relief against his neck.

He continued to groan and shudder through his own release while I devoured every inch of it with my eyes.

When he finally regained his senses, he gazed at the camera. "Come home."

My heart did a swoopy thing in my chest. "I... I'm trying." I swallowed and tried to come back down to earth. "Besides, you're not even there."

"I'm headed there as soon as I can."

It took me a minute to realize he meant "home" as in… Majestic. "It probably makes more sense for me to go back to the city instead of all the way to Wyoming."

A little crease formed between his eyebrows. "And miss Lellie's birthday? It was one thing when you were going to be meditating with Chaska, but you can't skip it just to stay in the city. You love that girl."

It was true. I'd been following Lellie's progress since she was an embryo, and Dev had put me in charge of making sure any child born out of his "donation" to his friend Katie was protected financially. I'd kept up a correspondence of sorts with Katie after Lellie was born, keeping up to date on her growth and welfare, and when Dev inherited custody of Lellie after Katie's death, I'd finally gotten to become an active part of her life.

I missed her… almost as much as I missed Landry.

Which was a sign I'd fallen way too far off the don't-give-a-shit wagon. This emotional nonsense needed to end.

I sat up and reached for a T-shirt, tossing it over my deflated dick. "I'm sure the Brotherhood doesn't need their trusty executive assistant at the birthday festivities," I said, wondering how to get off this call now that we'd had our fun.

"Dammit, don't do that," Landry snapped.

I blinked at him. "I beg your pardon?"

"After all this time, after everything we've been through, you're going to act like you're nothing more than our assistant? Are you fucking kidding me?"

This was veering dangerously close to emotional territory, and my mental sirens began clanging. "Ah… I think I'm due for a meditation session right now," I said, looking around for my phone. It took me a few beats to realize it was the thing with the angry naked man on it, propped on my bedside table.

Fuck.

"Do not hang up that phone," Landry warned. "We need to discuss this. Kenji—"

I reached for the red button and ended the call.

I squeezed my eyes shut and cursed myself for being an idiot for inadvertently revealing too much.

I blamed effing Landry, with his rare vulnerability and his stellar orgasms, for this moment of weakness.

Of course I knew that I was more than "just" an assistant to the Brotherhood. They trusted me with their secrets. They relied on my advice. They respected my loyalty. I felt valued—more than valued—and it showed in the outrageously high salary that I made sure I *earned* every single day. I couldn't have imagined being this happy or professionally fulfilled back when I was a desperate twenty-something New York newbie accepting a temp job.

But.

Was there a part of me that sometimes watched the five of them together—these men whose friendship had been forged through unimaginable wealth and incredible pain, whose bonds were so deep they called each other *brother*—and felt like a bit of an outsider? Maybe. Yeah. A little.

Was there a part of me that wondered, if I hadn't spent my college years scurrying from job to class to job, or every free moment in my current life devoted to the Brotherhood—if I actually made time for socializing—whether I could have had friendships like theirs? Yeah, okay, maybe that, too.

So, it simply worked best to remind myself from time to time that their friendship wasn't meant for me. That I had a different role in their lives and them in mine. *Creating boundaries that protect my peace*, like Chaska said.

Landry tried calling me back, but I sent it directly to voicemail. Unfortunately, while my finger was on the screen, a new text message popped in from Dev's fiancé, and I inadvertently opened it.

Ugh.

Below the text was a picture that wasn't just cute but *criminally* cute. Lellie's chubby face grinned up at me, her hair in a waterspout pigtail on top of her head. She wore a red-and-white-striped shirt with a white Peter Pan collar that I'd given her at Christmas, when I'd taken every opportunity to hold her and tell her how much her mother had loved her and how much her dads and uncles loved her, too.

It was one thing to try to keep boundaries with the adults in my life, but this happy toddler with her cheek-smacking kisses was a boundary-destroying machine.

She was also a potent reminder of the future I'd always wanted —a large, boisterous family to make up for the oppressively quiet household I'd grown up in, a devoted husband, a house that felt like home—but seemed unlikely to ever have.

In order to make it happen, I'd have to find someone interested in being the primary caregiver for our children. And they'd have to be okay taking second fiddle to my commitment to the men I worked for. They'd have to be responsible, caring, selfless, capable, *committed.*

Essentially, a unicorn.

Hence, my single life... *and* hence my inability to seriously consider Landry Davis as a serious potential partner. While I knew he also wanted kids one day—and was annoyingly great with them—he wasn't in a position to settle down. Or maybe it was more accurate to say he didn't show signs of wanting to settle down.

Although he did retire from modeling…

I blew out a breath and stood up. It might be late in England, but the sun was still up here in San Cordova. While I wasn't due for a specific class, there were always meditation sessions I could join. It seemed to me this would be the perfect time to try and get back into a more grounded headspace.

One in which I stopped imagining what it would be like to settle down and have kids with Landry Davis.

I'd come here to focus. To evaluate. To strategize.

I hadn't come here to fantasize.

———

"Let the sweetness of the drink remind you that joy is found in the simplest of moments. Cheers."

Jamie's voice was softened by the alcohol as well as the teasing grin on his face.

"This can't be your first retreat if even your toasts sound like Chaska's wisdom," I said with a laugh. Jamie and I had shared several good conversations since arriving, and when he'd suggested drinks at the pool bar after our meditation session, I welcomed the distraction. That had been four fruity cocktails ago, and we were now knocking back fresh drinks and a tower of chicken nachos at a table between the bar and the sun loungers.

"Believe it or not, I was a retreat virgin before this. Although with views like these and company like yourself, I can imagine they're addictive." Jamie shot me a wink as he reached for another chip.

Island music played from hidden speakers while the warm breeze blew away the heat from the sun, and I decided maybe Jamie's fake Chaska quote was right on the money.

I settled back in my chair and focused on being present in the moment.

The slight spice on the chicken. The cool sweetness of the rum punch. The low hum of conversation. The utter lack of needing to be anywhere other than here, indulging in this beautiful location with an attractive man who shared my interest in Chaska Inira's ideology.

"You told me you live in New York, but you never mentioned what you do for a living," Jamie said, stretching back in his chair and angling his long legs to catch the sun.

"I'm an executive assistant," I said for what seemed like the millionth time on this trip. Asking someone's occupation seemed the go-to conversation starter. "What about you?"

Jamie motioned to the bartender for another round of drinks. "I'm a finance director at an investment firm in London."

"Ah. That explains how you can afford to spend a month at a place like this."

He studied me with a grin. "And what's your excuse?"

I shrugged modestly. "I'm well compensated. I also work my ass off. It took a team of five people to fill in for me this month."

"You must be very good at your job." The grin he shot me was halfway between flirty and merely friendly. "Do you like it? Are you achieving *small daily fulfillments*, as Chaska advises?"

"I *love* what I do. I love being essential to the smooth running of the business." I grinned. "Some people might say I'm a workaholic, but I prefer to say I like being busy. Being busy and vital makes me happy."

"Same. The men and women I've dated have rolled their eyes at me for being too ambitious, but personally, I think there's nothing sexier than someone who knows what they want." Jamie's gaze met mine, and he lifted his glass in a little toast before draining the rest of his drink.

My face went hot, and I was grateful when the bartender appeared with fresh drinks and set them down in front of us with an easy smile. The local man stayed and chatted for a moment about the weather and locally sourced produce, his relaxed attitude reassuring us that whatever civil unrest was happening in the town of San Cordova was far removed from our experience here on the resort.

When he'd departed, Jamie glanced out at the water for a moment. "In yesterday's session, Chaska asked us to consider what aligns with the person we wish to become. I've been thinking about that. What aligns with the person you wish to become? What would you need to be happier?"

I considered it for a minute. The alcohol—not to mention the lingering effects of my conversation with Landry—made my lips a little looser than normal.

"I'd like to find a partner and start a family," I admitted. "But I don't want to give up my job. It's not about the money, and I'd give up city life in a heartbeat since I don't really want to raise kids there anyway, but my job..." I shrugged. "Making my bosses' lives easier aligns with both the person I am and the person I wish to become. As Chaska—and Marie Kondo—would say, it sparks joy."

We shared a laugh, the kind that bordered on a giggle due to the sheer amount of fruity drinks we'd consumed.

"What about you?" I asked, sobering. "Do *you* want a family?"

Jamie's hazel eyes crinkled at the edges as he smiled. "That's a pickup line I've never heard before, Kenji."

Heat rushed to my face again. "Not a pickup. I promise."

He leaned forward and put his hand on my arm. "What if I'd like it to be?"

Suddenly, my relaxed good time came screeching to a halt. Jamie was an attractive, charismatic man. Blond and broad-shouldered. Wealthy, successful, and interesting. I should be excited by his interest... but instead of excitement, I felt a strange kind of discomfort.

"Oh," I said stupidly. "Well. I mean..."

Jamie's fingers brushed down my arm until they reached my hand where it rested on the table. "I came here to focus on myself, not hook up with people, but, as Chaska would say, '*Desire is a natural and beautiful part of the human experience. If your heart and mind are clear, and both souls involved embrace the connection with honesty and respect, then there is no need for justification.*'"

I narrowed my eyes at him. "You're using Chaska wisdom to pick me up?"

His teeth flashed in his tanned face as he laughed. "Is it working?"

I let out a breath. "It *would*. It definitely *would*. You're very charming. But, ah..."

"Oh." His smile dimmed.

I opened my mouth to say some variation of *It's not you, it's me*, but then I closed it. "It's complicated," I said instead, parroting Landry's words from earlier.

"There's someone else."

I winced. There *shouldn't* be, but... "Yeah," I admitted.

Jamie tilted his head. "So what's the complication? Is he a bad boy? A married boy?"

"A stupid boy," I muttered.

When the easy rumble of his laugh assured me he wasn't too upset at my rejection, I forced myself to lower my shoulders. Jamie leaned back and reached for his drink, swirling it with his hand until the ice cubes tinkled in the glass. "Tell me about the stupid boy. What's he done that's so bad?"

"God, where to begin?" I jabbed my straw into my glass and tried to assemble my thoughts. The warm, bright sunshine and the cold alcohol made it difficult. "First of all, he's beautiful."

Jamie blinked.

So did I. I hadn't intended to say that.

Just how much have I had to drink?

"Sounds awful," Jamie said mildly.

"Well, it *is* awful," I said, doubling down. "He's got these eyes that just... *boom!*" I thumped myself in the chest for emphasis. "And don't even get me started on the rest of him. His mouth, his abs, his voice?" I shivered. "Ridiculous. Worse, *excessive.* No one should have all those things."

"Outrageous," Jamie murmured. "How dare he?"

"He's wealthy, too. I'm talking more money than sense sometimes. Mostly." I leaned forward and whispered, "The man bought me a Louis Vuitton suitcase."

"And you... don't like it?" he guessed.

"What? No, I love it. It's a *Louis Vuitton suitcase,*" I repeated, like Jamie was being particularly dense. "The thing glides like butter. It's fucking perfect. The absolute pinnacle of luggage. The Prince Charming of carry-ons. It's the kind of thing I would never, ever buy myself. And now that I have one, no other luggage will ever compare. Which is why—" I jabbed my straw harder. "—he has no business giving me something like that and letting me get used to it in the first place. You see?"

Jamie wrinkled his nose. "Not entirely, I'm afraid."

I ran a hand through my hair. "This isn't coming out right. Just... trust me when I say, he's a playboy, okay? He's not about commitment."

"Ah." Jamie's expression cleared. "Well, there you go. If the guy's sleeping around when that's not your arrangement..."

"No, it's not like that." I waved a hand. "Technically, we've been monogamous for the last three years. Not because it's a rule." I pointed a finger at Jamie for emphasis. "It *isn't.* It's a choice, with no expectations or promises. A choice he happens to have made repeatedly for the past three years, and so have I. But that's all."

"That's all," Jamie echoed. "Three years."

"The question is, how long is that likely to last, really? You know?" The setting sun was doing strange things to my eyes, making Jamie's face double, then merge again with every blink. "He's not ready to settle down. He *isn't*. No matter what he said to me at Christmas or how sweet and sad he looked when he said it."

"Riiiight." Jamie stretched the word out. "So, you're saying... he's not interested in having kids like you are?"

"No, he is. I mean, I think he is. Eventually." I rolled my eyes. "I'm sure he hasn't given a single thought to how to make it happen, though."

"Okay, now I get it." Jamie nodded sagely. "He's not a go-getter. It's hard to be a high achiever in a relationship with a person who doesn't support your ambitions. I feel that, believe me."

"Weeelll..." You couldn't say a man who'd graduated from Yale, become a self-made billionaire before age twenty-five, and mustered the self-discipline to become one of the world's highest-paid models wasn't a high achiever, could you? "He has achieved some things. More things than I have," I admitted.

"And is that a problem? Does he want you to give up your work?" Jamie was sitting back in his seat and looking at me strangely now, probably because I was attempting to murder my fruity cocktail with my straw rather than drink it.

"Oh, good god, no. He's not jealous, and he'd *die* if I quit." I snorted to myself, just imagining it. "He loves that I'm so good at what I do. Frankly, I think it turns him on. And he sometimes looks at me like I'm a superhero, which turns *me* on. And when you think about it, he's probably the only man on Earth who wouldn't care that I'm married to my job because it'd almost be like being married to *him*... except that we're not married and never will be for all the reasons I mentioned." I gave the icy remnants of my drink one last poke and set the glass on the table. "Now do you understand?"

"I think I'm beginning to." Jamie smiled—a smile that was pure friendship and no flirtation whatsoever. "Poor stupid boy." He sucked up the last bits of drink in his glass. "And poor you."

I wanted to argue with this—clearly, I'd given Jamie some misconceptions about my situationship with Landry over the course of the conversation if he was feeling sympathetic toward him, and it seemed important to correct this—but when the bartender brought us yet another round, the thoughts flew out of my head like ripples across the pool, there one minute and then gone so quickly I couldn't remember what we'd even been talking about.

By the time the sun went down, we'd been joined by several of the other retreat attendees. A local band came in and played live music while the warm breeze blew across the pool terrace from the beach.

Everyone was easy and friendly, and I realized I was glad I hadn't been able to fly home early after all. Maybe there was something to this relaxation thing. I had another two weeks to enjoy my time here, learning and meditating during the day and then practicing having a social life at night. Maybe by the end of the remaining two weeks, I might feel less like a stiff workaholic and more like a regular human being with a work-life balance, and maybe this distance from Landry would eventually help me let go of him... though, admittedly, I hadn't been doing great at that so far.

As I stumbled back to my room well past midnight, I overheard two resort employees whispering in a dramatic way. I glanced over at them to try and determine what was going on, but they immediately stopped their discussion, smiled, and wished me a good night.

I was too drunk to think much of it.

When I got back to my room, I forced myself not to check my phone. That way lay madness in the form of another jerk-off session or possibly phone sex, and I was too drunk to trust myself not to blurt out something I might cringe to remember. Instead, I used my remaining energy to wash my face, brush my teeth, and pass out.

If only I'd checked my phone.

By the time I woke up late into the morning, the resort was in chaos, San Cordova was under martial law, and all communication with the outside world had been shut down.

SIX

LANDRY

As soon as I returned from my run the following afternoon and turned off the workout app that blocked my notifications, I immediately knew something was wrong. I almost always had a couple of new texts or news alerts chime through when I came back online; I'd *never* had two dozen texts and missed phone calls, most from the Brotherhood, asking me to call ASAP.

My first thought was that it had something to do with Lellie, so I didn't bother checking any other alerts. I set up my laptop on the table by the settee in my bedroom—my usual spot for doing videos since it hid the rest of the room's distinctive antique furnishings from view—and started a video call without even bothering to shower.

"What happened?" I demanded.

Silas's forehead creased in concern. "We can't get in touch with Kenji."

"Oh." My heart gave a little jolt, but I reminded myself I'd spoken to him less than twenty-four hours before. He'd been fine then—pricklier than a cactus, sexier than any three men put together, and saying utterly infuriating things about where he fit in our lives, but otherwise *fine*—and he'd assured me he was safe. "He's keeping his phone turned off because of the retreat," I reminded them. "I'm sure he'll—"

"Landry," Way interrupted. Silas's husband's face was so serious my lungs squeezed immediately. "San Cordova's under martial law."

"But..." I shook my head. "Kenji's at a luxury resort."

Even as I spoke the words, I knew how foolish and flimsy they were. Money and privilege could only protect you from so much.

The members of the Brotherhood, their various partners, and Foster, who happened to be the local sheriff, were all arranged around the large kitchen table at Dev and Tully's place, and they'd set up the webcam at the end so I could see everyone. We'd done this kind of thing many times before... but I'd never felt nauseous in one of these impromptu meetings before now.

"You're in Europe, right? I don't know if you've been following the news," Silas began, "but there's a copper mine—"

"Yes, Jesus. I know," I snapped, texting Kenji when a call wouldn't go through. "The miners are protesting unsafe working conditions."

Are you okay?

I closed my eyes and sent another one.

Text me if you can.

Unsurprisingly, he didn't immediately write back. The messages didn't even say Delivered.

"He can't reply, Landry," Silas called, immediately realizing what I was doing. "They've shut down all nonessential communication."

"Fuck." I threw my phone down on the cushion beside me and

raked my hands through my hair before looking back to the laptop. "What's the latest? Tell me everything."

Way leaned in and rested his elbows on the table so I could see him clearly on the camera. "The protests turned violent overnight with the murder of the labor secretary in his home. The president panicked and declared martial law, but then his personal security team decided to move him to an undisclosed location on the island. It's a little unclear if they're with him or against him."

He continued. "Meanwhile, their military leaders are apparently a mix of government loyalists and islanders whose families work in those mines or live close enough to be impacted by the toxins. So it's hard to say what side everyone's going to come down on. Right now, it's very up in the air with the possibility of more violence, a coup, you name it."

My head swam with the thought of Kenji in danger. "What do we do? How do we get him out? What's the State Department saying?"

Silas sounded more unsure than I'd ever heard him, which ratcheted up my fear by a thousand. "I don't know, Landry. This is usually when we'd all ask Kenji how to handle a situation."

"We need to call our attorneys," I said helplessly. "We need to find someone in the State Department."

Silas nodded. "Does anyone have any contacts—?"

Bash narrowed his eyes in thought. "I have an acquaintance. He might be able to—"

"Wait!" I blurted, pacing back and forth in my bedroom. "Wait, wait. We all have kidnap and ransom insurance! Let's use that. They cover stuff like this. The company will go in and extract Kenji—"

"He hasn't been kidnapped." Dev's voice was a deep, worried rumble. "You said yourself, he's at a luxury resort. That's still the case... as far as we know."

"Also... Kenji doesn't have that kind of coverage, Landry." Silas winced and shrugged. "It never occurred to anyone he'd need it. He's not a high-value target."

"Fuck off!" I snapped, not thinking rationally. Everyone's eyes widened in shock, but I didn't have time to manage their reactions. "This is Kenji we're talking about. The center of *every*-fucking-thing for every person on this call. He's high-value. He's the *highest* value!" My voice cracked a little, but I couldn't bring myself to care about that either.

I forced myself to blow out a breath, to think about the situation logically. "We need to get him home safely as soon as fucking possible. What are our options? Can we hire the same kind of company to go in? Don't they just need a boat or something?"

All eyes turned to Ryan since Zane's bodyguard and boyfriend had the most experience with personal security, but he shook his head. "It's not as easy as they make it sound on TV. We don't have a relationship with any of those companies, and we don't know if Kenji's actually in danger..." He glanced at Zane, who was watching him with pleading brown eyes, and broke. "But I can make some phone calls," he agreed before giving Zane a kiss and walking out.

Bash stood up and pulled out his phone. "I'll reach out to the guy at the State Department."

Foster leaned forward, a coffee mug held between his hands on the table. His sheriff's uniform gave him an air of commanding competence. I vaguely remembered he had excessive training in search and rescue, so I focused on him, eager for his input.

"I know it's stressful, but let's try and keep a level head. I think contacting the State Department is a good idea. I can't imagine the US has an embassy there, but they'll have other US citizens in San Cordova to be concerned about, too. We need to make sure Kenji's name is on that list so he's involved in anything they do."

"Right, good." Ordinarily, at this point, it would be Kenji taking over the meeting, fingers flying deftly over his tablet as he researched what we'd need with one hand and somehow managed to get it for us with the other. I felt completely inadequate to the situation. "I'll, ah... look up embassies and see if the US has one there. Silas, maybe call our attorneys? See if they have any ideas?"

We spent the next several hours banging our heads against the wall. Ryan's security contacts came up empty, and after waiting on hold with the State Department, we were told they'd add Kenji's name to the list of citizens "possibly" in San Cordova. There was no embassy there, and the closest one wasn't in a position to get involved yet.

After tracking down Kenji's travel information, we called all of our contacts back with proof of his visit, copies of his passport, and everything else we could get our hands on.

Throughout it all, I kept texting Kenji.

> Please, Kenj. I'm worried.

I knew it was pointless. I also knew it wasn't his fault he couldn't get a message out. But I craved something, anything, from him.

At one point, Tully returned to the table with Lellie on his hip. "Say hi to Uncle Landry," he murmured, waving her little hand toward the camera.

"Hi, Lanny," she said softly before tucking her face into Tully's neck. I couldn't help but be grateful for this one happy spark in an otherwise awful day.

Spending time on the video call with my friends, my found family, was healing in a way, but I couldn't shake my fear for Kenji. Yes, he was at a luxury resort, but from everything I'd managed to read, San Cordova was a developing nation without reliable infrastructure and adequate resources to handle a situation like this.

Bash came in from another room where he'd been on a call.

From the look on his face, I could tell it wasn't good. "I got an update from the guy I know. Armed personnel have surrounded the resort where Kenji is. It's unclear whether they're protecting the tourists or holding them."

My stomach plummeted. "Surely Kenji's not the only American there," I asked. "The government has to have a plan to get them out."

"Unfortunately, the State Department isn't willing to act until there's a clear indication they're in danger," Bash said. "Fucking bureaucracy."

Foster pressed his lips together. "Yeah. You know if there was a *famous* American there, they'd already have a plan to get boots on the ground. We receive way more resources to find lost rich kids than poor ones. And if there's a celebrity involved? There's no limit to the amount of money and personnel involved in a rescue operation." He glanced between us. "Does anyone know if Kenji's retreat had anyone famous attending?"

"The guy putting on the retreat is famous," I volunteered. "Chaska Inira."

"He's Peruvian, though, isn't he?" Bash said. "The US isn't going to foot that bill."

"We don't know who else is there," Silas said. "None of us have talked to Kenji in two weeks."

"I have," I admitted. "But you know Kenji's not the type to name-drop celebrities. How do we figure out who else is there?" I asked.

"People like that might use hashtags on socials," Zane suggested.

"I don't think they're allowed to use their phones," Dev cut in. "Screws with the meditation vibes."

This was true... but I happened to know at least one person who hadn't been able to grind out four whole weeks of mindfulness. I was willing to bet there were more.

"It's worth a try," I told Zane. "You guys search for San Cordova hashtags, and I'll look for ones for the resort."

We quickly discovered a young Chicago socialite named Lindsey Graves, who had a significant following on social media and had been posting practically nonstop since landing on the island... at least until yesterday.

I wasn't sure she was enough of a celebrity to prompt State Department involvement, but I couldn't help scrolling her retreat photos anyway, hoping to catch a glimpse of Kenji in the background. Instead, I found a different familiar face in one of her posts. The guy had changed a lot since Eton, but his square jaw and thick blond hair had stayed the same.

I felt a new spark of hope.

I sent the photo to the Brotherhood. "This is Jamie Winthrop. His father, Jim, is the CEO and co-founder of Winthrop & Meyers, a large investment firm. They're American expats in London with plenty of money. Winthrop's a pretty powerful businessman. I'm guessing he'll do whatever it takes to get his son back. He's probably already working on it."

Foster sat back in his chair. "Is he influential enough in London or the States to pull some strings? If so, maybe we could get Kenji out with the Winthrop kid."

Silas's eyes flicked to mine. "Landry, do you think this Jim guy will take a call from us?"

I hesitated. "I don't know."

Jim had spent a lot of time and money trying to establish himself in London's financial market over the years, including several attempts at influencing my father's votes in Parliament. This had led to a very open rivalry between the two men—Jim had dismissed my father as an old-school traditionalist while my father referred to Winthrop as nouveau riche and implied Jim's thirty-year-old company was too new to take seriously—which was one of the reasons Jim's son and I hadn't run with the same crowd at

Eton. I'd come up with the boys from old families while he'd stuck with the other expats and new-money kids.

Between not knowing Jim personally and his contentious history with my father, contacting him would have to be a last resort.

I opened my mouth to try to explain some part of this but remembered at the last minute that I couldn't. As far as the Brotherhood was concerned, I was a poor kid from the wrong side of the council estate.

The lie was a familiar bitter lump in the back of my throat, but it felt larger than ever now. Hard to swallow around. Hard to breathe through.

I clenched my back teeth. There was someone other than Jim Winthrop I could call for help. My father had been friends with the current prime minister for as long as I could remember. "Guys, I have an idea. Let me see what I can do."

After a quick shower, I threw on clean clothes and went searching for Nan. As soon as she saw the look on my face, she dropped her affectionate smile.

"What's going on?" she asked, closing her laptop on the desk in her office.

"I need to get in touch with Teddy Baines."

"We should get our PR team on hand before you announce anything," she said hesitantly. I realized she thought I'd meant to call the prime minister to start the process of taking a spot in Parliament.

"Not about that. It's about Kenji. He's in San Cordova, caught up in a violent protest."

She opened the laptop again and went searching for the information I needed. "Oh, Landry. I'm so sorry. I've got Teddy's mobile number right here."

"Thanks, Nan."

"Of course. Let me know what else I can do."

After retreating to my bedroom again, I took a shaky breath and called the prime minister. It immediately went to voicemail, which didn't surprise me since I was calling from an unknown number.

I texted.

> It's Everett Davencourt, Viscount Hawling. Need help re: San Cordova. Please.

"Everett?" Teddy asked gruffly as soon as I accepted his call.

"Yes, sir."

"I'd ask where you've been, but I have bigger concerns right now. Who do you know in San Cordova?"

I swallowed. Calling Kenji a friend would sound stupid and unimportant and was patently untrue, so I avoided calling him anything.

"His name is Kenji Toma. I want to know if you have a plan to get anyone out of there."

"I've already heard from several other British families affected by this situation. Send the info on your friend. UK passport number would be ideal, but if you—"

"He's American."

There was a pause. "Everett, I'm sorry, but I can't—"

"He's my fiancé," I blurted, shocking myself as much as Teddy. "We're getting married. He's my partner. I need to get him out. Money's no object—"

"It's not that. This is a delicate situation because of our history with San Cordova," he said. "In addition, the political ramifications of expending our resources on an American—"

"I'll do anything," I said in a low voice. "Pay any amount of money. Make any calls. Just tell me what to do, and I'll do it."

I knew it was unwise to give someone carte blanche like that, but I meant it. I would burn the world to bring Kenji home.

Teddy paused. "I need your father to retire—"

"That's already in progress," I assured him. "His health is... precarious."

"—and I need you to take his place."

Fuck. How had I not seen this coming?

I closed my eyes and covered them with my hand. "I-I'm not ready, sir. It's one of the reasons I haven't stepped forward as the head of the family—"

"I understand. And I'm sorry about Ed. He's a good friend and a good man. But I need some energy in the Lords. Allies to outweigh the antagonists. I've been following your career, and you're quite popular with young people. You acquitted yourself well at Yale, and I know you've been working diligently on the Davencourt holdings behind the scenes since then. I think you could do a lot for the party... and for the country."

"Sir..." I hesitated, my stomach twisting with nerves. "Even if I agree to run, there's no guarantee I'll be selected—"

"Leave that to me," he said. "At least tell me you'll let me submit you to the Clerk for consideration."

Panic flared beneath my skin, but what else could I say? "I... yes. Alright."

"Excellent! Come to Downing Street and bring your man's information. We'll see what we can do."

When the call ended, I raced to my closet and grabbed the nearest things, for once not caring whether any of it went together. Then, I made my way through the city.

After giving Kenji's information to an assistant, I was escorted to a conference room where several people were gathered. I immediately recognized Jim Winthrop. Before I had a chance to greet him or anyone else, one of the officials in the room quirked her head at me. "You're Landry Davis."

"Yes." I nodded, knowing where this was going.

"But..."

"I am also Everett Davencourt," I explained. "Everett *Landry* Davencourt."

She paused while trying to work it out. "Bit like a stage name, I guess. And it's your fiancé in San Cordova?" Her eyes went wide. "Oh, wow. Did you give the coordinator his information?"

I nodded as the prime minister entered the room.

Teddy came over and shook my hand. "Everett, welcome. Have a seat."

"I prefer Landry to Everett, sir."

"Noted. Helen, do we have any updates on the situation?"

The woman nodded and returned her focus to the laptop in front of her. "The protesters want to use the resort tourists as a bargaining chip. They're demanding a repeal of the decision to allow the copper mine to operate without the proper safety measures. The companies who purchase from that mine are involved now, and they're in the process of trying to balance putting pressure on the San Cordovan government without..."

As she continued to explain the geopolitical complexity of the issue, it became clear that there were more players involved in the crisis than I'd expected: various countries and companies, not to mention the upset workers and locals.

I glanced across at Jim Winthrop, whose nostrils were flaring in annoyance. He finally cut in. "Sir, bottom-line this for us. Are you sending in a team to get our people out of there, or are you leaving it up to the private sector to solve?"

"Right now, we're still assessing the situation. As you can imagine, it's a delicate matter, considering our history with San Cordova and our relationships with various players. Our hope is that the corporate customers involved will put enough pressure on the company to do the right thing in regards to the safety protocols. We need to give them time to do it. If we get involved prematurely, it could be considered an aggressive act by a foreign nation."

Jim folded his arms across his chest. "How much time?"

Teddy met his eye. "That remains to be seen. Thus far, we have no reason to believe there are British citizens in immediate danger."

I leaned forward to remind him, "The protesters murdered someone already. That seems like danger."

Teddy turned toward me. "I understand. But they murdered someone they felt had caused the problem. The tourists aren't part of this conflict."

Jim's tone was incredulous. "Except for the part where they're being held as a bargaining chip!"

He was right. As Jim did his best to convince Teddy to send in a team, my head began to pound. I didn't have the capacity to be patient. I wanted to fly to South America, source some especially lethal weapons, tactical gear, and a speedboat, and take things into my own hands, vigilante-style.

When the discussion turned into a repeating loop, Teddy and his team left to take a call and gather updated information. I met Jim Winthrop's eyes before moving closer to him.

"They're not going in anytime soon," I said. "Have you contacted Executive Rescue? I assume you have a policy on Jamie."

He nodded once.

"What do I have to do to get my fiancé on that boat?"

He eyed me as if suspicious I had an ulterior motive. "Rescuing two instead of one would increase the risks."

I clenched my back teeth and tried to restrain my temper. "Then I'll get another Executive Rescue team together, and I'll offer them ten times whatever you're paying to get my guy out first."

Jim didn't seem impressed with my bluster. "You're threatening me while asking me a favor? You really are a Davencourt, aren't you?"

"You'll never insult me by comparing me to my father." I stood and gathered my things. "I have to go. Apparently, I have a call to make and a company to bribe."

"Wait," he barked. "I didn't say I wouldn't do it." He glanced at the door before lowering his voice. "I need you to find us a plane that can get us from London to Ecuador as fast as possible. I sent mine to San Cordova with Jamie, and we need to get in the air in the next couple of hours if possible."

That was easy. "Done."

"You'll owe me a favor, Davencourt. A big one. And you'd better hope nothing happens to my son because of this."

I took a breath and steeled myself. The only favor I could imagine a finance executive like Winthrop wanted was political influence. It sounded like I was going to be forced to consider serving in Parliament sooner rather than later, no matter who helped get Kenji out.

But did it really matter who I owed a favor to if it meant keeping Kenji safe?

"Understood," I said. "We can discuss it on the plane."

He met my eyes. "This is going to upset the prime minister. There could be fallout for both of us."

I nodded. He was right, but I didn't much care. Maybe an upset prime minister would be the key to releasing me from parliamentary expectations.

I quickly texted our pilots before texting Nan to have a bag packed and sent to the airport for me. Jim did the same on his end, and within an hour, we were on the plane, awaiting the pilot's final checks.

After ending a call with Executive Rescue, I tried texting Kenji again, though I knew it would be fruitless.

I glanced at my screen in shock as Kenji's photo appeared a moment later. I quickly answered the incoming call.

"Baby?" I blurted, scrambling to keep from dropping the phone. "Are you okay?"

Kenji's voice was unusually harried. "Landry, fuck. I can't believe I got through. They have us all locked in our rooms. Men with guns. They... it's bad. They hit a man in the head with the butt of a rifle and shoved a woman down onto the pavement." He swallowed a sob, and the sound nearly brought me to my knees. "There's a rumor they killed someone in the government. Now, there are men with guns patrolling the hallway outside our rooms. They don't look like military. I need you to call a company called Executive Rescue. See if you can—"

"Already did," I said, interrupting in case we got cut off. "I'm working on getting you out. Stay safe, please. And if you get put into a group, find a guy named Jamie Winthrop and stay close to him."

"You know Jamie?" he asked in surprise.

"His father and I are working together to get you both out of there. And Kenji—" I hesitated.

How was I supposed to explain all the things I hadn't told him over the past ten *years*—who I truly was, how I felt about him, why I hadn't said anything before now—when we might only have ten *seconds* before we were disconnected?

In the end, we didn't even have that long.

"Someone's coming," Kenji said, nerves clear in his voice.

"Find a weapon," I instructed. "Corkscrew near coffee stuff, maybe? Your razor? What else?" I racked my brain to think of what he might travel with that could be used as a weapon, but I drew a blank. "Grab your portable phone battery in case they move you. Put the phone in your sock or something."

"Wait, they're..." I heard fabric sounds like he was moving the phone down against his chest. The sound of muffled shouting came through the phone, making me break out in a cold sweat. The pilot was waiting for me to finish my call before we could take off since even on a private plane, I wasn't supposed to make cell calls. I worried about Kenji trying to reach me while I was in the air. The flying time to Ecuador would be at least fourteen hours.

"Kenji," I pleaded softly.

"They're pulling people out of their rooms, Landry. What do I do?"

My jaw ached. My throat felt like it was filled with cement. "Can you hide?"

"No, there's nowhere to, oh *fuck!*"

I could hear the shouting clearly enough to recognize the Spanish words for *go, ransom, now,* and *hostage.*

"Kenji, I'll pay it! Whatever they ask. I... I... Kenj—"

A loud slamming sound was accompanied by more shouting, the sound of Kenji exclaiming in surprise, and then nothing.

I stared at the phone in horror when I realized the call had ended. I didn't dare try calling back in case, by some miracle, he was able to hide his phone on his person before someone saw it and took it away.

My hands shook, and my skin prickled under a cold sweat. I finally glanced up at the flight attendant. "I'm ready. Let's get this plane off the ground *now.*"

He nodded and turned toward the cockpit.

Jim leaned forward, pressing his hands flat on the small table between us. "What happened? Was that him?"

I tried to control my breathing to keep from panicking. "Yeah. He... they... it sounds like there are armed men taking the tourists hostage. At first, they were locked in their rooms, but he said they're pulling people out of their rooms now. It didn't sound good."

Jim's face turned florid. He took out his phone and began

typing, presumably sending texts or emails to update the rescue team and urge them to move faster.

I closed my eyes and leaned my head back as the plane chased the sunset. I thought about the sun setting on San Cordova, about how violence increases at night, and how the island nation was several hours from Ecuador by boat.

Mostly, I thought about how I wished I'd told Kenji I loved him so that he fully understood that I would do anything in my power to get him out safely... including telling the British prime minister he was my future husband, making a deal with one of our family's political enemies, and agreeing to throw off years of silence to finally claim my public role as the heir to the Davencourt earldom and serve in the House of Lords.

As the plane shot through the night, the intricate house of cards I'd been building meticulously for fifteen years came tumbling down, leaving a single joker lying facedown in the rubble.

SEVEN

KENJI

I was shaking so hard my teeth were rattling. One of the older men I recognized from the retreat was pale and sweating. His poor wife seemed justifiably concerned for him, but she was obviously too scared to draw attention by asking for help again. The first time she'd tried it, the closest gunman had gotten in her face and barked at her in Spanish while pointing the muzzle of the gun at the husband's forehead. The woman had quickly clamped her mouth and eyes closed, leaving fat tears falling, accompanied only by the sounds of her jagged breathing.

There were half a dozen armed men in the room, but they didn't appear to be under any kind of organized command. Several of them were in street clothes, and others were in quasi-military garb. It was unclear who exactly they were or what their plans for us were.

"You're bleeding," Lindsey whispered from beside me.

The lively influencer I'd met on the airport transfer van two weeks ago looked shaken and hollow-eyed now, barely recognizable.

I felt the heat of her stare on the side of my face, where the blood was still warm and sticky at the edge of my hairline.

"It's fine," I said as softly as possible, keeping my eye on the nearest gunman. My head throbbed from where it had hit the corner of a decorative statue when one of the gunmen had shoved me into the resort's open-air restaurant. Now, we were all lined up side by side against the long interior wall while the gorgeous summer day and pristine turquoise water outside mocked us.

Here against the wall, there was no breeze to mitigate the oppressive humidity, and I was already covered in sweat and sand. Thankfully, I'd had an elastic band around my wrist when I was pulled from my room, so I was able to get the hair off my neck, at least.

"How long can they possibly keep us?" she asked.

I refused to answer such a ridiculous question. How the hell should I know? It wasn't like I'd ever been held at gunpoint by an angry mob before. Besides, we wouldn't have to worry about being released if they killed us first for talking.

"I wish I had my phone," she whined softly, not for the first time.

I didn't dare mention I had mine in the pocket of my running tights alongside my passport and a credit card. I'd quickly yanked off the long-sleeve half-zip I'd gone running in and tied it around my waist to hide the phone-shaped bulge on the outside of my thigh.

There was a sudden commotion in the doorway to the restaurant as they brought two more guests in and shoved them toward the group with a shout.

One of them was Jamie.

My heart rate picked up. When he hadn't been in the group of resort guests, I'd worried something had happened to him, so I was relieved to see him alive and well.

Thankfully, he noticed me, and I made a quick "come here"

gesture with my hand. Jamie moved toward me quickly and took a spot on my other side.

"Thank god you're alright," he whispered, nudging my shoulder with his.

"Same." I lowered my voice further and took the opportunity to say more while the guards were talking amongst themselves. "Your dad's working on a plan to get you out."

"My..." His eyes widened. "How do you know that?"

Before I could answer, a woman's sobs filled the air—the same woman from before with the sick husband. The entire room held our collective breath to see what the gunmen would do to her.

One of the gunmen stepped aggressively in her direction. "*¡Cállate!*"

She nodded frantically and turned to bury her face in her husband's shoulder. Thankfully, the husband didn't look any worse. While the man didn't look great, he wasn't clutching at his chest or arms, so I hoped he wasn't as ill as he looked. I silently urged the crying woman to settle down so they didn't get hurt.

Lindsey muttered under her breath, "How's she supposed to be quiet when her husband's probably dying of a heart attack?"

Over the next two hours, they brought in the rest of the guests to the restaurant. During that time, three different men had tried to be a hero and had gotten shoved, punched, or pistol-whipped for their efforts.

Part of me wished I was that kind of guy—the brave hero type—but the other part of me wasn't stupid enough to put myself in the crosshairs. And I wasn't cocky enough to think my efforts would have any impact on half a dozen armed and angry men.

"You okay?" Jamie asked softly a couple of hours later. The guards had stepped far enough away that the whispering didn't seem to be a problem.

"No," I admitted.

He moved a little closer and leaned his shoulder into mine. "How do you know about my father's plans?"

I looked down at my clasped hands, wishing one of them was held safely in Landry's larger ones. "Stupid boy told me."

Jamie met my eyes. "Not so stupid, then?"

I shook my head and tried not to cry.

He was right. Landry, the man I'd told myself for three years was "unreliable," was the one working to save me from this night-mare... and I knew without a shred of doubt that he'd salt the earth to get me to safety.

Over the next several hours, I thought back to all the times Landry had tried to turn our enemies-with-benefits situationship into *more*. There'd been the conversation at Christmas—the first time he'd actually asked me in so many words—but there had been a dozen smaller attempts before that. Invitations to dinner, to long weekends away, to be his date at various galas. Each time, I'd turned him down with an eye roll, and each time—until Christmas —he'd grinned and laughed like it was all a joke, cementing my belief that I couldn't take him seriously.

But if he wasn't trustworthy or responsible, why was I suddenly so sure I could count on him? Why had I been fighting so hard to keep our relationship as shallow as possible?

Because the truth was my feelings toward Landry weren't meek or mild. They were fraught and passionate. Deeper and more possessive than I wanted to admit, even to myself. Love and hate were two sides of the same coin, and I suddenly felt like the coin had been tossed high in the air.

Fuck.

What did it say about my real feelings if Landry was the one person I wanted to see, when my moments left on Earth might be limited? That the memory of being in his arms was the happy place I wanted to escape to?

I'd spent years fighting my attraction to Landry, afraid he'd let me down if I dared give him my heart. Now, I wondered if life was too short to be so cautious and if I'd been wasting time.

Maybe I needed to give Landry a chance. Allow myself to trust him. Maybe he'd grown up and was ready to take things more seriously.

He was great with Lellie, and he'd proven himself a steadfast friend to the Brotherhood in recent years, especially Zane. He was protective of him and seemed to always be there for him.

Could I let him do the same for me?

Lindsey shifted next to me and whispered, "If I can find a way to get out of here, is there anyone you want me to call for you?"

I blinked at her. "What?"

She firmed her jaw. "Next time they take us to the bathroom, I'm going to find a way to sneak out. I'm just saying, I can call someone for you."

"How... generous," I murmured.

I used to think Landry was the kind of guy who would take off and leave his friends behind, but hearing Lindsey's plans to do it made me realize Landry would never leave a friend behind like that. If anything, he was too generous, buying drinks for the whole bar, contributing anonymously to every charity that contacted him, and starting an education fund for Lellie even though her own father was a billionaire.

I'd always interpreted those things as signs he was careless with his money, but in reality, they were signs of selflessness and affection.

The night was a long one. Thankfully, we were allowed a trip to the bathroom every few hours in small groups, and they let us stretch out and lie down, in case anyone could possibly sleep in this situation.

My head throbbed from where I'd hit it earlier, and my thoughts raced with a lifetime's worth of regrets.

Sometime in the middle of the night, when several people

were sleeping and the restaurant space was nearly silent, three of the gunmen got into a rapid-fire argument that escalated in volume enough to wake everyone up. They shoved and threatened each other with their weapons until the noise brought in another gunman from outside. As soon as that man entered and shouted at them, one of the fighting men turned his weapon and shot.

The noise made everyone jump. Screams rang out. The man who'd entered the restaurant was on the ground, writhing in pain, clutching his side. Blood began puddling under him.

The other gunmen shouted at each other even more, presumably blaming each other. When they finally decided to help their friend, two of them dragged the man out of the restaurant, leaving a giant smear of blood on the tile floor. I squeezed my eyes closed and tried not to think about the escalating tension. None of the men holding us seemed calm or rational. They were angry and uncoordinated, which made the situation even more dangerous.

"You okay?" Jamie asked again.

"No," I said as emphatically as I could without making noise.

"I'm scared," Lindsey whimpered from my other side. "What are we going to do? We need to get the fuck out of here. If only I had a phone, I could livestream this shit and get us some news coverage."

"Assuming they don't still have the communications locked down," Jamie said.

"I managed to get a call out earlier," I admitted. "For about two seconds. News outlets already have the story. But even if someone sent a rescue crew, it would take time to get here."

In the end, I was right.

Late the second night, when half the room was asleep again and my stomach was grumbling after only being given some bread and an apple all day, the room suddenly exploded in blinding light and deafening noise.

I was yanked off my feet and thrown over someone's shoulder

before my brain came back online. I was too terrified to protest or ask questions, wondering if I was being taken to my death or to safety.

It wasn't until I was placed in a small inflatable boat that I realized the people taking me were speaking English. They were also wearing clean, black tactical gear and speaking into advanced comms equipment.

My eyes were fucked, and my head rang like a bell.

"What's happening?" I asked stupidly.

"Name?"

I nodded and swallowed. "Kenji Toma."

He turned to someone else. "And you?"

"James Winthrop."

I turned to see Jamie huddled on the opposite side of the boat. It seemed as though we were the only ones who'd been taken.

The man in charge snapped orders into his comms, and within seconds, we were speeding away from the beach. Water sprayed over the edges of the boat, making me just wet enough to start shaking from the cold. The night air had been plenty warm in the protected area of the restaurant, but it was freezing as we raced over the water at top speed.

There were four men in the rescue group, and they all seemed busy with various jobs. I didn't dare interrupt them to ask questions.

Jamie wasn't so hesitant. "Where are you taking us?" He had to shout over the sound of the outboard motors and the wind.

One of the men glanced over at Jamie. "Manta, Ecuador. There's a plane waiting to take you home."

Jamie nodded as if all of these arrangements were standard fare instead of miraculous and amazing. "How long will it take to get to Manta?"

"One hour to the ship. We'll load into a helicopter. After that, should be two hours to Manta."

"Th-thank you," I said, still speaking in a low voice out of habit.

The man glanced at me and noticed I was shaking. "I have an emergency blanket in my kit." He found the packet and opened it, fighting the wind to get the thing wrapped around my shoulders. As soon as I pulled it close, I closed my eyes in relief. It wasn't necessarily cozy, but it made a huge difference.

I tried to zone out and calm down now that we were relatively safe, but I couldn't help wondering what would happen to the other resort guests.

"Do you know if they're going to let the rest of the hostages go?" I asked. "Are they asking for ransom or are they trying to get the toxin safety rules back in place? What do they want, exactly?"

The man shot me an apologetic look. "Not sure. We've been head-down planning this op. The bigger-picture stuff is above my pay grade."

I nodded. Selfishly, I was glad to be out of San Cordova, but the guilt was eating at me. It wasn't fair that money had saved me and had left many others behind.

For the remainder of the wet ride, I tried to meditate and manifest a safe outcome for everyone we'd left behind. While it might not make a damned bit of difference to the situation, it would at least keep me from spiraling into a panic attack.

After we met up with a larger military-type ship, I tried calling Landry to let him know I was safe, but my phone was completely out of charge.

We moved onto the ship and waited while the rescue team dismantled and deflated the boat before transferring to a very large helicopter on the top deck of the ship. Within half an hour, we were airborne.

The rescue crew handed us each a paper bag with food and a bottle of water in it. I devoured the sandwich, cheese and crackers, banana, and cookies before washing it all down with the water.

I was exhausted from not sleeping for the past two days, but there was no way I could fall asleep in the current conditions. As a result, by the time we landed on the helicopter pad in Manta, I felt like the walking dead. My clothes were rough from dried sea spray, my hair was a tangled mess, and I probably had an entire luggage set under my eyes.

When we stepped off the helicopter, a handful of official-looking people were waiting for us on the tarmac, but I paid no attention. All I wanted was to get to a hotel to shower, sleep, and, most importantly, talk to Landry before finding a way back to the States. I knew if I could just hear his voice, something inside me would settle.

Long blond hair blowing in the wind caught my eye, and I took a closer look at the assembled people.

I blinked. Was I tired enough to hallucinate Landry?

I squinted into the morning sun. He was wearing familiar designer jeans and a Zee Barlo concert tee, faded to a soft black from the wash. My eyes filled as I let out a little whimper.

And then I started running.

EIGHT

LANDRY

When I saw Kenji climb down the helicopter stairs, I closed my eyes and thanked fate, Jim Winthrop, Executive Rescue, and the Brotherhood's invention that had given me enough money to hire them.

I opened my eyes in time to catch Kenji as he crashed into me, nearly knocking us both down. My arms wrapped around him and held him tight.

"Fuck," I breathed. "You smell awful."

He gave a startled hiccup of laughter, and I tightened my grip even more until I worried he couldn't breathe. Thankfully, his arms were around me just as tight.

"I hate you so much," Kenji said with more love in his voice than I'd ever heard. "Thank you for getting me out of there."

I turned my head and pressed a long kiss to his temple, trying to settle into the reality of having him safe in my arms, *finally*, when I realized I tasted blood. "Kenji, what the fuck?" I pulled away just enough to notice the dried blood at his hairline. "What did they do to you?"

Who the fuck do I need to murder?

"I'm okay, I promise. I need to find somewhere to shower and sleep." He sounded exhausted and defeated—two words that should never be used to describe Kenji Toma.

"You can do both on the plane." I pointed to the far side of the small airport, where the Brotherhood's private jet was waiting.

Kenji must have recognized it and remembered it held a private suite with not only a bed but a bathroom and shower. He quickly began walking in that direction, but I nudged him toward the small airport building instead, where we had to go through a more official process before we could board the jet.

On the flight over, I'd told Jim about my preference for the name Landry. He'd agreed easily enough, but I knew it was only a matter of time before he told his son who I really was.

My stomach churned nervously. I couldn't calm down until I'd explained everything to Kenji.

When we finally got on board, Kenji offered Jamie the first shower and took a seat in one of the leather chairs to wait. Fortunately, Jim didn't attempt to make conversation since he was busy calling people to provide updates.

As soon as Jamie came out wearing clean clothes, the plane took off. The moment the flight attendant gave us the go-ahead to get out of our seats, Kenji bolted back to take his own shower.

I followed him into the suite in time to see him yanking off his clothes and leaving them in a pile on the ground. That was not like Kenji. The man was meticulous. Even during our most passionate encounters, he'd taken the time to set his clothes aside neatly.

He knew I was in the room with him, even though he didn't acknowledge my presence. I moved over to the cabinet where my own clothes were and pulled out a soft hoodie and the shortest pair of joggers I could find so he'd have something clean to wear.

Then, I pulled off my own clothes and followed him into the shower stall. "Kenj—"

He turned and leaned into me, burying his face in my neck

and letting out a sob. I held him tightly again and let him cry as the hot water streamed over us.

"Shh, it's okay," I murmured. "You're safe. It's over."

He sniffed and pulled out of my arms. His eyes were full of anguish. It was more emotion than I'd ever seen him express, with the sole exception of the times he'd lost his chill and yelled at me about a fuckup. "It's not over, Landry. There are a lot of people back there who are still in danger. There's a man who might be having heart problems and a woman who…"

He shook his head and stepped back into my arms.

After a moment, I explained that the prime minister was following the developments and had hopes the situation would be resolved soon. "There is a lot of pressure to reinstate the safety measures at the mine. Global sentiment is on the side of the locals, not the government officials."

He shuddered. "I hope they get it resolved before anyone else gets hurt."

"Do you want to talk about it?" I asked gently.

He shook his head.

I reached for the shower gel and managed to fill a washcloth without letting him go. As I scrubbed his back and arms and ass, I couldn't help but get even harder than I'd been watching him undress.

I wanted him so fucking badly, but I wasn't going put the moves on him while he was so vulnerable and when I had so much I needed to tell him. Instead, I worshipped his body with the soapy cloth, moving him this way and that until I'd cleaned his entire person.

Once we were both clean, I dried him off with one of the thick towels, then pointed to the clothes I'd set out for him. He pulled them on before crawling into the bed and pulling the duvet up to his chin.

I watched him while I dried myself and dressed again. He

looked tiny on the large bed, which was also unusual. Kenji was technically small in stature, but he always stood up straight and wasn't afraid of taking up space in the world.

Kenji didn't *do* vulnerable, and seeing him this way made me want to erect a force field around him, to protect him from any further discomfort or upset.

I closed the window shades and turned off the lights before sliding into bed at his side. He immediately reached for me and yanked me closer until I was spooned around him.

I held him close and nuzzled my nose behind his ear. His damp hair was in a knot on top of his head, otherwise I would have gladly eaten mouthfuls of it if I could stay close and give him the comfort he so clearly needed.

We both drifted off to the sound of the airplane's white noise. A couple of hours later, I woke up, suddenly remembering I hadn't updated the Brotherhood on Kenji's rescue.

I snuck out of bed as quietly as I could and made my way to the main cabin. Jamie was asleep on one of the sofas, and his father was sitting at a table working on his laptop.

When I took the seat opposite Jim, he glanced up. "Is he okay?"

"Not really. What about Jamie?"

He shrugged. "He'll get on with it."

I blinked. "They saw some bad stuff, Jim. They feared for their lives. That kind of experience isn't easy to set aside."

"I'm sure he'll handle it."

Instead of arguing with him, I pulled out my laptop and started a group message to the Brotherhood to let them know Kenji was safe on our plane.

SILAS

What happened? How'd you get
him out?

I sucked in a breath. How the fuck was I supposed to explain the situation?

> Long story. I had to pull some strings to make this happen and now I owe someone a favor.

SILAS

Is he hurt? Upset?

I thought back to the image of Kenji alone in bed.

> He has a cut on his temple. Not sure what from. He hasn't said much yet. Showered and went right to sleep.

BASH

Is he coming here or going to NY?

> We have to drop some people off in London first. Will update as soon as we know.

They asked a few more questions I didn't have answers to before I ended the chat by saying I'd explain more after getting some much-needed sleep.

The next message was easier to send. I pulled up the contact information for Kenji's grandmother.

> I don't know if you've been following the San Cordova story, but I wanted to let you know Kenji is safe.

MRS. TOMA

Thanks for letting me know! Will you ask him to call me?

> We're on a plane so he can't call until we land, but I'll tell him as soon as he wakes up.

MRS. TOMA

Are you with him?

Yes.

MRS. TOMA

Thank you, Landry. Please take good
care of him.

That's an easy promise to make.

After the chat ended, I messaged Nan and Cora to update them on the situation. Nan wasn't thrilled that I'd made a deal with the devil, but she promised she'd have a room set up at Hawling House, where Kenji could rest.

After reassuring anyone who needed to know that Kenji was safely away from San Cordova and messaging Kenji's assistant to upgrade the damned Wi-Fi on this plane to allow for video calls, I made my way back to the bedroom, stripped down to my underwear, and slid into bed again, trying to figure out the best way to tell Kenji the truth about who I was.

Unsurprisingly, no magic words occurred to me. It was as impossible to know where to begin as it ever had been.

I must have drifted off because I woke up to the shocking sensation of a hot mouth on my cock.

At first, I assumed it was a dream. "Kenji," I groaned when the fantasy mouth pulled off me.

"Need you. *You*," he said before sucking me down again.

My eyes flew open. Even in my dreams, Kenji had never talked like that.

His hand cradled my sac as he teased me with his mouth. I tangled my fingers in his long hair and bit out a curse. The man was naked and sucking my cock like he was trying to win a competition.

"That feels so good. Fuck. Let me... oh fuck."

After a few more pulls, he lifted his head and met my eyes. His face was flushed, his mouth wet. "Want you to fuck me. Hard."

I understood the need to reconnect after a harrowing experience, but I worried about the fervor in his eyes. "Kenji—"

"Don't you dare deny me this, Landry. Or I will go out there and ask Jamie Winthrop to take your place."

It was an empty threat—we both knew he wouldn't do that, especially under these circumstances—but we also both knew I wouldn't reject him. I never had.

I quickly sat up, grabbed him under the arms, and yanked him up, manhandling him onto his front beneath me before moving down to spread his ass cheeks apart.

Kenji sucked in a breath right before my tongue landed on his hole. Then, he let out a debauched whimper that changed into a groan. I ran a hand up his spine and pressed down firmly between his shoulder blades. Then, I moved his knees up underneath him until he was exactly where I wanted him, face and chest down, ass up.

I felt instinctively what he needed, and I did my best to give it to him. Thankfully, I had lube in my bag. After several long minutes of enjoying his ass with my mouth and tongue while listening to his needy sounds, I grabbed the travel-sized tube and moved up behind him.

Kenji reached his hand back for mine. I held on tight while I used my other hand to line my cock up with his hole.

Over the past few years, we'd had many frantic interludes like this—quick, desperate fucks that scratched an itch for one or both of us. But never had Kenji seemed so *emotionally* needy, so in need of reassurance and comfort.

It unsettled me... and lit a fire inside me at the same time.

I leaned over him as I pressed myself inside. "Okay, babe?" I demanded breathlessly.

His hand squeezed mine and pulled our joined hands under

his chest. I curled around him and pressed kisses on his shoulder and neck as I thrust in and out, finding a rhythm that seemed to hit the right spot.

I tried not to make too much noise, remembering our audience in the main cabin, but the familiar grip of Kenji's body, the clean heat of his skin, and the sheer level of his need made it hard to keep from crying out.

I released his hand so I could grab his cock and stroke it.

"Please, Kenj. I need you to come," I croaked in his ear. "Not gonna last. You feel too good."

Kenji's hand joined mine on his shaft until I felt his release hit. I quickly moved a hand up to clamp over his mouth as he let out a hoarse shout.

For the briefest moment, I allowed myself to imagine what we would look like to anyone who saw us this way. Kenji, a pliant, boneless sprawl of limbs, me fucking him into the mattress. That was all it took to push me over the edge.

The only time Kenji ever surrendered his rigid control was when he was in bed with me, and the image of it never failed to make me come.

It had been over two weeks since I'd felt an orgasm this strong and satisfying. But on the heels of my release, I realized my time with Kenji would inevitably come to an end when he realized I'd spent the past ten years lying to him about who I was.

I moved off him and stepped into the bathroom to wet a washcloth. When I came back into the bedroom, Kenji was on his side, watching me, his expression softer than usual.

Affectionate. Strangely, heart-racingly affectionate.

"Why are you looking at me like you don't want to murder me?" I teased as I nudged him over so I could clean him off.

"I don't want to murder you."

I avoided his eyes and attempted to tease. "Give it time. You will."

"I'm actually feeling very fond of you right now."

I swallowed. "Maybe it's a variation of Stockholm syndrome."

"Did you send in a SEAL team to rescue me? What was that?"

I finished cleaning him up and yanked the duvet up to cover him before looking around for my clothes. "Executive Rescue. Jim already had a team in place, and I managed to get you a spot in their rescue."

"How? I don't have a policy with them."

I glanced at him while I finished pulling on my clothes. "You do now."

Kenji reached for my hand and pulled me down until I was lying next to him on the bed. "Thank you."

Then, he leaned in and did something he'd never done in three years of passionate encounters.

He kissed me.

On the *mouth*.

It started off hesitant until he pressed closer and deepened the kiss. I made an embarrassingly desperate sound in my throat before grabbing him by the back of the head to keep him from pulling away.

I knew Kenji had never wanted us to kiss because he'd wanted to keep things very clear regarding what we were (and weren't) to each other—hookups, not lovers. Definitely not *in* love.

It hadn't worked. At least for me.

The kiss I'd given him in New York before he left had been born from my fear that, in addition to him leaving, he would also move on to someone else.

But now, he was here in my arms and in my bed again, kissing me voluntarily. I wanted to know what it meant, but there was no way I was going to end it prematurely to ask questions.

A loud knock on the door made us both jump and pull apart.

"Sir? We're preparing to land in London," the flight attendant called through the door. "We need you to buckle into a seat."

Kenji glanced at me as he climbed out of bed and began pulling on his clothes. "Why London? Did you need to get back to your family?"

I was trying to wrap my head around the fact we'd practically slept the entire flight away without realizing it. There was so much I needed to explain. "Yes... and no. We left from London. That's where the Winthrops live. And... and I kind of owe Jim a favor for including you in the rescue."

I didn't take the time to explain that the favor Jim had asked of me involved reconnecting socially—and very publicly—with my fellow peers in an effort to spread the good word about Winthrop & Meyers investment management over the next few weeks.

Kenji ran long fingers through his hair to straighten it. "As much as I want to go home and sleep in my own bed, I'm not sure I want to turn right around and spend another ten hours on this plane."

"You don't have to. We'll go to my place. I can introduce you to my dad." I watched his reaction.

"Really?" Kenji's face softened into a smile. "I'd like that."

I swallowed. "But there's something you need to know first."

Kenji moved past me and opened the door to the bedroom. "I already know about the Alzheimer's. It's okay."

I opened my mouth to correct him, but he'd already walked out to the main cabin, and I had no choice but to follow.

Once we got there, Jamie Winthrop's eyes caught mine. I could tell by his expression his father had explained who I was.

I grabbed Kenji's elbow in an effort to pull him back into the bedroom, but the words were out of Jamie's mouth before I could prevent the catastrophe.

"Everett Davencourt. Fuck, I had no idea!" He grinned like we were all in on the same joke.

Except it wasn't remotely funny.

And we weren't *all* in on it.

"You mean Landry." Kenji chuckled lightly, though his forehead crinkled in concern, maybe wondering if Jamie was confused after their ordeal. "This is Landry Davis, Jamie. The man I told you about."

"This is... No way!" Jamie laughed. "Everett Davencourt is your stupid boy? Holy shit, you look different from our Eton days!" He reached out a hand to shake and shot me a genuine, friendly smile like he wanted to put aside our schoolboy animosity or, worse, reminisce about it.

I gave him a half-hearted handshake, my stomach in free fall. "Stupid boy?" I repeated under my breath, feeling the familiar sting of Kenji's rejection.

Kenji narrowed his eyes and hissed, "Everett Davencourt? From *Eton?*"

He dropped into the seat across the aisle from the Winthrops. I took the seat beside him like a man approaching the gallows.

Jim's and Jamie's eyes moved between the two of us like they were watching a tennis match. I shot Kenji a look, silently begging him to save this conversation for a private moment. He closed his eyes and inhaled as if trying to seek patience from deep within.

"Is there an update on San Cordova?" Kenji asked, opening his eyes and looking at Jim as if the name debacle had never happened.

Jim glanced between us before giving an update. "The San Cordovan government has rescinded their exemption, which means they're now requiring the safety measures to be put in place before allowing the mine to return to operation status. Half the tourists will be released in the next twelve hours—including anyone in need of medical treatment—and the other half are scheduled to be released when the representatives from the mining company land on the island and sign new contracts. That's expected to happen tomorrow."

Kenji let out a breath and nodded. "Thanks for letting me

know." He turned and looked out the window, where the London sky was its usual winter gray.

"Let me explain," I said in a low voice. "Please."

His nostrils flared, but he wouldn't look at me. "No, thanks."

"Kenj—"

He held up his hand to stop me. "I do not have the mental bandwidth to deal with your bullshit right now, Lan...whatever-the-fuck your name is."

We landed within ten minutes at the small private airport. As we stepped off the airplane, it seemed the air in London might have been even colder than Kenji's mood. We hurried into the small terminal building and then stopped short.

There in the lobby was a crowd of reporters and camera people. As soon as they spotted us, their voices tumbled over each other in a bid for attention. The noise made Kenji startle, so I reached out and grabbed his hand in reassurance without thinking. His hand tightened in mine as he shrank closer to my side.

It took me a minute to understand what they were shouting.

"Which one of you is the long-lost viscount?"

"Lord Hawling, over here!"

"Is it true you flew all the way to San Cordova to rescue your fiancé?"

"Isn't that Landry Davis, the supermodel?"

"Which one of you is heir to the Winthrop fortune?"

"Is the Davencourt heir engaged to the Winthrop heir?"

Kenji stood frozen at my side. There was a momentary hush before Jim stepped up and held out his hands in a calming gesture. One reporter asked, "Mr. Winthrop, can you tell us what the situation is in San Cordova and how you managed to get your son out of there?"

Jim pulled Jamie close and put his arm around him. "As you can imagine, my son, Jamie, is exhausted from his harrowing experience. He and Lord Hawling's fiancé, Kenji Toma, were held hostage at a resort in San Cordova. Jamie and Kenji are simply good friends who happened to be at the same spiritual retreat. We have heard that the remaining hostages will be freed within the next twenty-four to forty-eight hours. It would not be appropriate for us to say more about the situation right now. Thank you for respecting our privacy at this time."

As he'd made his comments, he'd gestured to me and Kenji, who stood wide-eyed, still holding hands like the betrothed couple he'd described. Kenji dropped my hand like a hot potato and stared up at me in confused panic. It was a look I'd never seen on his face before.

Kenji was always Mr. Capable. He never panicked. When the rest of us were clueless about how to handle a situation, he was the one we turned to for direction. I hated knowing that his reaction now—in front of the press, no less—was my fault.

The reporters turned to me and started shouting out more questions. So much for "respecting our privacy at this time."

"*Landry, is it true you're really Everett Davencourt, Viscount Hawling, heir to the Davencourt earldom?*"

I felt Kenji begin to sway on his feet, so I placed a hand on his lower back to keep him from toppling over. "No comment."

"*When's the wedding? Will it take place at Davencourt Park or Hawling House? And does the King know?*"

"*Will you and your fiancé be at the Hearts of Hawling Dinner together?*"

"No comment," I repeated, trying not to lose my temper.

I tried moving through the crowd toward the exit, wrapping an arm around Kenji's slender form to keep him protected. The sound of snapping camera shutters followed us as we pushed past the reporters and reached the door.

Thankfully, my Range Rover was close to the valet stand. I yanked open the passenger door and hustled Kenji inside. Just before I got his door closed, one more nail was banged into my coffin.

"Is it true you plan to take your father's place in the House of Lords this year?"

I felt the air whoosh out of my lungs as I stalked to the driver's side of the vehicle and climbed inside. My hands shook as I started the engine and put the vehicle in Drive.

It wasn't until we were out of the small airport and making our way through London's city streets that Kenji finally spoke.

"Take me to Heathrow. I want to go home."

NINE

KENJI

I was numb with shock.

Learning the extent to which Landry had lied to me—to everyone—was almost worse than being held hostage by gunmen in a foreign country. At least with the gunmen, it hadn't been personal.

"No," Landry—or whatever the fuck his name was—said between clenched teeth.

"No?" My nerves were fading away, to be replaced with sharp rage. "*No?* What? You're going to keep me hostage, too? News flash, Landry. You don't have a weapon."

Which was, of course, a lie. His weapon was his stupid fucking mouth and the bullshit he spouted. Apparently, it had the ability to pierce deeply because I felt like I'd been stabbed in the chest and was bleeding out right now.

I was ashamed to admit that when Jamie had first called Landry by a different name, I'd been sure he'd made a mistake. That was how stupidly far I'd let myself go down the path of trusting Landry. Of letting myself believe in the possibility of a future with him. Now, I didn't just feel betrayed and angry; I felt like a fool.

"I will send you home on our plane tomorrow," Landry said. "After the pilots get a fresh sleep window. In the meantime, I need you to let me explain—"

I ignored the strange thread of vulnerability in his voice. "Pretty sure I got all the explanation I needed from the circus back there. Did they miss anything? Did they get anything wrong? Let's see... are you, in fact, Everett Davencourt? Yes or no?" I didn't bother addressing the rumors of a fiancé since that one was obviously so far out of the realm of believable as to be laughable. And I knew from experience during Landry's modeling career and Zane's music career that the press would do anything to provoke a response, including telling a bold-faced lie.

Landry's jaw ticked for a beat. "Yes."

"And are you a fucking *viscount?*" I spat the word like it was disgusting. Because the idea he was a British peer instead of the poor kid he'd pretended to be to the Brotherhood at Yale was unimaginable. *Unforgivable.*

"Kenji—"

"Yes or no, Lan... *My lord!*"

"There's more to it than that," he snapped, hands gripping the steering wheel until his knuckles were white. "I need to explain."

"Was your father *recently* established as an earl?" I asked, suddenly wondering if it was possible he was right. That there was a reasonable explanation behind the secret. "So recently, in fact, you simply haven't had time to tell me about it?"

Landry's nostrils flared. "No."

"When, in fact, was the earldom established in your family?"

He didn't speak.

The London traffic moved at a snail's pace. I turned to look out the window as my head pounded.

Landry's voice was subdued when he finally said, "Sixteen hundred and twenty-four."

It took me a minute to realize he was referring to the year. It was impossible to wrap my head around. "Your family has been in the British peerage since the time of fucking *Galileo*?"

I stared at his profile, wondering if there was a famous painting in a museum somewhere with the same noble features, passed down through aristocratic lines from important men who'd done any number of impressive or nefarious things throughout the years.

"All this time, no one knew?" It was unbelievable. "No one said, 'Hey, that model in Times Square looks a lot like the nineteenth earl of whatever-the-fuck'? I just don't understand."

Suddenly, I realized maybe it wasn't a secret. Maybe the Brotherhood had always known and *I* was the one on the outside looking in. My head felt airless, and I made a strange sound in my throat. "Wait, do they know?" I asked in a strangled voice. "Does the Brotherhood know?"

Landry's head snapped to me. His eyes widened in concern. "Kenj. Breathe, baby. Do you want me to pull over?"

"Do they know, Landry? Am I the only one who—"

His hand grabbed mine and squeezed. "No! No. They don't know. No one but my family." He swallowed. "And, well... the King. And, uh, the prime minister."

I yanked my hand out of his and buried my face in my hands. I needed to be alone. I needed space. My world was no longer safe in so many more ways than I'd expected only a week ago. "Drop me at a hotel, please."

"I can't do that, Kenji. The paps will find you, and they won't give you any peace. There's security at the house, and there's plenty of room for you to have your own space. I promise."

Within a few minutes, he pulled through a gate into an alley that led into a small underground garage. A young man in a uniform came out of a nearby door and waited for us to pull to a stop.

"Welcome home, sir," he said to Landry as he opened the driver's door.

I stared at the kid, my mind going off on a million tangents. How was it possible there was an entire—giant—aspect of Landry's life I'd had no exposure to? I knew he'd been keeping his personal life close to the vest, but *this*?

It was impossible to wrap my head around, and my heart ached when I tried.

"Thanks, Simon," Landry murmured, handing the man the key before coming over to my side as if he was going to open my door. Instead of waiting for him, I hopped out and moved toward the door to the building. Landry let out a sigh and followed me. "Simon, this is Kenji Toma. He's allowed full access to the house and vehicles. Please treat him like family, okay?"

The young man's eyes widened. "Yes, sir. Welcome to Hawling House, Mr. Toma."

I nodded at him and let Landry lead the way into the vestibule, where there was a small utilitarian office and an elevator. We entered the elevator... and came out in a completely different world.

If I'd ever imagined what a historic home in Regent's Park would look like if it had been held by the same family for hundreds of years, this was definitely it. Old paintings and framed vintage photos lined the walls. Intricate lamps stood on large antique tables with brass knobs mottled from age. Even the air smelled like old wood and leather. The elevator seemed to open off to the side of the entry hall. A giant vase of fresh flowers sat in the middle of a round table in the center of the open space, and a lush circular rug covered the old wooden floor. A graceful curving staircase led upstairs on the opposite side of the hall, and the ceiling was at least four stories above us. Weak winter light came in through windows on either side of the intricately carved double doors leading to the front walkway.

I could see a sliver of a uniform on a woman dusting a table in a nearby room, and a different woman's laughter drifted from the back of the house.

"Are you hungry?" Landry asked. "I can introduce you to Nan, who kind of runs this place, or I can take you upstairs to a room..."

He looked nervous, which made it a little harder to hate him... but only a little. "I'd like some privacy to call my grandmother."

"Of course." Landry gestured for me to follow him up the wide staircase. "I texted her from the plane to tell her you were safe, but I know she'll want to hear from you."

I stopped on the bottom step. "You did?"

"Yes." He frowned down at me. "I didn't give her any details," he hurriedly assured me, as though *that* was what might be giving me pause.

But I was too angry and hurt to be swayed, even by his consideration for my Baa Baa. I waved a hand impatiently for him to continue up the stairs, and neither of us spoke again until we'd reached the right level and walked far enough down a quiet hallway to a guest room.

"There should be a phone charger in the nightstand and whatever toiletries you need in the bathroom," he offered quietly from the hallway. "There's also a minifridge with drinks and snacks. If you want anything else to eat, just text me. And I'll grab you some more clothes."

Landry shifted his weight from side to side and kept his eyes on the floor. I refused to feel sorry for him when he was the architect of his own misery.

"Fine." I stepped into the room and closed the door between us before letting out a breath. My shoulders were around my ears, and I was fighting the sensation of feeling trapped.

The room was more than a guest bedroom; it was a *suite* of

rooms that included a sitting area, a walk-in closet that was more of a dressing room, and a giant, luxurious bathroom with marble floors and antique porcelain and cast-iron fixtures. Everything was well maintained and luxurious in an understated way.

It still felt like a prison since I wanted to be anywhere but there.

I muttered to myself, "I can leave anytime."

I moved over to the windows in the bedroom and looked out at the barren trees across the street. Several umbrellas bobbed down the sidewalk opposite the house as cars drove by in the afternoon drizzle. It was warm and dry in the house, but February in London was a stark contrast with the sunny weather I'd experienced in San Cordova. It never failed to surprise me how you could travel between such vastly different places in the span of a day.

Just like you could go from thinking you knew a person to feeling like they were a complete stranger in the span of five minutes.

I'd always known Landry was hiding something, but never in a million years did I think it was something like this. I still couldn't wrap my head around how a British peer could hide while also being on magazine covers, billboards, and the side of London buses. It defied all logic.

And the better question was, *why* would he hide it?

My head swam with exhaustion and confusion. Maybe it was *me*. Maybe I was too tired, too overwhelmed by what I'd learned and what I'd been through, and too worried about what was happening in San Cordova to process anything more.

After plugging my phone into the charger, I threw myself on the bed and sank into the luxurious bedding. Despite the sleep I'd gotten on the plane, part of me wanted to curl up under the covers, but I knew my grandmother needed to hear from me directly before she'd believe I was safe.

I dialed her number the second my phone had enough power to turn on.

"Kenji, sweetheart." Her voice was so familiar and warm my eyes stung.

"Baa Baa. I'm okay. I'm safe."

"Where are you?"

"London. I'm... I'm with Landry."

"Ahh. Good. *Good.*"

"Not good. But safe. Sort of." I let out a frustrated breath. "It's a long story. Look, I don't know if Mom and Dad heard about this on the news—"

"Don't worry about that," she interrupted. "This is probably the silver lining of them being too frugal to spring for the Wi-Fi package on the ship."

I laughed, but it came out creaky.

"Aw. You sound so tired, honeybunch. Maybe you need a vacation from your vacation now."

I could hear the teasing smile in her voice. "That's an understatement. But I think I'd prefer to get back to work."

"You and your work," she scoffed. "Someday, you'll look around and wonder why the fax machine doesn't love you back."

I snickered. "I won't wonder. I'll know it's because the fax machine has been dead lo, these many years. May it rest in peace."

She gave a soft *hmph.* "Fine. The Xerox machine, then. You get my point."

"If your point is that you haven't been in an office since 1986—"

"You said you would let me fix you up with a nice man when you returned from your retreat, Kenji."

I blew out a breath. "That's the last thing I need right now."

"So you say. When are you coming home? Agatha next door says her nephew lives in Brooklyn and would like to take you to dinner at a place that has live jazz music. Doesn't that sound nice?"

It did sound nice. More than that, it sounded normal.

"I should be home in a couple of days. I'll let you know when I get back, and maybe you can give Agatha's nephew my number." In the meantime, I would make sure not to answer any unknown calls.

"I'm glad you're safe, sweetheart."

After the call ended, I lay back on the pillows and stared at the ceiling. It was made up of warm wooden panels with intricate carvings. My headache lingered, so I eventually got up and made my way to the bathroom sink to fill a glass with water.

I drank as much as I could stomach while eying the deep bathtub. It was too tempting to pass up. While I waited for it to fill, I poked through the luxury toiletries displayed in a nearby wooden box and found a Molton Brown bath oil.

Within a few minutes, I was sinking gratefully into the warm, fragrant water, safe from the dreary winter day outside and well on my way to blocking out the reality of my current situation.

I focused on regulating my breathing and beginning a meditation. Chaska's words ran through my memory.

Close your eyes and settle into the present moment. Feel the ground beneath you, steady and supportive, holding you with care. Take a deep breath in, drawing in peace and clarity, and let it flow out slowly, releasing all tension and worry. With each breath, allow your body to soften, your mind to quiet, and your heart to open. Be here, now. This is your sanctuary, your time to simply be.

My conscious mind fought me for several long minutes, repeating the ludicrous statements the paparazzi had shouted at the airport and reminding me of Landry's shocking reveal. I wanted to rage, to host entire arguments in my head with Landry, but I hadn't spent the past few weeks at Chaska's retreat without learning the power of meditation.

I needed a clear head before I could tackle this situation, and there was no better way of clearing it than meditation in a warm bath.

Within moments, I was relaxed to the point of sleep. I didn't even realize I was dozing until Landry's voice startled me awake.

"Kenji? Fuck! Kenji, wake up. Are you okay? Fuck!"

I woke up to the sensation of being pulled out of lukewarm water and banging my elbow against the old cast-iron tub. Landry lost his grip on one of my arms when I flailed. Water splashed over the floor and wall as I scrambled to keep from slipping.

By the time I was safely on my feet on the bathmat, dripping water everywhere, my heart raced, and any benefits I'd received from the meditation had been washed clean away.

"What the fuck, Landry!" I snapped, knowing full well he'd done the right thing in waking me up.

"I sent someone out to get you some clothes, but you didn't respond when I told you I was leaving them on the bed. I called through the bathroom door, but you didn't answer. And then I fucking thought you were *dead* in the bathtub. Jesus."

I grabbed a towel and threw it around my waist. Yes, Landry had seen me naked hundreds of times, but that didn't mean he had carte blanche, and currently, he was *all* of the names on my shit list.

"I'm fine," I bit out.

His eyes were wide with concern and the vestiges of fear. "You were asleep in the bath. I read an article about this once. It's incredibly dangerous."

"I wasn't *asleep*. I was... meditating."

He paused. "Meditating."

"Yes. With my eyes closed." I lifted my chin and crossed my arms in front of my chest.

Landry narrowed his eyes. "Is drooling while meditating an

advanced technique you learned at your retreat?" He lifted one eyebrow in challenge and reached out a thumb to wipe the corner of my mouth. "You've got a little something right here."

A shiver ran through me that made goose bumps prickle over my skin at the lingering touch.

From the chill of the room, I told myself.

Landry turned to grab a thick bathrobe from a hook on the wall, whipping it around me and pulling it together in the front. "You're cold."

"I'm fine."

"You almost drowned," he growled.

"I'm fine."

His eyes flicked up to mine. "Careful. You sound like Zane."

I clenched my back teeth until my jaw ached.

"Did you call your grandmother?" he asked in a softer voice.

"Yes."

"Good."

His hands were still on the lapels of my bathrobe. From this distance, I could smell the familiar hand lotion he used. I could see the small red spot next to his nose that was usually covered meticulously with concealer. And I could see the darker roots beneath his famous blond locks.

I tried not to remember all the times I'd run my fingers through his long hair. The times I'd gripped and tugged it during sex and the softer times I'd caressed him when he was safely asleep and not able to misinterpret the gesture as anything other than... a moment of weakness.

We stood awkwardly before he cleared his throat and patted the robe's lapels. "Right. Okay." He stepped back. "I'll let you..." He exhaled and turned to go.

I almost called him back. Almost called out... *something* that would soften the tension between us. But I wasn't ready for that. I didn't trust myself not to temporarily "forgive" him just to get the benefit of his comfort.

That wouldn't be fair to either of us.

As I stood there staring at the empty doorway, it suddenly occurred to me I'd meant what I'd said to my grandmother. I missed my job. My job was something I was good at. It grounded me and made me feel competent and capable. So what the hell was I doing wallowing in a bath when there was work I could be doing?

I had to wait until morning before I could take the Brotherhood's plane home, but I could work from my phone now that it was fully charged. I propped myself up on pillows and opened my inbox.

But the soft bed and my heavy eyelids conspired against me. I only managed to return one email before the phone fell on my face and shoulder. My eyes slid closed as I sighed in frustration.

And then it was morning.

The sun shone more brightly than I expected... until I realized it was well after 9:00 a.m. and I'd slept longer than I'd meant to. I quickly texted the flight crew to let them know I was on my way and that I'd update them as soon as I had an ETA from my rideshare app.

After throwing on the clothes Landry had left for me last night, I slid my phone and passport into a pocket and tidied up the room as well as I could. By some miracle, I found my way back to the main-level foyer, only to discover the front door was locked with a set of antique fittings I couldn't figure out, and the elevator had a numeric keypad instead of a simple button.

In hopes of searching out a back door or someone who could release me, I followed the sounds of talking deeper into the house until I found a narrow hallway that led to a large, open kitchen where an older gentleman sat at a table reading an honest-to-god newspaper. A slightly younger woman looked up from where she was working on a laptop and smiled at me. "Oh hello, you must be Kenji."

I nodded. "Yes. I'm sorry to intrude. But—"

"Nonsense," she said, standing and waving me forward. "Please make yourself right at home. I'm Nan, and this is Edward. Ed, this is Everett's friend Kenji."

No one had to explain that this man was Landry's father. Not when he had eyes that were a slightly watered-down version of Landry's aquamarine. It was strange to see Landry's eyes in another man's face but even stranger to realize that this man, Landry's father, had been here all along. Right here in central London, all these years. I'd been in town countless times with Silas and Bash on business or with Zane and Landry for a concert or appearance, yet Landry had never once mentioned his family or brought us here.

I held out my hand to Ed. "It's nice to finally meet you," I said, the words nearly choking me. I wanted to apologize, somehow explain the rudeness of taking nearly a decade to finally make Landry's father's acquaintance. But of course, it was none of my business.

And I was leaving anyway.

He smiled at me. "Friend of Everett's, you say? From university?"

"No, sir. I w-work for him. In New York."

Landry hustled into the room behind me with an Apple Store bag on his arm and four large Starbucks cups on a takeout tray. He handed one of the coffees to me before setting the rest on the table, placing the Apple bag on the floor by my feet, and pulling off his jacket and knit cap. His blond hair came tumbling down into a runway-ready look. "He doesn't just work for me, Dad. Kenji is my good friend. Remember I told you about the Brotherhood? Kenji is part of that group."

"Not really," I said quickly. "I work for them. That's all."

"That's *not* all, *really*," Landry said hotly.

Nan's eyes flicked to Landry's and back to me. Her smile was one of understanding, as if she knew some of the history between Landry and me. "Landry speaks very highly of you, Kenji," she offered. "It's nice to finally meet you in person."

I felt incredibly awkward. Was I supposed to let on that I knew next to nothing about them? That Landry had kept everything a secret for all these years? Or did they already know?

"Are you hungry?" Landry asked eagerly. He gestured toward a man in a chef's coat washing dishes in a far sink, and the man seemed to pause as if waiting to hear my response to the question.

"No, thank you. I was just leaving."

The man returned to his dishwashing.

Ed's smile wavered as he looked between Landry and me. "Nonsense. We'd be *shockingly* terrible hosts if we let you leave before you eat, and Reggie makes an excellent omelette... or he could even do the full English if you're hungry."

The man in the chef's coat smiled at me. "We've got streaky rashers or sausages."

I nodded at the Starbucks in my hand. "This'll do me, but thank you. I have a flight to New York to catch."

"Kenji..." Landry's eyes held emotions—hurt, confusion, frustration—that I had no intention of acknowledging.

Stay strong, dammit. "I need to get back to work."

"Then I'm coming with you. Give me a minute to pack my things," Landry said before disappearing back toward the stairs.

I could feel Nan's eyes on me. When she spoke, her voice was kind. "At least have toast or a muffin." She stood and pulled out a chair, nodding at it like a friendly but firm schoolteacher.

I sat and reminded myself the man at the table with me, my host, was an earl. If ever I was going to remember my manners, maybe it should be here and now. "Toast, please. Thank you."

Ed studied me, a crinkle of confusion between his gray eyebrows. "You a friend of Everett's? From school?"

I opened my mouth but didn't know what to say. "N-no, sir. We're f-friends from New York."

His eyes widened like it was the first time he'd heard this information. "You're the friend in trouble? He was very upset, you know. I haven't seen him that upset since his mother... well, anyway." He cleared his throat and pulled the newspaper back up.

Nan plucked one of the cups out of the Starbucks tray and handed it to the man in the chef's coat while he bustled around to make my toast.

"It's true, you know," Nan said quietly, returning to her seat. "Landry was devastated when he discovered you were in danger. He raced to Downing Street, met with Teddy. If he hadn't worked something out with Jim Winthrop, he was prepared to contact the Palace. He was terrified for you."

I stared at her. When she said *Teddy*, did she mean...?

A younger woman with wild brown curls came hustling in as Nan finished speaking. Her eyes lit on the remaining Starbucks, and she quickly plucked it from the tray. "Sweet relief," she murmured before taking a sip and closing her eyes. "Nan, we have a serious problem."

Nan cleared her throat and straightened up in her chair. "Cora, this is Kenji Toma. Kenji, this is Cora Davencourt, the earl's niece and Landry's first cousin."

Cora's eyebrows winged up toward her hairline as she noticed there was a stranger in her midst. She glanced from me to Nan and back. "You're Landry's guy?"

Nan nodded. Reg moved toward me to place a collection of very elegant tableware in front of me, dropping a linen napkin in my lap before setting a plate of toast and accoutrements next to it.

I glanced back at Cora. "What do you mean, Landry's guy?"

Cora and Nan exchanged a look before Cora spoke. "Oh. The,

uh... guy Landry was... ehrm, worried about. That's all." She flashed her teeth at me in a grimace-smile combination that showed she was a terrible liar.

I sighed and focused on eating some toast. From the corner of my eye, I saw the pretty gray-and-white cat Landry had been cuddling the other night lift its tail and skulk out of the room like it didn't want to be associated with our bullshit.

I couldn't blame Turkey. If it weren't for the ridiculous locks on the front door, I'd escape, too.

Cora looked at Nan before tilting her head toward me. "Back to the problem..."

I blinked. Was she saying I was the problem?

Nan took a sip of her tea. "The crisis management team is on their way. We'll discuss it when they get here."

Crisis management? I opened my mouth to politely ask what the fuck was happening when Ed lifted his head from the *Financial Times*.

"Kenji? Is that Japanese?"

Finally, a question I understood.

I took a sip of my latte. "Yes, sir. My paternal grandfather was born in Misawa in northeastern Japan. My grandmother was American, but she lived in Japan for a while, and that's where they met."

"Oh, really?" The corner of Ed's newspaper dipped in interest.

I nodded. "Her father was stationed at a nearby air base. My grandmother used to run English classes for some of the local kids and—according to her—one particularly persistent and handsome fisherman who was the worst student she ever had." I smiled. "When she moved back to the States, her persistent fisherman came with her."

Cora and Nan continued speaking in hushed tones, but Ed seemed to ignore them, so I did, too.

"Your grandfather must have been very brave to move to the United States and learn a completely different culture and language."

"He was brave, yes... and also a little sneaky." I smiled wider, remembering. "It turned out he'd known English for quite some time—he'd simply wanted an excuse to spend time with my grandmother. And he got it. Forty happy years, until he passed away shortly after his retirement."

Ed set the newspaper down completely and leaned back in his chair. "What a wonderful story. You know, Landry's mother was an expat as well. It's a unique experience. Obviously very different if you already speak the language."

I glanced at Nan and Cora, but they were still lost in their own conversation. "How did you and your wife meet?"

Landry strode back into the room, typing something on his phone, but I resolutely ignored him.

Ed's face softened into a nostalgic smile. "Olivia saved my life. Well, after she nearly killed me." He let out a little laugh. "I was preparing to cross the road, you see, when I caught sight of her. She was laughing. Her hair was blowing in the wind, and the motion caught my eye."

I thought back to the day before when I'd noticed Landry's hair blowing in the wind in Manta. My eyes flicked to Landry against my will. Fortunately, his were still focused on his phone.

"She was here on a school trip," Ed continued. "I found that out later. But I stepped into the street to cross, not realizing I was still staring at her. She grabbed me and pulled me back before saying, 'Look right,' as if I was an American tourist." He chuckled again. "Can you imagine? The American was telling *me* to mind the direction of traffic. I was so embarrassed."

Nan looked away from Cora to glance at him affectionately. "But not too embarrassed to ask where she was staying."

"No," Ed said. He shot Nan a charming wink that was a

perfect template of the one his son used. "I was embarrassed, not stupid."

Nan glanced at me. "They became pen pals for five years, if you can believe it. Letters. That was before the internet, of course."

"Did you know her, too?"

She chuckled. "Oh god, yes. Liv and I were thick as thieves for years. She was a good woman. Funny and smart. Kind and generous. And a hard worker, like this one," she said with an affectionate smile now pointed at Landry. "He's just like her. Looks like her, too. I'll have to show you a picture of Liv. There's the painting in the drawing room, of course, but there's a photo album that has some good candid shots of her as well."

Cora chimed in. "I wanted to be Aunt Liv when I grew up. I always thought she was a celebrity. Like a movie star. It's no wonder Landry inherited that face."

Ed turned to Landry. "Your mother was a beautiful woman, Everett."

Landry glanced up and nodded. "Yes. I remember."

"Did I ever tell you how we met? Funny story, that. She was here on a school trip..." He went on to tell the exact same story again.

My stomach dropped with sympathy, and in spite of myself, I looked to Landry to gauge his reaction. I expected to see him upset —worried, sad, embarrassed, annoyed, or some combination—but instead, he smiled at his father affectionately.

"Bet you never forgot to look right after that, did you?" he teased in a gentle voice. I could only imagine how many times he'd repeated those words.

"No, I did not." He chuckled and went back to reading his newspaper.

Nan caught my eye and gave me a small smile of acknowledgment before standing and taking her own mug to the sink. When she came back, she checked her phone, patted Landry's shoulder, and lowered her voice, presumably so Ed couldn't hear. "Now that we've all pretended nothing's wrong for a few minutes, maybe we can address the looming public relations situation before you faff off to New York? A crisis management team is waiting in my office."

TEN

LANDRY

I was drowning. Normally, Kenji managed my fuckups. When I made a colossal mistake, Kenji was the one to put it to rights. So I had no clue where to even begin sorting out a fuckup that involved ruining Kenji's life by accidentally throwing him straight into the trash-fire that was the British press.

The photographers and reporters who'd been at the airport had been busy all night while we'd slept, and the headlines and social media stories were outrageous. Kenji couldn't have been online this morning, or he wouldn't have been able to calmly eat toast and talk with my father.

He proved this a moment later when we reached the hallway outside Nan's closed office door and he stopped her with a friendly smile.

"Thank you so much for your hospitality last night, Nan. Obviously, if there's a public relations situation involving—" He waved a hand in my direction but didn't turn his head. "—I'm happy to help. I'm kind of an expert in cleaning up his messes by now. It's literally my job."

My gut clenched, my whole body hollowed out by regret and

pain. The situation was even worse than I'd thought. His tone was cold. Precise. Businesslike. As though his body hadn't dissolved under my touch yesterday. As though the unguarded looks and smiles he'd given me on the plane had never happened.

As though all he was to me was an employee.

"But I'm sure you understand that I need to get back to New York," Kenji continued politely, "so if we could coordinate our response remotely—"

"Kenji." Nan hesitated, glancing back and forth between us before focusing on him. "I can't begin to imagine what you've been through in the last few days, and I *do* understand your desire to be back on the other side of the Atlantic, but I cannot stress enough what a terrible idea that would be right now. The press is absolutely salivating over your story—"

He shook his head. "They can salivate all they like. I have no comment about San Cordova."

"Not that. I mean *your* story." She ticked her finger between Kenji and me. "Surely you understand that when the heir to an earldom reappears out of thin air, whilst announcing an engagement to an unknown American, no less, the vultures will circle."

Fuck. "Nobody announced anything—" I protested.

Kenji spoke as if he hadn't heard me. He didn't so much as spare me a look.

"The reporters at the airport yesterday saw us holding hands and standing close. They made up a narrative." His dismissive tone was a dull blade shoved smoothly between my ribs. "There is no story there."

I dropped my chin to my chest and tried not to remember the feel of his lips touching mine. Was it really just yesterday?

"The less we say about it, the quicker it will disappear," Kenji continued. "No one will actually believe—"

"They will," Nan said bluntly. "Since the prime minister's office, while refusing to give an official comment on your release or the hostage situation, did wish all the best to Lord Hawling on 'his fiancé's safe return.'"

Kenji's body froze, and he let out a strangled puff of air. "The... he... what? Why would he—?"

"Because I told him we were engaged," I admitted. "I... I had to convince Teddy to put you on the rescue list. He wouldn't add an American, so I... improvised."

"Jesus." Kenji rubbed at his forehead, still without looking at me—*fuck, why wouldn't he look at me?*

Cora came up behind us, waving her phone. "It's all over the internet and social media. I'm afraid the world thinks you're engaged whether you are or are not. It's actually quite sweet. They're comparing it to Harry and Meghan—a royal romance of sorts. 'The Long-lost Lord and his American Sweetheart Reunite After Harrowing Ordeal in San Cordova.' You have to admit it's ready-made clickbait." She sighed. "And the photos. Fucking Christ, Landry. You're pretty and all, but did you have to have a beautiful boyfriend, too?"

Kenji's body stiffened. "I'm *not* his boyfriend," he hissed in as polite a tone as possible. "We need to clear this up before it goes any further."

"Clear it up?" Cora's eyebrows lifted. "You think Landry should admit he lied to the prime minister?"

Kenji opened his mouth and shut it again. His face flushed.

The new housekeeper appeared around the corner from the main part of the house, wringing her hands. "Pardon me, my lord, but there's a Mr. Jim Winthrop here to see you."

I glared at her. "Mrs. Ashcombe, we've talked about this. Will you please call me Landry?"

Her eyes widened in a combination of shock and offense. "I apologize. I will certainly try to remember that... my lord."

Cora murmured under her breath. "Might as well ask her to pole dance for cash, Landry. Christ."

Nan hushed us both. "Mrs. Ashcombe, please let Mr. Winthrop know Lord Hawling will meet with him in the Anning Room in five minutes. Thank you."

Mrs. Ashcombe raced off, her sturdy heels click-clacking on the worn tiles of the house's lower west wing where our offices were located.

I glanced at Nan. "I thought we were meeting with the crisis management team."

She shook her head. "It wouldn't do to keep Jim waiting. We can get started without you."

"You're worried about upsetting Jim Winthrop?" I asked, surprised. "Since when?"

Nan's face pinched. "Who do you think was responsible for informing the media who was on that plane yesterday and when it was landing?"

My stomach dropped. While my night had been long and rough, my thoughts during those hours had been centered on Kenji, not the paparazzi. I hadn't even considered how they'd known to be there. In my world of modeling and my friend Zane's world of musical celebrity, the press were like ants at a picnic—always where you didn't want them to be. But this wasn't a nightclub, a party, or even a commercial flight. So who had tipped them off?

The only people who'd known about that plane landing in London yesterday and who was on it were our own pilots and flight attendants, who'd been loyal to the Brotherhood for years... and Jim and Jamie Winthrop.

I bit out a curse. "I'm going to kill him," I growled, turning down the hallway to follow Mrs. Ashcombe... until Kenji laid a hand on my arm.

I stopped instantly.

He stood straighter and threw his shoulders back. "You're going to kill him *with kindness*," he instructed. "You're going to spoon-feed him the story you want the media to know in the nicest way possible."

Was he serious? Jim Winthrop had been so eager to use his son's kidnapping to raise his profile he'd invaded our privacy—*Kenji*'s privacy—and made Kenji a media target. I was ready to tell him where he could shove the favor he thought I owed him.

I shook my head once, nostrils flaring. "Sorry, no. I'm not capable of playing nice right now."

Kenji's hand tightened briefly on my arm before he stepped away. "Then you're going to let me lead."

I watched the slight bounce of his ass as he preceded me down the hallway, for all the world as if he knew where he was going. His sleek black hair swung from shoulder to shoulder the way it did when he was on a mission.

It was sexy as fuck.

But despite the momentary relief of having Kenji back on my side, even briefly, I recognized that this was Kenji's MO. Throwing himself into work to avoid unpleasantness was his wheelhouse, and "managing Landry's messes" was his quintessential life's work.

I moved up beside him to guide him to the proper room.

When we entered, Jim and Jamie were standing near the fireplace.

Jim's face lit up. "Ah, good to see you both. I assume you're well recovered after a nice night's sleep?"

Kenji turned on a smile. "Much better, thank you. I'd like to apologize for not thanking you yesterday for spearheading the rescue. I'm indebted to you for including me in the rescue." He reached out a hand to shake.

Jim's ego was immediately stroked. He shook Kenji's hand before moving to shake mine. "Happy to help. Everett—sorry, Landry—here has already agreed to do me a big favor to show his gratitude. Maybe you wouldn't mind helping him with it."

I opened my mouth to remind him that there'd only been *one* person offering *one* favor in this scenario, and Kenji hadn't had a part in any of it, but Kenji clasped his hands around my forearm. His touch was enough to stop me in my tracks.

His smile stayed calm and genuine. "Why don't you tell me what you had in mind, and I'll see what I can do to help? Please, have a seat, and we can all talk for a few moments."

As we moved to take seats in twin settees opposite each other over a low coffee table, Jamie leaned in and pressed a kiss to Kenji's cheek. "You sure you're okay?" he murmured to him as they pulled apart.

Needless to say, I wanted to rip his fucking head off and chuck it in the fire.

"Definitely. Thank you for asking," Kenji said before taking the seat next to me.

I wasn't surprised to see Kenji lie to him, but I was secretly chuffed.

Jim rubbed his hands together before leaning forward and placing his elbows on his thighs. "Alright, here's the plan. Landry agreed to accompany us to several high-profile social events over the next few weeks to help Winthrop & Meyers break into the old-money set. But seeing the media's reaction to your..." He waved a hand between Kenji and me. "Your love story has made this even more exciting. The two of you are about to be the hot ticket in town, the perfect mix of old and new. What better way to make the case that an old, storied family from the peerage is embracing new ways of doing things than to have both of you accompanying us?"

Once again, I opened my mouth to give this man a piece of my mind, and once again, Kenji stopped me again with a hand on my arm. "The problem is that the media has gotten it wrong. We're not actually, ah..."

My jaw ached from where I forced my mouth not to stop him. To plead with him. To beg the universe to make it right.

He cleared his throat. "Engaged."

Jim frowned. "You're not? But..."

Jamie ignored his father's confusion. He looked at Kenji strangely for a long moment, then smiled. "You know, I did wonder if there was some misunderstanding, given our conversation the other day. This media circus must be a nightmare for you, then, Kenji." He wrinkled his nose sympathetically. "But I think I have an idea that will work out well for everyone."

"You do?" Jim asked.

"You do?" Kenji echoed, narrowing his eyes suspiciously.

Jamie nudged his father. "We'll tell the press they got it wrong and it's actually Everett and *I* who are together. That *I'm* his American fiancé who was being held. It'll be brilliant."

Jamie and me? I nearly snorted in surprise. "Sorry, how would that help anyone?"

"Well, if we really sold the bit, it would mean Kenji could go back to his life in America unmolested by the press. And Winthrop & Meyers would get plenty of publicity." Jamie pursed his lips thoughtfully. "I figure we'll need to do a few casual appearances together to make the paps believe it. Exchange a few smiles, a few loving glances. Wrap our arms around each other, you know? Oh, and definitely hold hands while we walk down the street." He glanced at Kenji's hands on my arm. "There'd probably need to be a few steamy kisses, too, I imagine, to seal the deal... but it wouldn't be *so* bad, Everett. I promise." He shot me a cheeky smile. "You might even like it."

I wouldn't. Not at all. But I'd agree to the pretense temporarily if it meant giving Kenji the freedom to go back to the States and get away from this mess. Nothing about this media situation was okay, but I'd signed up for it willingly in exchange for Kenji's safety. I hated that I was bringing Kenji down with me when he hadn't been the one making up lies.

"That would be—" I began.

Kenji clamped his hands around my arm like an angry bear trap. "Awful," he said through his teeth. "Utterly terrible. Because... because the reason we aren't *engaged* is that... is that..." He forced a laugh. "Is that we're already married."

I turned to stare at him, wondering how it was possible to mishear someone from eighteen inches away. "We... what?"

He blinked slowly, as if he'd surprised himself as much as everyone else in the room. "I, ah... I know you didn't want to tell anyone yet, b-baby, but now the media have gotten a hold of the story, it's only fair to make it public."

Sharp sparkles of bright light flicked at the edges of my vision. "What?" I asked again, very stupidly. Because I knew I hadn't heard it right, but my brain couldn't figure out what words he'd actually said or meant.

Someone in the back of my brain was doing a swoon about the "baby" he'd dropped. What would I have to do to get him to say that to me and mean it?

Kenji's eyes met mine, and the force of it, after a morning of him refusing to look in my direction, hit me like a fire hose. The combination of emotions swirling in his gaze was hard to interpret, but there was for sure something fierce in it. "I'm not letting you go to those events with Jamie Winthrop on your arm," he gritted out before remembering himself and plastering the polite smile on again while turning back to Jim and Jamie. "When I'm happy to take my rightful place there."

He transferred his double grip to my hand and pulled our joined fists into his lap.

I glanced to the Winthrops, expecting to see them laughing. Instead, Jamie looked almost smug, and Jim looked relieved.

"Even better," Jim said. "And congratulations. I was almost positive you'd said fiancé when we were at Downing Street—"

Kenji answered while I continued to stare at Jim in continued shock. "No doubt he did, in an effort to protect me," Kenji explained, sitting up and taking on an all-business tone. "Right, darling?"

It took me precious seconds and Kenji's nearly painful squeeze of my hand to realize *darling* was... me.

"Uh, yes. Definitely. Always," I said, meaning it.

Kenji inhaled sharply. "You see, the wedding was an impromptu affair, and I haven't had a chance to tell my... my grandmother. But now, the cat's out of the bag. I'll call her after our meeting."

Jim's smile faded. "When exactly did you—"

My brain finally kicked into gear. I *did* want to protect Kenji, even if I had no idea what he was trying to accomplish at the moment.

"None of that is important right now," I told Jim firmly. "What's important is planning out our appearances for Winthrop & Meyers so Kenji and I can get back to the States as soon as possible."

Jim frowned. "I thought you hoped to take your father's place in Parliament. Teddy seemed impressed by your resourcefulness regarding the hostage situation when I spoke to him this morning. He said something about bringing that energy to the Lords."

The sparkles returned to the edges of my vision, only this time, they were accompanied by an anvil in my stomach. "That remains to be seen—"

My father's voice rang out behind me. "Jim Winthrop? What are you doing here?"

Kenji's hand tightened around mine as I nearly lost my shit completely. I stood up, releasing Kenji's hand before it could cause my father further confusion. "Dad. I wanted to thank Jim for his help getting Kenji back from San Cordova."

"Oh. Kind of you, Winthrop." Dad walked further into the room and held his hand out to shake Jim's. I held my breath and hoped he wouldn't say anything to reveal his fragile grasp on the present.

In the end, of course, Kenji saved the day. He stepped forward with a warm smile as my father finished greeting Jim and Jamie. "Ed, I'm sorry to be rude to the Winthrops, but would you mind showing me that portrait of Lady Davencourt you told me about this morning? I'm desperate to see it so I can tell my grandmother about it when I call her."

He gracefully distracted my father from any confusion he may have had about being ushered out of the room. Once they were gone, Jim looked back at me, his head tilted in confusion. "Why did Kenji rush your father out of the room?"

I froze for a minute before remembering that I had, in fact, had many, many sessions of media and PR training, not only in my job as a model but as the son of a British peer.

I lifted an eyebrow at him and grinned. "I believe he's trying to protect me from the earl's wrath if my father learns I've made a deal with the devil."

The three of us sat back down. Jim chuckled. "Fair enough, I guess. Although he'll see the media coverage of the two of you with Jamie at these events."

I nodded. "At that point, I can explain we've mended bridges after San Cordova, maybe even as a result of today's meeting. Now. What events did you have in mind?"

———

Once they were finally gone, I made my way to Nan's office to discover her conference table full of people working on laptops and tablets. My mood was at the bottom of the Mariana Trench, and I anticipated it going even lower once Kenji got a hold of me.

"Oh good," Cora said, spotting me from across the room. "The happy husband is here."

I closed my eyes and took a deep breath. "About that—"

"Yes," she said with obscenely wide eyes. "We were just discussing with the PR team how to announce your nuptials with the *least amount of personal details possible.*"

Her eyes frantically flicked to one side, trying to send me a message I was struggling to interpret. I followed her twitch to see a familiar messy bun in one of the seats. Kenji had removed his sweater and rolled up his sleeves. His hair was mostly off his face with only a few wispy strands escaping the hairband, and a laptop lay open in front of him. Discarded Apple Store packaging lay to one side.

"You found the computer," I said, meeting his eyes.

"Yes. Thank you. Uh, darling." He winced as the word clanged awkwardly around the room. "I explained to the team that we needed to wait for you before continuing to strategize because I wasn't sure what you wanted me to tell everyone about the question of you... uh... running for..." He glanced at Cora. "Or, er... being selected for..." He closed his eyes and seemed to take a moment to come up with the word "Parliament."

"I'm not ready to address that," I said quickly. "That's not on the table."

His eyes met mine. "Are you running or not? A PR campaign works better when all the cards are on the table."

I walked up to him and reached out a finger to brush an errant strand of hair behind his ear. His eyelashes fluttered.

I suddenly had a ridiculous idea. If everyone in this room thought we were actual newlyweds, we needed to act like it.

He smelled like the fancy toiletries in our guest bathrooms as I leaned in and ran my nose across his cheek. "Are we putting *all* the cards on the table," I murmured into his ear. "*Husband?*"

And then I kissed him on the mouth. Soft and sweet at first but then firmly enough to assert a microscopic amount of control back into the situation.

A puff of air came out of his nose as he surrendered to the kiss. As soon as he did, I pulled away quickly.

"Alright," I said, addressing the room. "My answer is no. I am not ready to consider a role in Parliament at this time. As the son of the Earl of Davencourt, I hold a deep respect for the role of hereditary peers in the House of Lords and the centuries-old traditions they represent. Serving in this capacity is a noble responsibility, and I have immense admiration for my father's dedication and service over the years. His tireless work and steadfast commitment to the House of Lords have set an extraordinary standard, and I do not feel that I would be able to live up to the expectations of his incredible reputation by acting too quickly. Will that do for a statement?"

Everyone, including Kenji, stared at me. Nan's face held an expression of resignation that made my hands clammy.

Kenji stood up and faced me. "Well said... husband."

He was so close, so mind-blowingly beautiful, it was impossible to think. "Well, you were the one who said the thing about the cards."

Kenji's hand slid into mine as he turned back to the team at the table. "I need to speak to Lan... Ev... Lord... my husband, for a moment in private." He turned to Cora and tilted his head at the door. "You're coming, too."

I clung to his hand, knowing it was all for show and wanting to wring every possible moment from the experience before he dropped it like a hot potato in the hallway. But once we were out of the office, he continued to hold it until Cora had led the three of us into the privacy of my office and closed the door.

Then he dropped it and returned to the familiar Kenji who was all about business strategy. "I need to know what Jim Winthrop said. What exactly are you on the hook for?"

"Why did you say we were married?" I shot back, suddenly feeling like I could speak freely. "I had it all settled. They offered us the perfect out, and you were free! All you had to do was go back to the States, and you wouldn't have had to deal with any of this shit. What the fuck, Kenji? Why did you do it?"

"Because... because..." He narrowed his dark, glittering eyes at me. "Because I couldn't leave you to your own devices in the middle of a PR crisis, could I? Are you insane?"

"Maybe," I breathed.

Honestly? I felt like it. What had happened to him "coordinating" things with Nan remotely?

My life was spinning wildly out of control, and all I could think about was the way Kenji's smooth skin felt against the pads of my fingers. The way his hair tasted when I kissed the back of his head as I pressed my cock deep inside him from behind. The small rush I felt whenever I called his phone to find out what ringtone he'd assigned me. The way I felt when he'd brushed his lips against mine and let out the faintest whimper of surrender.

"Kenji's right," Cora said matter-of-factly, reminding me of her presence in the room.

"He usually is," I agreed, trying to shake myself out of my obsession.

"No, but, like, this is perfect," she continued. "He'll be next to you for all of these public events with the Winthrops and can..." Her eyes flicked to Kenji.

"Manage me," I said drily.

"I mean... kinda," Cora said with a guilty shrug.

"You do realize we're not married," I stated. "But the entire Crisis Team seems to think we are. Does that not wave red flags and clang noisy sirens to you?"

Kenji propped his hip on the edge of my desk. "I made a judgment call. It's not ideal, but we're going with it. When the interest in our story dies down, we can let it slip that the 'wedding' was never official or legal or whatever but that we'd simply had a ceremony among close friends. People will be disappointed, and then they'll move on."

"Until Landry decides to serve in Parliament," Cora pointed out.

"I'm not doing that. And even if I wanted to, I wouldn't get elected."

Cora huffed out a laugh. "You forget that what Teddy Baines wants, Teddy Baines gets. If he wants you in that spot, he'll find a way to make it happen."

Kenji didn't say anything.

Cora looked between the two of us and sighed. "Fine, we'll punt that. First, we need to decide if you're Landry or Everett."

"Everett," Kenji said at the same time I said, "Landry."

His choice was hurtful. As if he wanted me to be someone I wasn't. Someone he didn't know.

"Landry," I repeated with a growl, piercing him with my glare. He could take over my life in a lot of ways, but not this. He couldn't tell me who I was *if he was going to get it wrong.*

"Cora," Kenji said in a lighter tone, as if there wasn't a stew of noxious tension in the room. "Would you mind terribly if Lord Hawling and I take a break for a couple of hours? I'm afraid the jet lag is getting the best of me, and I need to lie down."

Lord Hawling? *Fuck.*

Cora bit her lip to keep from grinning. "'Course not. Take all the time you need."

I followed him through the house and up the stairs like a petulant child. I knew I was in for a brutal tongue-lashing once we were alone. Kenji was going to ream me out. Flay me wide open and take me to church about secrets and betrayal. About lies and disrespect.

But when we entered his bedroom and closed the door, that wasn't *exactly* what happened.

ELEVEN

KENJI

This day had gone completely off the rails. I prided myself on being able to roll with the punches, but even I couldn't absorb this many hits without taking a few moments against the ropes to recover.

"Don't talk to me," I snapped before reaching for the buttons of my shirt and kicking off my shoes. I had one destination in mind, and it was the now perfectly cleaned and pressed bed I'd left several hours ago.

"Are we having sex?" Landry asked incredulously. "Now?"

I closed my eyes and sent up a prayer to the universe to have mercy on Landry whatever-the-fuck his name was so that I didn't strangle him right now with the lavender-scented sleep mask that was resting on a porcelain tray on the bedside table.

"You may be," I said in a clipped tone. "I am not."

I yanked off my shirt and dropped it on the floor before shoving my pants down and stepping out of them. My underwear and I climbed between the heavenly sheets and let out an involuntary groan of relief. "Thank fucking Christ for this bed and everything associated with it," I breathed, settling into the luxurious bedding and closing my eyes. "Pull the curtains closed, please."

"You were serious about napping?" Landry asked.

"I wasn't until I saw the bed," I admitted. "But I'm known for my adaptability."

The light dimmed behind my eyelids as I heard the soft clink of metal curtain rings sliding across rods.

"We need to talk about this," Landry said. "There's time to correct this. To let you go back to the States."

I kept my eyes shut as I listened to him yank another pair of curtains closed. I refused to acknowledge that I'd been planning to do exactly that—leave Landry and his *lordly* crisis management team to handle the boots-on-the-ground work while I did my part remotely.

More to the point, I refused to consider why I'd changed my mind.

"And leave you here to turn this into an even bigger cluster-fuck?" I scoffed. "I don't think so. You pay me to keep your life from imploding, Landry. Remember?"

The sound of fabric moving against fabric continued as he moved around the room. "I think everyone would agree pretending to be my husband is a bridge too far, Kenj."

I shrugged, snuggling deeper into the mattress. "Silas did it for Way. What's the difference?"

The mattress dipped on the far side as Landry slid between the covers. My lungs seized in surprise, leaving me unable to snap at him or tell him to get the fuck out of my napping chamber.

Landry's voice was deep and familiar. And close. "The difference is the two of them were actually married," he said, moving closer until his hand grasped one of my wrists and gently began moving my body where he wanted it.

My heart rate skyrocketed. "I'm not... we're not... this isn't... you aren't the boss of me."

I bit back a groan. He was literally the boss of me.

"I am your husband," he said in a voice full of knowing, full of heat. Full of something I wanted more than I would ever admit. "And you will go where I put you."

I was still angry. So, so angry. And hurt. And embarrassed.

But my dick was already half-hard, and Landry's deep voice commanding me in bed was enough to make the blood abandon my brain with all haste and hotfoot it down to the fun party as fast as humanly possible.

I opened my mouth to snap, "You are not the boss of me," until I realized I'd already said that *and* already reminded myself it was untrue. And I was probably too far past the point of being allowed to speak with any semblance of self-respect.

"Norf," I said instead.

The low rumble of his laugh hit the back of my neck on a hot breath. "That right?"

"*Eing.*"

"Let me have you," he pleaded in a soft, desperate voice. "Please."

"Call me husband," I said, trying to make it sound snarky and sarcastic. Trying and failing. It came out in a drug-slurred voice, low and wanting.

Landry's hands moved around to my chest and stomach. "Do you have any idea what I want to do to you, *darling husband?*"

Wavy air filled my head, and hot fire lit my cheeks. "*Nuhfh.*"

His hard cock pressed against the top of my crack and lower back. The warmth of him surrounded me as his lips teased my ear and neck.

I tried to clear my head, at least enough to make me stop spouting nonsense and set some boundaries. "This doesn't mean anything."

"Of course not, darling," he soothed.

"No, I mean... *oh, god...*" His hand moved down into my boxer briefs to grasp my cock right as something in my brain suddenly served up the realization that while I'd been meditating in the bath yesterday, Landry had acquired my preferred brand of underwear, pants, shirts, and sweaters. He'd somehow managed to buy shoes in my size, the exact model of computer I used, and everything else he thought I might need for the less-than-twenty-four-hour time frame I'd planned to be here. How had he done that? Why had he? "...h-husband," I finished.

The word shouldn't have come out sounding so real. Sounding so right.

I shook my head. "No," I breathed into the sheets.

He froze. "Kenj?"

Suddenly, I realized he'd interpreted my *no* the wrong way. I grabbed his hand to keep it on my cock and reached back with one leg to wrap my foot around his ankle.

He released a sigh of relief. "Tell me to stop if you don't want this."

"Don't stop."

"You know you can tell me to stop." His voice had taken on a knowing, teasing quality I didn't appreciate.

I tightened my grip around the hand he had around my dick. "Don't. Fucking. Stop."

It was his low chuckle that finally threw me over the edge. I lurched forward and grabbed the sleep mask off the table before turning and shoving it over his head. "You don't get to watch."

I yanked it into place on his head, trapping his hair in the strap so he looked ridiculous, and then I shoved him onto his back and moved down his body, nipping and teasing him with both lust and anger in my heart until I got to his cock.

And then I went to town on his gorgeous fucking cock in a way that was aggressive and brutal. It wasn't the first time I'd done this with him. In fact, he'd come up with a name for it about a year into our... encounters.

The Spite Suck.

Whatever. My purpose was to bring both of us to completion as swiftly and brutally as possible. Before anyone caught feelings. Before it had a chance to mean anything. Before—

"Fuck, baby, you feel so good around my cock. So good for me."

A humiliating noise came out of my throat. Landry was doing this on purpose. He knew what words like that did to me.

I moved off his cock completely.

Fuck him.

Instead, I traced the seam of his sac with the tip of my tongue as lightly as humanly possible. But it turned out the joke was on me because seeing the skin crinkle as his balls drew up only made me harder.

I reached back to slide a finger over my hole, remembering the times he'd teased me with his fingers.

"Dammit, Kenji. Suck my cock." His voice was graveled with need. "You know you want to feel my dick on your tongue. You know you want to make me come."

I bit the inside of his thigh lightly, appreciating the swift intake of his breath. His hand found my head, tangling fingers in my hair. "Baby, careful," he warned, even while he spread his thighs further.

I moved down to take one of his balls into my mouth, reaching up to stroke his shaft with one hand while continuing to tease myself with the other.

"Are you touching your cock, Kenji? Are you imagining my fingers on you?"

"I need you to stop talking," I snapped. Except my voice sounded panicked and high-pitched. Something in it made Landry yank his mask off and reach down to grab me under the shoulders, yanking me up his body and flipping us around until we were face-to-face with him peering down at me.

His hand gripped the back of my head. Instead of kissing me, which was what I expected, he lifted my chin so that I had to look at him. "Tell me you want this."

I blinked at him. Usually when he did this, when he called an end to my attitude and manhandled me where he wanted me, there was an unspoken agreement that all verbal communication was over and he was in charge. I went where he put me and took what he gave.

As long as he didn't give me attitude or emotion.

"No," I said automatically, regretting it the instant it was out of my mouth. "Wait!"

His eyes widened a split second after I'd seen the spark in them dim. My heart thundered. *Is he going to call a stop to this? Do I want him to?*

No. Hell no.

"I..." My chest heaved with rapid, shallow breaths. "I want this."

"But you're still angry at me."

"Yes."

He stared into my eyes. His own were glassy pools of verdant water on new grass. "Do you have any idea how much I want you? How much I've *always* wanted you? How scared I was when you—?"

My heart climbed into my throat. "Landry, stop talking. That... that isn't what we're about—"

His big hand moved between us and pressed firmly against my mouth. "I need *you* to stop talking. I don't want to hear your lies."

My lies? *Mine?* The irony of Lord fucking Landry saying those words was galling.

But at the same time, I had to admit... he wasn't entirely wrong. I was a lying liar, too.

I'd come to some realizations in San Cordova about why I'd been holding myself back where Landry was concerned. For years,

I'd accused him of being incapable of commitment and taking a relationship seriously while I'd been the one tap-dancing around the truth.

I cared about Landry. A lot. Too much.

Which was why it hurt so fucking badly that he'd been hiding such a large part of himself from me. His family. His name. His whole second life.

And while my anger was justified—*more than justified, damn it!*—it didn't change the facts.

We weren't enemies with benefits. Not anymore, if we ever had been.

I could tell by the look on Landry's face he wasn't going to leave me hard and aching, but I could also tell he was as angry and hurt as I was.

He'd been lying about who he was, yes. And I'd been lying about who he was *to me.*

He moved down my body, leaving his hand on my mouth with his impossibly long arms, and proceeded to wreck me with his mouth.

He took me to the edge over and over again with long sucks, breaking off as soon as I gave any wordless indication that I was on the precipice. Then, he'd tease me with short strokes and a grip that was just one degree too loose to bring me any relief while delivering teasing licks to my balls, my taint, and my hole that made me writhe with a different kind of pleasure. Just when I was ready to scream in frustration, he'd suck me down and begin the beautiful torture all over again.

Every time I bit out my frustration in a curse, something inside me realized that no one knew how to take me apart like Landry Davis. It was a masterclass in my own destruction, as if he'd been studying me for the past three years.

Landry had never edged and teased me for that long before because I'd never allowed it. If he'd drawn a sexual encounter out to the point I felt vulnerable, I'd always done something to provoke him into finishing because I'd known on some level that if I'd truly put myself in his control, all of the barriers I'd erected between us would come crashing down and leave me in the dust.

And it turned out I'd been right.

By the time he took mercy on me and finally let me come, his hand was long gone from my mouth, and I was clamping my own hand over it to keep from crying out. When the aftershocks of my orgasm subsided and I felt his hot, sticky release on my leg, I turned to thank him...

And found an empty bed.

———

After pulling myself together and cleaning up, I still couldn't bring myself to show my face downstairs. The knowledge that I'd hurt Landry left me feeling like I'd just stepped onto a boat in unknown waters during a squall. I didn't know how to navigate this.

While it was very tempting to believe my own excuses about why I'd blurted out the marriage lie in front of the Winthrops—that Landry needed my help—the truth was, I'd been suddenly, shockingly, viscerally jealous.

Jealous like a pampered dog guarding purloined table scraps. Irrational and primal. Unnecessary. Ridiculous.

But the feeling had been so sharp and bitter I hadn't been able to stop myself from blurting out the word *married*, verbally pissing on the man, because what I'd really wanted to say was *Mine*.

Mine, mine, mine.

Had I really claimed Landry publicly just to reject him? Was that who I was? Was that actually what I wanted?

I sank down on the little couch in my guest room and tried to marshal my thoughts. I was fueled by organization and logical efficiency. But when I tried to think about Landry objectively, to make a pros and cons list, I couldn't stop remembering earlier today, when Cora had brought the three of us to a little office.

I hadn't noticed much about our surroundings at the time, too overwhelmed by the man beside me and the fallout of my possessive overreaction. Now, I considered the details of the room itself.

A familiar crystal statuette shoved to the back of a bookshelf had been one of Landry's Model of the Year Awards.

The stack of spiral-bound reports on the desk with their unique mottled blue-green covers were the annual reports from Sterling Chase, the Brotherhood's shared venture capital firm, which I prepared for them at the end of each year.

The scattered hair bands beside the stack of opened mail in the antique wooden desk box were the type Landry used.

The tiny mason jar filled with candy dicks was a gift Silas had given the Brotherhood for Christmas.

The room we'd escaped to had been Landry's office, not Cora's. And it was obviously well used.

He'd brought the candy and the reports with him to England, even though he'd stopped in New York between leaving Majestic —where he'd received both the candy and the reports—and arriving here.

Hell, I was surprised he hadn't left the reports in a recycle bin at Dev and Tully's house. I'd never known Landry to pay much attention to the Sterling Chase business details.

My fingers initiated a phone call to Bash before I could stop to think about it.

"Thank god you're okay," he said as soon as he picked up. "You *are* okay, right? Landry said you weren't hurt."

I reached up to touch the edge of my forehead where the cut had disappeared into my hairline and the bruise was easy to hide. "I'm fine."

"Good. Are you back in the city, or are you headed to Majestic? Rowe and I are still in Majestic and think it would be a good place for you to recuperate. But if you're in the city, don't even think about going to the office."

I walked over to the window and pulled back the curtain. Deep shadows cut across the view of Regent's Park as the sun slipped behind the buildings.

"I'm in London."

Bash hesitated. "Wait, still? I thought that was just a temporary thing."

A couple walked hand in hand down the sidewalk. The woman chatted excitedly while the man shifted a tote bag on his shoulder without losing his grip on the woman's hand.

"Landry had some things he needed my help with," I said, remembering Chaska's wisdom. *Clarity comes in simplicity.*

"Oh, well, good. I hope it's not too demanding. I'm sure he could use your help with his statements to the media and whatnot. As long as you get some time to recover."

For a split second, I thought he knew about Landry being a British peer and about our sham engagement-slash-marriage... but then I realized he must have been referring to Landry's retirement from modeling.

Bash obviously hadn't seen the news yet, but then again, it was early in Wyoming, and when the guys were together at Dev and Tully's house, they were more likely to be focused on Lellie than their phones.

I cleared my throat. "Actually, we have a situation here. I thought the Brotherhood might need to be aware of it."

"What is it?" Bash asked, his need to control coming to the surface in his tone.

"We landed in London to a bit of a media frenzy," I began. "There are some wild headlines floating around—romantic headlines—and we're currently strategizing with a PR team to figure out the best response."

"Romantic headlines? You mean, about you and Jamie Winthrop?

Landry told us about the rescue plans. Did the press think you and this Winthrop guy were together just because you were rescued together?"

I wanted to laugh, bark out a snort, and then explain it was all a big joke. If only it were that simple.

"No, actually. I, ah... I was holding Landry's hand when we stepped off the plane. There was already a misunderstanding, and the image of the two of us together added fuel to the fire. It's kind of exploded."

Long story short, the world thinks we're married.

Bash's voice carried a smile. "Holding hands, huh? You mean you finally threw Landry a bone?"

I heard Rowe's voice in the background making a *bah-dum-bum* sound.

"I beg your pardon?" I asked, sounding more like a ninety-year-old butler than myself. I closed my eyes and breathed through my nose.

"Come on. Landry's a good man, Kenji, and he's pretty obviously had a *thing* for you for a while. Maybe don't be so hard on him."

Rowe's snickering intensified. "No pun intended," he called out.

"He's a child," I insisted, unsure whether I was referring to Bash's husband or Landry.

"Landry's a hard worker, and you know it. Unless you've forgotten about Milan Fashion week two years ago when he added a charity sponsorship to his already overpacked schedule, resulting in his working around the clock for two straight weeks while nearly comatose from jet lag. Or the times he's had to skip our vacations to check on his dad back in England. Or that time he skipped the opportunity to be seen at the Oscars so he could bring you zosui soup from Hirohisa when you had the flu. *Or the time he hired a fucking SEAL team rescue for you on the other side of the world.* Or the time he got Rowe into that backroom couture lingerie sale so he could get—"

Rowe squawked in the background.

Bash sucked in a breath. "Never mind. That's... private. Anyway. Landry has a giant heart, an impeccable work ethic, and an overwhelming crush on his executive assistant. The two of you either need to fuck and get past it or go on a date. But stop whatever the hell this is because it's killing Landry. He looked like a kicked puppy at Christmas."

Another couple on the street had entered my field of vision. Two women walked arm in arm, bundled up in coats and scarves. They were talking with their heads together, unsmiling but obviously close. They reminded me of a couple who'd lived in my apartment building until last year when they'd decided to move to Vermont in search of a slower-paced life so they could spend more time together.

At the time, I'd thought they were crazy. I'd fully expected them to be bored within a month, but here we were, eight months later, and their Instagram feeds were full of photos of their happy life together in the mountains. Their house had a wide, sweeping view of a meadow leading to low peaks where the sun painted swaths of warm colors every morning and night.

It reminded me of the painting of Three Daughters in Majestic that hung over my bed.

Maybe I'd never let myself imagine a life like that because I didn't think it would ever be within reach.

Maybe it never would be if I kept throwing up roadblocks and pretending I didn't care when I did.

"Landry wanted me to go out to eat with him," I admitted softly. "Like... like a date."

Bash's voice held a smirk. "For real? You have to admit it would be kind of funny if Landry never needs to reveal the secret of the Brotherhood billions to his life partner because the guy already—"

Rowe squealed again. "Oh shit. Oh shitttt. That's what he meant! Landry said at Christmas his partner already knew. Omigod omigod!"

At the time, I'd thought Landry was just being dramatic. I hadn't been able to allow myself to consider any other reason for his comment. But now... "He told me he wanted to have a relationship with me. Something more than physical." I swallowed. "He wanted me to be his boyfriend."

There was silence over the line. I knew Bash well enough to know he was either lecturing himself in his mind to tread lightly, or he was staring wide-eyed at Rowe while mouthing *what the fuck do I do?*

"And you... declined?" he guessed.

"Obviously."

"Why?"

I huffed out a laugh, causing the glass windowpane to fog in front of me.

All the reasons I'd given myself for years danced in my brain. I *knew* Landry Davis, I'd told myself. Knew everything about him. Landry was a playboy who didn't know what responsibility was. Who didn't take anything seriously. Who wasn't the settling-down type. Who didn't know what long-term commitment even looked like and wasn't a family man.

But not only had Landry been faithful to me for three freaking years, but he was obviously dedicated to his family. And if there was anything that screamed long-term commitment more than a centuries-old family legacy, it was having a man lie to the freaking prime minister *for me.*

The true answer was *because I'm a fucking idiot.*

But what came out of my mouth was, "Because he's a freaking

lord who's going to get talked into serving in Parliament, and I wouldn't make a good countess. I have to go."

I ended the call and threw myself onto the bed again, yanking up the duvet and trying hard not to feel the tsunami of guilt pour over me.

I really was a fucking idiot.

And it was becoming clearer and clearer to me I was also in love with one.

TWELVE
LANDRY

I would not love him against his will.

Alright, fine, I *would*, only because I couldn't help myself, and I'd been doing it too long to stop now, but I wouldn't let it show. I wouldn't keep trying to get him to love me back. That way lay madness.

Kenji didn't want me. Not for anything but sex. And after three years, I finally accepted that.

So instead, I would guard my heart—build an impenetrable fucking fortress around it—and get on with the next chapter of my life.

Moreover, I would accept the fact that this next chapter would not involve Kenji Toma.

I'd always known, in a half-formed sort of way I hadn't fully acknowledged to myself, that stepping into the public role of Viscount Hawling, heir presumptive to the Davencourt earldom, would mean stepping away from the possibility of anything romantic with Kenji. That was part of the reason I'd fought it for so long.

Now, though, I was relieved I could throw myself into something so demanding, so all-encompassing, it wouldn't leave me a single moment to consider crawling back to Kenji and begging for scraps.

I cleaned up in my room after having what would no doubt be my last sexual interlude with the world's coldest man, then headed down to Nan's office, entering the room with as much command and confidence as I could.

"Alright, I've made some decisions." I glanced around at the assembled crisis management team. "First of all, if I am going to begin representing the Davencourt family in public, my preferred name is Landry. Not only is it the name everyone in the world associates with this face, but it's also the surname of the original Viscount Hawling, who was granted the viscountcy after he famously rescued a kidnapped peasant girl who turned out to be a daughter of Queen Anne, secreted out of Windsor dressed in rags. The name Landry has been in my family for over three hundred years, and I rather like being associated with someone who rescued the sole living child of a woman who'd lost seventeen others."

That got everyone's attention.

"Needless to say, we don't need to explain all that," I went on. "Simply release the news that while my name has not changed, I prefer my middle name, Landry, to Everett. Secondly, if the prime minister calls on me to serve in the House of Lords, I will accept with pleasure. We will announce my recent marriage to Kenji and use it to project stability onto my image to help smooth the transition from model to peer. However, if I'm elected to Parliament and begin serving, Kenji will not be part of it. My intention is to help him retain as much privacy as possible after this initial introduction into society." I didn't explain to them that there would come a time in the not-too-distant future when we would end the sham marriage and quietly go our separate ways. That was a problem for a different day. But I did want to set the expectation now that Kenji would not be a part of my long-term publicity plan.

Cards on the table, as Kenji said. Not all the cards, but most of them.

Despite what Cora believed, I had no expectation that I'd actually be chosen to fill my father's spot, but the process of going through the by-election would at least tick the box on my familial expectation and perhaps bring my father a small amount of joy and comfort.

The heat of Cora's surprised stare seared the side of my face. I ignored it along with Nan's look of tender concern.

"So we need a plan to announce those things and address my duplicity. I think we keep it simple and explain that I wasn't trying to trick anyone; I simply wanted a chance to succeed on my own merit. Now that my father is retiring, it's time I set aside my childish ways—as they say—and accept the honor and responsibility of helping improve things for the country. I'll be honest. I don't believe I'll be selected, but I'm happy to tell Mr. Baines and Baroness Colborne they can consider me for it."

Several faces brightened with excitement and began strategizing. Nan stood and approached me. "We need to talk to your father."

She was right, but the reminder deflated me a bit. "Yes. Is he available now?"

Nan, Cora, and I spent the next couple of hours in my father's study discussing his retirement and future plans. Thankfully, he was in a clear frame of mind and able to discuss it in great detail, and Nan had the foresight to call in our head solicitor to witness and record the conversation with Dad's permission. The solicitor consulted with Dad's office to create the appropriate correspondence to send out after notifying the necessary people.

Nan had already floated the retirement idea to a few people to let them know it was in the works, and I'd done the same with the prime minister.

By the time we finished, my poor father was done for the day. Nan took him to his suite and ensured Reg sent up a meal.

"Where's Kenji?" Cora asked, meeting me in the kitchen for a curry dinner.

I shrugged. "I asked Mrs. Ashcombe to notify him that dinner would be at six thirty in the kitchen. If he's not here, that's his business."

She lifted an eyebrow. "That's a fine way to treat your husband."

I focused on splashing a generous serving of sauvignon blanc into a goblet. "Don't start."

"Landry," she said in a softer voice. "I know you're frustrated and things haven't, ah... worked out as you hoped—"

I snorted at this understatement.

"—but Kenji's been through a lot, and he stepped up for you today. Maybe you should go easy on him."

"Kenji doesn't respond to 'easy,' I'm afraid. Soft emotions like kindness, empathy, and tender regard tend to make him angry. I've decided his love language is bitterness and froth. Add in low-key declarations of war, blatant disrespect, stark rejection, and a high-brow sniff of disdain, and you can *almost* get the man in bed. But nothing, and I mean nothing, will get him to agree to a dinner date. And he didn't step up today out of any higher feelings for me, I assure you," I added. "He's just programmed to clean up my messes."

I tilted the bottle at her in a *want some?* gesture.

She nodded. "Have you considered he might have legitimate fears holding him back?"

I shot her a flat look over the wineglass. "Have you considered he's just not that into me?"

Her cheeks dimpled, reminding me of the days when she carried more baby fat in her face. "No. Because every time he's around you, he touches you. Yes, he's a bit... prickly... toward you, but he's definitely always aware of where you are in a room. He won't let himself look at you directly, but his eyes rarely leave you."

The wine was cool against my tongue and throat as I swallowed. "He's spent years babysitting me, Cora. Don't confuse management with love. Besides, the plan is for me to live here and serve the people, remember? Kenji has no interest in being a... countess." The very idea made wine shoot up my nose...

Which was why, when Kenji walked into the kitchen in search of dinner a beat later, I was choking and sputtering.

Cora's face lit up. "Kenji! Come sit by me. Reg is making one of my favorite curries. Do you like curry?"

The two of them talked about Indian dishes as if there wasn't a giant, undetonated bomb sitting in the middle of the table.

I stood and approached Reg. "Need any help?"

He didn't take his eye off the naan bread he was grilling. "Not as much as you do," he muttered before tilting his head back toward the table. "Go sort your own affairs. Dinner's almost ready, and I've a date with a pint down the pub."

"Take me with you?"

He snorted softly. "I take you with me and I'll never find a woman to share my bed. No offense, but you've got to be the worst wingman ever."

"I'm gay," I reminded him.

He rolled his eyes and nudged me out of the way to cut the naan bread into halves on the clean wooden counter. "Even worse. You think that means the women are going to leave you alone? They'll be asking hair advice and taking selfies with you for their Instagram."

I patted him on the shoulder. "Thanks for the ego stroke. I'll take it where I can find it."

After scrolling through my phone, peeking out the back window to check the weather, and straightening the cord behind the kettle, I finally slunk back to the kitchen table and tried to act aloof.

Cora glanced over at me. "The tailor will be here in an hour to do Kenji's fitting. Do you need him to do you as well, or do you have the clothes you need for Winthrop's little PR campaign?"

She pulled her laptop over from where it had been pushed to the side on the table and began going over the events as Reg set the food down in front of us.

"I have the clothes I need," I murmured, hoping I hadn't gained any weight since last wearing my tuxedo.

"Just leave the dishes," Reg said before heading toward the back door. "I'll get them later. Ta."

The kitchen seemed eerily quiet without him there.

Kenji studied the laptop screen. "I recognize most of the events from Landry's calendar in previous years, but what's the HoH Dinner?"

Cora frowned at him. "Hearts of Hawling? That's the big annual fundraiser for our family's foundation. It's one of London's most coveted charity events. Surely you've had to schedule around it in the past."

Kenji darted a glance at me, then looked away quickly. "Not as such. I do recall Landry marking off a 'spa weekend' this time last year, though."

The silence got much weirder as the bomb finally detonated and shrapnel hung still and jagged in the air, quivering in place as if waiting until everyone breathed again to strike.

I stood up and took my still-full dishes to the sink before depositing them and disappearing upstairs.

It wasn't mature. It wasn't professional. It wasn't the ice-cold persona I'd hoped to project.

But it was ten times better than listening to myself make up a new pack of lies to defend the old.

When I made it to my room and closed the door behind me, I finally exhaled.

———

At one in the morning, I gave up trying to sleep and made my way up two flights of stairs to the home gym. My father had arranged for it to be installed the year I'd left Eton to study at home, even though we hadn't ended up staying in the city long enough to use it much.

In the years since, I'd managed to make up for it by using the hell out of it. Every time I came through London on the way somewhere, I tacked on a few days to visit, using the gym to stay in top shape as my job had required.

There'd been times over the years I'd paid handsomely to upgrade the equipment or add to the tech, but in the end, it was an old, stuffy room that carried a familiar gym stink.

I started with a warm-up on the treadmill. My headphones were cranked up to damaging levels, and Beyoncé pumped through me, speeding up my stride as the song changed from "Beautiful Liar" to "Break My Soul." When "Crazy in Love" started, I barked, "Fuck!" and nearly chucked my phone across the room.

Instead, I quickly changed to Eminem's "Houdini" and moved from the treadmill to the chest press machine. The reflection in the mirror mocked me.

My hair was pulled back from my face and neck by a large elastic hairband, the mashed-up waves causing it to stick out like a lion's mane. I couldn't decide if it was fierce or pathetic, but at least my face was clear, and my skin glowed.

How many years had I done an instant inventory when faced with my reflection in the mirror? How was my hair? My skin? My weight? Were there circles under my eyes? What was my muscle situation? My veins? Did I need manscaping? A salon visit? *Waxing?*

As of a week or two ago, I'd actually thought I was done with all of that.

And now here I was, being thrust back into the public eye. Being photographed. Judged. Criticized down to the length of my fingernails and eyelashes.

I blew out a breath and stood up, moving to the bench to do tricep curls.

Suddenly, I stilled. They would criticize Kenji like that, too.

My stomach twisted. *Fuck.* I didn't want Kenji to go through that. What the hell had I been thinking when I'd enlisted him in...?

But I hadn't enlisted him in anything. He'd been the one to say we were married. Because he hadn't trusted me to navigate this situation on my own.

Well, fuck him. I'd been born to navigate the British press. And this wasn't my first rodeo. Not by a long shot.

As I put myself through the paces in the gym and diligently avoided all the Taylor Swift songs in my playlist, I remembered something I'd read in Kenji's Chaska Inira book.

"When the task feels impossible, remember: you carry the strength of every challenge you have already overcome."

I'd been in sticky situations before with the media. And I'd learned early on that the key to lowering their expectations and boring them to tears was to act shallow and stupid.

In this particular case, if the world thought Everett Landry Davencourt, Viscount Hawley and heir apparent to the Earl of Davencourt, was a pretty face with nothing behind it, not only would they lose interest in him more quickly, but the powers that be in the British government would stop hoping for him to take his father's place in Parliament.

I blew out a breath. There was no way I would let my father

and my name down by acting stupid on purpose. Chances were I'd act stupid enough by accident.

When I finally made my way back downstairs to my bedroom, I thought I heard a whimper coming from Kenji's guest room. I raced down the carpeted hall and pressed my ear against the door. As soon as I had confirmation I hadn't been imagining things, I would open the door to make sure he was okay.

I listened for an embarrassingly long time.

And didn't hear a sound.

I finally made my way to my own room, took a quick shower, and fell into bed.

But it was hours before sleep finally rescued me from my thoughts.

THIRTEEN

KENJI

After Landry stormed out of the kitchen, Cora and I talked. And talked.

She told me enough about Landry's visits "home" for me to realize just how complex it must've been for him to hide his second life all these years. It wasn't that he'd walked out of his life as a member of the esteemed Davencourt family and pretended to be someone else instead. He'd been both Everett Davencourt *and* Landry Davis.

The man had spent *years* running the Davencourt holdings, managing investments, hiring and firing land stewards, and consulting Cora on projects at the foundation... while also running around the globe as one of the world's most in-demand male fashion models, taking part in events on behalf of Sterling Chase, and staying actively involved in his friends' lives.

And I'd never had a clue.

All that time, I'd thought he was fucking off to the Med to spend a few days on a yacht with booze and boys or spending a long weekend in a luxury hotel somewhere, catching up on sleep.

Never in a million years had I imagined he was in a stuffy

office in Regent's Park reviewing performance reports and signing legal paperwork to expand the family's real estate holdings. Or helping his father navigate the ever-changing landscape of British politics and critical alliances.

"I can tell this is hard for you," Cora had said kindly, handing me a mug of tea after the tailor had finished sticking me with dozens of pins. "We begged him to tell you."

I'd pressed my lips together. "Landry couldn't trust me."

She'd disagreed, but it was true. And I couldn't blame him. I'd never given the man a real chance.

I'd slept horribly after that, waking over and over from stress-fueled nightmares that interspersed terrifying scenes from San Cordova with scenes of me panic-running through an empty city, unable to find Landry.

Before the sun rose, my eyes opened in the darkness as a memory served itself up with particular cruelty.

Landry and I had been hooking up for about six months when he'd begged to stay over at my place after we'd fucked.

"I'm bone-tired, and it's cold as balls out there," he'd murmured, eyes already closed.

"Tired? Haven't you just spent the past week on the coast holding down a sun lounger? Get up. I have to be at the office before six tomorrow."

He'd turned and snuggled into my shoulder. "Kenj, please. I was up for three days straight trying to navigate an easement deal in Torquay."

It had sounded so ridiculous I'd assumed he was already half-asleep and dreaming. "We have an agreement," I'd insisted, nudging him off me to keep from wrapping my arms around him and begging him to stay. "You nut, then you go."

He'd hauled himself out of my bed with a sigh.

"You never let me stay long enough to talk to you," he'd complained as he'd yanked on his clothes.

"This isn't about talking. I don't need you to talk. I get enough of that during the day," I'd said, scrolling through my phone to keep from watching his beautiful abs disappear under a sweater and jacket.

His *pale* abs, I realized now, years too late. Not the sun-kissed abs of someone who'd been in Puerto Vallarta but the winter-pale abs of a man who'd been on the coast of *England* in Devon.

As I lay there in the darkness, I remembered another time, when I'd overheard Landry and Silas talking out by the pool at Bash's house in the Hamptons. Landry had asked Silas a question about real estate investment trusts.

My attention had floated in and out, but I remembered hearing Silas explain REITs were like mutual funds but for real estate.

Landry had replied, "I understand what they are and the tax advantages. My question is how to optimize the structure of a REIT. If seventy-five percent of its assets have to be in real estate, cash, or government securities and seventy-five percent of its income has to come from things like rent, interest on mortgages, or property sales, and ninety percent of its taxable income has to be distributed to shareholders annually, is it possible to structure a REIT around historic properties with strict preservation regulations? How do you ensure an adequate occupancy ratio in order to meet the requirements?"

Silas had seemed just as surprised by the question as I had. I'd pretended to be engrossed in my work, sitting off to the side at an umbrella table, but it had been one of a handful of moments when I'd stopped and reminded myself this guy had been admitted to and had graduated from Yale.

Landry wasn't stupid.

So why the hell did he act like it sometimes?

I wiped my leaky eyes with the duvet, then tossed it aside. Today was our first command performance as a couple. The plan was to take a simple walk, hand in hand, to a local place for brunch and then enjoy our food while acting like normal newlyweds. The press would be tipped off to find us there and shout questions at us as we prepared to leave and walk back to the house. We would pretend to be surprised when encountering Jim and Jamie Winthrop on their way in for brunch, and we'd agree to linger for another cup of coffee.

Considering Landry hadn't spoken to me since yesterday afternoon, I was unsure of the success of the plan. But the official press releases had already gone out, and the game was afoot regardless of how I felt about it.

I dressed in another of the outfits Landry had purchased for me when we'd first arrived in London. Well-fitted jeans, surprisingly similar to a pair I owned at home that he'd complimented me on several times, and a white turtleneck sweater.

If I spent a little extra time at the vanity, it was only because I was going to be on camera later today, and I needed to be attractive enough to make it at least semi-plausible that someone as beautiful as Landry Davis... Davencourt, would actually choose me.

After an hour of fighting with my hair and face, I gave up and made my way downstairs to the kitchen.

Nan's face lit up when she spotted me. "Kenji, you look wonderful, dear. How are you feeling?"

Landry's luminous blue-green eyes glanced up at me, but his face remained expressionless.

My breaths came a little quicker than before... because I'd just walked down the stairs. *Obviously*.

"I'm fine," I replied belatedly. "Thank you."

Cora moved her laptop out of the way and pointed to the seat next to her. She set a Starbucks cup in front of it. "Sit here. Landry got you a coffee."

I glanced at Landry to thank him, but he'd already turned his attention back to his phone.

"Thanks," I murmured anyway.

"Mph," he grunted back.

I closed my eyes and inhaled. This wasn't going to work.

Cora pulled her laptop closer. "Okay, I'm writing up some profiles for our media kit. Kenji, I have all of your education and work history. Can you give me some interests outside of work?"

I opened my eyes and blinked at her. "What, like hobbies?"

She nodded. "Yes. Like... gardening, hiking, reading, crossword puzzles, swing dancing lessons... you know, that kind of thing. What do you like to do for fun?"

"I'm kind of a workaholic. I don't have hobbies."

"We need something to put here. Surely you have some kind of interests? Are there any shows you like to watch or charities you volunteer with?"

I thought of the charity runs I did every holiday season, but they seemed too silly to include. "I took a shodo class once. It's like Japanese calligraphy."

Landry didn't look up from his phone. "It's a type of Zen practice. He also practices mindfulness and meditation, specifically following the wisdom of Chaska Inira, who believes that fostering peace and understanding can create a world of greater connectedness."

I stared at him. "Yes," I breathed.

Cora typed into her laptop. "That's good. I like that."

Landry took a sip of coffee. "He also raises money for LGBTQ military groups by doing virtual 5Ks during the months of October, November, and December, but he donates anonymously. And he volunteers at a youth suicide hotline, but he's not going to let you write that down. And he sends strongly worded letters every quarter to a particular senator, but that obviously can't be included. He's an incredible chess player who was once ranked, even though he won't say how high, and he rarely plays anymore. Oh, and he also sends strongly worded letters to the company that makes the copy paper we used to use in our corporate office, even though they already changed their policy on—"

"I take pictures of sunsets," I blurted. "And I make birthday cake kits for a local food bank."

Cora typed happily into her laptop as I let out a breath and took a sip of my coffee. After a moment, I could swear I felt Landry's eyes on me, but when I looked up, he was focused on his own cup.

"I also house-sit for friends," I admitted, watching him. "I swing by their place when they're out of town and do their laundry, change their sheets, grab a few grocery essentials before they come home. That kind of thing. And sometimes I... I go into their Netflix and click around in it until their suggestions are full of things I think they'd like."

Landry's eyes slowly lifted from his cup to meet mine. My heart skipped erratically like it was going to wing itself off the nearest overpass.

Cora made a dismissive sound in her throat. "No offense, Kenji, but that last part sounds a little OTT."

She was probably right. Thankfully, Reg distracted me by setting a plate full of food in front of me. "The full English. Cora said you've got a busy day ahead."

I murmured my thanks out of habit before remembering our morning "date."

"Aren't we eating breakfast out?"

Cora waved a dismissive hand in the air. "You won't be able to eat much, and you have to order specific menu items that you may not like."

Landry took another sip of his coffee, which was no help at all.

"Specific menu items?" I prompted.

She nodded. "To cause the least amount of offense to viewers as well as not looking disgusting in a photo. The PR team has settled on the french toast with banana and berries for you. Don't put too much syrup on it. If you must have it, drizzle sparingly. And Landry will get the açaí bowl. Then he'll adorably ask to take a bite of yours."

Landry didn't seem surprised by any of this. "And do not eat any food with a skin or a leaf unless you can swallow it whole or bite only with your back teeth. I went semi-viral once with a blueberry skin stuck between my teeth. Haven't eaten blueberries in public since."

I dug into my full English while I had the luxury of privacy.

Cora continued to outline the reminders from the PR team, even though I'd already read through them in my email during one of my midnight wakings. Touch Landry, but not in strange or "exotic" places like his inner thigh or armpit. Smile a lot, but not maniacally or showing too much teeth. Be sure to listen to what the other says, but remember, active listening includes eye contact, avoiding interrupting, and leaning toward the speaker rather than away from him.

By the time Cora herded us out of the kitchen toward our command performance, I was convinced I was going to fuck it all up.

"You're trembling," Landry murmured as he reached for my hand in the foyer. "Do you need a warmer coat? I have one in my—"

"No, no. I'm fine. I'm not cold."

Landry's eyebrows dipped together before winging apart in surprise. "You're nervous!"

"I'm not good in front of a crowd."

"Neither am I," he insisted. "But you get used to it. Smile and look pretty. Works every time."

I rolled my eyes. "It works for you because you're beautiful."

Cora bustled past us and opened the front door just as Landry turned and cupped my cheeks in his warm hands. "You are the most gorgeous man I know, Kenji," he insisted. "Do you remember when I hurried you away from that lunch restaurant in the Village last year? And you got angry thinking I didn't want to be seen with you in public? You were right, but not for the reason you think."

His voice was low and calm, as if there weren't suddenly cameras and reporters only feet away on the sidewalk.

"Why, then?" I breathed.

"Because I was meeting with my agent and the hiring director for a project. The Breitling job, remember? And I was afraid if the man saw you, he'd want you instead."

Something about that didn't sound right. "First of all, don't be ridiculous. Second, I would have never accepted an offer for a modeling job. And third..." I stopped because I was surprised by my own thoughts, even though they were true. "You'd never begrudge a friend an opportunity like that. Especially me."

"The man is a player. He would have wanted you not only for the project but also in his bed," he growled.

I blinked at him as he continued.

"And I wasn't about to share you."

His mouth came down on mine, hungry and possessive. The crowd around us went crazy. For a split second, I wondered if he'd orchestrated that moment for maximum effect, but then I quickly realized Landry Davis, *my* Landry, wasn't quite that good of an actor.

The kiss was quick but borderline feral. When he pulled away, it left me gasping and off-balance. He reached for my hand and threaded our fingers together before pulling me forward and grinning at the cameras.

"Ya found me," he said with a bright smile as if this was all *so much fun.*

A reporter in the front could be heard above the rest. "Landry, are you, in fact, Everett Davencourt, Viscount Hawling?"

He nodded. "I am, and I'm on my way to breakfast this

morning with this beautiful man, so I only have time for one or two questions."

Another reporter asked, "Is it true the two of you are engaged? Can you introduce us?"

Landry released my hand and slid his arm around my waist. "I'd be happy to introduce you, but we aren't engaged." The collective group seemed to deflate a little. "We're recently married."

Maybe Landry was a better actor than I gave him credit for. He seemed to have a flair for dramatic timing.

The reporters began shouting again until one won out over the others. "When did the two of you marry?"

"Kenji and I met through work many years ago, and we married over the holidays with only friends and family in attendance."

"Is the rumor true about your father retiring? Are you going to try to take his place in the Lords?"

He tilted his chin down, not taking his arm from around me. "My father is retiring. As to whether I might find myself in Parliament, well, that is a question for the people and for the leaders of our government. Now, if you'll excuse us, I'd like to get my beloved husband out of the blustery cold. Thank you, everyone."

He clasped my hand again tightly and pulled me forward. I tried to project an air of friendly and polite calm. An agreeable helpmeet rather than an awkward math nerd who had a secret collection of handy spreadsheet formulas tucked away in a file labeled *SumThingSpecial.xlxs*.

I was not the kind of guy who had fancy London brunch with a supermodel boyfriend.

Husband.

"I can't feel my legs," I said almost too softly for my own ears to pick it up.

"You're doing fine," Landry murmured, tightening his grip on my hand. "It's only two blocks away."

"They probably think I'm mute."

"I can assure them you are not," he said in a particular tone. I glanced up at him and noticed his plastered-on smile didn't meet his eyes.

"You're still angry."

He turned his unsmiling eyes on me and grinned wider. "Darling, I could never be angry with you."

And then he leaned down and pressed a kiss to my lips.

I stared at him as he pulled away to continue walking. *I think I'm going to be sick.*

"I'm sorry," I breathed.

"For what, sweetheart?"

My eyes stung, and I tried to think of something else, something besides hurting the one man in the world who loved me unconditionally.

"Did you know that Excel will let you undo up to one hundred actions?" I asked.

Landry's smile wavered. "Excel... the spreadsheet software?"

I looked off to the side, taking care to continue smiling even though I worried the gesture wouldn't be good at containing vomit. "It also has over five hundred built-in functions, including one for gamma distribution, which I've never really understood. But there's also the Unique function, which quickly deduplicates lists and helps with things like RSVPs. That one I use often."

"What are you... *Kenj.* Look at me."

I turned reluctantly to face him, taking great care to look at the place where his red spot had been carefully covered with concealer. His mouth was still smiling playfully, but his eyes showed concern.

"I'm making conversation," I explained softly with my smile in place.

"You're scaring me," he grumbled, turning away and continuing our progress. Thankfully, the security personnel Nan had arranged for us were keeping the reporters far enough away from us not to hear our conversation. "I forgot spreadsheets were your security blanket. Continue. Maybe you can explain why every time I change a cell's format to currency, it automatically shifts everything to one side."

I happily explained the importance of aligning the decimal point in a currency column, and by the time we reached the restaurant, I probably looked as happy as a clam, even though my heart still felt like it was being squeezed in a giant vise.

We took a seat at a small table for two by the window. Everything had clearly been arranged ahead of time, and I was grateful the paparazzi wasn't allowed inside.

"Thank fuck," I muttered, exhaling and perusing the menu. "Think I'm allowed a hot chocolate?"

"No whipped cream unless you want an adorable spot on your nose I can kiss off," he said blandly into the menu.

I reached across the table and took his hand in mine. His eyes widened in surprise as he looked up at me.

"I'm sorry I messed up your plans," I said. "I'm sorry I blurted out the marriage thing and I'm..." I sucked in a breath. "I'm sorry I hurt your feelings. I'm having trouble—"

"Welcome to Drunch. What can I start you with? Coffee?"

Landry turned on the charm like I'd seen him do a million times. "Hello! I'll take some coffee, but my husband here would like hot chocolate with extra whipped cream, please."

I blinked at him and opened my mouth to correct him but felt the warning squeeze of his hand. I clamped my mouth closed after murmuring my thanks.

Once she was gone, Landry glanced back at me. "You're having trouble...?"

I felt the eyes of the media on us through the window. This

wasn't the time to explain that I was having trouble sleeping. Having trouble breaking the habit of holding him at arm's length. Having trouble not throwing myself into his arms and begging him to build a life with me for real.

The weight of everyone's expectations pressed down on me, and I remembered the purpose of this outing. We were supposed to be selling our romance.

I picked up Landry's hand and pulled it to my lips, kissing each knuckle one by one without taking my eyes off his.

"I'm having trouble keeping my hands and mouth off of you," I said with a teasing, flirty smile.

Landry's eyes heated, but his smile didn't return. I reached for his other hand and began doing the same.

Until I came to a warm gold band on his ring finger.

My stomach lurched with a silly, lightning-fast worry he'd somehow either gotten secretly married when I wasn't looking or he'd been married all along. But then my brain kicked back in, and I shot him a look.

"Fuck," he hissed, pulling his hands back to fumble in his pockets. "I have one for you, too."

"Baby," I said between my teeth, still fronting a smile as the server approached. "Tread lightly."

He spoke at a normal volume as he pulled something out of his pocket with a dramatic flourish. "I just got this back from the jeweler. Apparently, the delay was due to its age and historical significance." He reached for my left hand and began sliding a ring onto my finger. "In the Victorian era, men wore wedding rings on their pinky fingers. Those would have probably fit your slender ring finger, but I didn't like any of the ones in our family collection."

It took a minute for the paparazzi to realize what they were seeing through the window, but once they did, they quickly scrambled to get closer.

I concentrated on keeping my hand from shaking. "So this one is...?"

His eyes bored into mine. "It is a gimmel ring from the eighteenth century. It's actually formed of three separate gold bands. My ancestor, the eighth earl, had it made as a symbolic gesture for his lady love. During the betrothal, he wore one of the bands, she wore the other, and the person who'd introduced them—who happened to be her brother and his friend—wore the third. During the wedding ceremony, all were placed in the bishop's hand for a marital blessing and then placed together, as you see here, on the groom's finger. There was a matching one for the bride, but it was lost after her death. We believe it was actually buried with her."

I glanced down at the design. Two hands were clasped together, almost like a Claddagh ring design but more primitive and blocky.

"There's a heart inside," Landry murmured. "Hidden beneath the hands. Each hand is on a separate band, and the heart is on the third. You can separate them to see when you take it off."

As soon as he released my hand, I pulled it close to my heart and covered it with my other hand. "Thank you," I said, forgetting for a minute that none of this was real. "I mean... I'll, uh... I'll take good care of it."

I stood and leaned over the table, grasping his face and kissing him tenderly. "Thank you," I murmured again softly. "You are a good man."

He stretched his head from side to side and cleared his throat. "Don't know about you, but I'm in the mood for an açaí bowl!"

As the performance brunch continued, I couldn't help but glance down from time to time to see the antique ring on my finger. No one had been within earshot when he'd told me the details of the ring. His description of its history hadn't been for the press. It had been for me.

My mind reeled with this new reality, the one in which

Landry Davis, *my* Landry, was heir to a long and storied earldom complete with a rich, chronicled history as evidenced from this piece and everything in Hawling House, as well as the kind of familial expectation and pressure I couldn't even wrap my head around.

I'd been under family pressure myself. Pressure to go to college, to graduate and get a good job. And then, when I'd given up the "good" job as an entry-level market research analyst to move to New York, pressure to find an even better one *and* meet a successful gay man I could settle down with, too.

Within a month of moving, I'd run out of money, not because I hadn't saved properly for my move but because I'd fallen for an apartment rental scheme and had been too mortified by my own stupidity to ask my parents or grandmother for help. I'd plastered the city with resumes and had taken a temp job as an assistant in the meantime... which was how I'd ended up at Sterling Chase.

"What are you thinking about?" Landry asked, shaking me out of my memories.

His hair was perfectly styled to look messy. His eyes were bright with curiosity, but his mouth was still set in a fake smile. My hand was loosely held in his as his fingers toyed idly with mine, rubbing every now and then across the patina of the old ring.

"I was homeless when I started working for Sterling Chase," I admitted.

His fake smile evaporated with the steam from his coffee.

My hand tightened involuntarily around his.

"I thought your father managed rental properties," I said, trying not to act as upset as I felt at not having known this. "How could you have been homeless? That was only ten years ago."

Kenji waved his free hand dismissively. "I didn't tell them. I was too embarrassed. And it wasn't like I was sleeping under a bridge. I'd met a guy at a bar one night who gave me the code to his building. I snuck in and slept at the bottom of the stairwell in the basement by the storage room door."

I ran through my memories of that time, looking for clues. "You... you had a resume. You'd worked for a consulting company. In market research."

Kenji sat back, as if my recall surprised him. Unfortunately, he took his hand with him. I moved both of my hands around my coffee to keep from reaching for him again.

"Yes," he said. "And I was looking for something similar in New York." He continued to tell me the story of how he'd wanted to live a bigger life, wanted to have his *Sex in the City* era, but had been taken advantage of after answering the wrong rooming ad.

Kenji shrugged, the movement drawing my attention to his elegant frame in the cream turtleneck sweater I'd picked out for him. He was so fucking beautiful it made my eyes smart.

"Then suddenly, I needed a paycheck, and I needed it quickly. I knew if I looked for a serving or bartending job, I ran the risk of never getting back into an office environment. So I signed up for a temp agency. Got sent to Sterling Chase that very first day."

I remembered Bash mentioning his "miracle" of a temp and how he'd burned a bridge with the temp agency by hiring the guy right out from under them.

"You impressed us," I said, remembering the younger, skinnier Kenji. The one in a hundred-dollar suit and a delicate nose ring that had made my dick perk up immediately. "Whatever happened to the nose ring?"

Kenji ran his fingertip down the side of his nose. "My father didn't approve. He suggested the reason I hadn't found a 'real' job yet was because I didn't project a professional appearance. Maybe he was right. When I removed it, I got an offer from Deloitte."

My coffee landed on the table with a thunk. "That was after you were working for us!"

He nodded calmly. "Yes."

Before I had a chance to ask him why he hadn't taken it, the server appeared with our food. We slipped back into the lie, pretending to eat our food while chatting happily about absolutely nothing.

I remembered to take a bite of his french toast. And he ended up with a dollop of hot chocolate on his nose. I leaned over and dropped an open-mouthed kiss there, tasting the creamy sweetness before moving down in search of more of it on his tongue.

We kissed longer than necessary. I was a victim of the heartbroken boy inside of my chest who insisted that kissing Kenji on the mouth was something we were meant to do. It was a god-given right we'd been denied for entirely too long.

When I sat back in my chair, I quickly grabbed his tall hot chocolate mug and made a comment about needing more of that sweetness, but in reality, I needed something to hide behind, if only for a moment.

He stole it back from me too soon, losing his smile for a second as he met my eyes.

The tension between us was excruciating, and I began to wonder how many hours we were expected to stay here.

Somehow, we survived long enough to make it to the door before running into the Winthrops. My stomach dropped with the reminder that we were only partway through this nightmarish ordeal.

Another half hour of chatting, of manly back-clapping and hearty handshakes, remained. My restlessness must have shown because Kenji grabbed my hand and held it tightly in his, running his other hand up the inside of my forearm under my sweater.

His nails dragged lightly up and down my skin. Up and down. Up... and down until my body hair stood on end and my dick swelled. I shifted in my seat, but Kenji only pulled me closer and continued the tender torture. He carried the entire weight of the conversation, asking Jim and Jamie about their business and discussing mutual colleagues known to Kenji through Bash and Silas's work with Sterling Chase.

"...looking forward to seeing Cora," Jamie said.

The mention of my cousin quickly doused the magic and returned my dick back to unimpressive proportions. "I'm sorry, what? You're seeing my cousin?"

Jim nodded enthusiastically. "I spoke with her yesterday. She's agreed to partner with Jamie for the sports day so you and Kenji can be together."

"Sports day," I repeated stupidly as the details mentioned in one of the PR meetings finally bobbed to the surface.

Kenji gave my arm one last squeeze before letting go and reaching for his glass of water. "The youth program receiving the foundation's endowment in a couple of days. Remember? You're giving a speech to the kids on healthy nutrition and exercise. It's part of the—"

"Darling, I can't possibly give a speech," I said with the same fake smile I'd been abusing all day. "How about money? I'm good at giving that."

Kenji gave an equally fake chuckle. "Don't listen to him," he told Jim. "Landry's good at doing both. We're looking forward to it. Cora is excited about the dedication, and I'll make sure Landry doesn't take the games too seriously."

Jamie leaned forward to tell Kenji a supposedly funny story about the time we played cricket during a heavy rainstorm at Eton. "We were all too competitive to call the match. I remember wondering if it was all of those years of family expectations and brinksmanship that made these baby lords insist on catching colds and making themselves miserable."

Jim and Kenji laughed politely as we all stood up to make our way out of the cafe.

"And what about you?" I asked Jamie as I helped Kenji into his coat. "I don't remember you giving up either."

Jamie met my eye and waited a beat for his father to step over to say something to the server. "You weren't the only one with family expectations, Ev... Landry," he said in a low voice. "You weren't then, and you aren't now."

We each played our roles as we sauntered out of the cafe and made a big production out of saying goodbye and wishing each other well.

"See you later this week at Killian Prep?" I asked Jamie with a smile as if we were suddenly great chums.

"Wouldn't miss it. See you then."

As soon as Kenji and I stepped onto the pavement, the questions started up again. This time, they were more focused on San

Cordova. On the violence and conflict. On whether or not we'd heard about the delay in freeing the remaining hostages.

Kenji seemed to shrink next to me, so I let go of his hand and wrapped an arm around his shoulders before ignoring the questions and setting off for Hawling House under the protection of our security personnel. The warm weight of Kenji against my side felt better as we made our way down Charlbert Street. Partway down the road, I pointed to a building behind scaffolding. "Did you know Zane once recorded a song in that recording studio when he was here between tour dates? Apparently, they'd messed something up on... what song was it?"

"Oh. Was it 'Ashes to Amen' and everyone started calling it 'Ashes to Omens' after everything went wrong?"

We laughed together, remembering. It felt good to have someone with a depth of shared memory. I was grateful to have Kenji and the guys in the Brotherhood. At a time when my father's memory was becoming unpredictable, I especially appreciated being able to reminisce with Kenji.

I would miss it when he was back in New York.

Kenji leaned over and kissed under my ear, surprising me.

"What was that for?" I said it in a teasing manner for the cameras, but his kiss didn't feel scripted or put on.

"I was in Florida when that happened with Zane. At my grandmother's bedside. She'd passed out at a luncheon, and her friends had worried it was a stroke, so I flew down to be with her—"

"Oh shit," I said. "Yeah. I remember now. I think I was in Milan or something. I know I wasn't in New York with you when you got the call."

He leaned into me even more, almost causing me to list sideways. "You were in Turkey. And I remember because I got a security alert from your credit card account asking if you'd meant to make a purchase on United Airlines for over two thousand dollars from somewhere in Turkey."

"Oh?" I felt his eyes on me.

"Yes. And I assumed the charge was fraudulent because you had the private plane with you in Istanbul. But when I got to JFK to check in for my flight to Florida—a flight on United Airlines, of course—they'd put me in first class."

My face heated. "Sucks to have long legs in coach," I muttered, grateful to spot our house at the end of the block.

Kenji's legs weren't all that long, but they still seemed it. He reminded me of a praying mantis sometimes, long and lean. Poised. Observant.

Before he had a chance to say anything else, we'd reached the house. I gestured the security personnel to the side so I could answer one of the shouted questions I'd heard.

Kenji stood close, his hand warm in mine.

"As you know, that was Jim Winthrop at the cafe, along with his son, Jamie. Jamie happened to be at the same retreat in San Cordova where Kenji was when the protests began. Jamie and I were at Eton together," I added, subtly reminding everyone I was the son of a peer, an old-money aristocrat rather than simply an American supermodel. I'd been to Eton. I'd been raised here, at one of the largest historical homes in London. It was the reason we took all of our questions here, on the front steps of Hawling House, instead of in front of a cafe that was younger than Zoom. "It was nice to rekindle our friendship. I discovered we're both involved in a youth charity event later this week. Killian Prep School has agreed to open their sports fields and swim facilities for use by the Crimstock and Fendall Primary Schools for their sports days. The Davencourt Foundation is donating equipment and other kit so more kids can enjoy outdoor sport. The Winthrops' own foundation has created a project to replicate this at other schools around London. They'll be announcing more information about it later this week. It's an incredible project."

Kenji piped up. "And Landry is giving a talk to all of the school children about the importance of healthy nutrition and exercise. Over the years, he's supported dozens of similar programs in the US and Latin America. You probably already know about his participation in the CFDA Health Initiative and Vic Machado's Shape the Runway program."

My face heated as I cut him off as quickly as possible. "We also discussed the upcoming Hearts of Hawling Dinner, which helps the Davencourt Foundation raise money to be able to fund projects like these. I made sure Jim and Jamie were both invited, and I'm looking forward to connecting with many other old friends there. If you have any other questions, please reach out to the foundation. Thank you."

I slid my hand onto Kenji's lower back and guided him through the front door and toward the staircase. Once the front doors were closed behind us, he turned to move toward the kitchen. "Don't you want to update Cora and Nan on how it went?" he asked.

"No. I want to get back in bed."

Kenji's eyes widened.

"Alone," I added quickly.

He rubbed his thumb across the back of the ring on his finger as if ensuring it was still there. "Fine. But I'm going to give them an update."

Kenji's legs ate up the distance to the back of the house, where I could hear Nan and my father talking.

"Trust me," I called after him. "You do not want to do that."

He waved a dismissive hand over his shoulder. I took a step in his direction before stopping myself. What I really needed right now was distance from him.

Kenji's hand in mine, his calm words praising me, and the

feathery touch of his lips under my ears had lured me down a dark path.

A false path.

We weren't actually in a relationship. Despite my wishes, despite years of hoping, and despite the farce enacted for the media, Kenji didn't want to be with me.

Breath struggled to move through my chest at the reminder.

What I needed was something to keep my mind off my fake husband. What I needed was to prepare myself for this absurd bid for Parliament. Even though my chances of getting selected were close to zero, I knew Teddy Baines wouldn't have asked me to put myself up for it if he didn't have a plan.

I turned on my heel and entered the code for the elevator. While I waited for it to come up from downstairs, I shot a text to Teddy's assistant.

> Please find me a few minutes in Teddy's schedule.

His team would have already seen the cheeky implication I gave to reporters before brunch and know exactly what I wanted to talk about.

Once I was ensconced in the Range Rover—with Simon at the wheel in case the area around Whitehall was too congested to park —my phone buzzed with a call from Zane.

The sight of his familiar face on my screen made me realize how much I missed the Brotherhood.

"Hey, you," I said, accepting the call. "How are things with the new label?"

"Fuck you," he said, emotion clogging his throat. "Fuck you so *fucking* much."

My chest constricted as I realized that in all of my plans, in all of the strategy meetings and discussions over how to reveal my hidden identity to the public, I'd never made the four most important phone calls.

"Zane," I breathed. "Wait."

I could hear his tears and his bodyguard boyfriend's angry grumbles in the background. "You stood there in front of cameras acting like it was no big deal. Like the fact that you and Kenji are... are..."

"We're not!" I said quickly, cutting him off, trying to limit what Simon heard since he'd only worked for the family for six months. "We're not. You need to let me explain, but I can't right now. I'm on the way to an important meeting and—"

"Oh," he scoffed with a bitter laugh. "Oh, sure. Well, if it's *important*, I guess you'd better go."

"Call Kenji," I begged. "Please. Please call Kenji right now and ask him to explain."

"Kenji's not my *brother*," he barked, voice full of betrayal. "Kenji's not the guy I thought understood me. The one who supposedly grew up poor like I did, who knew what it was like to wonder where his next meal was coming from."

Shame washed over me, leaving me hollow and light-headed. "Zane."

I heard Ryan in the background. "Hang up. He's not fucking worth it. C'mere, sweetheart."

Tears welled in my eyes as I looked up at the ceiling of the Rover in hopes they wouldn't spill out and get caught on someone's camera.

"He's right, Z," I said, pretending to smile in case anyone was watching. "Listen to the man."

I ended the call.

The minute I walked into the kitchen, I was bombarded by the one-two punch of Nan and Cora demanding to know every detail of every moment we were in the public eye.

"I... uh... think so?" I replied, wondering why it was important which reporter asked which question. "She was wearing a fluffy hat over her ears, so I didn't see what color hair she had. But she was tall."

"That's Janice," Cora said, nodding as she looked down at her phone. "There's a picture of her in the hat. I recognize it from the Fulham art gallery thing."

Nan's eyes pinned me, even though her expression was kind. "Next time, try to remember to marry your knife and fork when you're finished eating."

I gave her a slow blink. "I'm... sorry? I don't..." I glanced at Cora for help.

Cora responded while typing something into her phone. "Put the knife and fork side by side on the plate to indicate you're finished eating. It's alright. I already scheduled an etiquette refresher for tomorrow afternoon. Then Henri will be back with the first suit fittings. After that, we'll have a formal-ish dinner party with just the Winthrops where we can practice the etiquette lesson. Sound good?" She glanced up and looked around for Reg, who was busy chopping something on a cutting board while talking to a younger woman who was also wearing a chef's coat. "That okay with you, Reg?"

He nodded. "It's one of the reasons Beth is here this week. Three or five courses?"

"Five."

One of Nan's assistants was busy tapping notes into a tablet as she stood next to Nan, asking questions. The housekeeper was fluttering in and out with various cleaning staff. Ed was filling out a sudoku puzzle in the newspaper with a sleek, ebony pen. A cooling cup of tea sat too close to his elbow, so I reached over and nudged it out of the way.

"Thank you, darling," he murmured without bothering to see who'd done it.

I noticed the meticulous care with which his face had been shaved and his white hair styled. Someone had pointed out Ed's personal valet at one point as he'd bustled through the kitchen on his way to the laundry, but this was the first time I'd stopped to think about the man. Ed's clothes were elegant and fine but also current. There was no way the earl shopped for himself, of course, and I'd already learned enough to know Nan didn't bother with minor details such as fetching clothes from Brooks Brothers or whatever.

Even *I* no longer did that for the guys in the Brotherhood. I had lower-level assistants who did it for me.

The Davencourt wealth was different than the Brotherhood's money in some ways, but in others, it was similar. I wondered now if that was—at least in part—because of Landry's influence on the Brotherhood.

Bash, Silas, Dev, and Zane all gave generously to good causes.

Much of their wealth was used anonymously for good, but enough of it was used publicly to keep the judgmental media off their backs. The same seemed to be true here with the Davencourt family.

"Did you leave an appropriate tip?" Nan asked.

It took me a minute for the words to compute. "I... wasn't the one who paid." I remembered belatedly something about this from all of their previous instructions, but I hadn't remembered it in the heat of the moment. "I forgot. Sorry."

Cora and Nan both groaned. "No," Cora said. "Remember we talked about this? We said you needed to pay to stave off any rumors about you marrying him for his money."

"The bill was probably less than fifty bucks," I said, losing my patience. "Who the hell cares? Landry always pays. He hasn't let me pay for anything in the ten years I've known him. None of the guys do. I work for them!"

A hush came over the kitchen as I realized what I'd said. "I mean, I *used* to," I quickly corrected, remembering one of the many lies I was supposed to tell. "So it's a habit for him to pay. Are we seriously going to pretend there's no income gap between us? He's a... a world-famous supermodel. A viscount. I'm an executive assistant. Let's be real here."

I'd almost let slip he was a billionaire in his own right, thanks to the software he'd created with the Brotherhood. The idea that he wouldn't be the one to pick up a simple brunch tab was laughable. A fifty-dollar tab to him was like spending a fraction of a penny. There'd been memes about how little the very wealthy felt day-to-day expenditures like the rest of us did. "Had I made a point of pulling out my card to pay for breakfast, it would have looked like the performative action it was."

Cora lifted an eyebrow. "Or it might have looked like you share his money now, and it doesn't matter who pays because it all comes out of the same account."

I felt off-balance and on edge. "I'm sorry," I muttered. "I'm not exactly used to being the one in the spotlight. I'll do better next time, I promise."

Ed spoke up without lifting his eye from the Sudoku. "Liv once asked for a ginger ale at Buckingham Palace. Drank it right out of the bottle before the server could bring her a glass. I thought my mother was going to faint dead away." He looked up at me and winked. "No one died. I can promise you that."

Nan gazed at him fondly. "No one died, but the headlines called her the Duchess of Canada Dry for about a week."

They chuckled and shared a few more memories before Ed left to take a walk in the park with his valet and a member of the security team.

A little while later, when I'd finally extracted myself from the interrogation, I slunk upstairs. Cora passed me in the hallway when I stopped at the door to my room. "Are Nan and your uncle together?" I asked her.

She glanced around us to make sure we were alone. "It's sort of an unspoken secret around here. Everyone suspects, but no one talks about it."

"Why not? It's sweet."

She hesitated. "Nan's worried about Landry's reaction. She doesn't want him to find out."

"He doesn't know?" I asked in surprise.

She shook her head. "And you can't tell him. He was very close to his mom, but he's always been close to Nan, too. It would be weird for him."

"He's a grown adult, Cora," I insisted. "He can handle the truth of someone else's relationship."

She tilted her chin up until she was looking down her nose at me. "We're talking about a man who changed his name and moved half a world away to avoid dealing with his mother's death. Are you sure?"

I opened my mouth to say I knew the man, I'd known him for years. But then I realized maybe I hadn't. Maybe the real man was the young, pimply boy out on the cricket field, drenched in rain to prove himself worthy in front of all the other mini-lords. Maybe the real man had hidden his pain and fear under highlighted hair, waxed eyebrows, fake tan, and a flippant persona. Maybe the real man had never felt safe enough in front of his judgmental executive assistant to talk about his real life.

After Cora left me and continued on to her own room, I moved into mine and closed the door. The sun lay warm stripes across the carpet, telling lies about what kind of day it was outside. Judging by the light, it would seem summer was almost here, but I knew better. The truth was if you didn't throw on plenty of protective layers when you went outside, you'd be vulnerable to a bone-deep chill.

———

I called my grandmother again to check in, but she didn't answer. Within moments, she texted me that she was getting her toes done and didn't want to be rude to her nail tech by talking on the phone.

BAA BAA

Congratulations on your marriage, by the way. That sounds exciting.

I stared at the text bubble before frantically typing.

It's not real! I would have told you if I was getting married, I promise!

BAA BAA

What do you take me for? A 14-carat sucker?

I closed my eyes and groaned. My grandfather had quoted an old movie from the fifties with that line for years.

> I promise I'll tell you everything. Just… don't worry. And please don't talk to any reporters.

BAA BAA

> Don't worry. I only spoke to the one lady from the Enquirer. But she seemed more interested in your chess-playing than your relationship with any British nobles. I told her about the tournament in Harrisburg. She was delighted.

I couldn't help but let out a laugh.

> Now I know you're lying. You would have never given up that story, upon pain of death. I made you swear on your air-conditioning unit, remember?

I pictured her there in the Nail 'N More outside of the Vista Bonita Active Seniors Community with her eyes crinkled in laughter as she gazed affectionately at her phone.

> I love you. Thank you for everything you've done for me.

BAA BAA

> Stop texting like you're dying, Kenji. You could do worse than an earl's son (who just so happens to be a fashion model) in your bed.

My cheeks flushed with heat.

> He's not in my bed!

Which was true at that exact moment... but, it turned out, not for long.

A couple of hours later, when I was recentered, manifesting calm confidence, and brushing my hair in preparation for returning downstairs, Cora knocked before rushing in. "Hey, sorry to bother you, but, uh... we have a situation."

"This entire situation is a situation," I said, setting the brush down on the dresser and sliding my shoes back on.

"I need you to pack your things—"

I stopped mid-shoe and nearly lost my balance until she continued.

"—and move your stuff to Landry's room. Nan overheard a few of the housecleaning staff gossiping about the two of you staying in separate rooms. Nan quickly interjected something about the terrible effects of your ordeal and jet lag on your sleeping patterns and that you were now sleeping in your husband's room."

I thought back to last night. While I would have loved to have blamed jet lag and my ordeal for the terrible tossing and turning I'd experienced, I was also aware that having Landry by my side might have made all the difference to a steady night's sleep. "Have you spoken to Landry about this?"

"I did, just before he announced he was going for a run. He agreed."

I moved back to the dresser and began to collect the meager belongings I'd accrued in the past two days. "A run? I thought he went out in the car."

"That was earlier. He went to Downing Street to talk to Teddy. Not sure how it went, but when he came back, he came straight upstairs to get on his running kit. He'll probably be gone already by the time we get to his rooms, and he's usually gone for a while on these runs. But you probably already know that."

I lingered over the pullover Landry had given me on the plane. "You know we aren't actually..."

She rolled her eyes. "I understand it's complicated, but I also passed by this room yesterday and heard just enough to know you'll survive a few nights bunking in with my cousin."

Heat rushed to my face. Hadn't Landry clamped a hand over my mouth? Jesus.

She found a cloth laundry bag in the wardrobe and handed it to me for my little collection before she reached for the few items on hangers. "Besides, there's a settee in his room. Make him sleep on it if you want. He practically bleeds good manners."

I snorted. "Landry? Good manners? He once ate an entire serving of edamame while flicking the shells out of a limousine window one at a time."

She lifted an eyebrow. "He's dined multiple times with the royal family without putting a foot wrong. He met and conversed with the president of Hungary when he was selected to join the man's tour of Eton. He was present at his father's Privy Council ceremony, which is an uncommon honor. And he—"

I cut her off. "You sound like Nan. I get it. He can fake it when he needs to. But the man also once deliberately farted in a business meeting to set up a good-cop, stupid-cop routine with Bash."

The edge of her mouth curled up. "He did that exact same thing when he was young to get out of going to tea with a friend of his mother's. Aunt Liv wasn't having it. She made him give up milk, ice cream, and cheese for an entire week to 'make sure he wasn't bothered by dairy.' I, of course, taunted him with every dairy treat I snuck from the kitchen like the supportive cousin I am."

We moved together out of the bedroom and down the hall. I didn't even know where Landry's room was, so I was reliant on Cora to show me the way.

"Sounds like the two of you were close," I prompted.

The old wooden floorboards creaked under the carpet runners in the hallway as we moved down the hall and around the corner to another part of the house. "Sort of. Uncle Ed brought us to live here when my dad died. I was fourteen, and Landry was ten, which meant I had no patience for him, and then we went off to different schools. It wasn't until later that we became closer."

"Well, I'm glad you have each other," I said softly.

Cora smiled. "I am, too. Sometimes it's hard to explain the pressures of a life like this to anyone who doesn't live it, not to mention the challenges that come from Uncle Ed's health and my mother's... other issues."

"Other issues?" I glanced at her in concern. All I'd heard about Landry's Aunt Lydia was that she was on vacation in the Maldives but scheduled to return in time for the Hearts of Hawling Dinner.

Cora caught my look and chuckled. "Oh, my mother's not ill, fortunately. She's just very, *very* involved in my life. You'll understand when you meet her." She threaded her free arm through mine and pulled me around a corner. "Landry's room is just—oh!"

The man himself appeared like we'd summoned him somehow, and those gorgeous aquamarine eyes met mine.

For a second, I forgot where we were. Forgot Cora. Forgot the clothes in my arms. Forgot everything but the way my chest ached at the sight of him.

Landry looked *exhausted*, like a hundred years had passed since we'd walked home from brunch rather than just a few hours. And it hit me like a punch to the ribs that he didn't just look tired; he looked heartbroken.

"Landry? Are you—?" I began.

Before I could finish the question, he reached out a hand to cup my face. His thumb traced the corner of my mouth, and his own lips tipped up in an impression of a smile.

"You," he said softly, "are a sight for sore eyes."

Then, his hand slid behind my head, his fingers threaded into my hair—firm, sure, *claiming*—and he pulled me into a kiss that made a whimper escape my throat and a flare of heat curl through my gut.

I could still count the number of kisses we'd shared on one hand, but something about this felt different than the others. It was passion and desperation and hunger, a demand, a *plea*.

I pressed myself into him and pushed up onto my tiptoes, wanting to give him whatever he was searching for—

But a moment later, he broke away. He stared at me, eyes wide, breathing heavily. Then, he cleared his throat.

"I'll see you at dinner, sweetheart," he said, and then he was gone.

I stood breathless and reeling. I'd felt that kiss fucking *everywhere*... and I had no fucking clue what it meant.

"Landry?" I called, turning. "Are you—?"

One of the maids stood halfway down the hall, biting her lip and blushing, clearly having witnessed the kiss—

The world snapped into place.

—having witnessed the kiss because Landry had *meant* her to witness it. It had all been for show.

Fuck.

"Dear sweet baby Jesus," Cora breathed. "That was—"

"Landry's room, Cora," I snapped, making a show of hefting my clothes. "Before my arms drop off, please?"

"Yes. Of course. Sorry." She jumped to attention and led me through the first doorway on the right. "Just here."

Landry's "room" turned out to be a suite of rooms, including a large bedroom with a sofa sitting area in front of a fireplace, a dressing room, and a sprawling en suite bathroom. Turkey was asleep in the center of the giant bed. She opened one eye and closed it again.

Cora was obviously familiar with Landry's rooms because she went straight into the dressing room and began hanging the clothes she'd been carrying while pointing me to an empty stack of drawers. The small space smelled like Landry, and I took a moment to close my eyes and inhale.

Leather. Laundry soap. Masculine cologne. The slightest hint of berry from the sugarless candy he stashed in pockets and promptly forgot about as soon as he tossed his clothes in the hamper.

Stop this madness, Kenji.

"So that was, um..." Cora began, eyes darting toward the hall.

"A thing that will not be discussed," I concluded crisply.

She sighed and worried her lip. "Do you ever... worry about him?" she asked, drawing my attention back to the moment. "I heard him up in the workout room late last night, and now he's out running again. Between all the exercise and his calorie restriction..."

I shook my head. If anyone was an expert sleuth in Landry's health, it was me. "He only calorie restricts when he's prepping for a job. If he was in the gym, it was most likely for strength training. An outdoor run is for cardio but also his mental health. He's running because he's upset."

When I felt the heat of her gaze on me, I squatted down to straighten my clothes in a drawer before continuing. Turkey wandered in and bumped my leg with her pink nose, rubbing her whiskers across my leg in clear demand for attention. I scratched her head and under her chin. "Landry's healthy. You know about his participation in the Shape the Runway program. He's fighting hard for better health standards in fashion modeling and recognizes one of the ways to do that is by modeling the right behavior. He takes his nutrition very seriously. Lamar—that's his agent—was specifically selected because he's also a certified nutritionist. I promise, he gets what he needs. He also has a fantastic physician who makes him come in quarterly for blood work."

Yes, I was babbling, but this happened to be a subject I had a secret PhD in. It was hard not to want to reassure her when my research and observation had been borne out of the same concerns.

The fact that it distracted her from asking about our relationship was just a side benefit.

And one that didn't last long.

She finished hanging up the clothes and leaned her hips against the island in the middle of the room. "Why aren't the two of you together? He obviously likes you very much, and the two of you have..." She grinned. "Chemistry."

"You're nosy," I pointed out, closing the drawer and standing up straight after a final pet of Turkey's head.

"I'm protective. There's a difference." She poked a finger in the air. "As you're well aware."

I blew out a breath. "I thought he was a playboy who never took anything seriously."

"Landry?" She let out a peal of shocked laughter. "No!"

"Yes. I admit he's not nearly as bad as he used to be, but there was a time when he was trashing hotel rooms regularly, getting arrested for disturbing the peace and needing me to bail him out, and sowing enough wild oats to end world hunger. Plus, I've always had the sense he was keeping things from me—" I cocked my head. "—which, wouldn't you know it, turned out to be true. So how was I supposed to trust him in a relationship?"

Cora winced. "I can see what you mean. But now that you know the truth...?" She pinned me with a somewhat familiar intense stare. "You care about him, I know you do. And that *chemistry*..."

"The chemistry is neither here nor there," I lied. I stuffed my hands in my pockets. "I do care about him. But Cora, the man lied to me—lied to all of us—about something huge. I know last night you said it wasn't about him not trusting me, but that's how it feels. Like I wasn't important enough for him to let me in on his secret.

And maybe that's partly my fault," I admitted. "I'm still hurt about it, though. And I'm angry. *And* he won't talk to me."

He just kisses me randomly in hallways and looks like his heart is breaking.

"Kenji—" Cora began.

I held up a hand. "Honestly, even if I could just shrug and roll with it, the two of us wouldn't work. In case you've forgotten, I live in the States. My job is there. My friends. My apartment. My grandmother. My history. And he's going to be an earl and an MP. He's running for fucking *Parliament*, for fuck's sake." Air rushed out of my lungs as I deflated. "Sorry for the foul language."

I didn't add how upset I'd been to learn of Landry's decision about Parliament on the fucking internet this morning, along with the rest of the world.

Cora's lips pinched together and moved from side to side while she processed my response. "He doesn't actually want to be an MP, Kenji. He's been avoiding it for years."

"Yeah? Then why's he letting them put him up for it?" I leaned back against the door, arms folded over my chest. "Is he doing it for his dad? Is the pressure that strong? I mean... if he's getting it from the prime minister *and* his own father..."

Cora's forehead crinkled in frustration. "Not directly. Uncle Ed encouraged Landry to go to Yale and helped him with the necessary documents to do it under a different name. He wants to see Landry happy."

"*Could* he say no if he wanted to?"

"To being an MP?" She met my eyes and nodded firmly. "Definitely. There's no legal requirement that he serve. But... growing up a Davencourt means growing up under the weight of history. You're not just part of a family; you're part of a proud legacy. Landry feels the pressure of that, even if it wasn't Ed's intention to force him into anything."

Turkey twined herself around my ankles and made a little *mrrp* sound for attention.

Cora leaned down and gave her a quick pet before straightening back up. "As Uncle Ed's memory began to decline, Landry took on more responsibility for the earldom behind the scenes, and he was brilliant at it. I think the family, including Landry, assumed it was only a matter of time before he moved back to England and took on the public-facing role as head of the family, including serving in the Lords." She caught one of Landry's shirtsleeves in her fingers and twisted it lightly. "Except he kept putting it off year after year, even when it became clear Ed needed to retire. And I realized that, for Landry, it's never been about deciding to serve in Parliament but about deciding whether he'll be the first Davencourt in four hundred years *not* to."

For the first time since learning Landry was a viscount, I could sense the invisible but undeniable burden of duty that came with his family's long history. It wasn't just a title. Not just a collection of estates. It was a part of who he was. Who he'd been raised to be.

And yet selfishly, I cared more about his happiness than any of those things.

"Landry's spent the past almost fifteen years outside of England, and he hates giving speeches," I muttered. "I'm sure he *could* be a good politician because there's not much the man can't do, but he'd be miserable."

"I know!" Cora threw up her hands, frustrated now. "And I thought for sure he was finally going to bring himself to say no. Then the two of you... did whatever you did in your bedroom that sounded like a bit of fun... and he came storming downstairs, declaring his desire to be the next Davencourt MP!"

I winced at the memory of Landry's pain yesterday. I'd been dismissive and prickly. But surely our personal situation hadn't been enough to cause him to do something as serious as running for the House of Lords... had it?

Fuck. Everything in me wanted to fix this for Landry, but I didn't even know what fixing it would look like. I didn't actually know what he wanted.

"I can try talking to him again," I offered, not believing for a moment that it would work. The man seemed hell-bent on ignoring me with the exception of his *performance* in the hall earlier.

"Yeah?" Cora's smile was wide, all straight teeth and sparkling eyes. "Excellent. But first, you and I are going shopping."

I bit back a groan. "For what? Please say shoes because that's the only thing I need more of, and I don't trust that tailor guy to pick ones that won't pinch."

She stepped forward and grabbed my arm to pull me out of the dressing room. Turkey had long returned to the bedroom for another nap, although this time, she was curled up on a window seat in the sun. "We can definitely do that, but we need you to pick out a gift for your beloved, remember? You and I are going to be seen shopping together to reassure everyone that the upstart American has been fully assessed and embraced by the family."

As we made our way back through the winding corridors, I thought about what I could possibly get for Landry that he didn't already have. It wasn't easy to buy gifts for a billionaire. Believe me, I'd had years of learning it the hard way.

But because of my experience, I'd learned a few tricks along the way. "Are there any photo galleries you recommend?"

She put on an exaggerated pout. "Yes, but I was hoping more for lingerie or novelty toys."

As we made our way into the Range Rover in the underground garage, my cheeks blazed. While there was no chance in hell I'd buy either of those things on a PR outing with Cora Davencourt, her teasing mention of it brought back a certain memory.

Which led to the entire ride to Bond Street being taken up

pleasantly with images of Landry modeling items he'd received in a gift basket from Véloce Intimates.

There were perks to sleeping with the most beautiful man in the world. Some nights, those booty calls were impromptu fashion shows of the very best kind.

SIXTEEN

LANDRY

"You're avoiding him," Silas said in a voice meant to intimidate.

Unfortunately for him, after dealing with Kenji's mixed messages at brunch, followed by Zane's heartrending phone call, the prime minister's polite yet powerful manipulations during our meeting, and that fucking kiss in the hallway that had frayed the last shreds of my control, I was done playing the obedient pup.

"Fuck you. You have no idea what's happening between me and Kenji," I snapped.

There was a long pause over the phone. "I was talking about Zane. He's been trying to call you back for two hours."

I glanced down at the phone and watched as sweat drops slipped off my nose, splashing on the glass.

There were three missed calls from Zane, two from Bash, and a text from Silas warning me to call *or I will track you down.*

I tossed the phone onto the bathroom counter before peeling my soaked running shirt off, careful not to dislodge my earbuds. "I was in a meeting, then I went for a run, and you know my workout app shuts off my messages. Listen... I'm sorry. I know I'm handling all this poorly. I should have called you and told you about... well, everything… and not let you find out through the fucking paparazzi headlines. I get it. I'm an asshole. I'm just… dealing with a lot of shit right now."

Silas's voice softened the barest amount. "It sounds like it. But you need to know we're not about to let you go without a fight."

"Go?" I asked, feeling a sudden and catastrophic cavern open up in my chest. "*Go?*"

"If you think you can just flip a switch and suddenly be this Everett Davencourt earl-type guy and forget everyone who cares about you back home, you can just—"

The dam cracked, and so did my voice. "Are you fucking kidding? You four—the Brotherhood—and Kenji, you're… you're my *family*," I said, feeling saliva pool in my mouth as my jaw tensed and my throat thickened. "You're the only fucking people who know me for who I truly am. I'm not going anywhere. I can't. I need you. Do you have any idea how much I need you? I'm fucking dying here, Silas. Jesus."

"Hey, hey. Okay. Okay. We're here. That's… fuck, that's what I was saying. You can't get rid of us that easily. We can be there by morning."

"No," I said quickly. "No, please don't. I can't… it's too much right now, alright? I can't add a pack of feral billionaires to this shitshow. Please just… just give me some time. I need some time."

Silence settled over the line as I reached for a tissue from a nearby box and swiped at my face. Thankfully, the overwhelming tide of emotion went dutifully back into its battered steel box.

"Okay," Silas said. "But you need to call Zane and tell him you didn't mean to hurt him."

"I didn't!"

"I know." He sighed. "Zane knows it, too. Just… call him. It's important."

He was right, of course, but that didn't make it any easier to dial Zane's number. Zane was the gentlest of my brothers, which made me feel that much guiltier. How could I apologize for such a huge lie of omission?

I took out my earbuds, put the phone on speaker and set it on the vanity, then perched on the edge of the tub. The cast iron was cold and solid through my damp running tights, but my stomach tumbled in free fall. Fortunately, Zane answered on the first ring.

"Thank fuck," he blurted, sounding relieved. "Landry, I'm sorry."

My palms slipped against the edge of the tub. "You... pardon?"

"I'm sorry." The voice that had sold a bajillion albums sounded hoarse and congested, like he'd been crying. "I should never have ended the conversation with you the way I did. I was pissed off, but I just kept thinking what if something happened to you and that was the last thing I'd ever said, and—"

"Zane." My own voice came out cracked. The steel box of my emotions was showing serious wear and tear. *Fuck.* "I'm the one who should be apologizing to *you*, okay? I should have told all of you the truth before you read about it online." I blew out a breath. "I should have told you a long time ago."

"Why didn't you?" he asked in a small voice. "I... I thought about it a lot after we got off the phone. I realized you never told us shit about your past. You never lied, at least, not that I can remember. And maybe we were the ones who jumped to all the conclusions—"

"Yeah, and I didn't correct you," I admitted. "I didn't know how."

I took a deep breath and stood to pace. "In the beginning, I was so scared of being found out, I tried to be as different from Everett Davencourt as possible so no one would guess the truth. So I let myself become Landry Davis—a guy who said what he thought without worrying that it would reflect badly on his family, and didn't hide that he was smart, and didn't only get invited to parties because some kid's dad wanted a favor from the earl. And it turned out, being Landry—being judged for who I was and not where I came from—was really fucking amazing."

"I get that," Zane said. "Not wanting to be judged by where you came from. Pretending things are fine when they're not."

"I know you do." I leaned on the countertop with my eyes closed, but tears still burned behind my lids. "That's why I liked you so much from the very beginning. We come from polar opposite places, but we're the same that way."

"Yeah," he whispered.

"And the friendships I found with you and the other guys... I'd never had that before. I'd been an awkward, spotty kid who'd grown up under a spotlight. I'd learned to pretend I was fine and keep everyone at a distance so they couldn't see the lie for what it was. Then suddenly, I was drinking Scotch on a snowy winter's day with these four amazing guys who thought I was funny and cool—"

Zane let out a watery chuckle. "Eh. Debatable."

"What? Please," I scoffed, trying not to laugh myself. "You were in awe of my cool."

He laughed harder. "Pretty sure no one who's actually cool uses the phrase 'in awe of my—'"

"Shut it, Zane. I'm attempting emotion here, okay?"

"Poor Landry," he teased. "Does it burn?"

"Ahem. As I was saying... suddenly, I was drinking Scotch with these three amazing guys *and Zane*—"

He laughed again, and this time, it sounded like a melody.

"You guys taught me what friendship was supposed to be about," I continued more seriously. "You taught me it was possible to have someone care about me without knowing who my family was. That it didn't matter who my family was. Then you guys and Kenji *became* my family. And for years, I've been terrified that if you found out the truth, you'd hate me for not telling you sooner, or you'd think differently of me, and I'd be alone again. So I..."

"Kept it a secret?" he said. "I get that, too. Landry, man, our whole Brotherhood has been keeping a secret for years. But you're not supposed to keep them from *us*, dumbass."

I snorted. "Yeah, I figured that out." I stretched my neck from side to side and finally opened my eyes. Late-afternoon sunlight I hadn't even registered earlier shone through the window, and the room seemed brighter than it had before.

"You should know by now that we'd love you no matter where you came from, Landry," Zane went on. "You're a hard worker. And smart. And kind. And yes, *cool*. But those things probably came from somewhere. From some*one*. And that's important, too."

I stared at the old brass fitting on the window clasp, fashioned into the shape of an elephant long ago. They'd been a gift to one of my ancestors from a visiting Indian diplomat as a symbol of protection for our home, and every window in my suite had them. My hand knew the shape of them without looking, the way they retained winter's chill even in summer. The metallic scent they left on my fingers. The cock-eyed stare of the one closest to my favorite spot in the window seat.

Important. Yes. My history was important. I'd spent years learning of its importance.

"Wasn't your mom from Connecticut?" Zane asked. "You mentioned it once when we asked about your accent."

I reached out to feel the elephant on the window latch. "Yes. Danbury. My grandfather was still alive when we were at Yale. I stayed with him one Christmas."

"What was your mom like?"

It occurred to me I could finally speak more openly about my past with the Brotherhood, but old habits of holding personal details close to the vest were hard to break.

"She was amazing."

"Tell me something specific. Do you have a memory of her doing something... oh, I don't know... admirable?"

Why was he doing this? Weren't there more interesting questions he could be asking me about everything? Hell, he hadn't even asked me what was going on between me and Kenji.

"She loved birds," I said, pulling an old memory out of the battered box in my mind. "Pet birds. We had a giant birdcage in the family room, and those fuckers never shut up. She would talk to them. Sing to them in hopes of getting them to sing back."

"Birds. Well, that's not my preference for pets, but if she wanted birds..."

"No, that's just it. She never got them for herself. She never set out to have a bird as a pet. She heard about someone who needed to rehome a bird, and she couldn't resist helping. 'Temporarily.'" I let out a laugh, remembering her stammering explanation to my father and the way he smiled at her with exasperated affection. "Then someone else needed another bird rescue and so on and so forth until the cage took up half the room and our eardrums wanted to burst."

I could hear the smile in Zane's voice. "Does your father still keep them?"

The elephant's chill had warmed under my touch. I traced a fingertip along the curve of its trunk before turning away. "No. They've all gone on to their sanctuary in the sky. And thank fuck because they really were a nuisance."

"She sounds sweet," he suggested.

"Yes. Unless it came to catching me with a hand in the biscuit tin after dinner. Or, god forbid, left the house without giving her a peck on the cheek. It didn't matter if I was late and someone important was waiting."

Zane let the air still between us for a beat. "She wanted to remind you what was important."

"Family," I murmured.

"Love," he corrected gently. "Connection. Affection. People."

I cleared my throat in hopes of dispelling the emotion there. "I hate you and all that you stand for, Zane Hendley."

"I love you more than you can know. My lord."

The call ended to the sound of his snickering.

I took a quick shower and threw on a bathrobe before settling into the window seat and sending Silas a text to let him know I'd called Zane and been forgiven, mostly because Zane was the forgiving type with a heart bigger than the night sky.

Silas's reply was instant.

SILAS

Good. Now call the others. Remember we're only a plane ride away.

I wasn't sure if that was a threat or a promise, but it made me grin anyway. I moved through contacting the remaining two members of the Brotherhood.

My call with Bash surprised me.

"I knew something didn't add up," he said. "There were a few times you said things that just... sounded wrong. When Dev tried to introduce us to polo, you were especially weird. But I remember you saying, 'That's a fine bit of tack,' as if you knew what the fuck we were looking at."

I winced. "I'm shit at riding horses, but I did try polo once when I was younger." I didn't explain this had happened at an event arranged by the Palace at Guards Polo Club for a group of young lads in the peerage. "It was fine until I bashed my own boot with the stick."

We chuckled over shared memories of similar polo injuries Dev had experienced over the years.

"We miss you, Landry," Bash said after a few minutes.

Before I could return the sentiment, he added, "But I want to hear about what's going on between you and Kenji."

I should have known Bash would be the one to ask the question no one else had dared to ask. He took his role as big brother of our group seriously.

I rolled my eyes and pressed the bridge of my nose between two fingers. "Join the queue, Sebastian."

"Listen, it's been obvious to the rest of us that there's something going on between the two of you, but I also know Kenji thinks he can't trust you. If you want him to give you a chance, you need to prove to him you're dependable and true."

I gritted my teeth. "I didn't ask for advice about my so-called love life. In case you haven't seen the entire fucking internet today, I have bigger shit going on right now than navigating Kenji's impossible requirements for potential life partners. Like, for example, convincing the world we're already *married* and that I'd be a good candidate for MP."

"Which brings me to my next question," he said dryly. "You're running for office? I wasn't aware you were interested in politics."

"I'm not," I bit out.

"Mm."

I stood up and paced, feeling the familiar dips and lumps in the ancient rug under my bare feet. "I'm sorry I didn't tell you about all of this."

"You already apologized," Bash said with a calm I didn't feel.

"But you can't understand the familial expectation and pressure I'm under."

"No. Probably not."

"Besides, it's different now. After some reform in the past twenty-five years, it's not like I just get handed the seat. I'd have to be selected from a hand-picked group of qualified people with impeccable connections. I have zero chance."

There was a beat of silence that probably only meant he was reaching for his water bottle or something, but I interpreted it as judgment.

"They won't pick me because everyone else will be more qualified," I clarified.

"Mm," he said again.

I clenched my teeth to keep from continuing my inane
excuses.

"Landry," he said. "I'm sure you know more about English
parliamentary by-elections, but if they're anything like... oh, I don't
know... *any other election in the history of humanity*, has it
occurred to you that someone who is popular, wealthy, beautiful,
and carries the historic significance of your ancestry might have
several legs up over candidates with stronger political resumes?"

He was right. Moreover, it wasn't anything I hadn't considered
already during the sleepless hours of the past few nights and
during my conversation with Teddy earlier.

"Do you have any idea how hard it is to break fifteen generations of tradition?" I asked with a humorless laugh. "Here I was
hoping I wouldn't get selected because I'm laughably unfit for
the position. It would be a nice, clean solution in which the
powers that be break the tradition for me. But maybe you're right.
Maybe I'll get elected. Not four hours ago, Teddy Baines assured
me he had a plan to get me in that seat with zero chance of
failure."

Which was why I was having a crisis of conscience, even
without the so-called help from my good friend.

"What do *you* want, Landry?"

I pulled my knees up and wrapped an arm around them,
leaning my head down against the soft cotton of my robe. "I want
Kenji Toma to be mine," I admitted softly. "I want to move to
Majestic and be surrounded by friends and family. I want to make
Kenji's wildest dreams come true. See Lellie grow up and maybe
have my own kids who can grow up with her. Watch Dev finally
shake his grief and Silas wear Way's cowboy hat unironically. I
want to stay connected to my father and my family here in

England and raise my kids to know their family history without feeling any pressure to serve it."

Bash let silence settle between us again. He'd always been good at letting silence do the talking in business meetings, and now I felt the power of its impact.

When he finally spoke, I was surprised by the words.

"If you plan on having kids one day, what will your choices in this moment teach *them*?"

His question echoed in my mind and heart as we ended the call and I moved into my dressing room.

As soon as I entered the familiar space, I stopped short. Kenji's meager collection of clothes hung in a previously empty spot, and the running shoes I'd picked up for him were neatly placed at the end of my own row of shoes.

I walked over and pressed my face into the fabric of the long-sleeved half-zip he'd been wearing when he was rescued. It had been washed, of course, so it smelled of Hawling House laundry soap. There was no trace left of Kenji's own scent or the Tide pods he used back home.

I was tempted to slide the garment over my bare skin, to flaunt the casual use of his clothes when I went downstairs, but I wouldn't dare. This and his running tights were the only articles of clothing he had of his own, and I could tell how much that bothered him.

After quickly throwing on a pair of trousers and a sweater, I called Dev. Thankfully, that call went way more smoothly, thanks to his distraction with Lellie who was playing in the background.

"I wish you'd told us," he said. "But I also understand. Grief is a heavy weight to carry, Landry. Sometimes the hardest things we face are the easiest to hide."

His words, like Bash's, stayed with me as I made my way downstairs to meet with Nan about tomorrow's sports day appearance.

Thankfully, Kenji was off shopping with Cora, so I was able to focus on Nan's words and learn all there was to know about the three schools involved, the Davencourt Foundation's history of programs like this one, the plans for future program expansion, and the names of all the key players I'd need to remember when I arrived.

"Now, let's go over your speech," Nan said, watching me carefully for my reaction.

I shot her a happy smile. "Don't worry, I'm too busy plotting Cora's downfall to blame you for this little detail. I'm well aware that she would normally be the one giving this speech."

Nan *tsk*'d me. "It's important for you to get the opportunity to speak of important issues so people can see you're more than a pretty face. I'm going to introduce you to Ned Pinchon, who's been selected to help write your statement to the voting members in the by-election. He's also taken a stab at your speech for tomorrow. The two of you can spend the rest of the afternoon sorting those things out."

The remainder of the day was more excruciating than the rest of the day had been, which was saying something. Ned was a fine man with excellent skills, but he took his job incredibly seriously. By the time I was called into dinner, my head was throbbing.

The throbbing turned to a relentless pounding when the first person I saw in the dining room was my Aunt Lydia.

"Darling! I'm thrilled you've finally finished that American modeling nonsense and are home for good."

I gave her the expected air-kisses before glancing around to find Reg's new sous chef setting a few serving utensils on the sideboard and Kenji standing alone nearby, pretending to admire a portrait of the ninth earl and his hunting dogs. I glanced back at Aunt Lydia. "Have you met Kenji yet?"

She tilted her nose up almost imperceptibly. "No, I don't believe we've been introduced."

I moved over to place a hand on Kenji's back, and he turned toward us. A mask of politeness fell over his features, dropping the temperature of the room a few degrees.

A small frown of worry creased the sous chef's face as she glanced between Kenji and Lydia, indicating some unspoken tension in the room.

"Aunt Lydia, may I introduce Kenji Toma? Kenji, this is my aunt, Lydia Davencourt. Cora's mother."

Lydia gave a perfunctory nod and fake smile without offering her hand. "I see. And you are Landry's assistant, correct?"

Kenji stumbled against my side, making me aware that I'd pulled him closer without noticing.

"Yes, ma'am," he began, the edge of his mouth curling up dangerously. "I assist him in quite a few things, actually."

The words were laden with innuendo.

Kenji's hand landed on my chest as he turned and shot me an adoring look. "Isn't that right, darling?"

I leaned down and pressed a kiss to his lips, surprising a breath out of him. Unlike our earlier kiss in the hallway, when I'd grabbed the man the way a drowning man gasps for air, heedless of anyone around us, this kiss was definitely intended for an audience. But it still lasted long enough for me to make my aunt uncomfortable, to establish Kenji was more than my employee, and to remind Kenji that even though I was angry at him and I was confident he was still angry with me, I was on his side no matter what.

When my aunt made a sniff of disapproval, I pulled back and met Kenji's eyes. My sweater was tangled in his grip, and his lips were shiny from the tip of my tongue. "Hi," I murmured softly. "Are you okay?"

He nodded silently, his eyes wide and a little dazed.

"Good." I turned back to Aunt Lydia but kept an arm around Kenji's waist. "I thought we weren't expecting you back from the Maldives until just before the Hearts of Hawling Dinner?"

She waved a manicured hand in the air. "Don't be daft. I obviously cut my trip short as soon as I heard your news. We need to present a united front as a family if you're to take up your place in the Lords. I can help plead your case, especially to the MPs' wives. You do know I'm on the membership committee of the Mayfair Ladies' Philanthropic League with Caroline Langhurst. Her husband is deputy leader. And I play tennis with Harriett Goldsmith on Tuesdays. Her brother is Lord Tremayne, senior deputy chairmen of... oh, I don't remember."

"Economic affairs," Kenji murmured politely.

I stared at him as Cora came bustling in. "Sorry, I'm late. Nan and Uncle Ed are right behind me."

Sure enough, my father and Nan completed our group. As soon as Dad reached his spot at the head of the table, he smiled and nodded at everyone in turn. "Welcome home, Lydia. Cora, nice to see you taking a break for once. Kenji, I hope your first foray into the lion's den wasn't too taxing. Everett, I had a call from Teddy this afternoon, full of praise and excitement about your willingness to help out. And Nan." His face softened into familiar affection. "If I haven't told you yet today, you're looking particularly lovely in that green. It sets off your eyes and reminds me of the Yorkshire dales in spring. Everyone, please be seated."

I stared at him, barely remembering to help my aunt with her chair before turning to do the same for my cousin. Unfortunately, Kenji was on the opposite side of the table from me, making up the traditional boy-girl seating order most of us had naturally drifted toward.

Before I had a chance to study Nan and my father more closely, my aunt began her interrogations.

"I thought this—" She waved a hand between Kenji and me. "—was all for—". She abruptly stopped speaking when the sous chef, who was clearly acting as server tonight, entered the dining room to begin serving the wine.

Aunt Lydia cleared her throat. "What I meant to say is, what do we know about the by-election, Everett dear? Has Teddy given you any idea of timing?"

At least this was a topic I could speak on. I explained the situation, my meeting with Teddy, his expectations for the process, and the PR campaign with the Winthrops.

"I don't understand," Lydia asked, setting her wineglass down carefully before allowing a carefully filled salad plate to be set in front of her. "Why are the Winthrops involved? What use have we for American new money?" She flicked a glance at Kenji. "No offense, Kenji."

His dark eyes widened, and his nostrils flared, but he didn't speak to oppose or excuse her.

"*I'm* offended," Cora interjected with a polite smile on her face. "Jamie Winthrop is a nice guy. We've met several times at London Funders meetings. The Winthrop Foundation is doing good work with—"

Aunt Lydia made a huff of impatience. "Yes, yes. Fine. My point is they're not involved with Parliament or the peerage. Why would they have anything to do with a Davencourt PR campaign?"

Kenji surprised me by speaking up. "Jamie and I returned together from San Cordova. The media is interested in some feel-good stories, and the PR team thought it would be a great way of getting Landry some positive press coverage. Two birds, one stone. Landry gets plenty of play as a doting husband, a caring friend, and an all-around good guy, without ever having to mention politics or Parliament."

Cora grinned. "Exactly."

Aunt Lydia seemed unable to counter his point, so she simply nodded before poking a bit at her salad. "Cora, dear, speaking of London Funders, Sir Malcom was asking after you. It turns out he is newly single after a breakup with... oh, what was her name? The one who showed too much décolletage at Ascot last year. Anyway, it hardly matters. He said he is looking forward to the Hearts of Hawling Dinner and hopes you'll save him a dance or two. Isn't that nice?"

"No, thank you, mother. Sir Malcom is not my type. Besides, I'll be too busy running around putting out fires to promise anyone a dance."

We spent the rest of the salad course with the two of them politely bickering about various titled men Cora should consider as husband material in the near future. By the time the main course was served, she'd poked me in the side of the thigh under the table with her fork twice.

I squawked the third time, finally realizing what she was attempting. "Yes, fine. So, ah, Nan... tell me about..." I inhaled, trying desperately to think about a new subject matter to introduce.

"Birds," Kenji finally suggested. "And cats. Cora told me about the birds Olivia used to keep. Was Turkey around for any of that? If so, what did she think of them?"

Cora and I both shot him a look of gratitude as Nan began telling stories of the various animals who had inhabited Hawling House in the past couple of decades. In addition to saving us from more pointed questions from Lydia, it also made my father laugh, which was always good.

Unfortunately, it only lasted until the dessert course, when Lydia interrupted to pepper Kenji with questions about his background.

By the time the table had been cleared, my thigh was bruised from Cora's fork, I'd called my aunt a regrettable name, and Kenji's teeth were probably broken from biting back retorts to her rude questions.

None of that did a damn thing to distract me from the way I felt every time I looked at Kenji. There was something about seeing the man in his element, calmly parrying jabs and answering questions with calm efficiency, that was hot as fuck. I'd had my hands and lips on him three times that day, and it had only whet my appetite for more.

I was still too angry at him—and at myself—to actually do anything about it, though.

I said good night as politely as I could, rounded the table, and grabbed Kenji's hand before pulling him up the stairs to my... *our*... room.

"I am so fucking sorry," I said as soon as we were alone.

Kenji shrugged as he headed toward the dressing room, his slender shoulders and movement graceful as always. "She's a product of her upbringing like the rest of us."

"I had a similar upbringing, Kenji, and I hope to hell I wouldn't be rude enough to ask someone how they could afford college."

I followed him into the dressing room to grab workout clothes. My hope was to do enough squats and leg curls that I would barely be able to hobble to bed later, much less fantasize about squatting over Kenji and railing him into the mattress. Maybe I could linger upstairs in the workout room long enough for him to fall asleep.

He shrugged again. "At least she seemed stymied a bit when I explained I'd paid for my degree with chess winnings. I didn't tell her they were from gambling with other students rather than taking prize money in tournaments."

"I love that story. Your grandmother told me—" I bit off the words, realizing he still didn't know I'd snuck down to Florida while he was in San Cordova.

He finished pulling his sweater off. "My grandmother?"

"No, sorry, I meant to say your grandmother was the one who encouraged you with chess, right? I remember you telling me about it." My face heated with the lie, so I turned away and busied myself in the far side of the room, rooting through a drawer for my kit.

"Yeah. She used to punish me by making me play against her. I loved it, though."

I turned to look at him over my shoulder, noting the long line of his back, the protruding angles of his shoulder blades, the way his waist nipped in, causing his trousers to sit low on his hips. The barest hint of an elastic band was visible over the waistband of the pants.

I stared at the rounded muscles of his ass, filling out the fabric and complementing the drape. My hands knew the shape of him and itched to cup and squeeze and caress. To move up his smooth back and into his shiny, dark hair.

"...cares about you. At least, I assume so."

I blinked and replayed his words. "Oh, Aunt Lydia? No. She cares about her reputation. She's nice enough, don't get me wrong. She's actually very loving and protective toward Cora, and she was in love with my uncle when he died. But unfortunately, she runs with a crowd that's all about status and rank. Her mother was the same way, pushed her on my uncle until he couldn't help but give in. They were lucky, though. The two of them made it work and eventually fell in love. Cora got sick when she was a baby. Supposedly, that brought my aunt and uncle closer."

I swallowed and remembered I was trying to keep my distance from Kenji, not tempt myself with sweet treats that were off-limits. "Anyway, Lydia's biggest goal in life is marrying Cora off to a title so she can go through her highlight reel all over again. Kids in all the fancy schools, exclusive invitations to the inner circle, lavish wealth and society intrigue, and blah blah."

He bent over at the waist and pushed his pants down, leaving me staring breathlessly at the cotton-covered bulge between his legs. Floaty bits of dust motes filled my head, and it took me a minute to realize he was saying something.

"Huh?" I said, licking my lips.

He turned and flicked his long hair over one shoulder. His

small brown nipples puckered in the chill space, and his winter-pale abs tightened as he twisted at his waist to reach for the pajama pants on the nearby counter.

"I said thank you for defending me." He slid his long legs into the loose pants one leg at a time like a goddamned torturer from medieval times. "You didn't need to do that, but I appreciate it."

My heart pounded in my chest, and my dick pounded in my pants. I held my workout clothes in a ball in front of me before quickly leaning over to grab my running shoes. "Yeah, sure."

"Landry... can we talk?" A flush rode high on his cheekbones. "I have some things I need to say—"

"I, uh. Maybe later. I'm going to work out right now."

"But you already ran today. Don't you think—?" His eyebrows scrunched in concern, and he reached out a hand to touch my arm.

I jumped away like he was contagious because it was that or throw him down on the bed.

"No!" I said a bit too loudly. "No. Thank you, but I know what I'm doing. Just... make yourself at home, and I'll..."

I gave up trying to find words and raced out of the room, up the stairs, and into the workout room before stripping off my dinner clothes and yanking on my athletic kit. I started with jumping jacks to warm up my muscles and punish my dick. By the time my muscles were loose, my cock was heavy and strangled in my tight pants.

"Fuck!" I adjusted myself and moved to the leg press machine. With every rep, I forced myself to imagine Aunt Lydia flirting with a young drinks attendant in the Maldives until my pants were loose and my stomach was vaguely nauseated.

Then I yanked out my phone and changed the song. Tank's "When We" moved slow and sultry through my earbuds. I used the pace to control my muscles, to focus on lowering my knees toward my chest as slowly as possible, holding it for a beat while it burned, and then shoving the plate up, pushing through my heels and squeezing my ass. I watched the muscles of my quadriceps contract and stretch.

With every repetition of the word *fuck*, I ground my teeth together, remembering.

Remembering the feel of Kenji's body as he let me in. As he begged me for more.

As he let me into his body.

While doing his best to keep me the fuck out of his heart.

SEVENTEEN

KENJI

I'd fallen asleep on the sofa in Landry's room, with one of his pillows under my head and his extra blanket over me. But when I awoke in the middle of the night with a full bladder, I was curled against his warm body like a sleepy but aggressive octopus.

I unpeeled my tentacles and snuck out of the bed.

"Baby," he murmured in a sleep-roughened voice. "Y'okay?"

My heart stopped before dropping into an embarrassing swoon as I said a quick "Yeah, gotta pee" and disappeared into the bathroom.

The marble tile was cool under my feet, a stark reminder that this wasn't Landry's luxury penthouse in Manhattan, where the bathroom floors had radiant heat. I emptied my bladder and moved to the sink, blinking at myself in the mirror in the dim light from the street coming in through the nearby window.

My hair was a rat's nest, and the T-shirt I'd stolen from Landry to sleep in was twisted around my neck. I straightened it and threaded my fingers through my hair before taking a long drink of water out of the tap.

"The sofa," I said firmly to my reflection.

But he's the one who moved me to the bed, I reminded myself.

"He was being a gentleman."

He's warm, I whined. *And lovely. And sweet. And he might need comfort after that conversation with Zane.*

"Boundaries," I hissed at mirror-Kenji. "You weren't supposed to overhear that. And he's angry at you. And he didn't ask for a roommate."

All of that was true.

None of it made the choice easier.

When Cora and I had nipped home midway through our shopping trip yesterday so I could drop off some purchases and grab a scarf, no one had warned me Landry was back from his run. I'd rushed upstairs and thrown open the door to his—*our*—suite, lost in thought and still low-key angry about Landry's lies and his Parliament run and that toe-tingling, performative kiss in the hallway.

Then, I'd heard Zane's laughter coming from the bathroom, followed by Landry's emotion-soaked voice saying, *"For years, I've been terrified that if you found out the truth, you'd hate me for not telling you sooner or you'd think differently of me, and I'd be alone again."*

My heart had squeezed hard—we're talking cardiac-event-hard—and I'd had to fight the urge to go into the bathroom and wrap my arms around Landry.

But of course, I hadn't. After all, I wasn't the one he'd chosen to get emotional with, was I?

No, I was the one he'd avoided talking to for days, except when the cameras were on, like whatever feelings he'd had for me had withered and died—

Landry shuffled into the bathroom behind me and caught me staring at myself.

"Get in the fucking bed," he muttered as he headed straight for the toilet, "or neither one of us is going to sleep."

I scurried out of the bathroom and dove into the bed. It was warm and soft. Heavenly.

And it smelled like my favorite combination of Landry and Kenji.

Fuck.

"Stop thinking so loudly," he grumbled, yanking back the duvet, climbing over me with no care for my personal space, and yanking the duvet back over us. "It's two in the morning. Apparently, I have to do *sports* in a few hours."

"You like sports," I reminded him, curling automatically around him again as if controlled by the feral octopus. I had no idea what kind of bed-sharing detente this was, but I wasn't going to question it.

Landry's arms wrapped around me and pulled me closer, tucking my head under his chin. "Not in London in February, I don't."

He was shirtless. My cheek tickled from his chest hair. I moved my face until I found a more comfortable spot.

"You're a nuzzler," he said, slipping back into sleep.

As soon as I opened my mouth to say, "No I'm not," he said the exact words along with me. *No I'm not.*

I sucked in a breath.

"Why can't you admit you like to cuddle?" he asked, turning us around so he was spooning me with his knees under mine and his arm holding my wrist against my chest in a loose grip. "You're so fucking obstinate."

"No I'm..." My voice trailed off as I fell into his trap. His chuckle vibrated against my back.

He pressed a kiss against my hair. "You're an elephant. Like the one guarding my windows."

This made zero sense. I couldn't think of an animal I was less like, and as far as I knew, elephants had nothing to do with windows. "You're already asleep, aren't you?" I asked, amused.

"Thick skin, nosy as fuck, highly intelligent, and... maternal."

I snorted. "Maternal makes me sound like a harried woman trying to get five misbehaving, sticky-fingered children into a minivan at the same time." I paused. "Come to think of it..."

His thumb holding my wrist made a gentle swipe over the center of my chest. "You mother all of us. You fuss and manage. Protect. Herd. Defend. Lead. It's nice."

A few minutes of silence fell when I didn't have the words to respond. Just when I thought he was asleep, he murmured, "You'll make a good father someday."

My heart hammered in my chest. "Do you want kids?" It was the first time I'd ever asked him outright, and I asked it so softly I wasn't sure it was even loud enough to be heard. But the only response was the rhythmic sound of his breathing.

I lay there wondering what the fuck this midnight interlude even meant. Was he still mad at me? Hurt? What did this mean for the two of us?

What did I want it to mean?

I tried to remember a time when we'd shared a bed all night without fucking. There'd been a night on a ski trip in Park City, Utah, when I'd brought some documents to his room to get signed and he'd been hot with a fever. I'd stayed next to him all night out of fear and because he hadn't let me take him to the hospital, worried about the possible social media frenzy from other tourists.

There'd been the night I'd snuck into his room at Bash and Rowe's house in the Hamptons for a quick fuck, only to find him on a call with a modeling friend who'd gone through a bad breakup. I'd lain down on the bed to wait for him to finish the call and had fallen asleep. He'd ended the call and stretched out next to me with the assumption we'd wake up at some point and fuck. But the scent of coffee had woken us instead, causing me to panic and race out of the room, nearly colliding with a house cleaner. I'd managed to stammer an apology and then stammer an unnecessary and detailed explanation to Bash about how I'd left my room before sunrise to be sure I was out of the way when the cleaners arrived because I was interested in taking sunrise photos. Which was only partially true.

Landry had overheard my stammering and gifted me a framed photo of a Hamptons sunrise the following Christmas, pointing out in front of everyone—with a perfectly straight face—that it had been the sunrise photo I'd taken that day, though it definitely hadn't been. "I'm just grateful to those house cleaners for sending you outside with your camera so early that morning," he'd said.

That was the same Christmas I'd given him a copy of *The Art of Stillness* in hopes he'd not only understand my obsession with meditation better but also realize how important it was to take some time alone, to slow down and focus.

As I lay there thinking back to my misperceptions of him at the time, a little over a year ago, I began to realize just how wrong I'd been.

First of all, he'd been too *busy* to be still. The man had been juggling two full lives. On the one hand, his life as Landry Davis, which included his found family—the Brotherhood, his somewhat silent partnership at Sterling Chase, and his modeling career, with its demanding nutrition and exercise expectations and aggressive travel schedule. On the other, his blood family, including his management of the Davencourt property and investment holdings Cora had described to me during our shopping trip, the expectation he'd eventually take up his family's legacy by serving in the House of Lords, and the heartbreaking reality of his father's Alzheimer's disease.

When he wasn't slammed with responsibilities from one, he was racing to stay on top of the other. And at every single moment of every day, he was hiding a piece of himself from someone.

I turned in his embrace and studied his relaxed face. My fingers found their way into his hair, brushing it softly back.

"Baby, fuck," he murmured without opening his eyes. "You're killing me."

"Before San Cordova, who knew that you were Landry Davis the model, Everett Davencourt the viscount, co-founder of ETC, heir apparent to an earldom, weird freak-boy about lobsters, oddly nervous about giving speeches even though he wants to run for office, and a guy who grew up with noisy house-birds? Who knew all of those things together?"

"No one. I don't exactly go around sharing the lobster thing." He paused as if searching for the catch. "Why?"

I wanted to cry. I wanted to cradle him in my arms and murmur promises that this man-boy, this tall, gentle lover of fun and shenanigans, this soft-hearted son and devoted friend, would never be so fucking lonely again.

"You don't have to hold it all in anymore," I whispered as carefully as I could. "There's one person who knows all of it now."

A puff of air escaped his nose, warming my hairline. "Yeah. And that person has kept me at arm's length for three fucking years. You make it sound so easy, Kenji. Know what's not easy? Racing with an egg on a spoon on only two hours of sleep. Close your eyes."

His large hand came up and covered my eyes for me, cutting off the dim light outlining the shadows of his face.

Instead of arguing, I let him dismiss my emotional plea, but I didn't follow him into sleep. I lay there thinking back over ten years of knowing Landry Davis, the Right Honorable Everett Landry Davencourt, Viscount Hawling. He'd been a grieving, confused teenager who wanted to escape the heavy mantle of familial expectation and have a normal life. A normal life that led him straight into another blatantly abnormal experience of almost-accidentally helping found one of our generation's most pivotal software systems, resulting in untold wealth he kept hidden from his family. A normal life that had tumbled him into the global spotlight for his good looks and charm, resulting in years of trying to keep his identity secret while under interrogation lights.

The man who spent years trying to be everything to everybody while pretending to flit around like a dilettante.

His story was unbelievable. And so incredibly isolating.

After a while, the door creaked open, and Turkey's heavy body landed on the mattress next to my legs. She wobbled over the folds and lumps in the duvet until curling behind Landry's knees.

I let out a breath. At least when he was here, he was loved and supported by his family. And when he was in the States, he was loved and supported by the Brotherhood.

My nose burned with emotion as my brain helpfully supplied the truth.

But not by you.

Landry was right when he said I'd kept him at arm's length. I'd believed the lies. I'd tried to protect myself from him.

What would it have been like if I'd given him a chance? Would he have ever confessed the truth of his identity to me? How long would it have taken? And how would I have reacted?

The answer to the last one was clear. I vividly remembered the things I'd told Landry in the car leaving the city airport. My first reaction had been to leave. To pick up my toys and go home.

To flee, like any other animal when scared.

I'd been an idiot.

And if that realization wasn't galling enough, I'd planted myself squarely in the center of a public farce where I had to pretend to be fake-married to the man just as I was finally realizing that he might, in fact, be the one for me.

It was like having everything you'd ever wanted dangled in front of you on a stick just out of reach. You could look but not touch. You could live adjacent to it but never claim it as your own.

My eyes stung from trying to see Landry's face in the dark.

But as hard as I tried, I couldn't make him out.

————

"Pretty sure consuming opiates before a public appearance is a bad idea," Cora murmured without taking her eyes off her phone screen.

The Range Rover smoothed to another stop as we made our way through London traffic.

"Fine." Landry shifted in the seat next to me and rubbed his hands up and down his thighs. "But we have time to stop at a pub for a quick pint. I just need to take the edge off."

"I don't understand," I said, not for the first time. "You've done things like this before. You helped Zane cut the ribbon on the community center in Barlo and then said a few words to the crowd about his generosity. You and the guys did a meet and greet last September for Sterling Chase employees and partners."

"Not the same," he grumbled, glancing out the window.

"How is it not the same?"

His chest heaved. "I didn't have to remember how to speak in exactly the way I'd been trained by political strategists while knowing people are fixated on my American accent. I didn't have to worry about making a stupid joke, or finding a way to drop a casual child poverty fact into my speech without scaring the children in the audience, or referring to three different schools without showing preference for one over the other. Or, god forbid, touching a child."

I reached over to take his hand, if only to keep him from ruining his pants, when I realized it was drenched in sweat.

"Hey," I said, reaching up to feel his forehead as if he was fevered instead of nervous. It was plenty cool, but I took secret delight in seeing his eyes flutter closed at my touch.

His reaction simply didn't make sense. "You've spoken publicly a million times," I reminded him again.

"I've thanked Calvin Klein for selecting me. I've joked about jet lag. I've announced my next appearance. I've thanked people for coming or congratulated someone on a job well done. Those are not the same thing."

"He's right," Cora called back from the front seat. "A lot is riding on this."

"Thanks, asshole," Landry groaned. He closed his eyes and leaned his head back. His skin had a slightly green pallor.

I scrambled to think of a way to help. "Focus on the kids you're helping. This program is a difference-maker. When I was in elementary school in Baltimore, we didn't have a place to play outside. There was a city park down the street, and the teachers would take us there sometimes, but it wasn't dedicated for our use at all, which meant we never knew what we were going to find."

As the Range Rover meandered through the congested streets, I told Landry stories of stray dogs nosing for food, homeless people under benches muttering to themselves, and the time Vonnie Cecil found a hypodermic needle and a candy bar in the same plastic baggie. I also told him about the time there was a random guy dressed as a clown doing cartwheels, the time a hot dog cart offered to give us all free dogs, and the day the sun shone down in full summer warmth on an early February day when the sky was a blinding blue.

"Being outside with your friends is where the good times happen," I said. "Those are some of the times we remember the most, right? Even you and Jamie went straight to a shared memory from being outside playing sports together in school. It's where kids connect and find joy. It's where they gossip and learn about betrayal and loyalty. And your family is giving that gift to kids from two different schools without dedicated outdoor play space."

"Pretty sure Killian Prep is doing it," he muttered.

"Pretty sure they only agreed after the Davencourt Foundation offered them a big donation," Cora added in the same snarky mutter.

"And I'm pretty sure there will be at least ten boys there who discover a little something about their sexuality when they see a real-life male model up close and personal," I teased. "You're doing the Lord's work, Landry. Worst-case scenario, you ruin your political future and your family's reputation, but you still help a few young people live a more authentic life. How about that?"

The poor young driver's ears turned red, but Landry's lips curved up a little.

Victory.

"You're lowering the bar," he accused with narrowed eyes. But then his grin widened, and he bounced his eyebrows. "I'm here for it."

My own sexuality wasn't immune to a reminder that I most definitely preferred men. I swallowed and looked away from him, focusing on the hodgepodge of signage plastering the windows of a nearby corner store.

I smiled to myself. "And if you feel the need to hug a child or clap them on the back, touch me instead. I'll take one for the team."

The sound of his soft chuckle mixed with Cora's laughter helped relax my shoulders. He would be okay. *We* would be okay.

When we got out of the vehicle in front of the school, Jamie Winthrop was there waiting with a friendly smile on his face. Landry's hand immediately reached for mine and took firm possession of it as we said our hellos and greeted the head of the school.

Paparazzi stood outside the school gates, but their manner was surprisingly mild compared to previous visits. I remembered from our prep for this event that there were strict rules about photographing children and schools, which was why there was an official photographer for the event and only one reporter recording the details.

After greeting the kids and moving up onto a raised dais where a podium had been set up, the head of Killian Prep stepped forward and welcomed us with a kind introduction.

"Lord Hawling and Mr. Winthrop would like to say a few words about our new program before we get started with our sports day."

The crowd cheered as Landry squeezed my hand one last time and left me to step up to the podium.

He leaned in and lowered his voice to a stage whisper. "Do I have poppy seeds in my teeth? Because I had a bagel this morning, and now I feel like my teeth are peppered with black spots. You will tell me, won't you? Or else they'll have a photo of me on the internet looking like a numpty."

The kids all laughed as Landry grinned and then quickly slapped a hand over his mouth in mock embarrassment, causing them to laugh harder.

"Right, no one said anything, so I'll assume I'm alright. Thank you for having me, my husband Kenji, my cousin Cora, and my friend Jamie here today. We are honored to start this program with you because we all believe that exercise and outdoor play are important.

"I grew up in Regent's Park, where I had space to run, space to move, and space to believe I could be something more. Later, I went to a school with Jamie here," he said, thumbing over his shoulder, "where we met and formed memories out on the field. In one particular rainy and cold cricket match, a young, strapping viscount claimed victory over a much less talented—"

Jamie blurted, "Oiy!" with a good-natured grin on his face.

The kids all laughed as Landry acted apologetic. "Alright, alright. Although I'm sure I won that match, only because he's one hundred percent American and I'm only half-American, how 'bout that?"

The kids cheered and agreed.

Landry was an incredible actor. There was no trace of nerves in his manner. "Every one of us should have a safe place where we can make connections. Where we can be bold, be strong, and believe in something bigger for ourselves, regardless of our postcode. Where we can take care of our bodies and improve our health while getting a break from the rigors of our academic studies. Which is why the Winthrop and Davencourt Foundations are helping Killian Prep enlarge this outdoor sports area and open it up to other schools. But this isn't just a sports area. It's a launchpad. Maybe you'll use it to train for something big. Maybe you'll use it to shake off a tough day. Or maybe, just maybe, this will be the place where you and your mates make memories that will last a lifetime.

"Access to safe outdoor spaces for exercise and play should not be a privilege. It should be a promise. A promise that you will have what you need to pursue a long and happy life with healthy habits.

"So today, when you run, when you kick a ball, when you cheer for each other—and hopefully for me because I'll need it against you lot—know that this space belongs to you. Because you deserve it. Because your future deserves it. And because I know you're going to do incredible things with your minds and bodies, if you use your imaginations and stick with your mates."

After handing the podium over to Jamie, Landry moved back to take his place beside me. I glanced up at him with affection and pride for an incredible job well done.

Which ended up being the photo from our sports day event that went viral.

Lord Hawling Dedicates Youth Sports Program While Devoted Husband Looks On

"Could have been worse," Cora said later while I had my final fitting with the tailor in the large laundry room behind the kitchen.

Landry scrolled on his own phone, his long legs spread out in front of him on the worn terra cotta tile. "True. They could have gotten a close-up of the fact that I did, in fact, have something in my teeth. What is that? A leaf? I ate oatmeal for this very reason."

"You look happy," she observed. "Which is more than anyone will be able to say for my mother when she sees the photo of me shaking Jamie's hand after besting him at archery. I can imagine the conversation now. 'Cora, dear, how do you hope to attract a titled husband if they think you might *shoot* them?'"

Landry snickered. "Well, from the dopey expression on Winthrop's face, he wouldn't mind being shot if you were the one holding the bow."

Cora smacked Landry's shoulder smartly. "Be nice," she commanded. "Jamie's sweet. And he didn't for one moment try to pretend he'd only lost because he was going easy on me, either. It was a fair contest, and he congratulated me like a true sportsman."

"Oh, it's *Jamie*, is it?" Landry teased, provoking Cora to smack his shoulder again, harder this time. "And do you want *Jamie* going *hard* on y—oiy! Leave off! Don't bruise the viscount!"

I barely paid attention to their sibling-ish squabbles. I was too busy staring at the photo of myself. I hated to admit it, but whoever was writing the headlines had gotten it right.

I huffed out a breath. "I never expected to be anyone's dutiful husband," I muttered. "It's embarrassing."

Landry quirked his lips at me while his eyes danced. "They didn't say dutiful. They said devoted. *Devoted*, Kenj. I'm sending the link to the Brotherhood. If anyone will laugh at the irony, it will be Bash and Silas."

I didn't mention that I'd already gotten a text from Zane with a row of hearts and swoony-face emojis and a long, drawn-out *d'awwww*.

"I *am* devoted to you," I said. "Devoted to your punctuality, your organization, your schedule, your dry cleaning, your..." My snark trailed off as a memory inserted itself front and center.

"I am devoted to your pleasure," Landry said with a teasing look on his face.

"Yeah, how about being devoted to getting me off as quickly as possible. I have a meeting in six minutes, and you're going to be late for your shoot."

We'd been in the executive restroom off my office, and Landry had been on his knees for me.

My eyes flicked to his and found deep aquamarine eyes staring back at me with knowing intensity.

The tailor was three seconds away from moving from my back to my front, so I shot Landry a death-ray glare and quickly imagined a quick plunge in an icy lake. It worked, but it left me feeling a little chilled.

I blamed Landry.

Just when I was poised to disappear upstairs and take some much-needed time to myself, Cora shot me a cheeky grin. "Etiquette lessons, remember? They were rescheduled when the sports day went long?"

I closed my eyes and bit back a curse.

Landry chuckled and moved past me. "Yeah, good luck with that, husband. It's a lot about utensil placement and proper address. Riveting stuff."

Cora caught his elbow. "You're in it, too. He's doing a dance lesson with it since the two of you will be watched like hawks at the Hearts of Hawling Dinner."

I silently cackled with glee when Landry did his cursing out loud.

The etiquette part of the lesson was easy enough. I'd picked up details here and there over the years that seemed to have covered most of it. The biggest challenge was the rules around addressing people properly and rank-based protocol. I planned to review a few of the finer points before the dinner since Landry was expected to spend the majority of the event introducing me and Jamie to as many peers as possible.

But the dancing part of the lesson... that one was brutal.

"Too close!" the teacher snapped for the third time, causing me to jump away from Landry. "This is not a brothel."

Landry's jaw ticked, but he kept his mouth closed.

"Again," she said, restarting the music on the Bluetooth speaker. "Forward, slide, close. Forward, slide, close. That's it. Keep tension in your arms. Just like that. Alright."

I lowered my voice to a nearly imperceptible whisper. "I notice the viscount is the man in this scenario. How unexpected."

His nostrils flared. "I am holding on to my patience with her by a thread, Kenji. Say the word, and I will let it go."

"Smile when you're talking!" the teacher called out. "Everyone is watching. Do you want to look like you're at the dentist, or do you want to look like you're in a happy marriage?"

"Is this when I casually let slip we're just fuck buddies?" I murmured. "If the ambulance comes, we might not have to do this for much long—"

"No whispering!" she warned. "Whispering is considered rude. You may speak of the weather, of sporting events, of a hobby such as gardening or visiting the theater, music. You may inquire about your partner's family, their recent travels, or their work. Stick to topics that can be overheard by others without causing harm."

Thankfully, Landry was now trying to stifle a laugh. As long as he was happy, so was I.

The day dragged on, ending in a formal dinner with five courses. The Winthrops had been invited, since Landry and Jamie's "rekindled friendship" had smoothed over any lingering resentment between Jim and Lord Davencourt, but their inclusion in the dinner meant Landry was even more stressed than ever, fearing Ed would get into a repetition loop that gave the Winthrops private insight into the real reason he was retiring from politics.

Jamie, his younger sister, and his parents were seated closer to Lydia and Landry, while Cora and Nan flanked Ed at the head of the table. I sat between Nan and Jamie's sister and managed to help steer the conversation. Every time Ed began to repeat a story, Cora, Nan, or I interjected to ask him about something completely different, sending him off in a different direction.

It was a long three and a half hours.

The Winthrops, minus Jamie, left soon after dessert, and Nan and Ed headed right off to bed. Cora, Landry, Jamie, and I made our way into a billiards room I'd never seen before.

"Thank you for that," Jamie said sincerely as he shrugged out of his dinner jacket. "My parents were happy to be invited and pampered, and my sister couldn't stop staring at all the paintings around the room and the sheer amount of silverware on the table."

Landry took both of their coats and mine and laid them over a leather chair in the corner. "Didn't she go to Wycombe Abbey? Surely they covered all of that there."

He nodded. "Yes, and she's friends with a couple of young women from titled families, but nothing like this. Dining at Hawling House is like dining in a Masterpiece Theater period piece."

Cora kicked off her heels and tossed a few of her bangle bracelets on the nearby wooden shelf before grabbing the wineglass she'd stolen from dinner and curling up on the sofa. "Maybe you can tell her the chair she was sitting in has been used to make epic pillow forts in the past."

"True story." Landry nodded sagely. "And a certain cousin of mine has also been known to deliberately grind mushy peas into that carpet in hopes the dog would eat them."

Cora nearly sputtered on the sip of wine she'd taken. "Aww, I miss Alfred. He was a good dog."

Landry nodded again, only this time, it was accompanied by a smile as he handed Jamie a pool stick and moved to rack the balls.

Jamie grinned at Cora. "Naughty girl. Does your mother know? Because I might enjoy being the one to tell her."

She knuckle-punched Landry's arm while laughing at Jamie. "Fuck off. My mother would punish me by forcing me to dance with every snotty lordling in town, so I try to stay in her good graces."

I could tell by his bright eyes when he looked at her that Jamie was especially enjoying Cora's company. "My lips are sealed, then, if only so I can take all your dances instead."

Cora's cheeks darkened. "Maybe not all of them."

Jamie nodded happily.

Landry gestured for Jamie to start the game. "As for thanking us for dinner," he said in response to Jamie's earlier comment. "I will forever be in your father's debt for getting Kenji out of a dangerous situation. You ready to break?"

My eyes stayed glued on Landry as he and Jamie began a friendly round of trash-talking across the pool table. His casual reference to the importance of my safety struck me as not only heartfelt but important.

He had been trying to tell me how much he cared about me for a long time.

But I was beginning to learn that actions spoke louder than words.

EIGHTEEN

LANDRY

It had been three days since the sports day at Killian Prep.

Three days of Kenji's attempts to pretend we were together, not only in front of the cameras but behind closed doors.

Three days of my blistering attempts at keeping myself so busy, so well exercised and distracted, I didn't dare peel him out of his damned pajamas when I finally snuck back to my suite after stalling in the workout room and moved the stubborn man from the settee to my bed.

I might have appreciated that Kenji was respecting my need for distance by sleeping on the sofa, but all it did was give me the opportunity to prove to both of us over and over how fucking weak I was by moving him to the bed.

During the day, my self-control had reached masterful levels. But at night, I wasn't able to sleep unless I was completely wrapped around him.

At least I could comfort myself that I did it without ever tearing his clothes off and begging my way into his body.

Kenji had tried at least ten times to talk to me about my motherfucking feelings, something I was absolutely not going to do. For three years, I'd hidden my hopeless love and feigned laughter to hide the sting of his rejections. Now, when everything in my life seemed to be teetering like my grandfather's old spillikins tossed on a narrow window ledge, poised to crash to the pavement at the mildest breeze, I didn't have it in me to laugh it off. Instead, I'd beg. I'd bargain. I'd sob.

If I shared my feelings with Kenji and he rejected me now, it would break me.

So maybe in a few weeks, after I'd finished my ill-fated attempt at becoming an MP, I'd be able to stomach some kind of final reckoning. I'd fly to New York and confess everything to him, and when he turned me down, I'd manage a dignified exit that allowed us to keep working together and remain friends. Then, I'd slink back to London and lose myself in family obligations.

But in the meantime, my self-control was all I had.

Unfortunately, that self-control didn't include moments in which the press dared to disparage Kenji Toma.

"Don't do it," Nan warned as I shoved back from the kitchen table in a fit of rage.

"This is unacceptable!" I spat, poking the screen of her tablet with my forefinger so hard the joint bent back a little bit. That was fine—the flare of pain only fueled my anger. "They do not get to make up blatant lies about my husband!"

It was late, and Kenji had already gone to bed. I could only hope he wasn't scrolling social media.

I'd come downstairs in search of ice for my recovery shake after my workout and found Cora, Dad, and Nan sharing a bottle of wine. It hadn't taken much convincing to swap my recovery drink for a glass of cabernet, and I'd enjoyed the normalcy of settling down to a bit of gossip.

Until Nan's tablet had buzzed with a salacious headline.

SLEEPING WITH THE HELP? NO, MARRYING

THEM! LORD HAWLING GIVES HIS COMMONER SECRETARY A NEW TITLE—HUSBAND! BUT TOMA IS ALREADY CONSIDERING OTHER OPTIONS...

Under the headline was a photo of Kenji standing next to Jamie Winthrop, beaming up at him. Jamie's face was creased in a grin, making it look for all the world like the two of them were flirting. Instead of the actual reason for their grins, which had been the fact the proffered cups of hot chocolate had featured soccer-ball-shaped mini marshmallows, for fuck's sake.

Now, obviously, I needed to murder a few people.

"Nan, get the crisis management people on the phone. No, don't tell me it's too late at night," I insisted when she opened her mouth to argue. "What's the point of having gobs of money if you can't get immediate response? I want this headline removed before the rest of the world wakes up, *and* I want a printed retraction and personal apology from this reporter, whoever they are. If they refuse, get our legal team involved. I will sue them so comprehensively their fate will become urban legend—"

"To be fair," Cora said mildly, swirling her wineglass in the air, "You *are* sleeping with the help. And Jamie Winthrop *is* attractive and charming."

I pierced her with a glare. "Kenji and I are not sleeping together."

Cora lifted an accusatory eyebrow.

"Fine," I gritted. "Technically, we're *sleeping* together. But we're not..."

Nan winced. "TMI, darling." My father grunted his agreement.

I ignored them since my face was already on fire from anger. "Kenji Toma would no more cheat on me with Jamie Winthrop than... than..." I blew out a breath. "Than he'd be caught dead at an all-you-can-eat buffet, or cut in front of a little old lady in a queue at the market, or put mayonnaise on literally anything. Or be late for a meeting. Or wear acrylic knits. Or sleep on microfiber sheets. Or marry me for real."

Now, it was Nan's eyebrow of judgment that winged up.

I deflated. "He just wouldn't. Not now. Not while he's pretending to be my husband. Kenji Toma bleeds integrity. He deserves better than this disgusting gossip-mongering."

Cora set her glass down with a *plink*. "You're acting like it's the first time any of us has been the subject of a disgusting headline."

Nan nodded and patted Dad's arm. "Cora's right. I remember your father asking me what a 'situationship' was when there was a rumor about you dating that singer friend of yours a couple of years ago."

If I wasn't so angry, I would've laughed at the memory of those rumors. Zane and I had been arrested together for causing damage to a hotel room, and even though plenty of other people had been involved, someone had snapped a chance photo of me with my arm around Zane. My head had been turned—shouting an expletive at one of Zane's misbehaving fans—causing the photo to look like I was kissing Zane's head.

I'd given a framed copy of the photo to Zane for Christmas recently with the innocently stated hope he'd hang it in his new place in Majestic. His bodyguard boyfriend had growled and toed the photo under the sofa in Dev and Tully's living room, and I'd laughed my ass off.

Now that Kenji was the one in the media's crosshairs, though, I understood Ryan's irrational anger and desire to salt the earth. It wasn't funny at all.

"It's more than one awful headline." I tried to explain. "After having his face splashed all over the internet and gossip magazines, he'll be recognized in public. Whispered about. He won't be able to move on after this without long-term repercussions."

Cora lifted her shoulders. "It's part of being a Davencourt. He'll get used to it."

"But that's just it—he's *not* a Davencourt!" I reminded her.

Kenji had a life to get back to, and I didn't want our fake marriage to ruin it.

My father leaned back in his chair, bringing his wineglass with him. "He could be. It's clear the two of you have serious feelings for each other."

I shook my head. "Not him. And he wouldn't want to be an MP's spouse or settle full-time in England anyway. Kenji has dreams that don't involve living in the center of a three-ring media circus."

My father tilted his head at me as if to understand. "Did I ever tell you how your mother and I met? Funny story, that. She was here on a school trip."

There was a silent, collective groan of disappointment in the room as he began one of his favorite story repeats.

I tried to focus on a centering technique I'd overheard Kenji describing one time—*Breathe in. Feel your feet. Exhale slowly*—but all I could think about was that my feet felt hot and humid in my running shoes after my workout.

That was a shit centering technique.

"What you may not know," my father continued, "was that I deliberately didn't pursue her at first."

I blinked at him in surprise. This was a new verse to his usual song. "You wrote her, like, a hundred letters."

He nodded. "That's right. But that's all I did. I was afraid if I pursued her, if she came back over here and married me, all the parts of her I loved, all of her spirit and playfulness, would be stifled under formality and the pressure of trying to fit into my world."

Nan didn't look surprised by this information, but Cora and I sure were. "I never knew that," I admitted. "So what happened?"

He scratched at an old scar on the table with a short fingernail. "She showed up on my doorstep."

Cora shook her head. "We know that part, but why didn't you turn her away if you were worried about it?"

His face softened with memory and old affection. "You must not remember your aunt. She wasn't the kind of woman who allowed anyone to turn her away." He looked up at Cora and then me. "I told her I hadn't wanted to throw her to the wolves by asking her out. She implied that she didn't need anyone making decisions for her, and she pointed out that if I liked her enough to write her a hundred letters and discontinue seeing other women for those five years, that was evidence enough that I was interested in her as more than a friend. And of course, she was right."

Their love story had been romantic and epic. Years after the press had gotten hold of it—leaked by one of my mother's American school friends—they'd gone on to compare Charles and Diana's love story to my parents', which had become more and more offensive as details of the royal couple's true relationship had come out.

It had taken them fifteen years—and countless losses—before my mother had become pregnant with me. My mother had always said the wait for me allowed her more time to spend with the love of her life.

Looking into my father's eyes reminded me that he'd had to spend the past fifteen years without his Kenji. How the hell had he survived?

His gaze was lucid and piercing. "Do you know what she told me that day? Sometimes choosing the path of happiness comes with unexpected sacrifices."

"I don't want him to sacrifice. I told you that."

Dad leaned forward and gripped my hand. "Darling boy. Whoever said I was talking about *him* doing the sacrificing?"

I stared at him. "I don't understand. You make it sound like I'm not willing to sacrifice anything for him, and that's simply not true."

He took a slow sip of his wine, the liquid leaving defined legs as it slid back down the bowl of the crystal glass. "Then why are you here in London playing a game only Teddy Baines will win?"

Once again, I looked at my father in shock. And once again, Nan didn't look surprised.

"I thank God every day that you are your mother's child, Landry," Dad said with a wink. "And your mother would advise you to choose happiness."

He turned to Cora with a smile and asked for details about her recent archery win, as though he hadn't just set my whole world on its ear... and called me *Landry* while doing it.

Nan shot me a warm look of understanding. "He meant what he said, Landry. Ed has only ever wanted your happiness. If you want a seat in the Lords, he wants you to have that. And if you want a life with Kenji, well..."

"It's a moot point what *I* want if the guy doesn't want me." I shook my head to clear it. "Meanwhile, this hasn't distracted me from the main point, which is this ridiculous media speculation." I pointed back to her tablet, where the headline and photo were no longer visible since the screen had gone to sleep. "We're going to ruin this reporter's career—"

Nan sighed and stood up, tucking her tablet under her arm. "We're not. Not tonight, anyway. Instead, we're going to put this in the hands of our crisis PR team *tomorrow* and let them respond with brains instead of..." She waved a hand at me. "Whatever this is."

I rubbed my face with both hands. "Fine."

It wasn't fine, but Nan deserved her rest. And I was perfectly capable of contacting the crisis team myself.

After retrieving my phone from the workout room, where I'd

accidentally left it, I poked my head in to make sure Kenji was asleep.

The little fucker was on the settee again. *Of course.*

Instead of risking waking him, I slunk back out of the room and closed the door.

And then got to work.

—————

The following morning, Kenji came striding into the kitchen, bright-eyed and gorgeous in a new outfit of wide-legged black trousers and a trim-fit toffee-brown sweater so soft it had to have been cashmere.

If I hadn't been so tired, I would have wanted to parade him around town and then pose with him for the cover of a magazine with the feature cover line claiming, "Legal Experts Agree: Kenji Toma is Off-Limits To Other Men."

"Good morning, everyone," he said cheerily, breezing past me to grab the sole Starbucks cup remaining in the carrier. "I would include my darling, *devoted* husband in that greeting, but he's currently dead to me."

"I am devoted to you," I corrected with a sleep-deprived grumble. "Devoted to your protection."

"*Mpfh.* I assume that's the reason Zee Barlo and an unknown woman from the Vista Bonita Active Seniors Community happened to leak photos of a certain viscount's cheaty husband within hours of each other?"

"You're *not* a cheaty husband," I muttered. "You'd never. That was the whole point."

"Oh my god, Landry, what did you do?" Nan asked, peering over Cora's shoulder at the laptop screen.

After a late-night Brotherhood strategy session, we'd come up with the right media distraction to pitch to the crisis PR manager.

Zane had, with his irresistible "oh shucks, he'll kill me for this, but you just have to see it" charm, sent old photographs of a knock-kneed chess geek winning prizes at various tournaments in the greater mid-Atlantic area circa 2002 to 2010.

Additionally, Kenji's grandmother, who'd still been awake, thanks to the time difference, had "accidentally" changed the security settings on a few Facebook posts featuring her chubby-cheeked grandson as an infant and as a gap-toothed second grader at Old Line Elementary School.

Cora gasped and clutched her chest. "Oh my god, the cowlick."

Nan leaned over and grinned. "That shirt collar makes your neck look as skinny as a pin. Aren't you just the *sweetest.*"

Kenji's glare was laser-hot against the back of my head as I turned to grab a breakfast sandwich from the tray. His voice was dangerously sweet. "This aggressive memory-lane campaign seems incredibly reactive, but I look forward to seeing the equivalent photos released of the Right Honorable Judas Iscariot in his infant dinner jacket and his prep-school tweeds. Maybe a shot of him playing polo, hmm? I heard he was incredible at it, and I, for one, would love to see a heretofore unseen shot of the viscount in his awkward prepubescent years."

Cora snorted, preparing to tell him the truth of my polo experience before I stopped her with a look.

Nan ignored the tension. "Look at you with your gran at your graduation. Och, such a lovely photo. She's obviously very proud of you, Kenji."

He took a breath. I imagined him doing a hard-and-fast scroll through his mental list of helpful Chaska Inira wisdom.

So I decided to help him out.

"*Fire cannot put out fire. Let the flames of anger pass before you speak, and you will not burn what you wish to protect.*"

His eyes widened in slow motion. "Did you just *Chaska* me?"

I bit back a smile. When an angry Kenji Toma was the match, I was happy tinder. "I simply believe in a tempered response. Consider meditation and reframing before—"

His slender nostrils flared with anger as he clapped a hand over my mouth. "Did it occur to you to consult with the person who was being smeared in the original headline? Did you ever stop to think that I make a living putting out fires and managing messes like this full-time? Or that we—" He made a jerky arm motion between me, Cora, Nan, and himself. "—have a crisis PR team on call right now who actually specializes in responding to ridiculous headlines like this?"

"I had their approval," I tried to say from behind his hand. But it came out sounding more like *M'adder proovuh*.

He yanked his hand away when I finally licked it. His voice was calm but with a clear thread of danger underneath. "Watch your back, *my lord*. You are on a very short list of extremely long and detailed revenge plans."

My dad wandered into the room with the *Times* under his arm and a mug of tea in one hand. After seeing everyone gathered around the laptop, he leaned over and lifted his glasses to get the right angle before asking, "What are we looking at, and why is my purported son-in-law upset?"

Kenji cleared his throat. "Sorry, sir. But you've raised a man-child who still needs scolding from time to time. I'm happy to take the duty off your shoulders."

I couldn't hold back a snort of surprise. Cora's face lit up with approval. It was nice to know Kenji wasn't intimidated by the fifteenth Earl of Davencourt.

"Don't I know it," Dad said with a grin before looking back at the laptop screen and Kenji's chess picture. "Wait a moment. That's a FIDE tournament. Just how good a player are you, son?"

Kenji suddenly lost his nerve and fiddled with his wedding

ring. "I, ah, didn't make Master. I stopped playing in tournaments halfway through college."

Dad reached out to squeeze his shoulder. "That's impressive. I'd love to take a lesson if you have time for a match with an old Cambridge lad. I'll certainly lose, but it will not be for lack of trying, only lack of practice. Maybe it will give the two of you a chance to cool off."

Kenji turned back to smile at him. "I'd love to play. I'm rusty, too. With the exception of playing against my grandmother a couple of times a year, I haven't played regularly in over a decade."

Dad clapped his shoulder and tilted his head toward the door to the rest of the house. "No time like the present. Come on, then."

He didn't give Kenji much choice, which brought back memories of my father's more commanding years. He'd mellowed quite a bit in the time I'd been away, but it was nice to see Kenji get a glimpse of who Edward Davencourt had been when I was younger, when he'd gone toe-to-toe with Lord Orren over critical energy proposals, changing the way England relied on foreign oil, or when he'd spent several days closed up with Dr. Frey and her husband hashing out details of a health initiative that provided additional funding to the NHS for research into rare diseases seen in combat veterans. In both cases, he'd argued staunchly in support of his proposed programs and won over an impressive amount of opposition to his causes.

I selfishly wanted Kenji to know that man. The smart, friendly, powerful fifteenth Earl of Davencourt. The man who'd made his mark on Parliament and on the legacy of our family.

The man whose reputation had made it so incredibly clear to me that no sane person would select *me* to take his place in the House of Lords when there were men like him who would do it a thousand times better.

I truly hadn't thought I had a chance at actually being elected as an MP, but after meeting with Teddy Baines yesterday, I had to acknowledge it was a possibility. Teddy was a smart man who hadn't ascended to the top of the government without being strategic and well supported.

While Kenji accompanied Dad to the library for a game of chess, I shoved the remaining bite of the breakfast sandwich down and refilled my empty Starbucks cup with black coffee before following Nan back to the office to review critical details of who would be attending tonight's Hearts of Hawling Dinner and how I needed to engage with them.

I felt like I was back in school, with lists of names to memorize and key details to retain for the exam. At one point, I took a break and headed immediately to the library, where Kenji was regaling my father with stories about the Brotherhood, about Lellie and Christmas in Majestic, and about the snow bunny I made for her using carrots for ears.

I watched them for a few minutes, out of sight behind the edge of the doorframe, and marveled at the lack of tension in Kenji's body. These days, the only time I witnessed him uncoiled was when he was deep asleep.

"Do you want children one day?" my father asked, gesturing to something. It took me a moment to realize there was a photo album on Kenji's lap. The one full of my mother's favorite pictures of me growing up.

Kenji looked down at the album. Instead of softening, he sat up straighter and closed the book, sliding it onto a nearby end table. "Yes, sir. I do. But I'm not sure my work life is compatible with a family."

"That's too bad. Children are a delight. I would imagine it's harder for you boys since you wouldn't have a wife at home to take care of them."

Kenji nodded, pressing his lips together. "Yes, sir. I'd love to have a partner who was able to stay home with our children... but then again, I wouldn't want to raise children in the city, and that's where my job is."

My father nodded and thought about it. "Tell me more about Majestic. Everett said it's got beautiful views. I'd love to visit one day."

Some of the tension bled out of Kenji's body. "It *is* beautiful. There's something both serene and inspirational about it. The views make you feel anchored but also... I don't know... adventurous? It's hard to explain. Lan... Everett would laugh if he heard me say that. I'm not exactly the outdoor adventure type. But being there makes my mind expand. I feel more creative and..." His voice trailed off as if he'd realized he'd run on a bit, but my father encouraged him to keep going.

Kenji shrugged. "I'm grateful several of my employers live there because it gives me an excuse to spend time in a place that feels very welcoming and therapeutic. It's quite a contrast from the city, as you can imagine."

As the subject changed and my father began telling a story about an adventure trip with his brother I'd heard a million times before, I continued past the library to my office and tried to put the conversation out of my mind. Hearing Kenji still refer to me and the guys as his "employers" galled me.

I checked in with the Brotherhood on a video call. They were all still in Majestic, awaiting Lellie's birthday celebration that night, though her actual birthday wasn't today.

"I told Kenji he should fly back for the party," I explained for the third time. "But he refused. We've been invited to a reception at Downing Street, kind of a political networking thing—"

Dev shook his head. "I still can't wrap my head around this. The man who once ran naked down the shore in broad daylight singing Monty Python's 'Penis Song' is going to don a powdered wig—"

"They don't wear wigs," I corrected. "And I'm not going to get selected."

Bash and Silas both stared into the camera with the kind of no-bullshit intensity they were known for. I glanced at Zane, whose face was creased in concern.

"But what if you are?" he asked. "What if you're selected and you stay in London full-time? Will we ever get to see you?"

"You'd be surprised at how many breaks they get," I assured him. "During the last session, they had about twenty weeks off. It's not a bad gig."

Silas's eyes narrowed almost imperceptibly. "So I guess there'll be time during those breaks to attend... oh, let's say a family birthday celebration?"

Dev shot him a look while Way reached over and shoved a cookie in Silas's mouth.

What they didn't realize was that the knife cut just as deep whether their hands were on the hilt with mine or not.

Tully, who held a wriggly Lellie on his lap, griped at Way for bringing out cookies and demanded one for his daughter if he was going to flaunt them.

I missed these guys. I missed them so much it hurt.

"I won't get selected," I said again, even though I was tired of being the only person who believed it. "There are several candidates in the running who are way more qualified than I am. They've been here for years, networking and establishing connections. Everything I've done here has been via email and phone calls only. Those relationships don't exist for me the way they do for the other candidates."

Silas shook his head. "The PM wouldn't have put his support behind you without being confident in your success."

"You're being naive, Landry." This time, the admonishment came from an unlikely source. Zane's boyfriend, Ryan, crossed his arms in front of his broad chest. "Politics is a chess game played by experts. They don't make a move without looking several moves ahead. Sometimes pieces are sacrificed to protect other pieces or moved to protect other pieces. And sometimes the move is a distraction tactic to make your opponent think you're doing one thing when you're actually doing another. I'm not saying Baines has any nefarious motive here, but I am saying—as I'm sure others have said already—there's little chance he's putting you up without believing you'll get the seat."

By the time I dressed for the dinner, I was in a shit mood. Not only was I tired from sleepless nights spent hard and aching against a man I couldn't have, but I was also finally coming to the conclusion that *I* was the one in denial about the House of Lords situation.

There was a very good chance I would get selected, not because I deserved it but because other people were pulling the strings.

I imagined most people would be happy in my shoes. In a way, I was happy myself. The position would keep me busy and distracted. It would let me continue a proud family legacy. It would let me do some good in the world.

But I'd be stuck half a world away from most of the people I loved, doing a job I didn't love, and depriving better candidates in the process.

Cora knocked on my bedroom door. "Landry? Kenji's been downstairs and ready for half an hour. What's taking you so long? The car is waiting."

I wasn't going to explain the elaborate dressing choreography I'd done to ensure I didn't see any of Kenji's bare body before he was safely out of the room. "Coming."

Cora's elegant gown looked amazing in the warm, dim lighting of the corridor.

"Is that Dolce?" I asked in surprise, recognizing the zebra chiffon. "I thought you were wearing Vivienne Westwood tonight."

As usual, she'd asked me to hook her up with some contacts in the fashion industry. She'd frequently claimed the only thing having a supermodel cousin was good for was the couture.

She flushed and looked away, her eyelashes fluttering inky black against her smooth cheek. "Jamie Winthrop suggested something a little more young and fun. Well, to be fair, I told him I wished I could wear this dress instead of the red gown but that I worried about upsetting our donors. He reminded me that charitable giving isn't just done by old fuddy-duddies. Do you think it's okay? Not too much?"

My cousin rarely expressed nervousness, and I wondered if my old Eton frenemy had some sort of scheme to use my cousin to get closer to my husband. "I think you look drop-dead gorgeous," I admitted, offering her an appreciative smile. "And if it makes your mother have a coronary, more's the better, right?"

She waved an elegant hand as we neared the top of the stairs. "She's already approved since it's from an established fashion house. Had the exact same dress been designed by an up-and-comer, she would have gasped and insisted I change."

I escorted her down the stairs where Kenji and Jamie Winthrop were standing, chatting happily. *Or possibly flirting,* some dark corner of my brain that had read too many scandal headlines suggested. *Maybe that reporter had a point.*

Knowing how irrational I was being only made my mood darker.

"You look amazing," Kenji exclaimed, eyes only on Cora. "That dress is gorgeous."

Jamie stared like a cartoon character with eyeballs on springs. "Shit."

Cora let out a nervous laugh. "That bad, eh? I look like shit?"

He strode quickly forward and reached for her hand, leaning in to press a kiss to her cheek and whisper something in her ear I couldn't make out. Whatever he said must have done the trick because she smiled and returned the cheek kiss.

"Right, then," I said quickly. "Wouldn't want to be late to our own show."

The next hour was a whirlwind of event-staff greetings and prep at the Royal Horseguards Hotel. The dinner itself would be held in the Gladstone Library, but the receiving line and cocktail hour were held outside of it in a different area. As we finally waited for the first actual guests to enter, Kenji stepped in front of me and reached out to fuss with my bow tie.

The upper half of his hair was pulled back neatly in a knot while the rest flowed down past his shoulders in a dark, glossy spread. His eyebrows were neatly shaped, his lips pink and full.

"You look fucking beautiful," I said under my breath.

He glanced up before focusing on the bow tie again. "You sound upset about that," he murmured.

"I am."

Though he rolled his eyes, his gaze didn't leave the tie. "I'd ask *why*, but since you're avoiding conversations with me—"

"Because every man and woman in this place will get the opportunity to flirt with you, to talk to you, to dance with you without being shot down."

His fingers spasmed, twisting my tie out of alignment.

With an epic scowl, he yanked it open and started tying it again. "I assure you, anyone looking for more than conversation will definitely be shot down."

I huffed out a humorless laugh. "Well, they can all join the fucking club. I'm the goddamned president of it."

His jaw ticked. "*You* haven't been shot down in days," he pointed out before glancing around and plastering on a fake smile. "In fact, if you'll recall, I'm the one who's been trying to talk, yet somehow, you're always conveniently too busy."

"Mpfh."

Kenji finally looked up at me. There was a toxic mix of anger, hurt, and lust in his eyes. The lust part threw me for a loop. "Landry, you can hardly be mad at me for looking my best when you clearly only need me to sit still and look pretty."

His words offended me deeply. "What the fuck?" I hissed. "When have I ever treated you like a prop?"

Kenji's eyes flashed as he finished the tie and put his palm below it on my chest, nearly high enough to strangle me. "When someone came for me with derogatory headlines and you decided to handle it yourself instead of bothering little ole me who... *makes a fucking living* putting out fires. No, instead of asking for my help or getting my *consent* for peppering every news outlet with awkward Kenji photos, you took it upon yourself to manage the situation."

Guests began entering the room, starting at the far end of the receiving line. I wrapped my fingers around Kenji's wrist to pull his hand off me and lowered my voice even more. "I don't want you to have to sort my shit for me."

If it was possible, he looked even angrier. "Did it ever occur to you that I *like*—"

"Oh, there you are, Landry!" Aunt Lydia's smile beamed as brightly as her glittering dress, but her eyes flashed a warning that she'd noticed our heated conversation. "You remember Lord Wymer, don't you? Lord Wymer, may I present Lord Hawling and his husband, Mr. Toma? If you'll excuse me, I see Lord Twetts over there, and I know he's been *so* eager to meet my Cora."

She melted away into the crowd, and Kenji's face lit up in a welcoming smile as he greeted the baron and baroness.

"Lord Wymer, it's been a long time!" I shook the man's hand. "Lady Wymer, don't you look lovely in blue? I believe I remember hearing you'd visited Fort McHenry when you were in the States last year, right? Well, Kenji here was actually born and raised in Maryland..."

The night spun out in a series of endless meet and greets like that one. With each subsequent introduction, I did my best to make a small conversational connection so that Kenji would be able to find people to talk to throughout the evening when I was pulled away for various reasons.

Tension vibrated between us despite the plastered-on smiles and deliberate touches intended to sell our "romance" to everyone there.

We finally moved from the receiving line into the library. Kenji was clearly still angry.

So was I.

How dare he get mad at me for trying to protect him. For trying to clean up my own messes for once. For keeping him from always having to take charge.

"There he is," Ben MacNeely said as I entered the large ballroom and took stock of the crowd. "We were just talking about our next MP, weren't we, Holmes?"

I reached for Kenji's hand as we approached the group of men clad in crisp Armani and women in sparkling couture gowns. "That can't be right. If I remember correctly, you were more likely lamenting Man United's embarrassing showing on Sunday."

Once everyone's laughter and teasing died down and I'd thanked everyone again for coming, Samuel Holmes pulled me aside with his wife, Laura. "So, Ev... sorry, Landry—that'll take some getting used to, won't it? Sorry. Anyway, Laura and I wanted to talk to you about a special measure coming up in regards to the transfer of water rights. Her parents' estate is on the Derwent and..."

He and Laura began appealing to me to support the special measure by explaining water rights in excruciating detail. I finally stopped him mid-plea.

"Sam, I understand riparian rights as I've been managing Davencourt Park for years, which stands on the River Wey. Unfortunately, I'm not able to dig into details about the special measure this evening, but did you know that the Davencourt Foundation funds clean water initiatives and ecological research? I'll have to look into it, but the Derwent might be on the list of rivers positively impacted by our efforts here tonight."

Kenji smiled and leaned forward. "Landry and Cora are also spearheading a project to establish new riverside walking trails. That project is near Epping, I think. Isn't that right, darling? The more funding the project gets, the more trails they can create, which fits right in line with Landry's personal hope of decreasing childhood obesity and increasing sustainable movement habits in adults."

As the cocktail hour continued, the situation repeated itself. Someone tried to pull me aside to ask a favor or win my support on something, and Kenji managed to turn the conversation back to the evening's purpose. Like a dutiful spouse.

He had to be hating every minute of this. It was an unwelcome reminder of all the other times in the past decade Kenji Toma had been forced to bail me out of scrapes. If only I hadn't dragged him into this mess by telling that one little lie about being engaged to him. And if only he hadn't felt duty-bound to double down on the lie with a bigger lie to try and fix things.

By the time I pulled his chair out at the dinner table, I was annoyed, anxious, and generally on edge.

It was probably for the best I wasn't able to sit with him. Instead, I was seated a few places away between Baroness Colborne and Teddy's wife, Kaveri.

Kaveri winked at me as soon as I inquired after her comfort. "I believe you're the one in the hot seat. How has the evening gone for you so far? Okay?"

I smiled and shrugged. "I can't say I'm not used to the scrutiny, although I've never had it focused on my brains over my brawn, so to speak."

The sound of her gentle laughter garnered attention from a few people sitting close to us. People's eyes had been on me all night, but the fact I was now seated between the prime minister's wife and the Lord Speaker placed me directly in the limelight.

"My lady, thank you again for coming," I said, addressing the Lord Speaker, Baroness Colborne, on my other side. "I understand from Teddy that you and your husband have recently returned from a holiday to Santorini. How did you find it?"

She and I both knew this was a dance in which a certain amount of small talk needed to happen before delving deeper. Teddy had arranged for us to have coffee in his office the following morning with a few other influential MPs, so it wasn't necessary to talk shop at tonight's event anyway.

While she explained her Christmas holiday and the joy her grandchildren found in visiting a place they'd only seen on television, I recognized the universal look of joyful affection on her face from sharing tales of her family with someone new.

I glanced over at Kenji and noticed he'd been placed close to Jamie Winthrop. The older woman between them seemed perfectly happy to be entertained by Kenji and Jamie sharing stories with her from both directions, and it was clear the three of them had created one of the more fun pockets along the large expanse of guests.

My fingers curled into a fist. I'd forgotten just how tedious and ridiculous these events were. Teddy leaned over his wife to ask me a question about whether a certain MP had contacted me to arrange for drinks the following week. He reminded me of several other contacts who were here tonight I hadn't had a chance to speak to yet.

As we spoke, my eyes kept moving over to Kenji, who was obviously having a grand old time yukking it up with Jamie. Jamie's face split into a happy grin, punching asshole dimples into his cheeks. Kenji's normally cool demeanor in situations like this was nowhere to be seen tonight. He was happy and talkative, warm and bright.

I wanted to absolutely murder someone. Everyone.

One person in particular.

How dare he tell everyone we were married, then turn around and flirt at my family fundraiser? Didn't he know everyone was watching? Didn't he know there would be more photos on the internet of him beaming up at the guy as if Jamie Winthrop was the greatest thing since Wi-Fi?

I was being irrational. I knew it, and I didn't care. The straight-jacket of my self-control was in tatters. The steel box where I'd been keeping my emotions was pulsing like a boiler about to explode.

It took me a moment to realize someone was tapping on my shoulder. Cora's strained smile alerted me right away to a problem.

"Pardon me for stealing your dinner partner away," she began, smiling to the ladies on either side of me. "But I need to ask Landry a quick question in private. Please excuse us."

I glanced over at Kenji's part of the table only to see his empty seat.

"What's going on?" I asked as soon as we were far enough away from the table.

"I have no fucking clue," she hissed. "But you're going to fix it. Your husband—you know, the one you've been glaring at for the past forty-five minutes—is in the cloakroom waiting for you. Figure out a way to get past... whatever the fuck is going on, and don't come back until you're ready to lose the murder face."

She walked away, throwing on a winning smile and flicking the skirt of her gown in place.

I stormed out of the library and down the hall to the coat room, which was really just a deep alcove in the ancient stone building covered by a heavy velvet curtain on a thick brass rail.

As soon as I entered the space and yanked the curtain closed behind me, I saw Kenji on the opposite end in front of a large window past neat rows of winter coats. He stood with his arms crossed in front of his chest.

"What the fuck are you doing?" we both snapped at the same time. Kenji's was more of a low hiss while, I'll admit, mine sounded a bit more unhinged.

His eyes darkened as he stalked toward me. "I'm trying to be a dutiful viscountess, my lord. Charm the masses. Look friendly and approachable. Convince a room of influential people that my husband is the perfect candidate for this cockamamie scheme."

I almost snorted at his use of *cockamamie*. It was a word I'd heard his grandmother use on the phone with him before. But I was ten miles past the exit on this bad-mood highway, and nothing was bringing me back.

"Oh?" I snarled. "That was you trying to help me? Flirting with every fucking man in the room?"

I hated how insecure I sounded. Somewhere in the back of my brain was a rational human wincing at my own words and unfair accusations. But that rational human had zero access to my mouth at that moment.

Kenji let out a soft laugh. "You're being a complete ass right now. I've been trying for days to talk to you. I've been nothing but friendly and agreeable tonight. I've tried to help you, but you can't—"

I took two long strides until I was right up in his face. "Help me? Help me? Eye-fucking Jamie Winthrop does not help me, Kenji. If anything, it's distracting me from being able to do my job," I growled.

He was so beautiful, so striking in the cool moonlight coming in through the window behind him. A few stray wisps of hair had come loose from the half knot and brushed the side of his face tauntingly. His lips were dark and his angled chin firm. I'd seen him in tuxedos before, but never one custom-tailored for his body. It fit him like a lover, like the way my hands knew him in the dark.

He took a breath as if trying to recenter himself and remain calm. "How would you like me to help you, then?"

My back teeth ached from biting back the words I'd wanted to say to the sycophants and the self-interested power brokers in the room. From biting back words I wanted to say to *him*.

From loving him for three goddamn hopeless years. From wanting him every minute of every day.

"You want to help me, Kenji?" I ground out, barely recognizing my own voice in the animal growl. "Truly help me?"

Kenji's eyes widened, and his calm facade wavered—a reflection on water disturbed by a ripple below.

I leaned closer until we were existing in the same space, breathing the same breath. "Then get on your fucking knees."

The air sparked around us, filled with the scent of perfume, faded cigar smoke, and leather. The sound of silverware clinking on china and conversations filled with bursts of polite laughter filtered into the curtained-off space. My cheeks heated with my own audacity, as if anticipating the rush of blood that would come when he slapped me. Hard.

But the slap didn't come.

Instead, Kenji lifted one eyebrow and whispered, "Yes, my lord."

Then, he sank gracefully to the carpet.

Landry Davis was one of the most laid-back people I knew. Nothing rattled him, nothing riled him. He was the textbook definition of go-with-the-flow... usually.

Now, rage coiled around him like a living thing, crackling in the air between us. After watching him bury himself in distraction and deflection for the better part of a week, the shift was electric. Raw. Unfiltered. And really fucking arousing. And I was so fucking here for it.

I wanted all that passion, all that pent-up frustration, to finally come out once and for all. My body hungered for his. My mouth salivated from the lack of his kisses. My skin prickled with need for his touch. And my heart cried out for any shred of affection he was willing to offer me.

I wanted his goddamn cock in my mouth.

So I knelt at his feet obediently and waited for him to take what he needed.

Landry's nostrils flared slightly. "*Now* you do what I say?" he murmured in disbelief. He shook off his jacket and flung it to the side before reaching for his shirt cuff to remove the antique silver link.

"Yes." My voice sounded sultry and breathy in the small space. "I... care about you."

Landry's jaw worked as he slid his cufflinks into his pocket and rolled up his sleeves. His forearms flexed as they moved. "*Care* about me? Give me a fucking break. You're the ice king, Kenji. You only care about getting off. Which is fine. It doesn't matter to me anymore." He eyed me up and down. "Take off your jacket."

Though I knew he didn't mean them, his hard words and dismissive tone hurt. I removed my jacket carefully, folding it and laying it down beside me on the floor. My cufflinks came off more quickly than his, but before I could get my sleeves rolled up properly, the metallic sound of Landry's zipper shot electricity through my veins.

I met his eyes and tried to stay calm. "I know you're lying. This matters to you. *I* matter."

My eyes focused on his strong hands reaching in to pull out his cock—hands that had manipulated me, commanded me, caressed and adored me. I wanted them on me again.

Landry's voice cracked over gravel. "I could fuck you right here, leave you on the fucking floor with my cum leaking out of you, and not give a single shit."

My cock throbbed between my legs. The man was lying, but he looked so fucking hot doing it.

"Okay. If that's what you want. If that would... *help*." I was provoking him on purpose, terrified he might change his mind.

I was on the cusp of getting a reaction out of him—of putting my mouth on him, of feeling his gentle fingers tangle in my hair—and I wanted him too wild with need to care how many wealthy nobles stood just beyond the thin curtain.

His aquamarine eyes darkened hypnotically. "It would *help* if you sucked me off," he gritted out.

"Yes, my lord," I repeated, fighting to keep the giddy joy from showing in my eyes.

He pressed the head of his cock into my open mouth, and my groan of relief was loud enough to carry through the curtain.

Landry shot me a warning glare but ruined the effect a moment later when his eyes fluttered in pleasure. "You look so good on your knees for me," he murmured.

After three years, I knew how to unravel him quickly and relentlessly. Within moments, he was gasping and begging, his commands jagged with desperation.

I relished the power I had over him like this. Always had. He was expressive and vulnerable in a way he rarely was outside the bedroom.

In a way I'd rarely let him be.

One hand slipped between his legs while the other rucked up his shirt, fingertips grazing taut muscle as his abs clenched beneath my touch. My gaze stayed riveted on his, holding him there and *making* him see me serving him, devoted to him, *his*.

I am yours.

I want to make you happy.

I will do whatever it takes.

Landry's eyes burned like liquid fire. Within moments, he pulled away from me with a glare.

"Stop looking at me like that."

Beyond the thin curtain, glasses clinked, laughter swelled and dipped, and the hum of polite conversation masked the ragged sound of my breathing.

I blinked up at him, jaw aching and lips slick, my head spinning from lack of oxygen... and lack of understanding.

"Like what?"

"Like you want something from me."

"But I do," I admitted softly. "I want you to admit you care about me."

Landry scoffed. "So you can reject me again?" He jerked his sleeves down and smoothed his cuffs as if he was getting ready to rejoin the party. "I could tell you I love you, and you wouldn't care. It wouldn't make a damned bit of difference."

I pushed off the ground to stand before him in the darkened space. The scent of perfume—something expensive and refined—drifted through the partition, reminding me that we shouldn't be here like this. But there was nowhere else on Earth I wanted to be.

My shirtsleeve hung open and crumpled as I wiped my mouth with the back of my hand.

"Try me."

He stepped close, his breath hot against my cheek. "You have no idea," he warned in a low, desperate voice.

I did, though. Or I was almost sure I did. And the way my heart flung itself around my rib cage at the knowledge should have been biologically impossible. "So tell me."

"Fuck you," he spat.

"Darling, I'd love nothing more..." I arched a brow and ran a casual finger over his shirt cuff. "...but it seems you're done using my body for the evening."

There it was. I'd finally found the hot button. And I'd pressed it long and hard.

Landry's eyes bored into mine, anger sparking anew. "*Using* your body? Never in the history of our time together have I *used* you! I have loved you from the very first time, Kenji Toma."

His eyes widened, and his voice broke, like he'd just realized what he'd admitted. But my Landry—my stubborn, beautiful reprobate—didn't back down... he *doubled* down. "I love you more than I can even put into words. I would give up my fucking future, my dreams, my family for you. I love you so much, I—"

I grabbed the front of his shirt. "Landry—"

He clapped a hand over my mouth. "No. Do not say a single word, or I won't leave here with my dignity intact. If you reject me again, that's it, and I'll dissolve into a pathetic, sobbing mess. If you don't..."

Landry frowned like he'd never let himself imagine the alternative, and my heart squeezed with something fierce and protective.

No one would ever hurt this man again, I vowed. Even—*especially*—me.

"If I don't?" I whispered against his skin.

He sucked in a breath. "If you don't, I will, quite frankly, experience a medical event and have to be carted out on a stretcher. Either way... please, baby. Please don't say it."

Every ounce of love I'd ever felt for him had to be apparent in my eyes. At least, I hoped it was. The words hammered against the back of my teeth, desperate to break free, but for him, I held them back.

He replaced his hand with his lips on mine and kissed me until we were both gasping for air.

I scrambled for my pants, yanking them open while Landry fumbled in his pocket for something. My idea was to relieve the tension with a quick frot, but he had something else in mind.

He spun me around, pressing me face-first into the thick wool coats. I grabbed onto them to keep from tumbling through them into the wall.

"*Lan—!*" I squeaked as a slick finger pressed against my hole. Relief and arousal hit me in tandem, sharp and dizzying. I didn't give a shit what he was using for lube as long as it worked.

"Shh," he cooed softly in my ear, his chin nudging my hair away from the side of my face. "That's it. Let me in, beautiful. Good. Just like that."

The feel of him inside me made my eyes sting, not from pain but from the sheer fucking rightness of it. I'd missed him so much —the way he took over, took care of me, made me feel like the center of his world and my pleasure was his sole focus.

"I love you," he breathed.

A whimper slipped from my throat.

Landry's low voice went straight to my balls. "Shh, don't say it. Don't."

My nose burned, eyes welling. He felt so fucking good as he worked his way inside me, slow and deliberate.

"I love you so much," he murmured. His cock felt like it was in my throat. The stretch burned, forcing me up on my toes.

"I love you," he said again, his voice raw and rough in my ear. "You have no idea what it does to me when you walk away like I don't mean anything. Like this... us... is only physical."

I opened my mouth to tell him he was wrong. That it had never been just physical. That saying otherwise had been the only way I knew how to protect myself.

But he slid a hand over my mouth. "Don't say it," he begged. "If you don't want a future with me, lock me out of the bedroom tonight. Because I'm too weak to stay away on my own, but I can't spend another night wrapped around my executioner."

His voice broke on the last word.

I reached back and palmed the back of his head, pulling him closer before turning and capturing his lips. The kiss was searing, desperate. He might have worried it was a goodbye, but I forced him to feel my surrender instead.

Without a word, I tried to tell him everything. That I loved him. That my future was his, however he wanted it.

His hand came around to stroke my cock, sending me immediately into the stratosphere. Landry clamped a hand back over my mouth to stifle the sound, but the restraint only drove me higher, wringing every last drop from me.

Just as his movements stuttered and his breath caught with his own release, voices broke through the haze.

A man's voice grew louder as he reached the curtain. "Your coat is in here, ma'am. Let me fetch it for you."

Landry ground into me one final time—a defiant, lingering pulse of pleasure—before reality crashed back. He pulled out and shoved me deeper into the alcove before snatching a coat off the rack. He threw it on and pressed me into the darkness of the back corner, hiding as much of me with his body and the heavy fabric as he could.

A woman's voice followed, far too close. "And my husband's also? His is a dark gray overcoat with a cashmere scarf tucked into the collar."

I held my breath and prayed the coat around us didn't have a scarf attached.

Rustling. A murmur. The sounds of a man checking tags.

Then, the woman let out a satisfied sigh. "Ah, lovely. Thank you very much."

Footsteps receded.

The curtain dropped closed.

And I exhaled.

"You're shaking," Landry murmured.

"I was almost the center of a global sex scandal." I was aiming for a joke, though it was too real to be funny. "But I suppose it would have quieted any concerns about how real our marriage was if we'd been caught, wouldn't it? We could've blamed newlywed passion." I laughed nervously.

Landry pulled back just enough to meet my eyes. Shadows sharpened the angles of his face. "Sorry I put you in this position." He brushed his fingers over my cheek, then pressed a lingering kiss there. He let out a soft laugh. "That's a blatant lie. But I *am* sorry we were almost caught."

I snorted and shoved him back as I leaned down to yank up my pants. He handed me a linen handkerchief before reaching into his pocket to retrieve his cufflinks.

After cleaning up as best we could and checking each other over, he leaned close and caught my mouth in a deep, slow kiss. "Please remember what I said."

And then he was gone.

I stared after him, heart pounding from the kiss. *What the fuck is he talking about?*

And then I remembered.

If you don't want a future with me, lock me out of the bedroom tonight.

A laugh bubbled up before I threw open the curtain and strode back to my seat. Halfway there, Cora stopped me.

"Everything okay now?"

"That depends." I grinned. "What's the opposite of locking someone out of a bedroom?"

Her eyes widened, and she looked around to make sure no one had heard. She might have blushed if her cheeks hadn't already been flushed from the chaos of running the event.

"I'm not sure I want to know in your case since you're sleeping with my cousin," she muttered. "But on a completely unrelated note, feel free to take the centerpiece roses home later. You know, in case you... need flower petals for any reason."

I laughed.

I floated through the rest of dinner, trying not to pay too much attention to Landry in case I giggled like a little girl.

He loved me.

He loved me.

The words weren't surprising, really, but he'd said them like a promise. Like he meant to build a life on them.

And I wanted that more than anything.

The remainder of the evening lasted a thousand years. I drifted through it in a daze, although my ass reminded me periodically that it would much rather be soaking in a nice hot bath—preferably with Landry—than standing around or dancing.

Landry, of course, looked impeccable. He worked the room effortlessly, always charming and composed, like a man used to owning a runway with poise and grace. Like a man who knew how to wield his rare combination of looks, brains, and charisma like a weapon.

Like a leader.

By the end of the night, my nerves were frayed. *Yes, he'd said he loved me, but what did that actually mean?* What kind of future did he envision? Was I really going to sign up to be his... what, viscountess? I'd made jokes about it, and obviously, that wouldn't be my title, but the truth was I'd be expected to shape my life around his.

Was that what I wanted?

As the night wound down, Lydia bustled over with my coat. "There you are. Cora said to fetch you. The viscount's gone— probably having drinks with a few MPs—and he suggested you ride home with us. Are you ready?"

I wanted to be annoyed that Landry had left without a word, but I couldn't be. This was to be part of his job—securing votes, playing the game. More than that, I guessed he was deliberately giving me space.

Space to decide. Without pressure or expectation.

Because for all his confidence, Landry was scared, too.

I nodded and slipped on my coat before following Lydia downstairs, where Cora and Jamie were waiting.

Cora held an armload of deep pink roses. Our eyes met, and she winked.

The ride home was a blur of exhaustion. I nodded off as the car slid through the city streets, lulled by the low murmur of Cora and Jamie's conversation and Lydia's occasional interruptions. When we finally pulled under the house and got out of the vehicle, the chilly night air jolted me awake.

As the elevator doors opened, Cora slid the flowers into my

arms and shot me a grin. "Put these in my room, yeah? Jamie and I are nipping out for another glass of wine."

I nodded, knowing she was only saying that to keep her nosy mother out of my business. I thanked her with a kiss on the cheek and rode up with Lydia. We exchanged polite, if cool, good-nights before going our separate ways.

I walked slowly down the hall to Landry's room, wondering how long I'd have to wait for him...

But when I opened the door, Taylor Swift's "Lover" played low and sultry. Candlelight flickered from candles over the mantel and bedside tables. Instead of a bottle of champagne or wine, a bottle of my favorite fruity water sat on a tray with cut crystal glasses.

My heart skipped.

I scanned the room... and there he was, propped in the doorway to his dressing room, watching me.

Landry's jacket was gone, shoes missing, tie and cummerbund nowhere to be found. His sleeves were rolled up again, forearms on full display.

He looked like he'd stepped straight out of a luxury campaign —the kind that made you want to buy whatever they were selling if it meant you could have the unattainably beautiful man in the advertisement too.

But the way Landry watched me—tense and wary, like someone who'd placed his final bet and awaited the turn of a card —it was clear he wasn't selling anything tonight.

I stood there dumbly, clutching an armful of roses. "I thought you were going to let me choose."

TWENTY

LANDRY

I shrugged. "Changed my mind. Figured I've let you choose for the past nine hundred and eighty-four days."

The air seemed impossibly thin, useless for breathing. Fear clawed at my ribs. But there was no way I was giving him the opportunity to make the wrong decision here.

I knew Kenji cared about me. That wasn't the problem. But loving someone didn't always mean you could build a life with them. And sometimes pushing too much, too soon, broke things beyond repair.

But I'd come too far to back out now. I had one move left. I'd already sacrificed my pawns, and now, I was advancing my queen —risking everything for the endgame.

I pinned him with my eyes as I stepped closer. "That's enough days, Kenji. And you're a terrible chooser."

He dropped the roses and leapt at me, wrapping his arms and legs around me so fast I nearly lost my balance. I barely managed to catch him, locking my arms around him as he clung tight.

Our kiss was fierce, a battle of lips and breath neither of us wanted to win. I spared a fleeting thought for the poor tailor who'd custom-made Kenji's suit before I tore it off without remorse. Within moments, he was on his back in the center of the bed, naked as the day he was born. His long black hair fanned across the pristine white pillows, his chest rising in rapid, uneven bursts.

He tugged on a strand of my hair. "I've always wanted to see you as a brunet."

"You'd hate me with my natural color," I said absently, leaning down to tease his nipple with my tongue.

He threaded his fingers through my hair. "Brunets have a more classic look."

Something about those words sounded familiar. I pulled back and met his eyes. "The Armani contract," I said, realization hitting. "I thought you were mocking my blond hair."

He smiled. "I wanted you to go brown. I was trying to be subtle."

I gaped at him. "There's such a thing as *too* subtle, asshole! Why didn't you just say, 'Hey, I think you'd look like a Greek god if you—'"

Kenji cut me off with a hard kiss, tumbling me onto my back. I wrapped my arms around his slim frame, hands roaming over his smooth skin. His hard cock brushed against mine, and I arched up, chasing more.

"Do you want to fuck me, Kenji?" I teased softly between kisses. "Press me into this bed and have your bossy way with me?" It wouldn't be the first time, but it wasn't my usual preference.

His hair fell around us like a curtain, cutting off the rest of the world.

"I just want to make you feel good," Kenji said, his eyes full of something so tender it made me feel warm and restless all at once.

I reached up, threading my fingers through his hair, imagining what we would look like together if I let my hair go brown again.

And then it hit me—*I could*. No modeling contracts to uphold, no secret noble identity to hide. I could be myself in front of the world, live fully in the light.

But what I wanted most was to be right here, with Kenji.

"What do you want?" he whispered like he could see my thoughts taking shape. "Landry? What's your fantasy?"

I studied him. *My fantasy?*

It wasn't a position or an act. It was *this*. It was *him*. Being with me. Wanting me—not just physically but in every way. It was Kenji Toma saying he loved me.

His hair was silk between my fingers as I pulled him down to kiss him deeply. His hard shaft slid against mine, his balls brushing against me. Our chests and bellies pressed together as I wrapped my other arm around his back, holding him close.

I kissed him until I couldn't see straight. Until three years of longing blurred into something softer, something real. Until his nose turned pink and his lips were swollen from my stubble. Until he melted against me, pliant in my arms.

Until his taste was imprinted on my tongue and my wildfire need for him dulled to a steady burn, one spark away from an inferno.

"Nrgh," Kenji said breathlessly. "*Nhnnh.*"

His eyes were dazed and half-lidded. He lay on his back, legs twisted with mine, my thumb tracing idle patterns on his chest and shoulders.

"*You* are my fantasy," I admitted. I leaned over to follow the path of my thumb with small, teasing kisses. "And making you say dopey words is one of my kinks."

"Please," he breathed as I moved lower, his cock hard and leaking.

I took him into my mouth, teasing the head with my tongue until he was back to intelligible sounds.

And then I took him apart piece by piece with my mouth and

throat, with my fingers and thumb, with every shred of love I'd ever felt for him.

I sucked and fucked him until we were both wrecked, sticky and spent, and then I half carried him into the bathroom for a hot shower, washing him clean with the same reverence I'd just worshipped him with.

When we didn't fall asleep immediately after settling back into the bed together, I decided to ask the question he'd dodged earlier in the week at the brunch spectacle.

"Why didn't you take the Deloitte offer?"

I'd always wondered why someone as smart and capable as Kenji had stayed with us all these years. Yes, we paid him an astronomical salary, but we'd also worried he wouldn't be content to be known as an assistant forever, no matter how much money he made.

He snuggled into my side, the dim city light outside casting just enough glow for me to make out his relaxed expression.

"The five of you were way more fun. And you paid me an obscene amount of money to fly around the world with a rock star, a supermodel, and various and sundry other billionaires." He stretched, voice lazy. "I weighed that against the corporate culture they were offering, and you guys won hands down. Do you have any idea how much action my hookup apps got during those early years because of my association with you and Zane? Almost as much as yours did."

I pinched his side lightly, and he laughed low and easy, which settled me more than the sex and shower combined.

"I didn't hook up nearly as much as you thought I did," I admitted.

His smile faded into confusion. "You did. I'm the one who arranged the NDAs, remember?"

I sighed, debating how much truth to reveal... but I was done with lies where Kenji was concerned. "Half those times, I was actually working on Davencourt business or traveling back here and needed a cover story. The other half, I was probably asleep before the deed was even done. Hiding all of this wasn't easy, Kenj."

His expression softened. He propped himself on an elbow. "I can't imagine how isolated you felt." He paused. "I wish you'd told someone. I mean, I wish you'd told *me*, but if it couldn't be me, then *someone*."

I tucked a strand of hair behind his ear. "I wanted to tell you," I admitted. A chuckle escaped as I remembered one of the times I'd chickened out. "Do you remember when Silas met Way and decided to pretend he was broke?"

"Of course. It made me *very* uncomfortable. The lies were impossible to keep track of. And it's not easy hiding that kind of wealth. It shows in every clothing choice. The way you move through the world."

"Right. Well, during that time, I said something like, 'Surely Way will forgive Silas if he cares about him,' and you said, 'Lying about something that important is a sign of lack of trust.'"

"It *is*," Kenji cried. "It *was*! We didn't know Way then, and we were talking about his legal claim on half a billion dollars!"

I nodded. "And then you said Silas was lucky Way was so forgiving because you weren't sure *you* would be."

Kenji grimaced but sat up, crossing his legs. "And that's true. Imagine you begin to care about someone and find out a decade later they didn't trust you with an entire part of themselves."

The vulnerability in his voice made my heart ache, even as it soared at his quiet admission of affection.

"I'm sorry, Kenji. I'm sorry I kept something so important from you." I shifted, sitting up against the headboard. "Part of me worried that if I began to talk about it in my American life, it would make it real and bring this timeline closer when I wasn't ready. Mostly, I was terrified my lies would confirm every negative thought you had about me and you'd be done with me for good."

Kenji moved closer, pulling our joined hands into his lap, above the duvet he'd yanked over our legs. "I was hurt when I found out," he admitted. "I thought it meant I wasn't important enough or that you didn't trust me."

"It was the exact opposite—" I began, but he stopped me with a smile and a raised hand.

"I *know* neither of those things are true. I overheard you talking to Zane on the phone, and I get it now." He took a breath. "Being here at Hawling House with your family—flipping through photo albums and hearing stories—makes me realize just how lonely it must have been. Your parents were so much older than everyone else's, which probably added to the formality and the weight of expectation on you. Even at Eton, you would have been surrounded by social pressure based purely on *who* you were, not *how* you were."

Kenji squeezed my fingers. "No wonder you were so afraid to tell us."

"I'd never had friends like the guys before," I admitted, feeling thready vestiges of that fear even saying it out loud. "What if they'd turned out to be like all the snobby assholes I'd grown up with? And it wasn't just my surname. People in the peerage judged me for having an American mother, too. As Zane's gran would say, 'I couldn't win for losin'.' And then, once I knew they were good guys, I was terrified of losing them because I'd lied."

"You never actually lied." Kenji arched an eyebrow. "Believe me, I raked through my memories, trying to build a *liar-liar* case against you, and I came up empty. *However*, I will now be submitting those fake hookup NDAs as exhibits one through ten thousand. Asshole."

I pulled him into my lap, wrapping my arms around him as he straddled me. "I plead guilty," I said softly. "If you need more evidence, I also lied every time I acted like I was okay with a purely physical relationship with you."

Kenji bit his lip. "Then it's my turn to apologize."

"What the hell for?" I asked, surprised.

"I never gave you a chance because I misjudged you. I thought you were reckless and shallow. A playboy who'd never commit, never take anything seriously, never be capable of devotion to his family. I was wrong. Impossibly wrong. And I'm sorry." His gaze roamed over my face. "I'm also sorry my rescue moved up your timeline."

I cupped his face and kissed him softly. "Nan was already pressuring me to come back. My dad needs to retire. They wouldn't have been able to wait much longer." I shrugged. "It was always going to happen at some point."

"It's *your* choice, Landry." Kenji hesitated like he wanted to say more but instead gave me a brilliant smile. "But if it's what you want, then I'm fucking here for it. I can help you accomplish your legacy, leave your own mark. You'll make an excellent MP, and I will make an excellent MP's spouse." He straightened, all business. "If you need to see my CV, I have extensive experience supporting great men's careers. Public relations, event planning, charitable endeavors, scheduling... I do it all." His smile turned mischievous. "Even the occasional posting of bail."

I barked out a laugh. "That was one time, Kenji. And there—"

"Three times, Landry," he sighed. "Three. What the fuck? How do you not remember being arrested two out of three times in your life?"

I ticked them off on my fingers. "The first didn't count because the airline decided not to press charges in the end."

"They banned you for life!"

I scrunched up my face. "Yet they'll still take my money for your first-class seats. Don't think I didn't notice and write them a strongly worded letter."

"And the second?" he asked, unable to keep from rolling his eyes.

"That's the one you actually posted bail for. And there were... extenuating circumstances." I deliberately didn't explain further. "As for the third and most recent, you weren't even there. And that one I also had a good reason for, if you'll recall. I was trying to let Zane get into a little trouble without getting into a lot of trouble like he wanted."

"Go back to the middle one," he said, narrowing his eyes. "Tell me what really happened. I always had a sense there was more to that story."

I scratched my neck and moved him off my lap. It was easier to focus when I wasn't distracted by his body. "Remember the Vencari contract a few years ago? The one where I did a catalog cover shoot, then Milan Fashion Week, then a shoot for a big formalwear ad spread?"

He frowned, trying to place it.

"And then suddenly, they added a swimsuit shoot and tried to pretend it was a language mix-up?"

I could tell by the sudden twitch of his jaw he remembered. "That guy was an ass, and your agent was even worse. Wasn't that the job that led to you hiring Lamar?"

I nodded. "That guy—the one who hired me, not my old agent —cornered me in a hotel room and tried to have his wicked way with me. I decided to turn it into a fistfight instead."

Kenji stared at me. "Please, baby. Please tell me you're pulling my leg right now."

I shrugged. "Wish I was."

"Why? Why didn't you say something? Call the guy out? Burn his career to the ground!"

My little hellcat was practically vibrating with the urge to Wolverine his way through an Italian fashion house, and honestly, the sight couldn't have made me happier.

I took his hand in mine and caressed it soothingly. "Because I didn't deserve the hit to my reputation."

"You were arrested for public intoxication and assault, Landry!"

I sighed. "Yeah, well."

"*Landry.*"

I cut him off with a firm kiss before pulling back. "I love you. They couldn't prove the intoxication, and the assault was pled down to disorderly conduct and probation. Remember?"

"Of course I remember! I thought you'd been in a fucking drunken fistfight with a colleague! I can't believe you didn't tell me the truth."

I couldn't keep my hands off him. With my fingers back in his hair, I murmured, "And what would you have done if you'd known? How would you have kept it quiet?"

This time, he was the one ticking things off with his fingers. "Homicide, for one. Kidnapping, for another. Bribery. And the most scathing and stealthy whisper campaign you can ever imagine. Which, by the way, has no statute of limitations, so I will be starting on my—*mpfh!*"

I tackled him onto the sheets and proceeded to distract him... *thoroughly.*

I sucked his cock until his threats turned to babbling nonsense, then flipped him over and ate his ass with my hand wrapped tight around his cock. As soon as his release hit, I moved behind him and jacked myself until hot spunk hit the crease of his ass and lower back.

We fell asleep empty and spent, and I woke up a short time later with a raging hangover—too much alcohol, not nearly enough water. I rolled out of bed in search of Kenji's fancy water, only to find the bottle empty and Kenji gone.

I threw on a bathrobe and made my way downstairs. As I approached the kitchen, I heard Kenji's voice.

"I heard she was a beautiful woman."

"She was," Dad said, "but so is my Nan, you know. Just don't bring a lobster near the girl."

Kenji sounded surprised. "Near Nan? I think you mean Landry. *He's* the one who doesn't like lobsters. Thinks they have nefarious intentions."

I grinned and stepped closer without entering the room. Was eavesdropping rude as hell? Yep. Was I going to do it anyway? Hundred percent.

Dad chuckled. "How do you think he acquired the shellfish bigotry, son? When he was little, we were in Padstow for a meeting at Prideaux Place. The lobster hatchery's nearby, so Nan took him over as a bit of a day jaunt while I was tied up in my meeting."

He continued to tell the story with impressive clarity… until he got to the punchline. "And wouldn't you know, Olivia ended up with several lobsters attached to her dress, all to keep the poor boy from going for a swim in the tanks!"

I saw the flicker of confusion on Kenji's face, saw him wonder if my mother had actually been there that day—she hadn't—or if my father had gotten confused, but he rolled with it.

"If she saved him, why did he end up with a lobster phobia?" he asked gently.

"Oh, Liv only kept him from a solid dunking. The boy still fell partway in and was covered neck to knees in baby lobsters. If only someone had captured it with a cell phone camera. But this was before everyone had one of those things, you know."

I decided to rescue them both. "And thank goodness for that," I said, strolling into the kitchen as if I'd just walked up. I caught Kenji's eye and winked. "Nan never wore that dress again, and she *definitely* didn't appreciate the donation we made to the hatchery in her honor that Christmas."

Dad laughed. "Too right, son. Speaking of lobsters, you should tell Kenji about your phobia." He turned back to Kenji. "We were in Padstow once. That's in Cornwall. Lovely area. I believe I had a meeting at Prideaux Place. Can't remember what it was about, but it wasn't something a boy of ten would have much interest in. So Nan decided to take Landry..."

Dad launched into the story again. I moved over to the refrigerator to find something cold to drink while Kenji listened, patient as ever.

"*Baby* lobsters?" Kenji laughed as if hearing it for the first time. "How did they end up traumatized if the lobsters were just babies?"

Dad chuckled, and for a moment, they shared a genuine laugh. I considered changing the subject to break him out of this memory loop but didn't have the heart. There was no harm in leaving it be if he was happy.

Movement in the hallway caught my eye, and I saw Nan rushing toward us in her bathrobe, a worried look on her face. She stopped short when she saw them laughing, pressing her hand on her chest and closing her eyes in relief.

When the puzzle pieces finally snapped together, I felt like the most oblivious human on the planet.

Nan only knew my father wasn't safe in his bed because she'd woken up to find him missing. She'd been sleeping in his bed. In *their* bed.

Maybe part of me hadn't wanted to see it before, but suddenly, I not only knew, but I also realized it had been going on for a long time.

I hurried to intercept her, gently gripping her upper arms. "He's okay. Just getting a glass of water and a sweet treat," I said in a low voice.

She shifted from foot to foot, glancing toward the kitchen. "I happened to pass by his room and..."

I didn't let her finish the lie. Instead, I threw my arms around her and hugged her tighter than I had in twenty years.

Emotion clogged my throat. "I love you," I croaked. "I love you so much, and I didn't know. I'm so fucking sorry."

Her arms tightened around me. She even smelled familiar, and I realized she'd been a part of my life as long as I could remember. She was as steady, if not steadier, than my own parents.

She was the rock of my family. And she'd loved me just as much as they had.

Nan pulled back, her eyelashes wet and her eyes bright. "I love you more than you can know, Everett Landry. And I know you love me. Still have a drawer full of your little treasures to prove it. Handprint cards, horrendous jokes written in your little-boy handwriting, salt-dough ornaments, and even the four-leaf clover charm that used to hang on my keyring."

After leading her to the kitchen and throwing back a large glass of water, the four of us returned upstairs. Kenji continued to laugh and swap stories with Dad until we stopped at the doorway to my father's suite. My father turned and smiled at Kenji. "You make a good viscount consort, Kenji. I'm proud to call you a Davencourt."

Kenji looked taken aback. "Thank you, sir, but we're not actually..." His voice trailed off as if unsure whether correcting him would only add to the confusion.

But my father reached up and softly tapped the center of Kenji's chest.

"You are where it counts, son. Good night."

Nan passed me, dropping a quick kiss on my cheek, then doing the same to Kenji before disappearing into my father's suite.

I stared at the closed door. "What the fuck."

Kenji reached for my hand and pulled me back to our room. Once we were settled in bed, with Kenji exactly where he belonged in my arms and Turkey shoving up between us, Kenji asked if I wanted to talk about it.

I told him what had happened in the hallway with Nan.

He didn't seem surprised.

"She's already running everything, Kenji!" I said. "The house, the staff, Dad's office staff, his social calendar. She makes sure I stay on top of the estate business and that Cora has everything she needs for the Foundation. She arranges the accountants, the solicitors, and..."

I stopped and took in a shaky breath. "And now she has to manage this, too? And the man she loves—who she didn't get to have for *years*, by the way—is..." My throat tightened. "It's not fair, Kenj. How can we ask this of her? It's too much."

For a long time, Kenji's fingers brushed through my hair, his nails dragging lightly over my scalp, causing me to fall into the in-between space of wakefulness and sleep. His voice was laced with warm, quiet amusement. "When it's someone you love, taking on their troubles isn't a burden. It's a blessing. You want to make their life easier. Fix their problems. Shoulder their worries. Lighten their load so they can live happy and free."

His voice soothed me. The rhythm and cadence lulled me further into sleep as his reassurance helped me let go of my stress about Nan.

It wasn't until the next morning, when I was on my way to an early breakfast meeting with Teddy Baines, that I fully processed the words Kenji had said.

And realized he hadn't been talking about Nan at all.

TWENTY-ONE

KENJI

After the tumultuous night, I slept in later than usual. But when I woke up, I felt like I'd stepped into a goddamned Julie Andrews movie. The hills were alive, and I might as well have had clothes made out of curtains for how joyful I felt.

"Oh dear god," Cora groaned when I swept into the kitchen and called out a cheery good morning. She dropped her head on the arms she had bent on the table. "He's one of *those*. Can we call a quorum to have him booted from the family?"

Nan looked up, amused. "Good morning, Kenji. Landry wanted me to remind you he had an early morning meeting at Downing Street. He said to let you have a lie-in, and I'm happy to see you got it."

I remembered Teddy's breakfast meeting—a chance to introduce Landry to a few key MPs. While I was disappointed not to see him, I understood this was his job now.

If he wanted it to be, a voice in my head whispered.

I'd meant what I told him last night. Whether to be considered for Parliament or not was *his* choice, and if this was what he wanted, I'd stand beside him and help make it happen. I still worried that he wouldn't be happy in politics—he'd been a tight ball of stress beneath his polished charm last night—but maybe the satisfaction of continuing his family legacy was enough to balance that out.

I wouldn't push him either way, but hopefully, now that things between us were finally, *beautifully* settled, we could talk about it more.

In the meantime, I had my own work to catch up on. It had been far too long since I'd checked in, and I had a Zoom meeting with my assistant later this morning. Time to start reclaiming some of my responsibilities.

"I feel refreshed and revitalized," I told Nan belatedly. "Thank you. It helped that I drank half a gallon of water in the middle of the night."

Lydia swept into the room, rustling like an expensive curtain. "Sit up straight, Cora, dear. You look like you're playing a bit part in a teen drama." She pulled out a thick, leather date book. "I've been poring over our invitations after last night, strategizing based on Lord Twetts's *keen* attentions to you. We'll definitely attend the Kingsleys' dinner party, and I think we'll have to at least pop in at the Willow and Ink fundraiser..."

Cora let Lydia prattle on while the rest of us focused on breakfast. Ed happily sipped his tea behind the paper, and I wondered whether Jamie had actually spent the night with Cora or not. I glanced around but didn't see evidence of him.

Finally, I nudged Cora with my toe and gave her interrogation eyebrows.

She squinted in confusion.

I widened my eyes and tilted my head toward the foyer— Jamie's most likely escape route, assuming he knew how to operate the damn locks better than I did.

Cora's hungover brain seemed to struggle.

"*Booty call,*" I coughed.

Her eyes widened, and her cheeks darkened. I tilted my head and blinked in silent demand.

She rolled her eyes and gave a slight nod before slumping over her coffee mug. "Mum, you have to stop. I'm not interested in Lord Twat. I mean Twetts. There is zero chance of a Davencourt-Twetts alliance. Please cease and desist."

Feigning ignorance, I mused, "I think it would be better if Cora made an alliance outside the nobility. But they *should* still be wealthy and powerful, of course. It wouldn't do to—*oof*."

The back of her heel connected with the front of my shin. Thankfully, she was still wearing house slippers.

She stuck out her tongue, and I fought a laugh, feeling lighter and happier than I had in weeks.

Which, of course, was the exact moment Nan sucked in a breath, eyes riveted to her tablet, and muttered, "Oh, bloody hell."

Cora and I scrambled around to read over her shoulder. As soon as Lydia realized what was going on, she pulled out her own phone to find out what was happening.

The headlines popped up one after the other in a series of real-time gut-punches.

'*Til Scandal Do Us Part! Davencourt Marriage a Complete Fabrication?*

Lords, Lies, and Lovers—Fellow Hostage Reveals Viscount Hawling's Faux Marriage!

From 'I Do' to 'I Duped You'—Viscount's Fake Marriage Exposed!

Parliament Rocked by Wedding Hoax

I stared at the screen until the words swam on the page and my pulse pounded in my ears. How did they know? How had we given ourselves away? What was Landry going to—?

"Who's Lindsey Graves?" Lydia asked.

It took a moment for the name to penetrate the blaring panic in my brain.

"Lindsey? She's a—" *Gossipy influencer,* I thought before remembering she'd been held in San Cordova several days longer than I had. I tempered my response. "She's a woman I met at the retreat in San Cordova. Another of the hostages. Why? What does she have to do with this?"

Lydia turned her phone toward us. In the video on-screen, a bare-faced Lindsey huddled in an overstuffed armchair, looking like the world's bravest little toaster.

"It was *awful,*" she said meekly. "I was held for days with barely *any* food or water. We were only allowed to use the bathroom *three times* a day." Her eyes welled up. "And I didn't even have my *phone.* I kept wondering why *some* people got to leave, but the rest of us were just forgotten." She sniffled. "For, like, *days.*"

A man's voice off-camera prompted, "You're referring to the hostages with health conditions, who were released as an act of good faith?"

"Not just them." Lindsey's eyes widened with innocent outrage. "Two men were rescued the *second night.* Kenji and Jamie."

"You mean James Winthrop, an American ex-pat living in London, and Kenji Toma, husband of supermodel Landry Davis, who's recently been revealed to be Viscount Hawling—" the off-camera voice clarified.

"Except they're *not* married." Lindsey's eyes flashed, and her cheeks flushed. "Kenji was flirty and chatty with me from the very beginning. And he specifically told me he and Landry weren't romantically involved at *all*—that he was just a *personal assistant* who helps with Landry's *public relations*." She helpfully provided air quotes. "In fact, he said he'd do *anything* for his employer, *including* crisis management!"

With an indignant lift of her chin, she went on. "Has anyone actually *seen* a marriage certificate? Because I wouldn't be surprised if this whole marriage *thing* was a stunt to distract from the fact that Landry rescued his *freaking PA* while the rest of us *suffered*." She sniffed delicately. "Not a good look for someone in his position, is it?"

No, I thought as Lydia stopped the video. *No, it wasn't.*

The room was silent, but I felt the weight of every gaze on me.

I shut my eyes and swallowed hard against the nausea creeping up my throat. My whole body had gone ice-cold.

Last night, Landry and I had fixed everything. We'd laid our cards on the table so we could build a future together. One where Landry could openly claim his proud family legacy.

Now, my hasty words had put Landry's reputation and political career in jeopardy.

"My fault," I whispered. My voice sounded distant, hollow. "All of this is my fault."

Somewhere in the house, a doorbell rang.

Nan turned to face me. "Don't panic. We're going to fix this." Her words were a statement of confidence.

"How?" I blurted. "How, when her accusations are true?" If anyone scratched the surface or demanded details, they'd learn the truth. No crisis management team could spin it away.

Before I could process that thought further, Jamie Winthrop strolled into the kitchen carrying a stack of bakery boxes tied with twine.

"Good morning everyone. Thought I'd bring you all a treat to thank you for a lovely evening last—" He stopped short, reading the room. "What's wrong?"

Shit.

I suddenly remembered there was another person from San Cordova who might be able to confirm Lindsey's statement. Jamie had gone along with the marriage thing and didn't seem the type to spill a secret maliciously, but if asked a direct question, what would he say?

Cora stood to help him with the boxes while I scrambled to figure out the most polite way to request someone not throw my fake husband under the bus.

"Oh, nothing." I forced a smile. My voice couldn't have sounded normal. "Just a regular day filled with ridiculous headlines. What did you bring? Croissants?"

Nan stood to refill her coffee. "Let's move to my office, Kenji, and call in the team."

I ran a hand through my hair. "I... I should get our attorneys on the line, figure out a way to make this woman stand down—"

"What woman?" Jamie looked between us. "Did I come at a bad time?"

Cora sighed. "Another of the hostages from the retreat, Lindsey Someone, is upset that you and Kenji were freed before she was. Now, she's claiming Landry and Kenji aren't married, which is—"

"True," I said flatly.

Silence fell. I met Jamie's eyes. "As I believe I told you in a drunken conversation where I listed all the reasons Landry and I could never be together."

Jamie tilted his head, considering. Then, he smiled. "Funny, that's not how I recall that conversation going."

"P-pardon?" I stared at him.

He shrugged. "You'd had quite a bit to drink, so maybe you don't remember the details. But *I* recall you spending ten full minutes telling me you were madly in love with the man."

Cora grinned at him like a lovesick fool.

"I..." My throat tightened. I scrambled to recall that afternoon. "Did I?"

"Oh, yes." Jamie grinned. "That's why I was so surprised when you denied being engaged when we met with my father the other day... and not at all surprised when you announced you were married."

"But—" I began.

"When my other friends tell me they are married, I don't demand paperwork. I believe them. And I know what two people in love look like." His sharp gaze pinned mine. "Which is exactly what I'll tell anyone who asks. Assuming, of course, that you *want* it to be the truth?"

Yes. God yes. All the yes.

Nan, ever the voice of reason, was more measured. "That's for Kenji to decide."

"Me?" I squeaked. "Landry's the one with a reputation on the line!"

Everyone in the room snickered, but it was Ed who spoke.

"Oh, Kenji. My son's talked about you for ten years—"

"Talked about?" Cora snorted. "You mean *gushed.* We didn't know it was a romantic thing until this visit, but he acted like you hung the damn stars."

"He once spent twenty full minutes explaining why Excel was better than Google Sheets," Nan volunteered. "And when I finally asked him why he was acting so belligerent, he threw up his hands and said, 'Because Kenji prefers Excel, and he's one of the smartest people I know.'"

"Three years ago," Cora put in, "he showed up here all in knots, muttering your name under his breath. We knew about the hotel incident with Zane and figured it had to do with that since you're the one who handled his bail." She rolled her eyes. "I asked if he was upset because you'd lectured him, and he immediately went off about how you weren't an unreasonable person and that if you were angry, it was for good reason."

Heat crawled up my neck. I remembered the night of that arrest. More specifically, I remembered how that "lecture" and the simmering anger I'd carried for him leading up to it had exploded into our first off-the-charts-hot sexual encounter.

"I did wonder why such a responsible lad had begun getting into so many scrapes he needed his assistant to get him out of." Nan shot me an innocent look over her tea mug. "Can you think of a reason, Kenji?"

Cora snickered.

"And just a week or so ago," Jamie added, not to be outdone, "Landry agreed to play fake boyfriends with me to give you your freedom and privacy back. Considering we were rivals up 'til then, that's a hell of a sacrifice."

The next volley came from an unexpected source.

Lydia circled the table and reached for my hand, running a manicured thumb over the top of my wedding ring.

"Everett was here in December," she said lightly, "before he went to Majestic for the holidays. He asked for my help in getting this ring resized safely since it has such historic significance. I'd hoped it was for Harriet Salvant since she's a lovely girl from such a good family—"

Cora rolled her eyes. "Mom. Landry's gay. He's not a politician who switches parties based on who's funding his campaign."

Lydia waved a hand dismissively. "There is such a thing as bisexual, darling, in case you haven't met your friend Jamie here—"

I barely heard their banter. I stared at the ring on my finger.

Landry had gotten it resized in *December*?

"Anyway, Kenji." Lydia squeezed my hand. "I apologize if I was frosty to you at first. I rather thought Everett had gotten mixed up in a scheme running counter to his best interests. Er, I mean, his heart. But even *I* figured out your relationship was real, even if your havey-cavey marriage wasn't. And there's no question Everett has true feelings for you if he gave you the Heart of Hawling."

I frowned. "The... fundraiser?"

Cora laughed and pointed at my finger. "The Heart of Hawling is the *ring,* silly. It's probably the most important heirloom the Davencourts have. Wordsworth even referred to it in one of his poems. And the family legend surrounding it is where the fundraiser got its name."

Overwhelmed, I stared down at it, instinctively curling my fingers to prevent it from slipping off, though it fit perfectly. "That's... that's..."

"A sign Everett wants your marriage to be real." Ed spoke with all the authority of the fifteenth Earl of Davencourt. It was impossible not to believe him.

He leaned back, casually plucking a piece of lint off his sleeve. "You know, Kenji, the Double Bishop Sacrifice was first played in Amsterdam in 1889. I've been reading up on it since our game the other day."

Cora, Nan, and I exchanged glances, waiting to see where this went.

Ed smiled, humor and steel clashing in those eyes that reminded me so much of his son's. "Any man who pulls that move against his father-in-law—real or imagined—in his very first match is someone who doesn't know fear. I have no doubt whatsoever that you'll sort this. You and Everett. And we'll do whatever it takes to help."

I blew out a shaky breath. "Thank you. Thank you all so much. But Landry and I didn't actually get married in Majestic over Christmas, as much as I wish we had. Even if Jamie corroborates our story, it's only a matter of time before someone looks for a marriage certificate. You can't just *invent* a wedding. You need witnesses, a license, a marriage certificate signed by a—"

I froze.

I *did* know a justice of the peace in Majestic, not to mention a small-town sheriff who owed me a favor and four upstanding citizens, plus their spouses and friends, who'd make unimpeachable witnesses. I was sure they'd agree if it meant helping Landry.

If I was being honest, I knew they'd do it for me, too.

"I've got to go," I blurted, dropping a kiss on Ed's cheek. "I need to fly home."

"Home?" Nan stood. "Kenji, let the crisis management team—"

I shook my head. "Not now. I'll explain it all later, but I need to set things in motion myself first." I grabbed her hand and squeezed lightly. "Let me do this for him, please," I begged softly. "It's what I'm good at."

"But don't you want to wait for Landry? Troubles are lighter if you carry them together," she urged.

"I know. And we will." I hugged her before stepping back. "I'm counting on it."

I grabbed my passport, laptop, and coat and was already at the door before I remembered something crucial.

"Someone needs to warn Landry what's happening before he leaves Downing Street." I met Cora's eyes. "His phone will be shut off, and I'm afraid he's going to walk out into a paparazzi firestorm. Tell him not to say anything."

Her brow furrowed, but she nodded.

On the way to the airport, my heart ached with thoughts of Landry. He didn't deserve the barrage of media inquiries this was going to bring and the potential derailment of his burgeoning political career. I shot him a quick text, knowing it might be hours before he was able to check his messages.

> I'm so sorry. I'll fix this. Come home as soon as you can.

It wasn't until I was in the Brotherhood's plane, winging my way west, that I looked down at the burnished gold ring on my finger.

Landry had told me a sentimental story about it but not its name. Not its full significance.

For the first time since he'd given it to me, I slid it off and examined it.

The three thin bands shifted apart, separating the two clasped hands and revealing a hammered metal heart nestled safely inside.

Along the inside edge of one of the bands was an inscription.

My beloved.

My breath caught. Landry had sized this ring for me back in December. When I'd still been trying to fortify the wall around my heart, he'd been determined to give me his.

Any lingering doubts about my plan melted away as I slid the ring back on my finger.

My husband needed my help.

And I couldn't fix this alone.

I set up my laptop and placed a video call to the Brotherhood.

When the first call connected, Bash squinted at his phone. He was shirtless and sleepy-eyed. "Why are you calling so early?" He squinted harder. "Are you on the plane?"

"Yeah. I need you to wake everyone up and put me on the big screen for a strategy meeting. And ask Way to get the sheriff there, too."

"Foster? What for?" He rubbed his cheek and yawned. "Where's Landry?"

"Back in England. He's okay, just... in the middle of something. Gather everyone, please."

Bash nodded immediately, used to following my lead, only hesitating when his husband's curly mop entered the frame.

"You guys okay?" Rowe asked, voice still thick with sleep.

I nodded. "We will be."

I disconnected so they could get some caffeine and regroup.

Fifteen minutes later, they called me back.

In that short time, the Brotherhood—apart from Landry—had all gathered around Dev and Tully's big table in their pajamas and sweats. Even Lellie was there, curled up in Dev's lap with her chubby hand clutching the faded equestrian logo of his old hoodie.

Seeing everyone there made my heart swell with warmth, as if love itself had gathered in that room. I couldn't wait to join them in person once this was handled.

Silas set two mugs in front of Way, leaned over to kiss his husband's head, and looked at the screen. "What's going on? And how are you video calling us mid-flight?"

Ryan cuddled a sleepy Zane on his lap. "Upgraded Wi-Fi on the plane. Remember Landry throwing a shit-fit after San Cordova?"

Everyone nodded and took sips of coffee. Tully walked in and handed a cup of milk to Lellie before taking the seat next to Dev.

"Is Foster coming?" I asked.

Way nodded. "He said the favor he owes you isn't a 'six-in-the-morning' level favor. I said if he needed extra favor credit, he could dip into all the shit he owes me after I had to listen to him cry over a straight boy last week."

Foster Blake was a good man. He might grumble and give his cousin a hard time about getting up early, but the truth was the sheriff had probably already been at work for hours.

"We have a problem, guys. Landry needs his brothers, and I..." I swallowed and took a chance. "I need my friends."

Slow grins spread around the table, but it was Dev who spoke first. "Took you long enough to call us that, fucker."

Zane nodded emphatically. "No kidding. All this 'I'm just an employee' stuff was getting old."

Silas sat forward. "We're here for you both, you know that. So... what's the plan, boss?"

My laugh came out shaky with nerves and relief. "Well..." I began. Then, I laid it out for them.

When I was done, Bash fixed me with an uncompromising stare. "This plan is absolutely insane, and I'm here for it." He grinned. "We'll make it happen, Kenji."

I really hoped he was right.

As executive assistant to five billionaires, I'd orchestrated countless impossible fixes.

But making this right for the man I loved... might be the biggest one yet.

TWENTY-TWO

LANDRY

When I walked out the door of Teddy's office, I felt utterly at peace. For the first time, I knew what I wanted. More importantly, I knew *who* I wanted.

And miracle of miracles, he wanted me back.

A Chaska Inira quote echoed in my mind: *"A heart at peace is the truest sign you have chosen well. Trust in your path, walk it with confidence, and let the universe meet you with open arms."*

I grinned as I reached the wide entryway leading to the street, wondering what Kenji would say if I told him I'd been thinking of Chaska unironically... and giddy to get back to Hawling House to find out. With any luck, he'd still be in bed.

"Lord Hawling?" A uniformed attendant hurried after me. "The prime minister had a message for you—"

I held up a hand, not slowing down. "I just finished speaking with him. Any convincing arguments he forgot to make can wait until I see him at the museum benefit in a few weeks."

I nodded at the security agent by the door, and he pulled it open, letting in a shaft of unexpectedly bright London winter sunshine. I smiled at him and stepped through—

And the world erupted.

A wall of camera flashes and shouted questions hit me before my foot touched the pavement outside the gate.

"Lord Hawling! Is the speculation about your marriage true?"

"Care to comment on the rumors?"

Reporters pressed around me, microphones outstretched. Tourists stopped mid-step, pulling out their phones in the hopes of capturing something newsworthy.

I had no idea what they were talking about. Had someone caught Kenji and Jamie smiling at each other the night before? The idea would have sent me into a green rage yesterday but almost made me laugh now.

"No comment," I said, scanning the street for Simon with the car.

"Do you have proof of your marriage?"

"Where exactly were you married, and on what day?"

"Does your husband know Lindsey Graves? Is her accusation true?"

I hesitated. *Lindsey Graves.* That name sounded familiar, but I couldn't place it.

Then, a reporter shoved a phone in my face... and everything clicked.

"He specifically told me he and Landry weren't romantically involved at all," the woman on the screen insisted. *"That he was just a personal assistant who helps with Landry's public relations. In fact, he said he'd do anything for his employer, including crisis management! I wouldn't be surprised if this whole marriage thing was a stunt to distract from the fact that Landry rescued his freaking PA while the rest of us suffered!"*

Fuck.

I remembered Kenji's concern about leaving people behind in San Cordova, and Lindsey Graves, the influencer we'd uncovered when we were trying to find him, had been one of the names on the list.

Had Kenji seen this video? Was he freaking out?

I realized I hadn't turned my phone back on after leaving Teddy's office, and as soon as I did, dozens of missed texts flooded in from Nan, Cora, and even Lydia.

The one from Kenji answered my earlier question.

> KENJI
>
> I'm so sorry. I'll fix this. Come home as soon as you can.

My heart rate kicked up. What did he mean, *fix this*? Fix it how? And why did I get the uncomfortable feeling he wouldn't be waiting at Hawling House when I got there?

I fired off a reply.

> Kenji, my beloved… what's going on?

"Is your relationship a scam?" a reporter demanded, shoving a tiny microphone at me.

"Absolutely not," I said firmly.

She didn't look convinced. "We have reports that your supposed husband has already left the country. He was seen leaving Hawling House and boarding a private plane. Can you tell us where he's going and why?"

I scowled. No, I *couldn't* tell them because he hadn't freaking told me.

Except…

Oh.

Come home, Kenji had said.

Not to Hawling House. Not to the city.

But to the place I knew had stolen his heart from the moment I first saw the painting of the Three Daughters on his apartment wall.

I blew out a breath. I trusted Kenji more than I'd ever trusted another living soul.

If he said he'd fix it, then he would.

And if my husband wanted me home... that's where I'd go.

"Was it all a hoax, or are the two of you truly together?" another reporter shouted.

I took a deep breath, the cool winter air energizing me from within.

If I knew Kenji—and I fucking did—he'd want me to be charming and noncommittal.

Unfortunately for him, I had no intention of avoiding commitment.

I grinned at the reporter. "You want the truth? Here it is: Kenji Toma is the love of my life. He will own my heart until the day the Earth stops rotating and our remains crumble into cosmic dust. And because he is the kindest, most generous, and most forgiving human on the planet, he loves me just as much. That's not a hoax. It's the most real and constant thing in the universe."

I graced them with the most lordly eyebrow raise I'd ever conjured. "Now, if you'll excuse me, I need to go join my husband. Our niece just had her second birthday, and she received a *shocking* lack of noisy toys to properly celebrate it. Kenji and I intend to rectify that."

The press erupted, firing off more questions, but for the first time since stepping out publicly as Everett Davencourt, I actually enjoyed the chaos.

No false identity to accidentally reveal. No modeling career to derail.

And, as of thirty minutes ago, no political campaign to fuck up.

There was just me, telling the world that Kenji was mine no matter what the paperwork said...

Before finding him and strangling him—lovingly, of course—for flying off half-cocked instead of waiting for me.

Simon pulled up, and I managed to make a smooth exit from the fray. "To Hawling House and then the airport," I said as he pulled away from the curb. "I need to be in the air as soon as possible."

As soon as possible turned out to be several hours, but only because the only commercial airline that still had a flight out today was the one I was contractually obligated to avoid.

Thankfully, Jamie Winthrop came through for me with his family's plane.

"It's not as nice as yours," he'd teased, "but it'll get you there by dinnertime."

As soon as the plane took off and the white noise of the engine was a steady thrum in my ears, exhaustion caught up with me. I slept for most of the ten-hour flight.

When I landed at the small Majestic airstrip, snow covered the ground, but the sky was dark and clear, with bright white pinpricks scattered from one horizon to the other.

I thanked the flight crew profusely, shouldered my backpack, and grabbed the handle of my large rolling suitcase to carry it down the stairs.

Unfortunately, the Winthrop plane hadn't had working Wi-Fi, but it had been a blessing in disguise. My shoulders had dropped once I was out of easy reach of the paparazzi and their endless bullshit headlines.

By the time I spotted Foster Blake's sheriff's SUV waiting by the tarmac, the urge to strangle my beloved had settled from a raging flame to a warm flicker.

"Let's go," Foster grumbled, reaching for my suitcase. "Everyone's waiting."

"Waiting? Who's everyone? How'd you know to pick me up?"

He snorted. "How do you think, Landry?" He tossed my suitcase in the back of the SUV and slammed the hatch. "Get in."

Once we were inside the still-warm vehicle, I shuddered in relief. There was London winter cold, and then there was Wyoming winter cold, and they weren't even in the same segment of the thermometer.

"Do you know what Kenji's planning?" I demanded.

"Yep," Foster said.

I huffed. "He hasn't replied to my text in twelve hours. And I know my phone is working because I got texts from Nan and Cora as soon as I landed."

"He's busy," Foster said.

When nothing more was forthcoming, I prompted, "Doing *what* exactly?"

After several more minutes of silence, I turned to the usually chatty sheriff. "Okay, what's going on? Why are you in a pissy mood? You're usually chipper and cheerful."

And *flirty*, but I didn't say that since I didn't want to imply I'd be into it. Foster was handsome as fuck but was about as toppy as they came, and more to the point, he wasn't Kenji Toma.

Foster cut his eyes to mine. "Have you ever had to sit through a wedding right after you'd gotten your heart stomped on?"

I blinked. "Uh, no? Why?" I glanced over at his stormy expression with a combination of panic and amusement.

Is he looking for relationship advice? From... me?

Foster didn't reply.

"I'd ask who's getting married, but I didn't think you'd been dating anyone," I went on. "So I assume this is a... metaphor of some kind?"

His hands tightened on the steering wheel. "Not dating. I just... I met a guy." He gritted his teeth and kept his eyes on the road. "Why are all the best men straight? And what kind of shitty-fucking fuckery is it for me to finally find someone who lit my fucking fire, only to find out he was fucking *engaged?* To a *woman!*"

I was having trouble following his disjointed complaints. "And you have to go to his wedding?"

"No! Jesus." He turned to me with a furrowed brow. "I'm going to *your* wedding, you idiot."

My hand rubbed down over my mouth and chin as I tried rearranging the conversation to make it make sense. It didn't work.

"*I'm* getting married?" My heart kicked into a furious rhythm. "Are you sure?"

Foster snorted. "Sure as the sunrise," he said as he turned down the driveway to Dev and Tully's ranch house. "Fastest wedding planning in Majestic history. But don't you worry. I bet Kenji magicked you a good one."

I stared at him for a long moment, jaw gaping, then turned my stare out the windshield.

I'd known Kenji would have a plan—a plan any war general would envy, complete with troop movements of his assistants, billionaires deployed like operatives, and multiple redundancies. I'd even assumed part of the plan involved fabricating some kind of marital proof.

It hadn't occurred to me that he'd plan us an *actual fucking wedding* without giving me advance notice.

Or, say, verifying that I'd be in attendance.

I hid my grin by turning toward the northern sky. "Yeah. He would have, wouldn't he?"

As soon as we pulled up beside the house, the front door burst open. Kenji came rushing down the steps to my side of the vehicle.

I jumped out and reached for him immediately. "Baby—"

He held up his hand, stepping back, though his eyes danced. "Don't you start with the *babies* right now, mister. We're on a schedule. Anna Kincaid is going to be here with her television crew in thirty minutes, and if we're not married by then, none of this will work."

"Married?" I was grinning madly. Couldn't stop myself. "Is this a proposal? Aren't you supposed to get on a knee?"

"Judge Whiteplume is willing to backdate the paperwork, but he insists on it not being a complete lie, so..." Kenji glanced behind us to make sure Foster couldn't overhear, then lowered his voice to a whisper. "...wife me now, Lord Landry, and I'll get on my knees later." He winked.

Since there was nothing I wanted more, I couldn't pretend to disagree, even in jest. I grabbed the front of his shirt and hauled him into me for a single hard kiss.

"Okay," I said softly. Happiness filled me like cotton candy on steroids.

Kenji's face softened for half a second before he rolled his eyes and pulled away. "Dammit, stop looking at me with that expression, or we'll never get it done in time. Now, go change your clothes into something that works for both a wedding and a global network interview."

He turned to hurry back into the house. My eyes went straight to his tight little ass.

I'd thought there was nothing hotter than watching Kenji Toma run the world, but I'd been wrong.

Watching him "magic" us a wedding was ten times hotter.

Foster caught up to me, still grumbling. "Stop being so in love. It's disgusting."

"Don't think I won't want the details about your Mr. Almost Right," I warned as he passed me carrying my suitcase with one burly arm.

"It's *Dr.* Almost Right," he muttered. "And I promise you, we'll never discuss him again."

As I entered the familiar house, Zane, Silas, Dev, and Bash all rushed me back to my bedroom and shoved clothes at me. I recognized the outfit as the one I'd worn for Christmas dinner and then left here. Since this house was kind of a second home for me, it was easier to leave an extra set of everything here on the off chance I could zip to Wyoming between jobs.

I wondered what it would be like now that I was more in control of my own schedule.

I guessed the answer depended on what Kenji wanted.

"Are you drunk?" Bash murmured as he leaned in to adjust a strand of my hair that had gotten displaced when I yanked the sweater over my head. I could smell traces of coffee on his breath. "Because I don't think I've seen anyone this happy to be force-married in my life."

I grinned at him, unsure if my cheeks would ever relax again. "Have you seen anyone force-married?"

Bash smirked and opened his mouth—

"Don't say it," Silas warned. "I was drunk, and you know it. I still maintain Vegas puts some kind of get-married drug in their drinks. Why else would so many people do it? It's weird."

Zane had full-on heart-eyes. "I think it's amazing. You and Kenji, both so clearly in love. *Finally*."

I tugged my cuffs, smoothing my sweater. "Do I look marriageable?"

"You'll do." Dev pushed off the wall and brushed invisible lint from my shoulders. "I'm so fucking happy for you." His voice was thick with emotion. "You deserve each other. And I don't mean that the way it sounds."

Everyone chuckled, stepping in to slap me on the back and fidget with my appearance.

I'd dreamed of a moment like this. Being surrounded by the men who loved me most in the world—with the sole exceptions of my father and Kenji. No longer having to hide who I was or who I loved. Getting ready to celebrate something real. Something joyful. Something forever.

My eyes burned. "I'm so sorry for not telling you guys. About London, about the earldom. About..." I stopped to take a shaky breath. "I was so afraid of losing you. *This*. What we have."

Bash's hand landed on my shoulder, firm and steady, like the big brother he'd always been to me. "I want to say it doesn't matter that you're a motherfucking *viscount*—" He rolled his eyes dramatically. "—but it does. It matters because it's a part of you. And I— *we*—love you."

"But if you think this means we're calling you *my lord*," Dev said gruffly, "then... you're absolutely right. I plan to be *obnoxious* about it."

My laughter came out slightly soggy. "I'd expect nothing less."

"If my brother is a viscount," Silas mused, "what does that make me?"

"Still a pain in the ass," Zane said cheerfully, then yelped when Silas pretended to lunge for him.

"This Brotherhood has been the greatest gift of my life. Until now," I added. "Thank you. For standing by me."

Dev smirked. "Where else would we be...?"

"Don't do it," Silas and Bash warned in unison.

"...*my lord?*"

Laughter exploded around us, unrestrained and giddy.

"Landry Davis... Davencourt... Whatever The Fuck, get your ass out here," Foster boomed through the door. "Let's get this show on the road."

My chest filled with something vast and unshakable.

I wiped my eyes, took a steadying breath, and grinned.

Time to marry my husband.

As we all filed out, Foster muttered something about me being better off just becoming a Toma. I could only imagine the look on my father's face if I even tried it.

Come to think of it, maybe he'd accept it better than Nan would.

Halfway down the hall to the family room, someone reached out and yanked me into a bedroom, slamming the door behind us.

Kenji was dressed in a crisp white button-down shirt and gray trousers with the slightest hint of a mustard and navy tweed plaid in it. His dark hair was pulled into a purposefully messy bun, and his collar was open just enough to reveal the dip between his collarbones.

He looked like someone who would upstage me on any runway.

"You okay, baby?" I shot him a smile that had to look smug as fuck. "I heard someone's forcing us to get married today."

His expression was serious. "I'll admit, I'm a little nervous."

My smile faded. "Hey. We don't have to do anything you don't—"

Kenji stopped me with a kiss. "Nervous I won't get this right." He brought my hand to his lips, then met my eyes. "But marrying you? I have never been more sure of anything."

He huffed out a laugh. "I may have been the last to know I'd been in a serious relationship for the last three years, but I see it so clearly now. Midnight snacks in my office. Lunch-break runs in the park. Bickering over takeout menus. Deep conversations about *everything*. Friday night sex that lasted until dawn on Saturday, and Saturday sex that turned into watching Sunday football on the sofa."

He swallowed, pressing my hand to the center of his chest. "I tried so hard to keep you from getting in here, Landry. So fucking hard. I was terrified I'd let myself fall and would never get back up." His lips curved slightly. "Turns out I fell a long time ago."

He stepped back, then sank to his knees. "I know it's cheesy, but I need you to know I am down on my knees begging because I love you more than I ever thought possible. I am yours for life, in whatever kind of life you want that to be. Everett Landry Davencourt, Viscount Hawling... will you marry me?"

I yanked him up and crashed my mouth into his, pulling him in so tight he had to hop up and wrap his legs around my waist.

"I love you," he murmured against my lips. "Love you so much, Landry."

The words poured over me, sinking into every parched, longing crack in my soul like cool rain after a drought.

"Of course I'll marry you. You're my fucking husband." I pressed my forehead to his. "But next time, baby, can you wait for me before flying off without saying a word?"

"Did you worry I was leaving you?" His eyes searched mine. "I saw the headlines. Right now, I might be in Mallorca with Jamie Winthrop—"

I snorted. "Cora might have something to say about that. No, Kenji," I said more seriously. "I didn't doubt for one second that you were off fixing things for me—"

"For *us*," he corrected. "Because fixing things for the people I love is what I do." He shrugged. "And we were kind of in a time crunch, you know?"

This man. This impossible man. *My* impossible man.

"How'd you even know I'd come?" I wondered.

Kenji slid down until he was back on his own feet. "Because I needed you. And being there when the people you love need you is what *you* do." He brushed a lock of hair off my forehead. "You're very dependable that way... even if it took me way too long to figure it out."

"I do love you," I whispered. "More than life."

"I know," Kenji said simply. "Now, c'mon. Everyone's waiting for us."

He tried tugging me toward the door, but I resisted. "You should know, I told Teddy I don't want to be an MP. I withdrew my name from consideration."

"Wait, really?" Kenji looked more concerned than surprised.

"What about your family's legacy? I was serious when I said I wanted to help you accomplish your dreams—"

"I know." I pulled him close and cupped his beautiful, dear face. "And that's what gave me the strength I needed to realize that you *are* my dream, and I want my legacy to be *this*. You and me. Us. The life we choose, the family we choose, everything we build together. You've already helped me accomplish so much, Kenj. Now it's my turn to support *you*."

As he stepped up on his toes to kiss me, I felt our love like a promise.

This, here, was our stated vow.

The actual ceremony was quick and cheerful. Each of the guys had volunteered to step forward and say something. Dev went first.

"*A strong marriage is not two halves becoming whole, but two wholes growing together.*" He nodded solemnly and stepped back.

I tried not to think that it sounded cliché as hell. And uncomfortably familiar.

Silas stepped forward and cleared his throat. "*Marriage is not about finding the right person... but becoming the right partner.*"

I narrowed my eyes.

Bash gave Silas a serious nod of approval before taking his place. "*Like a river and the shore, true partners shape each other with time and grace.*"

Foster muttered, "Mostly through years of gentle erosion."

Were they joking? Had these come from the back of a soda can?

Zane stepped forward. "*Love is the seed... but commitment is the garden.*"

Ryan reached out and yanked Zane back as everyone tried not to howl with laughter.

Kenji snorted but tried to maintain his composure as the men who were supposed to love me most in the world spewed Chaska Inira bullshit all over my wedding.

Kush Whiteplume, the judge most likely to throw back a beer or three with us on a Saturday night in town, rolled his eyes at Foster before looking back at Kenji and me.

"It's a blessing to solemnize a relationship in which I've been able to witness the, uh... *seed flinging* for a couple of years. May you live long and prosper with a sense of humor and a heap of patience. By the power vested in me by the great state of Wyoming, I now pronounce you... two wholes. Growing together. Or whatever the hell Devon said. Now... go on and kiss. You two earned it."

Everyone burst out laughing as I grabbed my *husband* and kissed him soundly.

Warm puffs of air escaped his nose as he laughed, and I wondered just how many times I'd get to experience such a thing.

"I love you, Kenji."

"I love you, too."

A champagne cork popped, followed by a whoop. Way's sister, Sheridan, and her husband brought out trays of appetizers and champagne glasses while Foster's mother, Jo, danced around with Lellie in her arms. "With this Ring" by the Platters crooned over the Bluetooth speakers.

Balloons and streamers in birthday colors hung from the ceiling and walls, ostensibly for Lellie's birthday but in reality for our wedding celebration. They had Kenji's fastidious nature written all over them, and they were definitely too fresh to have been left over from her birthday party.

Kenji grinned up at me, his arms still wrapped around my waist. "You don't seem bothered by all this. Just used to me telling you what to do?"

"Maybe," I mused. "Or maybe I'll do anything to be in your presence, including getting ambushed into marriage before giving a sit-down interview with one of the most intimidating media personalities alive today." I narrowed my eyes. "Speaking of, how did you get Anna Kincaid to Majestic, Wyoming, on such short notice, anyway?"

"Zane called in a favor with Jude Marian," he admitted as someone pulled us apart long enough to shove glasses into our hands. "Apparently, she did his original coming out interview, and they stayed in touch."

"Speech!" Tully cried.

Bash and Silas gave their vocal agreement, and Dev pulled out his phone to take pictures.

I wrapped my arm around Kenji's waist. "I'd like to say thank you to everyone for pulling this together so quickly. Thank you to Judge Whiteplume for the incredibly expedited paperwork." I shot him a wink, earning an eye roll and a grudging nod. "Thank you to Foster for being a rock-solid witness at our, ah, *December* ceremony. And mostly, thank you to my beloved husband, Kenji, for always rescuing me from the many scrapes I get into." I lifted my glass. "Including this one."

Kenji's cheeks darkened as I gazed at him and continued, "Did you know lobsters shed their shells to grow? In the meantime, they're left vulnerable. Their mate holds them and protects them until it's over." Just as his eyes softened, I grinned. "And then they mate for several days."

Everyone groaned and clinked glasses while Kenji grabbed the front of my sweater and pulled me in for a punishing kiss.

The toasts, laughter, and celebration continued until the television crew finally arrived.

Kenji and I sat down with Anna Kincaid in Dev and Tully's study. The built-in bookcases filled with legal books and a wide variety of novels made a perfect backdrop—serious enough for a news interview, cozy enough to remind us we were exactly where we belonged.

Her crew worked fast, setting up and rolling cameras before we had time to overthink. The interview passed quickly, and afterward, Anna stayed for dinner, where everyone wove in references to our beautiful December wedding.

The following morning, with all of us in our pajamas and sweats, we took turns reading out the headlines from the internet.

Landry Davencourt and Kenji Toma Face the Nation with Receipts!

The Earl's Heir Fights Back Against Fake Marriage Claims!

Davencourt Heir Picks Love Over Legacy in Political Shockwave!

Grave Mistake? Lindsey Graves Caught in Royal Wedding Hoax!

A Modern-Day Fairy Tale? Landry & Kenji Prove Their Love

I had to admit, the last one was my favorite.

"Wait," Zane said a moment later as he continued to scroll on his phone. "Landry, didn't you model for Vencari?"

"Yeah, why?"

We were curled up on one of the big sofas together, enjoying coffee and leftover wedding cake, and I was busy walking my fingers under the edge of Kenji's oversized hoodie to find warm skin underneath.

"Here's a headline about that guy you got in the fistfight with," Zane said. He cleared his throat and read:

***From Designer Suits to Dirty Secrets: Vencari Power
Player Accused of Misconduct!***

***Behind the Velvet Curtain: Vencari Talent Scout Faces
Scandal Over 'Special' Model Selections!***

I shot Kenji a glare. "Seriously?"

He shrugged. "You know what's better than cold revenge?
Really cold revenge. Icy. Freezer-burned, in fact."

"Please tell me that's the worst of it," I begged. "We just got
out of one scandal. I don't want to hop right into another."

Kenji shrugged but didn't look up from his tablet. "Depends
on which is worse. Losing your professional reputation or your
hair? His barber might accidentally swap the shampoo for hair
removal cream at his next appointment at four-thirty on Tuesday
afternoon. Who's to say?"

I mock-shuddered. "Remind me never to cross you, husband."

He looked up and met my eyes. His mouth curved into a delicious, affectionate smile. "Just don't withhold information from me
ever again, and we'll be fine."

I threaded my fingers through his messy, beautiful hair. "Then
I guess I should probably tell you, now that you're officially my
husband... I'm kind of a secret billionaire."

Kenji didn't even blink. Instead, he smirked, reached for his
coffee, and murmured, "As Chaska Inira says, 'Nobody likes a
sarcastic asshole.'"

I laughed, pulling him in for a kiss. "That is absolutely not a
real quote."

Kenji kissed me back, smiling against my lips. "It is now."

And over the course of our long marriage, it would become the
Chaska quote used most often in our home.

EPILOGUE
KENJI – TWO MONTHS LATER

"A little bit of you makes me your man…"

"Mambo No. 5" suddenly blasted through the car speakers, scaring the absolute shit out of me. I clicked to accept the call and didn't even let Landry get a word in before shouting.

"Are you fucking crazy? Stop changing my ringtone, you asshole! I almost wrecked the car!"

His honeyed voice came through the speakers, calming me against my will. "I'll be honest. I feel a little bad about that one because I didn't mean to imply that 'a little bit of you' referred to a certain body part. No worries, I've discovered a song called 'My Dick's Too Big' by the Saddle Tramps to undo the damage. I can switch it out when you get back to the house. Wait. That still sounds like an insult? Maybe I can—"

I pushed the button to end the call.

Three seconds later, the ringtone blared again. *"A little bit of you makes me your man…"*

I jammed the button. "Goddammit, Landry. What do you want? This is honestly worse than the time you made me watch a reality show about artisanal salad crafting, aka twelve hours of my life I'll never get back."

"I wish you hadn't brought that up."

"It's triggering, I know," I agreed.

"Because now I'm craving honey ginger dressing and pepitas." His voice sounded muffled like he was turning away. "Tully, do you guys have pepitas for a salad?"

I hung up the phone before remembering the damned ringtone.

"A little bit of you makes me your man..."

Now that I was married to a billionaire, I was tempted to throw my phone out the window just to be rid of the nuisance. But I was neither wasteful nor a litterbug.

And I was still, in fact, a phone addict.

"Everett Landry Davencourt," I gritted after answering the call. "You're the one who sent me to the store for red peppers and corn because... you know what? No. I'm not getting into another salad argument right now. I am one minute from turning into the ranch. Can you slow your fucking roll and wait for me to get there? I know you're in a hurry to show me something, but—"

He cut me off, his voice suddenly sounding serious. "Don't turn into the ranch. Keep going straight for one more mile and then turn left when you see the old wooden barrel."

I knew the barrel he meant. It was sun-bleached and weather-worn, sitting crookedly at the end of an abandoned gravel drive. In summer, it sprouted colorful volunteer wildflowers that tossed their heads in the breeze. In winter, it was mostly buried by snowdrifts.

Now that it was very early spring, I imagined it was dark with damp from the recent snowmelt.

"What's wrong?" I asked quickly, already assessing what our options were if there was an emergency.

"Nothing, promise. I just want to show you something."

Landry's calm tone immediately set my mind at ease. Despite the stress of the past two months—of traveling back to New York for work, returning to London for Ed's retirement dinner, and sitting through hours of legal work with Tully in Majestic to update Landry's and my estates—I was happy.

Our hope was to split our time between Majestic with the Brotherhood and Lellie and London with Landry's family. Yes, I would still continue to travel back to New York periodically to oversee Sterling Chase administrative personnel, but my hope was to do most of that work remotely.

Landry had already had my apartment moved in its entirety to his penthouse, which had resulted in a highly inappropriate but admittedly very satisfying Spite Suck in the men's room at Liberty London while I was picking up a few things for my grandmother's birthday.

Of course he'd waited until we were in public to tell me about it, which meant, in addition to the semi-public fellatio, I decided he could spring for a Birkin bag for my grandmother after all.

Which reminded me...

"I was thinking about heading down to Boca a few days earlier than we planned," I began, seeing the low outline of the old barrel in the distance. "My grandmother has a friend named Agatha, who has a nephew—"

"No."

I glanced at the phone display on the dash in surprise. "No? No, I can't travel of my own free will to visit my grandmother a few days early for her birthday? I'm sorry. Since when are you the boss of me?"

And why do I always turn into a petulant teen in an argument with him?

"You're not going early because I need you here. And whatever your plans were with Ethan, you can forget them."

My chest lightened as I realized I wasn't the only petulant teen in this relationship.

"But he sounds so lovely," I said, putting as much earnest naiveté into my tone as possible. "Did you know—" My brain screeched to a halt. "How do you know his name is Ethan? I didn't even know his name."

Landry hesitated. "Mpfh. Just made it up. Lucky guess. Don't give a fuck. Where are you?"

As I reached the turn, I noticed the broken barrel had a shocking display of fresh daffodils in it, set off in the warm light from the setting sun. "Turning in now, but how the fuck does this barrel have bulb flowers in it? Someone must have put them in last fall. I don't remember any daffodils last year. It was mostly..." My voice trailed off as the driveway curved around a stand of large trees and revealed a breathtaking view of the mountains.

A *familiar* view of the mountains. In fact, this was the exact view of Three Daughters that had graced my bedroom wall in my apartment and that now hung in our bedroom at the penthouse in New York.

Now that I was here in person, I could see there was an old barn off to one side that made the scene even more charming despite the fact it was clearly on its last legs.

"Park the car, sweetheart," Landry murmured, a smile evident in his voice.

I threw the car into park as soon as I saw him step out from around the old barn. He strode toward me with a bunch of daffodils in his hand and a giant grin on his face.

With the whirlwind surrounding our marriage and then all of the travel, we hadn't celebrated Valentine's Day. Was this some kind of belated romantic gesture? Him finding the view from my painting and surprising me with it?

It was sweet, of course, but trespassing wasn't my idea of fun.

"Please tell me you got the owner's permission for us to be

here," I begged. "Because Foster's been in a mood lately and would like nothing better than an excuse to arrest us after he caught us kissing at lunch yesterday. And homeowners around here shoot first and ask questions never."

Landry pulled me into his arms and pressed a warm kiss against my cool cheek. "I didn't get permission from the owners, but how about I do that right now?"

As he began to pull back, I reached up and grabbed his face, pulling him back in for a proper kiss. If I was going to get shot to death, I wanted the taste of Landry's lips on mine first.

I took my fill of him before finally allowing him to make his call.

He dialed the number and held the phone up to his ear.

"A little bit of you makes me your man..."

My phone rang at the same time, so I stepped away to take it. Cora had sent me information about a joint charity effort that I hadn't had time to look over, and it would be just like her to...

Before my brain kicked in to remind me that the ringtone was only for Landry, I saw Landry's face on the screen.

"What are you doing?" I asked him, not bothering to answer the call.

He grinned at me like a loon. "Asking the owner for permission to bring my husband here."

I waved my phone in the air. "You accidentally dialed me, asshole."

It took me a beat to realize I was the asshole. "Wait."

Landry slid his phone back into his pocket and nodded. His newly brunet hair caught the setting sun, throwing off threads of chestnut and auburn that hopefully represented the natural colors that would emerge as his own color gradually took over the color-corrected brown his stylist had done.

"Wait," I said again, glancing back at the view of Three Daughters. The one from my painting.

The river was still partially frozen as it meandered between the flat land and the foothills. The distant peaks of Three Daughters were white-tipped but bathed in orange and pink. It was a slightly different angle from the one at Dev and Tully's and a completely different one from Silas and Way's place.

It made sense Landry would want to build a place here, too. A place just for us.

On my dream spot.

"You bought us a place in Majestic?" I asked, the words tumbling out of me without passing through any filtration system. "Without asking me? Without consulting me at all?"

His smile faded a little. "Not exactly. I didn't buy it for us. I bought it for you. Last year, in fact. I couldn't consult you because you would have murdered me for my presumption."

My eyes snapped back to his. "Last year?"

He shrugged and looked off to the mountains. "I, uh... yeah. I mean... You said something about it being the place you went to in your mind when you meditated, and I thought it would be nice if you could go there in person, whenever you wanted. But that prick McCusker wouldn't sell. It took me over a year to wear him down."

He'd bought it last year. Which meant this gesture actually went back to the early days of our time visiting Majestic.

"Why didn't you say anything before now?"

Landry shot me a look. "Well, first of all, I wanted to show you in person, and we've been a little busy the past couple of months. Before we were together, I couldn't think of a way of gifting you a large parcel of prime Wyoming acreage without you immediately refusing me and calling me names in the process. Are you suggesting you would have accepted my gift?"

I stepped closer and threaded my arm through his, clasping his hand and looking out at the view from his side. "Not sure I would have been able to say no."

He huffed out a laugh. "Liar. You were, and still are, entirely capable of cutting off your nose to spite your face. In fact..." He turned and tweaked the tip of my nose. "I believe that's why it's so petite."

I swatted his hand away and moved into his arms. "I might have refused it at the time, yes. But I'm definitely not refusing it now. Thank you. Thank you so much."

He kissed me for a long time before pulling back with a murmured "Welcome."

I inhaled the still-cold mountain air and spun slowly to take in the entire vista as his generosity sank in. "How much of this is ours?"

He turned to take in the expansive view. "Forty-eight acres. It goes to the base of the hills." He gestured to the foothills leading to the mountains. "All of that is forever wild. And to the south is Dev and Tully's ridiculous acreage. To the east is the road to town. Which leaves our neighbors to the north, and they can't ever build too close to the river, which leaves us plenty of—"

"Nobody cares about your neighborhood roster," Foster called, stepping out from behind the barn. "Let's get this show on the road. It's going to get cold as balls once the sun goes down."

I glanced at him in surprise. "You invited Foster?"

Not that I didn't like the guy. I did. It was just that he'd been ornery as hell since he'd gotten back from his vacation in January, and we all considered him the Man Most Likely To Kick A Puppy these days.

Way had kindly reminded us that Foster's actual puppy—a bloodhound in training for search and rescue—didn't seem the worse for wear, but we all kept an eye out just in case.

"Not just Foster," Landry said, pulling me by the hand toward the barn.

Others began streaming out from behind the barn. The Brotherhood and their partners, Way's sister Sheridan and her crew, Foster's mother and sister, and...

"Baa Baa?" I squeaked, recognizing the woman on Bash's arm. Her wide grin and open arms were waiting when I ran into her embrace. "What are you doing here?"

"Your husband sent the plane for me. Said he figured you'd need expert advice on how to design a home that had just the right space for visiting grandparents."

Out of the corner of my eye, I noticed Ed, Nan, Cora, and Jamie laughing and talking with Landry. It was clear he'd already greeted them.

"Where did you all come from?" I asked in happy disbelief. Landry opened his mouth, but I cut him off with a raised palm. "And if you say, 'From behind the barn,' I will cut you."

Cora bounced over and gave me a tight hug. "We've just landed about an hour ago. Landry said he arranged for some people in town to delay your progress through the store."

As I hugged and greeted everyone, I thought back to Natana Whiteplume's odd request for my help selecting between two identical boxes of penne pasta because one of them looked "shifty." Lake McNair's insistence that I look at an astronomical number of ultrasound photos their surrogate had sent that seemed to only feature one cell, though Lake had insisted it was an entire fetus. Kicky Winshaw's long, drawn-out retelling of local gossip, including my own surprise wedding that she <cough> hadn't <cough> been invited to.

Jo Blake waited for everyone to finish saying hello before beaming at me and squeezing my shoulders. "I'm so happy the two of you are building a home here. When my nephew brought back that ornery city boy from Las Vegas a while back," she said, thumbing over her shoulder at Silas, "I never expected he would bring such a cast of characters with him. We are so happy to have you all here in Majestic."

She leaned in and gave me a tight hug before Dev approached her and handed an eager Lellie off to her. "Your turn,

Auntie Jo. If you're going to promise this girl candy, then you can take her."

"Lollypop!" Lellie said, beaming at Jo. "Lollypop!"

As Jo walked away, chatting happily and pulling a toddler-safe lolly out of her pocket, I noticed Foster staring after her with a mixture of emotions. Envy, longing, wistful happiness maybe.

But there was also exhaustion and defeat, which I hated to see on a friend's face.

"Foster," I began, stepping toward him.

His expression shuttered on a blink and was replaced with a friendly but polite smile. "Congratulations, Kenji. Mom is right— we're grateful you're here. Welcome." He held out his hand for a shake.

Now wasn't the time or place to press him on whatever it was that I'd seen on his face. Instead, I asked about his new pup. "Where's Chickpea?"

He rolled his eyes and sighed. "Jesus fuck. That dog. Don't ask. I'll be lucky if she can just stop tripping over her ears by summer, much less come when I call her."

Landry returned to me and took my hand. "Foster was right about it getting cold if we stay out here much longer. There's a special dinner planned back at Dev and Tully's place to celebrate. I got a stack of house plan magazines and some huge sheets of paper to sketch ideas on. You ready to head back to the house?"

I glanced around at the people we loved most in our lives, all gathered here in one place. The sun was slipping ever lower, casting shadows everywhere, but there was still plenty of light.

"First, I want to get everyone together in a picture," I said, quickly directing everyone to stand exactly where I wanted them.

Somehow, Way was able to move his truck around from behind the barn to the right spot so I could prop my phone on it for the group photo.

When the shutter sound finally began clicking, everyone was

laughing and teasing. The smiles that resulted were my absolute favorite, and I hoped the photo would be the first in a years-long series of annual shots taken in that exact spot, ones that would feature the kids Landry and I had already shared dreams about, Lellie and the siblings I knew Dev and Tully wanted to give her, and any other beloved additions to our family. Photos that would include Cora and Jamie, even though their duties at Davencourt would grow to eventually include the earldom. Photos that would include Foster's own happy-ever-after one day.

My dreams of those photographs came true over time, starting with Foster, whose love story began sooner than we expected. And I wasn't the only one who took incredible pleasure in watching him fall.

Because it turned out the straight guy who'd had him tied up in knots wasn't so straight after all...

And the key to our sheriff's heart was a man named Tommy Marian.

Looking for a little more Landry and Kenji? Click here to see what happens when they decide to cross the line... → https://readerlinks. com/l/4632788

Tommy Marian, you say? Grab your copy of the first book in the Made Marian Legacy series, Rescuing Dr. Marian *here → https:// readerlinks.com/l/4632691*

And make sure to check out the first book in the Made Marian series, Borrowing Blue *here → https://readerlinks.com/l/1437615*

LETTER FROM LUCY

Dear Reader,

Thank you for reading *Finding Lord Landry*. I am so happy with how this story turned out! We waited through four books before finally getting to see these two get their happily ever after. I hope you found it as satisfying as I did.

I do have a few notes for those of you who are interested. First, during the process of writing this book, the actual "real life" process of hereditary peerage "by-elections" in the House of Lords changed! For that reason, consider this a fictional account. Additionally, it's not easy for a woman to be a hereditary peer, but it is possible. Let's just imagine that's the case for our fictional Davencourt family.

Second, there is a Spotify Playlist with all of the songs mentioned in this book. You can find it here: https://readerlinks.com/l/4614922

Third, OMG SQUEEE!!!! We are getting a second generation Made Marian series!!!! OMGOMG! I can't wait. I've been sitting on this news for so long, and I am thrilled to finally let you in on it. Every time one of you posted in my FB reader group asking if Foster was going to get his own book, I wanted to scream and giggle and dance a little jig.

Depending on when you read this, I may have other exciting projects in the works like special editions, Kickstarters, Patreon exclusives including NSFW artwork, etc. Be sure to sign up for my newsletter to get all of that news and more, including discounts on the next releases!

You can also follow me on your favorite retailer site to be notified of new releases, and look for me on Facebook for sneak peeks of upcoming stories. You can also join me right now on Patreon for exclusive content and behind-the-scenes glimpses.

Please take a moment to write a review of *Finding Lord Landry*. Reviews can make all the difference in helping a book show up in searches.

Feel free to stop by www.LucyLennox.com and drop me a line or visit me on social media. To see inspiration photographs for all my novels, visit my Pinterest boards. The Pinterest board for *Finding Lord Landry* can be found here → https://www.pinterest.com/lucy_lennox/finding-lord-landry/

Finally, I have a fantastic reader group on Facebook. Join us for exclusive content, early cover reveals, hot pics, and a whole lotta fun. Lucy's Lair can be found here.

Happy reading!
Lucy

ABOUT LUCY LENNOX

Lucy Lennox is the USA Today bestselling author of over fifty gay romance titles including the GoodReads Hall of Fame winner Wilde Love. Born and raised in the southeast USA, she is finally putting good use to that English Lit degree she earned before the turn of the century.

Lucy enjoys naps, pizza, and procrastinating. She stays up way too late each night reading romance because it's simply the best.

For more information and to stay updated about future releases, sales and audio news and to grab some free and bonus reads, please sign up for Lucy's author newsletter on her website at LucyLennox.com or to stay in the know, join her exciting reader group, Lucy's Lair on Facebook.

facebook.com/lucylennoxmm

instagram.com/lucylennoxmm

amazon.com/Lucy-Lennox/e/B01N0IOYPT

bookbub.com/authors/lucy-lennox

patreon.com/lucylennox

pinterest.com/lucy_lennox

ALSO BY LUCY LENNOX

Find me online → https://linktr.ee/LucyLennox

Read my books:

Made Marian Series

Forever Wilde Series

Aster Valley Series

The Billionaire Brotherhood Series

After Oscar Series (with Molly Maddox)

Twist of Fate Series (with Sloane Kennedy)

Licking Thicket Series (with May Archer)

Champion Security Series (with May Archer)

Honeybridge Series (with May Archer)

Find a complete list of my stand alone romances and novellas at www.LucyLennox.com along with audio samples, freebies, suggested reading order, and more!

www.ingramcontent.com/pod-product-compliance
Lightning Source LLC
Chambersburg PA
CBHW060647190726
48289CB00002B/298